Turbulent Priests

Colin Bateman was born in Northern Ireland in 1962. For many years he was the deputy editor of the *County Down Spectator*. He received a Northern Ireland Press Award for his weekly satirical column, and a Journalist's Fellowship to Oxford University. His first novel, *Divorcing Jack*, won the Betty Trask Prize.

D0474628

COLIN BATEMAN

TURBULENT PRIESTS

HarperCollins*Publishers*

HarperCollins*Publishers*
77–85 Fulham Palace Road,
Hammersmith, London W6 8JB

www.**fireandwater**.com

This paperback edition 2000
1 3 5 7 9 8 6 4 2

First published in Great Britain by
HarperCollins*Publishers* 1999

ISBN 0 00 649801 9

Set in Aldus

Printed and bound in Great Britain by
Omnia Books Ltd, Glasgow

For Andrea and Matthew

PROLOGUE

It started with Cliff Richard, as things often do.

Moira had always been a fan. She was only in her early thirties, so she hardly remembered him as the teen idol rockin' with The Shadows, but she used to watch the movies on a Saturday afternoon when she was a kid – *Summer Holiday* in particular – and then he was on *Top of the Pops* doing 'Power to All Our Friends' with his silly little dance and she loved it. All her friends were into trendier, younger groups, but Cliff was for her. He'd always been a Christian, and she became one too, and that set her at odds with the rest of the island – they were all resolutely Roman Catholic – Christians as well, she supposed, but the God Cliff worshipped seemed so different, warmer.

Then, one Christmas, Cliff came to play in Belfast, at the King's Hall. The tickets had gone on sale nearly a year in advance and she'd managed to get one. There was nobody else she wanted to take, it was between her and Cliff. The ticket sat on her mantelpiece all through those traumatic months when she found she was pregnant, tearing herself apart trying to decide what to do, refusing to name the father, fighting with her family, then nearly losing it, but hanging on in there, always with Cliff as that light at the end of the tunnel.

Come the day of the gig, Moira was eight months pregnant, and heavy with it. She took her ticket, packed a small holdall, and caught the ferry across from Wrathlin to Ballycastle, then took the bus to Coleraine and finally boarded the train to Belfast. She arrived in late afternoon, it was snowing, lovely and Christmassy, but cold too and not really the time for walking the streets looking for a hotel. She hadn't booked one in advance – silly, in retrospect, as she tramped from lobby to lobby – but she'd made the trip on spec many times before, shopping, and never had a problem getting a bed for the night. But this time everywhere was booked up – between those die-hard fans travelling to see Cliff, the hordes of Christmas shoppers up from the South taking advantage of the weak pound, and the thousands attending the World Toy Convention at the Waterfront Hall, there wasn't a bed to be had.

Still, she was sure it would all work out. She got herself a nice tea, then took a taxi to the King's Hall. She would see Cliff. Everything would be okay. Her seat was in the second row.

He was *magnificent*. They all held lighters aloft and sang 'Christmas time, mistletoe and wine . . .' except Moira dropped hers and her shape didn't allow her to bend quickly to retrieve it. Then somebody kicked it away. No matter. It was only a lighter. When he sang excerpts from his musical, *Heathcliff*, he reached down from the stage to shake hands and even though it hurt like hell, stretching her stomach across, she managed to grasp his hand and was astonished to feel the warmth of the man course through her.

She was so happy.

She skipped through the streets later, or skipped as much as an eight-months-pregnant woman can, back down into the centre and started looking for a hotel again. It was late, the trains were long stopped, but there were lots of new hotels in Belfast now, since the cease-fire, and there were always cancellations, she knew that.

But everywhere she went, no room. They did their best to help, they phoned other hotels, but everywhere, no room.

She was getting very tired then; the elation hadn't gone, but it was well hidden. It was snowing harder. It was freezing. She needed to put her feet up, her ankles were up like baps. She came, eventually, to a restaurant-disco-hotel called *The Stables*. There was a Christmas party throbbing away, there were three big bouncers on the door who made cracks about her going for a boogie in her condition, but in reception the story was the same. No room. *Sorry, love, no room.*

At that point she broke down. She couldn't go any further. She rested her head on the counter and cried. The manager looked at the assistant manager. The manager said, 'There, there.' The three bouncers looked in and said, 'Are you okay, love? Will we get you a taxi?'

'To Wrathlin?' she wailed.

They all looked at each other.

One of the bouncers whispered to the assistant manager. The assistant manager whispered to the manager. The manager shook his head. The bouncer said, 'It's *Christmas*.' The manager shook his head. The bouncer said, 'I think you should reconsider,' with enough menace for the manager, who paid a lot in protection money every month, to reconsider.

After several moments, just long enough for it to look like it might actually be *his* decision, he put his hand on Moira's shoulder and said, 'If you're really stuck, we do have a storeroom. It's full of crap at the minute, but we could clear a bit of a space, haul a spare mattress down . . . if you're stuck?'

Moira looked up, smiled through her tears, then kissed all of them.

An hour later, with the last of the stragglers going home from the disco, with the road outside under three inches of snow, Moira snuggled down on her crisp white mattress, her fluffy pillow, looked up at the great piles of cereal boxes and catering-size tins of baked beans which filled the storeroom, and thought about how lucky she was and how wonderful people were.

Then her waters broke.

And the contractions came like very fast contractions.

The bouncers heard the screams first, and came running, then the assistant manager, then the manager, and they all stood squeezed in the doorway, not knowing what to do.

'We have to get her to a hospital!' the manager wailed.

'No!' Moira yelled. 'It's coming!' Then screamed again.

'It can't be coming! You've only just start . . .'

'It's fucking coming!' Moira yelled.

They panicked. They ran about getting clean towels and hot water. The manager called for an ambulance anyway, but the hospital was already snowed in. He called for the police but there had been a riot at an ecumenical midnight carol service and they were all tied up.

'It can't be coming yet!' the assistant manager yelled, taking his cue from the manager.

One of the bouncers looked a little closer at Moira, who, in agony and beyond modesty, had removed her maternity dress and pants. The bouncer's eyes widened. 'I think I see someone waving at me,' he said, and they all started to giggle, even Moira, between screams.

And then the baby came, quick as a flash, no trouble at all, and the bouncers delivered it, three ex-paramilitaries with tattoos on their tattoos, they delivered it, and were as pleased as punch.

An hour later, babe in arms, Moira sat up in her bed. There was a doctor on the way, finally, and the three bouncers cooed around her. They were all drinking champagne.

The manager and the assistant manager stood in the doorway, grinning. Everybody felt good.

'You know,' the manager said quietly to his assistant, 'this is just like the baby Jesus, born in a stable.'

'Born in *The Stables*,' the assistant manager grinned.

'Born to a single mum too . . .'

'Mary . . . wasn't a single mum.'

'No, but she was a virgin.'

'I don't think Moira claims to be a . . .'

'No, I mean, metaphorically speaking . . . there's no husband, no father present, so it's like a virgin birth . . .'

The assistant manager nodded, because he was an assistant manager.

'So we have *The Stables*, the virgin birth . . . now look at our three bouncers.'

The assistant manager looked at Lenny, Jugs and Ripley Bogle.

'They're all hoods, right.'

The assistant manager nodded.

'And what're hoods called in Mafia flicks?'

'Mafia flicks? Ugh . . .'

'Wise guys, right?'

'Ugh . . . right.'

'And where are they from?'

'Italy . . . New York . . .'

'Not the Mafia – Lenny, Jugs . . .'

'Oh. Just round here. Jugs is Newtownards Road, Lenny's . . .'

'East Belfast. All from East Belfast.'

'Okay. Right.'

'So the three wise men from the east.' The manager smiled widely.

'I think you might be stretching . . .'

'Hold on, I'm not finished. What was the first thing she wanted after she gave birth?'

The assistant manager thought for a moment, then it came to him. 'A cigarette.'

The manager nodded. 'And what did she light it with . . . ?'

4

'She couldn't find her lighter, so Lennie gave her his, told her to keep it, a present . . .'

'It was a gold lighter.'

'Gold-ish.'

'Stick with me. A gold lighter. So after that, what did she want?'

This time the assistant manager's brow furrowed, he couldn't think what had been next.

'After all that screaming and shouting . . . ?'

'I don't . . .'

'She wanted to fix her face. So she asked for . . .'

'A mirror!' He said it a little too loudly and the bouncers scowled round, then returned to their cooing. 'But . . .'

'Don't you see?' The manager tutted. 'Look, the virgin *Moira*, comes to the city, finds no room at the inn and has to sleep in *The Stables*, she gives birth and the three wise men from the east bring her gifts of gold, frankincense and mirror.'

'*Frankincense?*'

'Well, I didn't say it fitted perfectly, but near as damn it. If you ask me, what we have on our hands here is the Second Coming. Mark my words.'

The assistant manager shook his head. It was late and he was tired and his boss was a raving lunatic.

He took a deep breath. He smiled across at Moira, babe in arms, and said, 'What're you going to call him, love?'

'*Him?*' Moira said.

1

Cardinal Tomas Daley, Primate of All Ireland and the hot favourite
to be the first English-speaking Pope since Robbie Coltrane, glanced
up from his desk. 'You look like you've been celebrating,' he said.

I nodded. It hurt. I had one of those headaches that begins
in your feet. Up top the Four Horsemen of the Apocalypse had
tethered their restless mounts to the back of my eyeballs. The
thousand curious little green woodpeckers cunningly masquerading
as summer raindrops thumping at the window didn't help.

'My wife had a baby last night,' I said.

'Really?'

I nodded. It hurt some more.

'Congratulations.'

He gave me the warm-hearted smile of a nice man with a problem
and turned perplexed eyes to the file lying open on the desk before
him. He made a note. I have never felt entirely easy with people
who maintain files on me. Particularly religious people.

'Thank you.'

I'd met him before, at some press conference or other, but he
plainly didn't remember. He was fifty-four years old. Plump, mostly
bald, pink-faced. He'd been Cardinal for ten years. He was mostly
based in Dublin these days but he'd managed to hang on to his
Northern accent. He still kept a house in Belfast. He'd done his
training up North. His first parish was in what he would call Derry
and he was still a regular visitor. Everyone seemed to like him. He
did a lot of good cross-community work, which you can file under
shaking hands with Protestants, a tough enough calling.

'Sure if you'd given me a call I could have rearranged this. You'll
be in no mood to . . .'

'I was curious.'

And I was. My dealings with the Catholic Church are few and far
between. I'd once survived for three days on nothing more than a

purloined bottle of red wine and some communion wafers, but it hardly amounted to religious fervour.

'Of course. You don't mind if all of this stays off the record, do you?'

'Why do all the best stories start like that?'

He smiled again. 'I know,' he said. 'But you'll understand when I tell you.' The Cardinal pulled at his lower lip for a moment. 'You're not a religious man, are you, Dan?'

In fact I'm the product of a mixed marriage. My father was an agnostic, my mother an atheist, although they still counted themselves as good Protestants. Protestantism never has and never will be about religion. It's about property and culture and spitting at Catholics. 'No, I'm afraid not,' I said. 'I was married in a Presbyterian Church, if that's any help.'

'But you're not a practising . . .'

'I was a practising footballer. There was a good church team.'

His eyes held steady on me, but it didn't feel like he was sizing me up; it felt like he'd made his mind up the instant I entered the room. The file, of course. The only thing that had surprised me thus far was his tardiness in offering me a drink.

'Would you say you had no real interest in religion then?' he asked.

'None at all, but I'll convert to anything if the price is right.'

He nodded glumly, which wasn't the response I'd anticipated.

'And what of the Catholic Church? Have you any particular views on it?'

'Nope.'

'But you're not anti-Catholic.'

'Nope.'

I took in some air. Musty air. There were big leather-bound books all around, the kind you could only pick up these days in the special offers at the back of the Sunday supplements. My head was threatening to start revolving. I was beginning to regret answering the summons. If it hadn't been extremely polite and cautiously mysterious I wouldn't have come at all. I had better things not to do. 'Is all this leading somewhere, Cardinal?'

'Yes. Sorry. Of course. I should get to the point. That's the problem with the Church generally, too much pontificating, though Lord knows I've done my best . . . ahm . . . Would you say you were familiar at all with the traditions of the Catholic Church in Ireland?'

'Nope.'

'For example, have you heard of Oliver Plunkett?'

'Nope.'

'The saint?'

'Did he take over from Roger Moore?'

'Are you joking me?'

'Partly.' I smiled. He smiled wearily back. 'I'm sorry,' I said. 'My head's not entirely with it. Last night 'n' all. Oliver Plunkett. There's a school named after him, isn't there?'

'Yes. Dozens of them. Oliver Plunkett was the last Catholic martyr in England. He had his head cut off three hundred years ago. It's miraculously preserved down in Drogheda. Looks just as he did the day he died. Kind of surprised. But it's one of the biggest tourist attractions on the island.'

I shook my head. 'I'm sorry. I'm sure it is.'

The Cardinal picked up a folded A3 sheet from his file and handed it across to me. 'Do you remember writing this?' he asked.

It was a reproduction of an article of mine from the *Sunday News*. The headline ran: THE LONELY VIGIL OF 'ORANGE' FLYNN. 'That's going back a couple of years,' I said.

'Three.'

'That long?'

The Cardinal nodded. 'Do you remember him, Father Flynn?'

'Yeah. Sure. Good story. I mean, good subject. The story's okay.'

'It caused a bit of a rumpus at the time.'

'Well, it would.'

I remembered it well. It had stood out from the usual round of murders and bombings. Frank Flynn had been an ordinary priest in a town famed for its extraordinary violence. In times of trouble people turn to religion, and Crossmaheart had only ever known trouble. Flynn's was a healthy congregation – those that were still alive – but he was not a healthy priest. A bad heart. It seemed he was on the way out when he was suddenly whisked off to London for a heart transplant. There followed a long period of convalescence. When he eventually returned to his parish he was a changed man: from the shuffling, wizened, pasty-faced priest, to a vibrant enthusiast with a face as pink and sweet as a fresh German biscuit. His close encounter with death had given him an insight into life, and he lost no time in trying to communicate this to his congregation. At first they'd welcomed him, pleased that he was returned to them and positively thriving. But then the sniping began, and for once in Crossmaheart it wasn't via an Armalite. The word was that the dour, cynical priest that had left the town had not just been cured, but had been cured with a Protestant's heart. His was a Catholic chassis driven by a Protestant engine. He had become the very antithesis of a Catholic priest. His congregation began to melt away. The sniping turned into scorn, scorn into hate. He was refused service in shops. He was cursed at. Spat upon. Convicted on the perfect evidence of rumour and spite. When I'd met him he'd been a lonely man in an empty church, supported only by his bishop. It had been a good article, rich in pathos, three hundred years of religious bigotry in microcosm. I'd done my research as well; and it was a Protestant's heart.

'As I recall,' I said, handing the sheet back to the Cardinal, 'he was a nice enough man, it was just that everyone hated him.'

'Yes. He was.'

'But now?'

'Well, that's harder to say.' He sat back in his chair and pulled at his lip again. Then he began tapping his index finger between the bottom and top rows of teeth. It wasn't a sound I needed to hear.

'Cardinal, why don't you just tell me what's on your mind? There are few things in life which can't be summed up in a single sentence. It's a basic rule of sub-editing.'

'Ah, if only it were that simple. The direct route isn't always the best, Dan. Father Flynn now, when you last met him his congregation must have been down to single figures.'

'Single figure. Himself.'

'Well, times have changed. In the end, though we were reluctant to do it, we moved him on. Back, in fact, to where he came from. You know Wrathlin Island?'

'I know of it. Can't say I've been there. A bit remote for my tastes.'

'And for most people. But that's his home. He's preaching every week to full houses.'

'Good for him.'

'Yes, well, that's the problem. He has distanced himself to a certain extent from our Church.'

'I see.'

'The thing is, Dan, the Church in Ireland has always been keen on its miracles. We've talked about Plunkett already, but to tell you the truth there's scarcely a year goes by without some tale of a dancing Madonna or crying Christ getting the pious moving. I'm sure you've heard of them.'

'Vaguely. Down South mostly.'

'Yes. Down South. There are blessed few miracles up here. The thing is, Flynn's gone down the same path. He's started having visions. Making all sorts of claims. And people are falling for them. It's just not on.'

'What sort of claims, Cardinal?'

'Well, that's the thing. Madonnas and such like, you can prove them to be false, eventually. I mean, we always do, but it's no bad thing to encourage the belief in the occasional miracle – it does wonders for church attendance, you understand?'

'Like a promotion gimmick in a newspaper. God's spot-the-ball.'

'If you like. Well, Flynn's just taken it a little too far.'

'Cardinal?'

'He believes that the Messiah has been born on the island. He says it's the Second Coming.'

2

It sat in the air for a while. The Cardinal's serious, ponderous eyes studied me with renewed interest, his cheeks pale pinky in a slightly embarrassed flush. I held his gaze, waiting for the spark of humour to cross his face. But it didn't come. I gave him a hint: I gave him a grin.

The Cardinal stood abruptly and moved to the window. The woodpeckers were still busy. 'Oh, laugh away,' he said, although I was far from it. 'I would probably see the funny side of it myself if it didn't affect me so directly.' He shook his head. He clasped his hands behind his back and was silent for a few moments. Then he turned back to me. 'The thing is, when Flynn lost the support of his congregation in the first place, I was the one who stood by him and I have done all along. Now he's talking about splitting from Rome altogether if we don't recognise the validity of his claims. I'm really in a most embarrassing situation.'

'I presume you've ruled out the possibility of it actually being the Messiah.'

'Well, of course I have.'

'But he must have some evidence?'

'Evidence? This is the Catholic Church, man, we don't need evidence. We need faith, we need belief, we need trust. Since when has evidence ever been a requirement of a religion?'

'But he must be basing . . .'

'On visions. On drug-induced visions.'

'Drugs?'

'He takes drugs for his heart. They must be affecting him. Or maybe they're not. I don't know. All we know is that he's gone doolally and we need to do something about it before his poison reaches across from the island.'

'You're that worried about it?'

'Yes, unfortunately. I know it sounds a little far-fetched, but I think we've all seen what a sudden outbreak of fundamentalism can do in the Middle East. It's a vicious, virulent plague and I really wouldn't like to see something similar happen here. Unfortunately there's no inoculation against it. It's early days yet, mind, early enough to nip it in the bud, before the McCooeys really take hold.'

'The what?'

'Yes. Sorry. The McCooeys.' He gave a little shrug. 'I know. The movement has to be named after someone. And the particular family involved happens to be called McCooey.'

I tried a little shrug as well, which was dangerous in my condition. 'Why not just excommunicate Father Flynn?'

'Daniel, have you any idea how rarely people get excommunicated from the Church? Have you ever heard of an IRA gunman or a Mafia assassin being excommunicated? Daniel, if Hitler were alive, and Catholic, he'd be on double secret probation. No, excommunication is out of the question – besides, in a roundabout way it might serve to legitimise his claims. What I'm looking for, Dan, is someone who can go in there, take a close look at what he's up to, and report back to me.'

'Which is where I come in.'

The Cardinal nodded.

'Why me?'

'Flynn has spoken very warmly of you. He very much appreciated the article you wrote on him – hundreds of people contacted him when it appeared, people from all over the world. I thought if you were to go over to Wrathlin, investigate what was going on, interview him if you like about what he's up to these days, then maybe you might get a little more out of him than we have so far managed.'

I shook my head. 'I don't entirely follow your reasoning. I mean, why not go yourself? Send a bishop. Send a priest. Send someone who can argue the bit out with him. Someone who can disprove the fact that this kid is the Messiah.'

'Daniel, we did send someone.'

'And?'

'He didn't come back.'

'Jesus. Excuse me. But . . . he was murdered?'

'Worse,' the Cardinal said grimly, 'he was converted.'

*   *   *

13

The city centre was jam-packed with shoppers. The cease-fire was good news for everyone but journalists. 'Armistice' Maupin, the French peace broker, was taking all the credit, but he'd failed to realise that even terrorists grow up.

I parked the Fiesta under the watchful eyes of a security guard in the grounds of the Royal Victoria Hospital. I checked my dank hair in the mirror, then reached into the back and lifted a brown paper bag. I climbed out of the car, locked up and pulled the collar of my black sports jacket up against the rain and walked quickly towards the maternity wing.

I took the stairs three at a time, but hesitated when I reached the swing doors to the wards. I peered through the clouded plastic window. I could just make Patricia out, half a dozen beds down on the left, sitting up, her head nodding at someone. I cursed under my breath and turned away. I followed the corridor on up to the incubator room and stood at the window for a while looking at the rows of tiny pink bodies.

I couldn't make out any of the names and could only guess which one was at least half a Starkey, and that only by marriage. I'd left the hospital the night before in a daze, for once not caused by alcohol. No one had prepared me – nor Patricia, for that matter – for the blood and the pain and the screaming and the mess. It wasn't like it was about life at all, but avoiding death. The fact that a baby was produced at the end of it seemed almost irrelevant. When he'd come he'd barely registered on me in the few seconds before he was taken to an incubator – more purple than pink, a shrivelled simian awaiting evolution.

One of the babies, closest to the window, had a hint of Patricia's scolding eyes. Another, nearer the back, was already sprouting her dark hair and thin-lipped pout.

A nurse tagged my arm. 'Father?' she enquired.

'Husband.'

A hesitant smile.

'Starkey,' I added quickly.

'Ah, yes! The little fighter!'

I nodded.

'Can you see him?'

I nodded vaguely in the direction of the pouting baby.

The nurse tapped lightly on the window. 'Such lovely red hair,' she said, pointing elsewhere, 'like he has a little rusty head.'

I nodded some more.

'Isn't he lovely?' she beamed.

'Delightful,' I said, and turned back to the wards. As I reached the doors again they swung open.

'Ach, hiya, Dan, how's it goin'?'

Patricia's father smiled up at me. He'd shrunk since I'd last met him. Within a year. Shrunk with age. Shrunk with living in a retirement community on the windy north-west coast. Shrunk with having his wife die on him. Shrunk with waiting for death.

'Hiya, John,' I said, 'you're looking well.'

'Did I see you looking through at us a minute ago?'

'Aye.'

He nodded. 'You went up to look at the kid.'

'Aye.'

'Lovely kid.'

'Yeah.'

He put his hand out to me and we shook. 'I know how it is, son,' he said.

'Thanks. I thought maybe you were, y'know, *him*.'

He squeezed my hand a little tighter, then let go. 'Aye, I know.'

'How is she?'

'Tired. Irritable. Same as ever.' He patted my arm. 'I'm sorry to rush on, but I've a train to catch.'

'I could give you a lift if . . .'

'Nah, never worry . . . away and see your wife.'

I smiled, we shook again, then he moved stoop-shouldered and stiff towards the stairs. I watched him negotiate the top flight, then pushed my way into the ward.

Patricia saw me immediately. She gave me a half-smile half-grimace which said it all.

I smiled at the woman in the next bed, and her visitor, then stopped at the foot of Patricia's bed and raised a hand in salute. 'Hail Caesarean,' I said.

The half-smile didn't develop much. 'Hello, Dan.' Her voice was weak, her face wan.

'I come bearing gifts.'

I moved along the side of the bed, bent and kissed her lightly on the lips, then handed her the paper bag.

She crinkled her eyes in mock delight. 'Thanks,' she said. She gave the bag an exploratory shake then set it down on the bed. 'Sit,' she said.

I pulled up a black plastic chair. 'Open it.'

'I'll look later, I'm just . . .'

'Go on, have a look . . .'

'Dan, I . . .'

'Just take a look . . .'

She tutted. She opened the bag and peered inside. She lifted out an egg, examined it for a moment, then replaced it and removed a handful of monkey nuts.

'Hard-boiled eggs and nuts, huh,' I said.

'What?'

'Hard-boiled eggs and nuts, huh.'

'Dan . . .'

'Hard-boiled eggs and nuts, huh.'

'Dan!'

'You don't remember?'

'I don't remember what?'

I puffed out my stomach, shook my head petulantly. 'Hard-boiled eggs and nuts, huh!'

'Dan!'

'Laurel and Hardy! Hard-boiled eggs and nuts, huh! Stan goes to see Ollie in hospital, he has his leg up in plaster, he brings him hard . . .'

She dropped the bag on the bed. 'Jesus, Dan, why do you always have to be different? You couldn't just bring me a bunch of flowers or grapes, could you? It always has to be something funny. Something witty.'

'You used to appreciate it.'

'I used to appreciate a lot of things.'

We glared at each other for a charged half-minute.

'I thought we were doing okay,' I said.

'Yeah.'

'I thought we were going through our second honeymoon period.'

'Aye, honeymoon cystitis.'

I slumped down in the chair and stared moodily ahead. Sometimes I genuinely don't love Patricia at all. It doesn't last very long, but it does happen. I looked across at the couple beside us. I could see now that she was cradling a baby in the folds of her voluminous nightie. The man caught my eye and smiled. I nodded.

'He hasn't been then?' I said.

'Who?'

I shrugged. 'I saw your dad.'

She nodded. 'He brought some clothes. Of indeterminate colour. He wasn't sure whether it was a boy or . . .'

'It doesn't much matter, does it?'

'I suppose not.'

'Insofar as nothing much goes with red hair.'

'Dan . . .'

'You might have warned me.'

'How was I supposed to know?' she snapped, then grimaced. 'It doesn't show up on a bloody scan. Tony hasn't got red hair.'

'It's in his DNA then. From flared jeans to flawed genes.'

'Does it really matter?' she hissed. Her face had acquired a little more colour. 'Jesus, Dan, I've just come through the most horrendous twelve hours of my life, pain you couldn't begin to comprehend, then you turn up here, stinking of beer, you give me a bag of eggs and nuts and start moaning about the colour of his hair, and all the time I'm still in fucking pain and that fucking wee tyke is still in there fighting for his life! Jesus Christ, Dan!'

I counted to ten.

It didn't work.

'Better dead than red,' I said.

She screamed and threw the hard-boiled eggs and nuts at me.

3

She had no idea what I was going through.

In the hospital café I got myself a Diet Coke and a Twix. I sat at a table and stared at a bare wall. There was spilt tea and sugar on the table and I'd an elbow in it before I realised.

She really didn't have any idea of what I was going through, although it should have been bloody obvious. But she was right as well. I'd no idea what she'd gone through either. I'd only had to watch and worry.

The other visitor from Patricia's ward set a cup of coffee down on the table and slipped in opposite me. 'You've still got some egg shell in your hair,' he said.

I brushed my head. A couple of brown fragments fell onto the table. 'Thanks,' I said.

He was a big fella. He'd a dark stubble. A knitted blue jumper over a white buttoned shirt. He hunched up his shoulders and leant forward, resting both elbows in the tea and sugar. He lifted them sharply. 'Fuck,' he said, wiping at them.

'I did that too,' I said.

'You think they'd . . .'

'Aye, you would.'

Bending his elbows had pushed up his shirt, revealing half of an IRA tattoo on his lower arm. I was going to suggest laser surgery or an IQ test, but decided against it. We nodded at each other for a few moments, then I rolled my eyes upwards and said: 'Sorry about all that.'

'Never mind, son. Sure I've seen it all before.'

'Not with hard-boiled eggs and nuts.'

'You'd be surprised. It's our seventh. Sure women are like that sometimes. Funny things happen when they have babies. It has something to do with the chemicals in their heads. You just have to remember to try and hold on to your temper. It just makes things worse. Give her time to cool off, then take her up a cup of tea and a bar of chocolate. A wee row. It's not the worst thing in the world.'

It wasn't the worst thing in the world. But it was part of it. The worst thing in the world hadn't even bothered to come and visit his son.

Once, long ago, I had an affair. It didn't work out. Patricia had one in revenge. It didn't work out for her either. We got back together, more in love than ever. But she was pregnant with his child. And he wanted to provide for it. I wasn't earning much money. He was. Patricia said he had certain rights as the father of the child. I said, has he fuck. But he remained a shadowy presence in our lives. I thought she was still in love with him.

'Hello again,' I said.

'Hello.'

'Is it safe?'

'Of course.'

'I'm sorry.'

'I'm sorry too.'

'I shouldn't have been so insensitive.'

'It doesn't matter.'

I took her hand. 'Are you very sore?'

'Someone ripped my bits open with a scalpel.'

'It's sore, then.'

She nodded.

'Tony hasn't come then?'

She shook.

'Do you want me to give him a ring?'

'Leave it, Dan.'

We fell to silence for a little while. I looked at the woman in the next bed. They'd taken her baby away and she now lay flat on her back, snoring gently. At peace with the world.

'This morning I had a private audience with the Primate of All Ireland,' I said, as if it were a regular occurrence.

'What?'

'Aye. Cardinal Daley.'

'Dan?'

'Just thought you'd like to know.'

'You interviewed him for the paper, you mean?'

'Nope, he interviewed me.'

'Dan?'

I clasped her hand in both of mine. 'Darlin',' I said, 'you know all I've ever wanted to do is write my book. Get away somewhere and write my book. You know that's been my dream.'

Patricia nodded hesitantly.

'And you know I've applied for every grant under the sun, but they've always turned me down.'

She nodded again.

'Well, Cardinal Daley administers an award on behalf of Co-operation North . . . you remember them?'

'Of course, yes . . .'

'It's for writers, new writers, it allows them to go away . . . and the thing is . . . he's offered it to me. At last someone thinks my writing is worth something . . .'

'Dan, that's wonderful . . . I really mean it . . . but we've just had . . .'

I squeezed her hands a little tighter. 'But don't you see . . . you can come with me, love. So can the little one. That's the beauty of it. For as long as we want . . . away from Belfast . . . our own little cottage, money to live on, peace and tranquillity . . . the perfect environment to bring up ba . . .'

She dropped her head into her hands. 'Dan . . . it's so soon . . .'

'We've a couple of months yet. Trust me, Trish.' I gave her the smile of the century. 'Have I ever let you down?'

4

The house felt empty.

It was, of course. Even with me in it.

As soon as I got home I opened a can of beer. Harp. I was collecting the ring-pulls. For every seventy-five you collected you could send away for a World Cup football. I had three hundred and eighty-seven but I was too lazy to post them. I put on some music. For once the guitar intro to The Clash's 'Complete Control' sounded too raucous and I switched it off. I went upstairs and stood in the baby's room with the can cradled against my chest.

Patricia had painted the room blue without any help from me. She'd had a hunch it would be a boy. We'd seen early scans, just enough to know the baby was healthy. The agreement was I would paint the room pink if she turned out to be wrong. Against one wall there was an old wooden cot which her father had presented to us. There were teeth marks on it. Hardy toys from her past were piled in one corner. In another, presents which we'd bought ourselves. Patricia had specialised in big cuddly toys. I'd provided the inappropriate contraptions with batteries. Mickey Mouse was stencilled onto every wall.

I felt alone; I felt as one, where I should have felt as three. I felt guilty for being a selfish son of a bitch. I have often tried not to be a selfish son of a bitch, but at the end of the day you are what you are and people love you for it or hate you for it. Occasionally there is a little mixing of the two emotions.

I should have been more understanding. I could see the pain and the hurt in her eyes, as if I had laddered the tights of her soul. I should have shown more interest in the baby. I should not have mentioned the hair. You could probably grow to love ginger hair.

But I didn't feel guilty at all for being economical with the truth about the Cardinal.

I hadn't lied. He *had* offered me a cottage. There *was* a writer's grant he administered. There is a saying that the camera never lies, but it does if you doctor the negative.

Sometimes wives don't need to know everything. They don't need to know about afternoon drinks. They don't need to know about night shifts spent watching football. They don't need to know about masturbation – when, where or how often, although they can probably guess.

She didn't even need to know about Father Flynn because I'd no great intention of spending my time on the island investigating him. What I observed in the course of living there could be relayed back to the Cardinal one way or the other, but I wasn't about to make it a priority. He was looking at my writing a book as useful cover for observing the renegade priest; I was looking at it as the principal purpose of my presence on Wrathlin.

Ah, yes. Wrathlin. That news still had to be broken.

She was probably thinking: scenic Donegal.

Or: boating on the Fermanagh lakes.

Or: when will I see Tony?

I went back downstairs and lifted Patricia's personal directory from beside the phone and ran my finger along the alphabet. When I found the number I took a deep breath and punched it in.

Fourth ring, a woman's voice, a solidly Belfast mouth fulla marlies.

'Hi. Is Tony there?'

'Yes, Anthony is here. Who shall I say is calling?'

'Uh, Willy. Willy from work.'

'Okay, just a second.'

She called out. *William from your office.* Too refined to shout. I heard hurried footsteps on bare floorboards. They would be French polished. There'd be lots of expensive antiques and tea in china cups. I sipped my beer.

'Who is this?'

'It's Dan Starkey.'

His voice dropped. 'Oh. Hello,' he said flatly, then followed it quickly with a chirpy, 'William. Yes. Indeed. What's up?'

'Patricia had a baby boy last night.'

He gulped. 'Mmm-hmm, yes, I phoned the hospital,' he whispered, then hurriedly added, louder: 'Yes, I know the file. Is it okay?'

'It was touch and go for a while, but I think he's okay now.'

'Good!' he boomed. 'I was hoping to get a good look at it earlier, but I've been tied up.'

'I think Patricia was expecting a visit today.'

'Mmmm. Yes. Indeed. Like I say. I've been exceptionally busy.'

'Listen. The little bastard's half yours, now get off your arse and go and see him.'

'It's been difficult to get away,' Tony hissed. 'I am married.'

'Yes, I know you're fucking married. So was I.'

'I didn't like to intrude.'

'If you hadn't intruded in her fucking vagina in the first place you wouldn't be in this situation, would you?'

Tony began some serious coughing. I held the receiver away from my ear for half a minute.

'Well,' he said eventually, loud again, 'I understood the file was closed. Obviously there are some loose ends that need tidying up.'

'You're a smarmy bastard, aren't you?'

'Obviously.'

'You owe her. You said all along you wanted to look after the child. You have a funny way of showing it.'

'Yes. Like I say, I've been tied up with those other files. But I'll certainly give that one my full attention tomorrow. It's good of you to take the trouble to call me at home. Yes. Indeed. See you soon then, William.'

'Aye,' I said and put the phone down.

I went to get another beer. Three, in fact. I needed another football.

Wrathlin sits about thirty miles off the north-west coast. It has a population of about a thousand, or had the last time I'd done any research on it: that was for a primary school composition. It's famous for two things, Robert the Bruce's cave, where he had an encounter with a spider, and the fact that Marconi, or at least some of his henchmen, carried out some of their earliest wireless experiments there. Oh yeah – and I remembered something fairly recently about Virgin boss Richard Branson doing one of his famous balloon crash landings there a few years back and the locals bartering a new community centre or something out of him in return for their invaluable help.

Not much.

Next morning, a Saturday, I wandered into the *News Letter* and sought out Mark Gale. Mark and I had trained together as reporters way back in the mists of time before the Pistols broke up.

He saw me crossing the newsroom. He sat back from his computer and stretched. He scratched idly at his paunch. Then he smiled at me.

'Dan, just the man. Perhaps you could answer a question for me.'

'Sure.'

'Who was Sam Andreas and why was it his fault?'

'I have no idea.'

'I thought not.'

I placed my thumbs on the edge of his desk and bent in over his computer. 'In that case,' I said, 'perhaps you could tell me who Sam Quinton was and why they hated every inch of him?'

'I have no idea.'

'I thought not.'

He reached for his cigarettes. Berkeley Mild. A healthier death. 'Maybe we could settle this by you telling me who Sam Francisco was and why they were going to him?'

I shook my head. He shook his.

'Busy?' I asked.

'Nah, you joking?' He offered me a cigarette. I refused. He lit one up. 'Ever since that bloody truce there's been nothing doing. The sooner they get back to blowing each other up the better. If you're looking for a shift you better give the Provos a call and demand a resumption of the campaign.'

I sat on the edge of his desk. The computer system the *News Letter* had recently installed was supposed to have created a paper-free environment and thus help conservation. Mark hated conservation. He liked things made with real trees. Rare ones, preferably. His desk had enough paper piled on it to reconstitute a small forest.

'Not interested in work, Mark. Just wanted to pick your brains. Do you fancy a pint?'

He shook his head mournfully. 'Off it for Lent.'

'Seriously? I thought Lent finished . . .'

'The wife insists.'

'Jesus. How the mighty have fallen.'

'Tell me all about it,' he said miserably. 'So. Pick away.'

'You're from Wrathlin Island originally, aren't you?'

'Sure.'

'I thought maybe you could tell me something about it.'

'Something?'

'I've been given this grant to write a book. It means living in a wee cottage on Wrathlin for a couple of months. Kind of like a retreat. Far from the madding crowd, as Oliver Hardy might have said. I'm just wondering what it's like.'

He smirked. I smirked.

'Have you ever been to Barbados?'

'Nope.'

'Good. It's nothing like that.' He rubbed his hands together, then held them up to his face and scratched at a heavy stubble. 'Ah, now,' he said, 'how do you describe Wrathlin? I suppose it's a pleasant little spot for a day out during the summer. When're you going, next summer?'

I shrugged. 'Sooner. A couple of months.'

He tutted. 'Coldy, coldy, coldy.'

'Bad timing? We go as soon as the baby's fully fit.'

Mark looked surprised. 'Oh, aye. I forgot Patricia was due. What'd youse have?'

'She had a wee boy.'

'Congrats. Everything okay?'

'Yeah. Great.'

'You don't look very excited.'

'It takes a lot to get me excited.'

Mark looked a little closer at me. 'You all right, mate?'

'Fine.'

'You're sure?'

'I'm fine.'

'My wife thinks you have a drink problem.'

I stood up. 'I don't have a drink problem, Mark. I have a hangover problem. It's a subtle but important difference.'

He looked a little bashful. 'Sorry, Dan, I didn't mean to . . .'

'Never worry. Tell me about Wrathlin.'

'Okay. Like I say, nice for a day trip when the sun's out and sea's calm. That's about a week every year. Rest of the time it's . . . well . . . a hole. Wind. Rain. Snow. Hail. Thunder. Lightning. Then you have your breakfast. Ach, maybe that's not fair. It's not so bad if you're keen on the island life – it's basic, it's primitive, its attitudes, its morals belong to the last century.'

'But it has electricity.'

'Yes, of course it has, Dan. It's not that bad. It's very insular, but then you'd expect that with, what, a population of about eight hundred it must be down to now. During the winter you can't even see the mainland much. Isolated is the word. It's a poor place. Not much work, and what there is is invariably seasonal.'

'Fairly religious, would you say?'

'Has its moments. For three hundred years it's been something of a refuge for Catholics from all along the north-west coast. Those that could afford to fled to England or France or down South to escape persecution. Those that couldn't ended up on Wrathlin. Most of them never left again. We're crocheted. They're close-knit.'

'You left it, though.'

'Aye. That's the problem with Wrathlin. It's not big enough to support a secondary school, so most of the teenagers get shunted off to schools on the mainland, they have their eyes opened a bit, and they don't want to go back. Population's dropping every year, I hear.'

'Your folks still out there?'

'Aye.'

'You ever go back?'

Mark shook his head. 'I should. Just never seem to get round to it. You know how it is.'

'Aye. I know.'

'You thinking of taking Patricia out there as well, then?'

'Yeah. And the baby.'

'You think that's wise?'

'You think it's not?'

'I wouldn't go that far. But Patricia . . . well, Patricia's a bit of a city girl, isn't she?'

'Yeah. I suppose she is.'

'Wrathlin's no city, Dan. You know they're still waiting for *Gone with the Wind* to arrive?'

I gave him the raised palms. 'Well, I've agreed to go. I'll jump the Patricia hurdle when I come to it.'

'And when'll that be?'

'In about half an hour.'

'Oh dear.'

'Aye. I know.'

There is a splinter group of the Ulster Volunteer Force called the Red Hand Commando. Sometimes it is referred to as the Barmy Wing of the UVF.

While the rest of the Province was celebrating peace it was planning murder. While I was lightly grilling Mark Gale about Wrathlin it was sending two gunmen into the Royal Victoria Hospital's maternity wing to murder a Republican activist.

The intended victim was the big woman in the bed beside Patricia's. They walked in cool as you like during visiting time, baseball caps, denim jackets and jeans, checked the chart at the foot of Patricia's bed, shook their heads, moved up to the next, where the woman was sleeping. Patricia shouted at them. The woman woke up. Woke up and looked into the barrel of the pistol. Not more than five inches from her head. Point-blank. Her mouth dropped open. The trigger was pulled. The gun jammed. Pulled again. Jammed again.

'One for luck, eh?' said the commando, and pulled the trigger a third time.

Nothing. He laughed. 'You're one lucky bitch. We'll get you next time. Have a nice day now.' He swiped her with the pistol, slicing open her scalp, then the two of them walked calmly off down the corridor.

When I reached maternity it was cordoned off by the police and army. It took some persuasion and a tantrum to get through.

When I finally reached Patricia she was in tears. Ginger was in her arms. She was rocking him nervously from side to side. He was crying too. There was no sign of the woman from the next bed. It was neatly made and her locker was empty.

'Take us away from here, Dan,' Patricia cried as I put my arm round her. 'I hate this fucking place.'

'It's okay, honey,' I said, 'we're going far away, just as soon as we can.'

God was moving in a mysterious way.

5

Everything was fine and dandy.

Patricia came home. The baby was doing great. We bundled him up and brought him out into the real world for the first time. The sun showed its face for the first time in weeks. Tony hadn't shown his. I'd cleaned the house. It had taken me eight hours, but I'd managed it. I'd discovered how the vacuum cleaner worked. It was a complicated procedure involving a plug and a socket. I lost three socks and a slipper in the process but I thought it was probably worth the sacrifice when I saw the look on Patricia's face as I led her into the lounge.

'You've cleaned,' she said, awestruck.

I shrugged.

She ran a finger along the arm of the settee. 'Really cleaned,' she said.

I shrugged again. I took Ginger from her. 'Will I put him in his cot?'

She nodded. Smiled. Kissed me on the cheek. 'Let's,' she said.

I carried him upstairs, Patricia on my heels, and entered the blue bedroom. He gurgled happily. I pulled back the blanket and set him gently down in the cot. Then I tucked him loosely in and stood back. He gurgled some more. Patricia gurgled back. I gave a little gurgle too. I surprised myself by not feeling stupid.

'Our whole life is changed now,' I said.

'Are you sorry?'

I shook my head.

'Are you sure?'

'Of course I'm sure.'

'I know it's been very difficult for you, Dan.'

'I know I've been very difficult for you.'

'But . . . you know what I mean.'

'I know what you mean.'

I took her hand. Later I bottle-fed the baby. Patricia put her feet up. She had cabbage leaves in her bra. I didn't ask why. I opened a bottle of wine. I cooked dinner and gave it to her on a tray.

'What's come over you, sweetie?' she asked.

'Nothing. I just love you.'

'I love you too.'

'Aw.'

I told her about Wrathlin.

She thought about it for maybe three minutes, not looking at me, but into her wine glass, slowly swirling the alcohol. Then she said, 'Okay.'

'What do you mean, "Okay"?'

'Okay. Fair enough. All right. I agree.' She squeezed my hand. 'What did you expect me to say?'

'I thought you'd tell me to fuck off.'

'Dan . . .'

'I thought you'd tell me to stick Wrathlin Island up my hole.'

'Dan, I . . .'

'I'm extraordinarily happy.'

'Good. So am I.'

We clinked glasses. 'I'm sick of this city,' she said. 'That thing the other day scared the shite out of me. Maybe we'll stay on Wrathlin for ever.'

'Let's not get ahead of ourselves, kiddo,' I said, stroking her leg. 'You don't know what you're letting yourself in for.'

She shook her head. 'I'll be with you. I'll be with my baby. That's all that matters.'

'Aw.' I looked into her eyes. 'Darlin', it's remote.'

'And sometimes, so are you.'

As the weeks sped by, Patricia got to grips with looking after a child. I put in a couple of hours as well. I also started packing up our possessions for an extended trip to Wrathlin Island. I kept it as best I could to the absolute minimum – baby things, women's things, men's things.

The Cardinal had described the cottage to me as modern and fully furnished, which cut down considerably on what we'd have to haul across to the island. I phoned him and negotiated for one of the natives to provide a cot. He agreed. He was anxious that I get out there as soon as possible. He even sent me a cheque to cover our stay on the island. It was three thousand pounds for ten weeks, which was pretty good, seeing as how the last advance I'd received for a book had been thirty-six pounds and a pot of strawberry jam.

Women, they're different to men. Say to a woman and her child, we can only take the essentials, and they'll totally agree with you, then they come up with enough essentials to relieve Mafeking. A man, now, can travel light. A good razor. Toothbrush. Some clean T-shirts. Jeans. A portable typewriter. Paper. A Walkman. Tapes of The Clash. Van Morrison. Neil Young. Oh, and a satellite dish.

There were some big fights coming up and they were only being covered on satellite. The heavyweight division had opened up a bit in the last few months, and even Belfast's own Fat Boy McMaster was back in the rankings. These I didn't want to miss. It seemed unlikely that anyone on Wrathlin would know what a satellite dish was. I'd heard they'd recently celebrated Yuri Gagarin's first circuit of the globe.

I don't know a lot about satellite dishes. My first instinct was to cut it off the side of my house with an axe, then Sellotape it to the side of the new cottage and hope for the best. But I thought it better to find out. There was late-night shopping down town, so I kissed Patricia and the baby goodbye and drove down to ask some advice from my friendly local dealer. He was very helpful. I nodded a lot, but most of it was beyond me.

On the way home I found myself whistling. It's not something I do often, or well, but it seemed appropriate. Everything was going well. I stopped at the off-licence and bought some wine for Patricia and twelve Harps for myself.

I was just pulling up outside the house when I saw Tony get out of his BMW and walk up to our front door. In the porch light I saw him nervously flick at his hair, then brush some raindrops off his Barbour jacket. I cursed and drove on. I circled the block, then parked several spaces down from our house. He was inside. I rolled down the window and spat.

I had a decision to make. The rain was beginning to come down in torrents. I was dry inside the car, but it might as well have been flooding in for the way my good humour had suddenly been washed away. I thumped the wheel. I thumped it again. Keith Moon was giving drumming lessons on my heart. My place was by my wife's side. But she would want to speak to him alone. My place was in there, defending my marriage. But Ginger was half his. I knew what I should do. I should give her the space. She'd told me she loved me. That she wanted to go to Wrathlin with me. But being suspicious was my forte, being the diligent cuckold was not. I shook my head. I opened a can of beer from the carry-out bag. She'd phoned him as soon as I left the house and he'd raced round. Even now they'd be . . . I slapped the wheel again. This time I hit the horn. No one seemed to notice.

I finished the can in double quick time and threw it into the back. I got out of the car and walked to our gate. I stared up at the house. The curtains in the lounge were drawn. I couldn't see any silhouettes against them.

I stood at the gate. I stared at my own house some more. I couldn't move. I got soaked. I stood for ten minutes staring at the door and windows, daring someone to move before them, to frame themselves. But nothing.

Tony's car was brand new. It looked sleek and cunning in the rain. I took my keys and scored a line along the driver's side. Then it didn't look so sleek and only half as cunning. I went back to my car and lifted out my carry-out then walked with it up the street. A couple of hundred yards up, there was a children's playground. I took a seat on the roundabout, started drinking my beer, and thought dark thoughts.

Two hours later I slopped up the street again. I'd done a lot of thinking but come to no conclusions, apart from the one that said that I could have achieved just as much by remaining dry in the car. It was close to midnight. Tony's car was gone. I let myself in. I shook myself like a dog. Patricia was standing in the kitchen doorway cradling Ginger.

'Where on earth have you been?' she demanded. Her voice was a rich cocktail of relief, anger, suspicion and concern.

'Does it matter?'

'Dan! Of course it matters. You're soaked!'

I nodded. 'And drunk.'

'Dan . . .'

'I saw his car, I didn't want to int . . .'

'Dan, I was waiting for you to come back . . .'

31

'I thought I'd leave you two . . . you three alone.'

'Dan, I wanted you to be here . . .'

'I thought . . .'

'Dan, you think too much, love . . .'

She ran forward and pulled me to her. We kissed.

'You're squashing the baby,' I said.

She laughed, pulled back and kissed him. 'You silly man,' she said. Then she took me by her free hand and led me into the lounge. I squelched along. She sat me down. 'Dan, you're one stupid, suspicious, crazy bastard,' she said. 'It's a good job I love you.'

'A good job,' I repeated.

'He phoned just after you left. He asked if it was okay to call round to see the baby. I said you'd be back in an hour and asked him to wait until then. But you didn't come.'

'I got delayed.'

'Tony said you called him.'

'He would. What'd he say?'

'He said you chastised him for not coming to see me.' She held my gaze for a moment. She had lovely eyes. Always had. 'He said you were quite right to have a go at him.'

'How magmaninous of him.' I silently mouthed the word again. 'Magnaninus,' I began again. 'That was big of him.'

Her voice was softly scolding. 'You didn't need to call him.'

'Yes, I did. You were pining for him.'

'Och, Dan, when are you going to understand me? I wasn't pining for him.'

'You were.'

'Dan, I . . .'

'Okay, you weren't. Whatever you say. I just geed him up. I thought he should come and see you.'

Patricia smiled. 'That was magnanimous of you.'

'Touché. Or is that touchy? It's all a matter of syntax. Or is that signtax?'

She set the baby gently on the floor, then leant across and kissed me.

'Thank you,' I said. I nodded at the baby. He lay peacefully, staring up at his mother. 'Isn't it time we put him to bed?'

Patricia nodded. She reached down and stroked his head. He gurgled. 'We're going to have to think of a name for him.'

'We had thought of one.'

'I know, but it doesn't seem appropriate now, somehow.'

'I hate to say it, but . . .'

'I know, it's the red hair.'

We'd thought of Richard. Richard Starkey. 'Richard doesn't go with red hair, does it?'

She shook her head. 'Red Richard roams round Wrathlin.'

'Rusty Ritchie recommends rabies.'

'No, Richard will have to go. Anything with an *r* will have to go.' She looked thoughtful for a few moments. 'One letter up. Sam.'

'Sam Starkey?'

'Samuel Starkey. Samuel S. Starkey.'

'S for . . . ?'

'S for . . . Steven . . .'

'Samuel after . . . ?'

'My uncle Sammy, runs the chip shop . . .'

'Steven for . . . ?'

'I don't know . . . Spielberg . . .'

'SS Starkey. Makes him sound like a ship.'

'Well, we're sailing to Wrathlin. Let's sail on the SS Starkey.'

And that, as they say, was that.

About five the SS Starkey sprang a leak and began sending out an SOS. Patricia slept soundly, spooned into my stomach. I lay for a few minutes, waiting to see if the crying would subside. It became a wail. I backed out of the bed as quietly as I could. Patricia grunted something and repositioned herself. I put on my dressing gown and padded into the blue room.

My mouth was thick with drink. I drew breath through my nose as I bent into the cot, thinking that might mislead him into thinking that his stepfather wasn't a drink-sodden fool. It didn't. But he stopped crying almost immediately and smiled as I picked him up and held him close. It was clear that he appreciated the aroma of stale alcohol.

'What's wrong, wee man?' I asked and gave him a cuddle.

'Dying for a fuckin' bottle, mate,' his eyes said.

I carried him down the stairs and prepared his bottle.

While it was heating, I changed his nappy.

'Don't get the wrong impression,' I told him. 'This is your mum's job.'

33

I fed him while I sat at the kitchen table. He was a warm little thing. While he eagerly sucked at the bottle I told him the things he would need to know to have any kind of a life at all: to never volunteer to do nets at school, to always be the striker. Told him that John Barnes was the best footballer ever to play for Liverpool, that George Best was the best since the beginning of time. That 'Anarchy in the UK', 'God Save the Queen' and 'Pretty Vacant' were the best sequence of singles ever released by a rock'n'roll band. That Sugar Ray Leonard and Muhammad Ali were the greatest boxers in the history of the sport, but that neither of them had retired when they should have. I warned him against ever perming his hair. Or wearing white socks. Of the dangers of flared trousers. Normally I would have advised him to be wary of people with red hair, but it seemed inappropriate. I told him that God probably didn't exist, but if he did his son was unlikely to live on Wrathlin Island.

I don't know how much of this sunk in. It would only become clear with the passage of time.

6

The *Fitzpatrick* was a converted trawler which crossed to the mainland twice a week, depending on the weather. It was just big enough to accommodate two cars and a handful of passengers. Islanders had long been campaigning for a larger vessel as an aid to kick-starting their tourist industry, but on that sun-kissed morning the need was not immediately apparent. Patricia, Stevie and I were the only passengers. We drove up from Belfast in the scattered light of dawn. As we rolled down into the harbour at Ballycastle the island was just appearing through a fine mist and we sat watching it from the quay for five minutes, just my wife, her baby, and three thousand tonnes of clothes to see us through the next ten weeks.

'It looks so peaceful,' Patricia said.

I nodded.

Charlie McManus was the *Fitzpatrick*'s skipper. He was a gnarled old gent with hair like an explosion in a mattress factory. He guided the Fiesta on board, secured it with lengths of chain, then circled it, shaking his head at the amount of luggage we'd managed to squeeze in.

'Are yees opening a shop or somethin'?' he asked. He had big, smiley eyes.

'We're staying in a cottage for a couple of months,' I said. 'I've some work to do.'

He looked me up and down and knew the answer before he asked the question: 'Yer not a farmer, are ye?'

'No. I'm writing a book. Peace and quiet and all that.'

He nodded, rubbed his chin for a moment. 'Aye, well,' he said, and climbed up behind the wheel to start the engine. It took a while to splutter into life.

We stood up front at first as Charlie piloted the boat out of the harbour, but as we hit the open sea a bit of a breeze began to blow up and Patricia snagged my arm and said she thought it was better

35

that she sat with Little Stevie in the car. I'd decided to refer to him as Little Stevie. It made me think of Bruce Springsteen and took my mind off the red hair.

I stepped up behind Charlie at the wheel. He nodded benignly as I joined him. 'Lovely morning,' I said.

'Aye,' he replied.

He had a finely cut beard, curiously at odds with his hair. 'You been doing this run for long?' I asked.

'Aye,' he said, 'long enough.'

'And how are things on the island?'

'Aye, well, not bad.'

'Good,' I said. He was the sort that wouldn't be fazed by the arrival of the Antichrist, let alone the Messiah. He'd say, 'Aye, well, another plague today, but there yees are,' and be more concerned about the boat leaving on time. I rejoined Patricia in the car.

'What's out of Captain Birdseye?' she asked.

'Nothing,' I said.

The journey took little over an hour. As pleasant a sea trip as I had ever undertaken. The sea undulated gently, the wind remained light and elbow-cooling. Gulls shadowed us the whole way, fooled by the old trawler and the fishy smell emanating from Little Stevie's nappy.

The harbour was awkward to approach, the currents forcing us wide. Half a dozen other trawlers were tied up on the quay. As Charlie ran the *Fitzpatrick* to the dock we left the car again and stood up front, picking out details ashore. The town itself – a village really – was tightly clustered around the harbour. Small whitewashed cottages faced the sea. Taller, more modern terraces, with ground floors speckled here and there with shops, ran back up a hill towards a crown dominated by a church glinting in the autumnal sun. It was a beautiful day. Patricia slipped her hand into mine. I squeezed it. She smiled up at me, then at the island. 'Lovely,' she said.

Charlie threw a rope ashore and a couple of young lads secured the vessel. Then he lowered the gate and I eased the Fiesta up onto the dock. He waved. We waved back. Stevie managed a gurgle.

'Welcome to paradise,' I said and we both laughed.

We were still laughing two hundred yards further on when we came to the pub.

I'd done my research. There was one pub on the island. Jack McGettigan's. He'd run it for thirty years. It was just a pub. He didn't serve lunch. He didn't have discos. There wasn't even a dart board. He served pints and shorts and that was it, and that was all you needed. It was certainly all I needed. I'd idly fantasised about doing my thousand words in the morning in my lonely garret, contented wife and playful child notwithstanding, then sauntering down to the pub for a few drinks, then meandering home for a few hundred more words, a cuddle with the wife and a tickle with the child, then spending the evening talking it up with the locals and old Jack himself over a few more pints; maybe even sticking my head out the door every once in a while to see if there were any miracles taking place up on the hill.

I stopped the car.

'What's wrong?' Patricia asked.

Suddenly I felt drained. Like Dracula had sucked me dry. 'The pub,' I said.

Patricia nodded. 'What of it?'

'It's closed.'

'It's early yet.'

I shook my head and opened the door. 'No, I mean, it's closed.' I stood in the road. 'It's boarded up. It's closed. Closed down. Look at it, Patricia.'

She looked at it.

'The fucking pub is closed.'

'So it is.'

'Did you know this?'

'Jesus, Dan, how would I know it?'

I left the door open and stepped up to the door. I pulled at it, but it was well secured. The windows too were boarded. 'Jesus,' I said.

The two young fellas who'd secured the *Fitzpatrick* appeared behind the car. One had a Royal Mail bag slung over his shoulder. There didn't appear to be much in it. He wore an Aran jumper and had curly hair which owed nothing to a hairdresser.

'What happened to the pub?' I asked.

'Shut,' he said.

'For good?'

'Aye.'

'Did Old Jack die?'

37

'Nah, he's around yet.'

They walked on. I got back in the car. 'Fuck it,' I said, and slapped the wheel. 'Is it too late to go home?'

Patricia snorted.

'This isn't funny. I didn't even bring a fucking carry-out.'

She squeezed my leg. 'Oh dear,' she said, without a trace of sympathy.

'Imagine closing a pub. Who ever heard of it? I mean, what do the people do?'

'Dan, they make their own. That's what they do in places like this. Poteen.'

'Bugger poteen. I want my Harp.'

'Dan, there's a boat in a couple of days. Go back and get some supplies then if you're that desperate.'

'That's a year and a day away, for God's sake. What am I supposed to do till then?'

'Suffer.'

'Thanks.'

I'd once tried to make poteen as a youth. It involved boiling a lot of potatoes and fermenting the residue. I didn't manage to create anything even vaguely alcoholic, though I did get a nice stew out of it.

I sat silent behind the wheel for a moment and tried to think things through. It wasn't that the beer was so important to me: knowing it was there and available would in reality have been sufficient; I didn't *have* to have it; but knowing that it wasn't there and it was a sea journey away, that was the killer. A real bloody killer. I slapped the wheel again.

'There's beer on this island somewhere,' I said. 'There must be.'

'Forget the beer for a moment, love,' Patricia said. 'It's time for milk.' She nodded down at Little Stevie. He started to cry. They had plainly rehearsed it.

Then it was Patricia's turn to girn.

We followed a winding road out along the coast for about a mile, then when we came to a lighthouse we turned inland. Another half-mile further on we came to Snow Cottage. Home.

There was a bath lying on its side in the front garden. It was half filled with murky water. The cottage walls had once been whitewashed but were now damp and dark. The garden was wildly overgrown.

'I don't like this,' Patricia said simply.

'Now don't jump to conclusions. It's probably a little palace inside.'

'Aye,' she said.

'You know,' I said, 'you can be very sarcastic when you try.'

'That wasn't even trying,' she spat, 'and if this place is a hole you're a dead man.'

Of course it wasn't a hole. It just wasn't a palace.

The key was being kept warm under the doormat by a couple of thousand woodlice. I didn't mention them to Patricia, they were probably just visiting. I stepped aside and made calming noises as she entered, Stevie in her arms, and began to storm from room to room, tutting. There was a fairly new bathroom suite, but the last bather had left a couple of layers of skin in it. There were dirty pans in the kitchen sink. A half-eaten bowl of Frosties sat on the kitchen table, the milk thick and stenchy.

'It's like the fucking *Mary Celeste*,' said Patricia.

I nodded. 'Could be worse,' I said

'How, Dan?' she demanded.

'There could be pigs in the parlour.'

'There have been pigs in this fucking kitchen, Dan. What am I supposed to do with this . . . ?' Her eyes darted suddenly with renewed intensity about the kitchen. 'Where's the microwave?'

'What microwave?'

'Dan, the microwave?'

'What microwave? Plainly, I would say from the evidence before you, there is no microwave.'

'But how am I supposed to cook?'

'With the cooker. Look. There. That thing in the corner. That's the cooker. It's plugged in. That's what real people cook on.'

'But . . . but . . .'

'Trish, it isn't difficult.'

'But I always use a microwave. I brought microwave meals.'

'Trish, they probably don't have microwaves here. They probably don't even have demi-waves.'

'I don't like this place, Dan. It smells.'

'It just needs to be cleaned up a bit, love.'

'Aye. And who's going to do that?'

'We'll both do it.'

'It's no place for a baby.'

'It'll be all right, love. It'll just take us a while to find our feet. Then we'll be laughing. Honestly.'

The bedroom was nice. A double bed. Made. No cot.

Patricia noticed first. She tutted. 'You promised.'

'The Cardinal promised.'

'The Cardinal seems to have promised a lot. Just get on the bloody phone to him, Dan, and tell him what sort of a state this place is in. It's a disgrace.'

She looked miserable. I pulled at my lower lip. 'I hate to point this out, Trish . . .'

Her eyes narrowed. 'What?'

'This business about phoning the Cardinal.'

'Yes?'

'It would really require a phone.'

'Dan . . .'

'I'm sorry, but I told you it was an isolated cottage, there's no . . .'

'But how am I supposed to phone . . . ?' She stopped. Bit it back. Silence hung in the air, hung on the dust.

'Tony?' I suggested.

'Dad, Dan. *Dad*. That's not fair. He'll be worried if I don't call.'

'So send him a pigeon.' It came out a little harsher than I intended. She looked hurt. I shrugged. 'I'm sorry.'

'You spend your whole life apologising to me.'

'I know. I'm sorry.'

The tears started to run down her cheeks. 'I want to go home,' she cried.

I went to her. The three of us nestled together. 'It'll be okay,' I said, without a great deal of confidence.

Little Stevie went to sleep on our double bed.

We decided to clean the inside of the house before unpacking our belongings. There were cleaning materials under the sink. Once we got stuck in it didn't take long to get the kitchen, then the bathroom, into shape. Then we took a break. We looked in on Stevie; he slept soundly. We brought some of our supplies in from the car. Trish made a cup of tea. I had a can of Diet Pepsi. It was warm, but it was still Diet Pepsi.

'It's not so bad, is it, love?'

'Mmmmm,' she said. Her eyes glazed over for a moment and she looked like she was drawing up a mental list of the things that *were* so bad. The noise of a car engine snapped her out of it. We peered out of the window. A Land-Rover was just pulling into the driveway. When it stopped a tall man in a pair of mud-spattered blue dungarees got out. He went round to the back of the vehicle, reached inside and pulled out a cot.

'Brilliant!' Patricia exclaimed and made for the door.

7

'I'm very sorry,' the big man said, 'I didn't think youse were coming until next week. I got the shock of my life when they told me in the shop you'd arrived.'

He held the cot in two massive arms. I went to help him, but he shook his head. 'Duncan Cairns,' he said, wiggling a couple of fingers round the base of the cot. 'I'm the schoolteacher. I should have gotten this place ready ages ago . . . but you know how it is.'

'Never worry,' Patricia said, reaching out and tweaking his little finger. 'It's good of you to bring it.'

Duncan smiled bashfully and manoeuvred the cot sideways through the front door. I thought it best not to join in the tweaking until I had figured out his sexual orientation.

Patricia bustled in behind him. 'It's good of you to bring it,' I mimicked behind her. 'You've changed your tune.'

'I'm only being polite,' she whispered.

'You could be polite to me,' I said.

'That'll be the day,' she hissed with enough venom to suggest a nodding acquaintance with the family *Viperidae*.

I shrugged and followed them in. It's funny how marriage vows give you a licence to be mean to your loved ones but polite to strangers. I have always believed and practised that it should be the other way about. Indeed, that I was within my rights to tell Duncan Bloody Cairns to stick his cot up his hole, as Oscar Wilde had once famously not said. But I held off. He had the flushed face and red-rimmed eyes of someone who might know where the beer was kept.

Duncan set the cot down in the bedroom, then stood back and admired it for a moment. 'It was mine when I was a kid,' he said.

'Aw,' said Patricia.

He looked at Little Stevie, sleeping soundly on the bed. 'Now there's a picture,' he said.

'Aye,' said Patricia.

I had done enough beating around the bush. I'd let him through my front door. I'd let him relax in his new surroundings and get to know us as friends. He'd crammed a lot into ten seconds. 'Listen,' I said, 'I'd offer you a drink, but there appears to be none on the island.'

'Naw,' he said with a slight shake of his head, 'there's not.'

'How come?' I asked. 'I saw the pub's shut on the way in.'

Patricia tutted. 'You've got drink on the brain, Dan,' she scolded. 'Would you like a cup of tea, Duncan?'

'If it's no trouble . . .'

'No trouble at all.'

She scooted off to the kitchen. 'What's with the lack of drink, then?' I asked.

'Aye, well, Old Jack McGettigan . . . he owned the pub . . . well, he kind of got religion and decided to close it down.'

'That must have gone down well.'

'Actually, it did, mostly. The Parish Council took a vote and decided to ban the stuff entirely.'

'Jesus,' I said.

'Something like that.'

He held my eyes for a moment, then turned and walked into the kitchen.

They had tea. I had another Diet Pepsi. If I ever do write my novel I will have to put 'with added Nutrasweet' on the cover.

'So who had the cottage before us?' Patricia asked, elbows on the table, fists bunched loosely beneath her chin. 'They left it in a bit of a mess.'

'I know. I'm sorry – again. A couple of young bucks over from the mainland rented it out. They seemed decent enough, but . . . you know . . . they weren't. They were asked to leave.'

'They seemed to leave in a hurry,' I said.

'Yes,' he said. He nodded once, as if to signal that the subject was closed. He looked about the kitchen. So did I. It looked a good deal better since we'd worked at it. 'So do you think you'll be comfortable here' he asked, 'what with the baby 'n' all?'

'Of course we will,' Patricia said, and gave his arm a little squeeze.

He was pleasant. Chatty without being gossipy. Interested without delving. Informative but not revealing. He didn't raise the subject of the child Messiah. Neither did I. It could wait. Even sitting, he was tall. He'd a shock of black curly hair. It was difficult to put an age on him, with his pale unlined face, but wind-hardened skin. He said he'd been a teacher in the school for six years. He was island born, bred and buttered. His parents were long dead and he now lived alone in a cottage at the rear of the school. The school itself wasn't much more than a room in which he taught pupils from five up to pre-teen. After that they were shipped off to the mainland.

'So where did you learn to be a teacher?' Patricia asked.

'Derry,' he said.

'But you came back here after you trained.'

'Yeah. That was always the plan. My dad was teacher here before me. It was kind of expected of me.'

'I think that's nice.'

'Well,' he said, and nodded once. His gaze lingered on Patricia.

My gaze often lingers on Patricia, but that is my right. I've paid the licence fee.

He turned to me. 'I thought maybe you could come along and read something of what you've written to the kids,' he said.

'You think they'll be into sex and drugs and rock'n'roll?'

'Oh,' he said flatly, and looked at the table.

'Dan . . .' said Patricia.

I shrugged.

'He's only teasing,' Patricia said. 'You'll have to get used to his sense of humour.'

Duncan nodded slowly. His eyes returned to me. 'So what are you writing?'

There are two ways to go when you get into a mood. You go with what comes naturally. Free flow. Stream of consciousness. Honesty. Say it with passion. Stuff the consequences. Or you can be polite. Sometimes you don't know until you open your mouth.

'I'm talking to Spielberg about a screenplay.'

Patricia tutted.

'It's an examination of the drink-sodden later years of Oskar Schindler. It's called *Schindler's Pissed*.'

'Dan . . .'

'I don't think that's funny,' Duncan said quietly. He didn't look at me. He looked at his tea. He stirred it slowly. With a spoon.

'I do.'

'You shouldn't make fun of a subject like that. Six million Jews died in the war.'

'Ach, lighten up,' I said and flicked my empty can at the waste bin in the corner. It missed. I went and retrieved it. Then I placed it carefully in the bin.

'He's right, Dan,' Patricia said, 'there's no need . . .'

'I have a close affinity to the subject,' I said. 'My dad fought in the war. While he was killing Germans, Spielberg was taking it easy in someone's womb.'

'Spielberg wasn't born until 1946,' said Duncan.

'It was a long pregnancy,' I countered. We were silent for a moment. Patricia looked daggers at me. Duncan continued to stir. So did I. Sometimes, once you're started, it's difficult to stop. You get in the groove. 'Sure how would you know anyway? There's not even a bloody cinema on the island.'

'I read a lot.'

'About movies?'

'Sure.'

'That's like reading about music.'

He stopped the stirring. He blew a rush of air out of his nose. Then he stood abruptly, knocking the chair back and over. 'I'm not going to apologise to you for life on this island,' he growled. 'You're the one who wanted to come here.'

He reached down and righted the chair. 'I'm sorry,' he said quickly to Patricia. 'Anyway. I must be off. I'm sure you've lots to do.'

'Nonsense, you . . .' Patricia began, but he was already turning for the door.

'I was only raking,' I said, belatedly. He nodded. I was starting to calm down. The little burst of temper helped.

Patricia walked him to the door.

I sat where I was. I felt a little stupid. I heard him say, 'I'm sorry, I get a bit defensive about this . . .'

'Don't say a word, Duncan, he hasn't been well. Just on a short fuse. We'll see you again, soon I hope. Why don't you come for dinner one night?'

I didn't hear a reply. A shake or a nod.

The door closed.

'What do you mean I haven't been . . . ?'

Patricia came back in and slapped me across the back of the head. 'What did you do that for?' she snapped. There was a squall on her face.

'I'm sorry. I just . . .'

'Why are you always so nasty to nice people?'

I bit at a lip. I rubbed the back of my head. 'I'm not comfortable with nice people. Nice strangers. You know that.' She was shaking her head. 'I think it's a self-confidence thing.'

'It's a bad manners thing. There's no excuse for it. You're like a child who won't share a toy. You were awful to Tony when you first met him as well. You tried to punch him.'

'He was sleeping with you, for Christ's sake!'

'He wasn't *then*, Dan.'

'Oh.'

'Your plain bloody nastiness drives people to extremes, Dan. Don't you know that after all this time?'

I shrugged.

'It's lucky I love you,' she continued, 'because you're a self-centred arrogant pig, and you've nothing to be self-centred or arrogant about. That poor man went out of his way to bring us a cot, his own cot for God's sake, and all you can do is try to be smart – and fail.' Suddenly she slapped the table. The surprise crack of palm on wood jerked me back. 'You'll go after him right this minute, and you'll apologise,' she snapped.

'I will not.'

'You will.'

Patricia can stare without blinking for longer than anyone in this part of the universe.

'Okay,' I said.

Patricia went into the bedroom to feed and change Little Stevie. Or change and feed. I hadn't quite got to grips with the running order. She closed the door behind her.

I wrote her a note. I'M SORRY. I LOVE YOU. I KNOW I'M STUPID.

46

FORGIVE ME. DUNCAN SEEMS ALL RIGHT. IF I'M STUPID AGAIN, I'LL SHAVE MY HEAD. In the grand scheme of things, it wasn't a great threat, but then Patricia knows how much I value my hair. I would have nightmares about it not growing back. Or growing back ginger.

8

It was getting towards dusk, a beautiful autumnal dusk with the sun slowly drifting down beyond the lazy waves, when I drove up the hill towards the school. I gave the pub a lingering look of regret as I passed. There was probably beer still locked up in there. If the owner had suddenly got religion, I couldn't imagine him having a closing-down sale. It might warrant further investigation if things got really bad. I laughed. I didn't really need it.

The shops on the Main Street, shiny in the heat, were closing up. I nodded at a couple of men. They squinted at the unfamiliar car for a moment, then nodded back. One smiled. One waved. I felt pretty good. The apology to Duncan was a bit of a bother, but I'd get that out of the way soon enough. Maybe he could help me suss out where the drink was. Then I could get settled into some serious writing. Perhaps the great Ulster novel wasn't entirely beyond me. Maybe it just needed me to get away from the temptations of the city, from the familiar distractions of friends and news and troubles. Wrathlin, a little paradise off the coast of frightened, bickering Ireland.

I parked in the school yard, a dusty little garden of feet-hardened and sun-baked mud. There wasn't much to the school. A room, just. I peered through the window. Desks. Chairs. A blackboard. Simplicity itself. It could have been my own primary school thirty years before, a time before video, a time before computers, a time before you could stab your teacher through the heart if you disagreed on a point of arithmetic. By the door there was a small cardboard box; toes of trainers poked out. Ah yes, that brought it back. The communal plimsole box, once a fixture of every school but outlawed since the great verruca epidemic of '71. On the desk at the front there was an upright wooden box containing half a dozen recorders, and beside it a bottle of Dettol. The instruments would be passed from child to child, dutifully dipped in the antiseptic fluid each time to clear out any lingering spit. The herpes epidemic of '78 had seen to that one too. It was like I'd passed through the Time Tunnel. Chalked on the blackboard, I noted, was the sign of the cross.

There was a small unevenly whitewashed bungalow behind the school, as if the paint had been applied by dozens of little brushes. And it probably had. There was space for a car, but no car. I rapped on the front door. No reply. Through the window: spartan lounge – sofa, one armchair, a foldaway desk with exercise books piled upon it. No TV. I turned from the window. The apology would have to wait.

I stood in the yard and looked down the hill over the town, serene, and out over the water to the mainland, now just a hazy blue line, like a distant fence keeping the troublemakers in. I looked up the hill towards the church, lonely, but confident, standing guard over the island. Perhaps subduing it. I started up through the long grass. There's no time like the present is a phrase which rarely enters my vocabulary. Any time but, is much more likely. Yet it was a pleasant evening, all was quiet, all was well, and if Father Flynn wasn't there there was the off-chance I might be able to locate some communion wine.

I was more than slightly out of breath when I got to the top of the hill. I would have to get back to the gym. Once I had enough strength to get the doors open. Luckily the church doors *were* open. As they should be. Once, years before, Flynn had offered me sanctuary in his church in Crossmaheart. It wouldn't have deterred any of the various shades of killer pursuing me at the time, but it was a nice gesture. Now I was spying on him.

Or not spying on him. There was no one about. I stood in the doorway and stared down the aisle.

I wasn't particularly familiar with the interior of any church, but I was particularly unfamiliar with the inside of a Catholic church. I grew up in a part of Belfast where there was very little cross-community activity. Just two cross communities. The one time I'd been inside a Catholic church was for a christening. There'd been a bunch of us, all branded Protestant by geography and parental affiliation, rather than religious fervour, but nevertheless we all clustered warily near the exit from the alien environment, ready to make a quick getaway if trouble flared. Throughout the ceremony – actually more spiritual than the Protestant version, a fine point to an atheist/agnostic – my friend Tommy Nailor had kept up a

whispered running commentary. 'He's lifting the baby now . . .
he's lifting the knife . . . he's slitting the throat . . . he's sucking
it dry . . .' We were laughing so hard, bent double, that when the
priest made the sign of peace and instructed everyone to turn to
their neighbour and shake hands we'd thought we were being set
upon and had bunched up ready for a scrap. Funny. Yeah. Someone
had burned down the church a couple of weeks later, although we
all had alibis.

I walked down the aisle. Pleasant. Cool. A half-dozen candles
flickered. Christ was on the cross. The Madonna. Their fiercely
Anglo-Saxon faces. Christianity wouldn't have got so far if Christ
had looked like Yasser Arafat.

I couldn't see any wine. Couldn't smell any. I walked back up the
aisle. I stopped for a moment by the font. I dipped my hand into the
water. Cold. I bent and sipped some up. Nice. Stony. I wiped my
mouth and looked up into the eyes of a child standing stock-still in
the doorway, his head back-lit by the last rays of the sinking sun.

My heart skipped a beat.

He couldn't have been more than five. His hair was blond, clipped
short. He wore a white T-shirt and blue shorts. He had plastic sandals
on bare feet. We held each other's gaze for a minute. His eyes were
deep blue, his stare intense.

'Hello,' I said.

He didn't react at all. I gave him a little smile. He didn't give it
back. 'What's your name?' I asked.

'What the fuck are you doing?' he demanded.

I relaxed. Probably not the Messiah.

'I'm looking for Father Flynn. Have you seen him?'

He shook his head warily.

'What's your name?' I asked.

'What's it got to do with you?'

He had a world-weary surliness not fitting for one so young.
'Well,' I said, 'I thought we could be friends.'

'Pervert,' he said, and turned on his heel.

I followed him back out onto the hill. He strode purposefully
towards the long grass I had previously tramped through. As he
reached it, three more boys rose slowly. They watched me sullenly
as their young companion rejoined them, then spoke together in
hushed tones. My young friend wagged a finger at me. 'We're

telling on you . . .' he shouted as they turned and walked slowly down the hill.

I started. I really did. 'I was only . . .' I began, and then stopped myself with a silent curse. I was trying to justify myself to a bunch of elves.

I stopped at a small grocery store at the foot of the hill. The owner, a big woman in a starched apron, smiled and welcomed me to the island. I said I was glad to be there. She said they were glad to have me. I said I was glad they were glad to have me. It could probably have gone on for ever, but I broke the circle by asking about the availability of mainland newspapers.

'I'm afraid we don't get them any more,' she said.

'None at all?'

She shook her head. 'No demand.'

I bought some cured ham. She looked pleased. I wasn't so sure. It still looked a little sick, but we had to eat. There were fish, of course, but we were a couple used to fish that came in fingers – indeed fish fingers that were charred black on one side and frozen on the other are a delicacy you can get in few other houses in Belfast – and I wasn't of a mind to buy fish as God had probably intended them. They lay on a metal tray, staring up at me. The woman did her best. Caught that morning. Absolutely beautiful fried in a little butter. I should have asked her to bone them, to poke their eyes out and cut their heads off, she could have done it without a second thought, but the first thought of it made me feel sick. As I turned to leave she tried to tempt me with a rabbit. It was no temptation.

When I arrived back at the cottage the Land-Rover was parked outside again.

Or not, as the case may be. It seemed to be the same vehicle as I approached it out of the growing dusk, but in the light from the front room I could see that there were subtle differences only the trained eye of an international reporter could detect. The front headlamp was smashed and the bonnet badly dented.

The front door opened before I could put the key in the lock. 'Thought it was you,' said Patricia, Little Stevie in her arms, a welcoming smile on her face. 'Visitor,' she said, a little quieter.

'Who?' I mouthed.

'Knows you,' she whispered.

I walked into the lounge. Father Flynn was sitting in the armchair, a cup of tea in his lap. He had the black shirt, the dog collar. For some reason I'd expected that he might have worn civvies. Or to have long flowing robes and a wooden staff.

I smiled and crossed to him. 'Hello,' I said, 'I'm . . . I know you, don't I?'

'Of course you do, Dan.'

I stood before him. I glanced at Patricia. Back at him. 'You're . . . ?'

'Crossmaheart, Dan.'

I shook my head. 'No . . . I . . . yes, of course . . . Father . . . Frank Flynn! Father Frank Flynn . . . God . . . sorry, yes . . . I'd no idea you were stationed here . . .yes, indeed, how's about you? How's the old ticker?'

Flynn set the cup and saucer on the floor and raised himself. He put his hand out. We shook. Firm grip. Warm grip. Bright eyes. He'd either had collagen treatment or he'd aged twenty years in the wrong direction.

'I'm fine, Dan, and you?'

'Great, just great.'

'I saw your name down for the cottage a couple of weeks back. I couldn't wait to see you. I've never forgotten what you did for me back in Crossmaheart.'

'I didn't do anything.'

He turned to my wife. 'He wrote the most wonderful article about me, Patricia. I don't know, maybe he told you about me? Anyway, the thing is, I had a heart transplant, got a Protestant's heart, and the local people didn't like it. Gave me a very hard time.'

Patricia nodded. 'I think I do remember . . .'

'He wrote a very sympathetic piece about me in the paper. People wrote to me from all over the world, you know? Offered me support, sent presents, even sent money. I was feeling so down. So lonely. It really did me the world of good. And I always did mean to come up and thank you personally – but you know how things are, you never quite get round to it. And here you are on my little Wrathlin. Such an amazing coincidence.'

'Indeed,' I said. 'Do you still enjoy an occasional whiskey, Father?'

'I haven't had a drink since the day I had my transplant, Dan. As you know, I emerged a new man.'

Indeed, a Paul Newman for his acting. I clearly remembered

sharing a glass or three of Irish with him. It was three years past, but I tend to remember drinks I've had in particularly important surroundings. I remember the seven shorts before my wedding. The first and last Bacardi and Coke which nearly killed me before my first date. The can of beer I had sitting with my father in his bedroom, just after he died. Crying.

'Oh, well,' I said, 'not that it matters. Prohibition seems to have returned.'

Flynn laughed. Patricia laughed with him. 'Yes, indeed,' he said, 'it's working wonderfully. You know there hasn't been one single crime on the island since we outlawed the booze?'

'Really?' I said.

'Just as it should be,' said Patricia. 'It seems a wonderful island. I think we'll love it here.'

'I'm sure you will.'

We chatted on for twenty minutes. He was good company. I walked him to his car.

I patted the bonnet. 'The teacher, Duncan someone, came to see us earlier. He had a Land-Rover as well. Just like this.'

'Aye, there's half a dozen of them on the island. We got an EC grant for community development. Bought a job lot. We'll be applying for some petrol next year.'

He laughed. I smiled.

'You seem to have had an accident,' I said.

'Aye. An EC grant's all very well, but there's no one on the island qualified to give driving lessons. We've all had a few scrapes.'

'It's hardly a scrape.'

'Aye, well.'

'The Lord drives in mysterious ways, perhaps.'

He was silent for a moment. He looked up at the darkened sky. Sighed. 'It's a wonderful night,' he said.

I looked with him. 'Aye,' I said. It was.

'Dan,' he said, casually, but not, 'I know why you're here.'

'That's good.'

'I know what you're here for.'

'I'm here to write a book.'

'Yes. I know you are. And you will.'

'Good.'

'But I know why you're really here.'

'Yes. You do. I'm here to write a book.'

He opened the car door and climbed in. Then he leant out again. 'I thought if you had a while to spare tomorrow I could show you a bit of the island. Go for a bit of a dander.'

'Sure,' I said.

'It'll be good to talk, Dan. Get it out in the open.'

'Get what out in the open?'

'Dan . . .' Shaking his head, he started the car. I waved him off.

Patricia was tucking Little Stevie up in bed when I went back in. 'Nice man,' she said, without turning.

'Yeah.'

'He invited me to come down to the church on Sunday.'

'I hope you told him you would rather burn in hell.'

'I told him I might,' she said and, turning quickly, kissed me on the lips.

'Why, Patricia,' I said, 'I'm most surprised.'

'Well, you shouldn't be, you fool. I do love you, even if it doesn't always seem like it.'

'Aw,' I said.

9

I suffer from techno-fear. I have it bad.

It is a genuine illness. It ranks up there with vertigo and shares a small room with claustrophobia. It's not that I dislike computers or videos or toasters. I'm no Luddite, it's just that I can't cope with them. I love the *idea* of them. It's the practicalities that get to me. Sometimes I can replace a light bulb. Sort of. I mean, I can twitch it about until it fits, but you wouldn't sit under a bulb I'd fitted, because it would get hot and fall out and singe a bald spot into your scalp. Similarly, I can wire a plug, but you'd have to watch it twenty-four hours a day to be sure it didn't burn the house down. I'm electrically illiterate. I've hands like feet. Patricia's the same. We once had to get The Man out to show us how to get a cassette out of the video recorder.

It was a foolhardy thing, then, to attempt erecting the satellite dish.

A swirly wind had blown up overnight and the delightful blue skies of the previous day were now an ominous grey. I manhandled the dish up a ladder and, perched somewhat shakily on the top step, I attempted to secure it to the cottage's front wall using a screwdriver, a hammer and a screw. I dropped the screw thirty-three times. I dropped the hammer twice. Once on my head. Patricia watched me for a while, sniggering, but then had to go to answer a scream from inside.

An hour after I started, and still up the ladder, I became aware of a man standing at the end of the garden. I sort of half-watched him out of the corner of my eye. He just stood there, staring. For a few minutes I tried to make it look like I knew what I was doing but then I realised that he might have been there for twenty minutes and already be well aware that I was a fool. So I turned my head.

'Morning,' I said.

'Morning,' he replied. He was small. About five six. Old. About six five. He wore an elderly denim jacket, jeans and a threadbare woolly hat.

'Bit chillier this morning,' I said.

'Aye,' he replied, and kept on watching.

I made a final determined effort to secure the dish to the wall. Determined efforts and techno-fear do not mix well. I whacked my thumb with the hammer. I dropped the dish. I sealed in the scream.

'What're you doing?' the man asked.

'I'm baking a fucking cake,' I snapped.

I dropped the hammer as well and set to sucking my thumb. He watched. After a few moments I said, 'Sorry.' He nodded. 'I'm not having much luck with this.'

'They're not allowed,' he said simply, and walked on.

Father Flynn arrived promptly at eleven. He parked his Land-Rover behind the Fiesta. I was shaving in the bathroom. Patricia answered the door. I heard him: 'Locked away writing already, is he?' Patricia, laughing: 'Aye, burning the candle at neither end.'

I finished up, came out, shook hands. Patricia saw us to the door. Patted my bum on the way past, which was a nice touch. Flynn cast an eye over the satellite dish as we left. It was firmly affixed to the wall. What's more, I could now get thirty-two different channels on my portable television. All of them static. Unless I met an expert, I would have to forgo the pleasures of world championship boxing. Flynn didn't say anything about the dish.

'You don't mind a bit of a walk, do you?' he said. His cheeks were flushed pink. He wore a green windcheater and trouser ensemble, with matching green wellington boots. I wore black jeans, trainers and a bomber jacket.

'I'm game for anything,' I said. And I was. For the first time in a long time there wasn't even a hint of a hangover about me. Apart from my thumb, I felt on top of the world.

We turned right at the gate and continued on up the road for about a hundred yards, then he guided me off along a muddy lane which quickly began to dip towards the coast. Before we'd progressed very far the mud had oozed up over the edge of my trainers. Flynn appeared not to notice. He strode along confidently while I slipped along uncertainly behind him. I hadn't walked in mud since primary school.

We started out with the usual small talk, but after a while it trailed away and on the odd occasion when I managed to stay abreast of the priest I could see that his face was grimly set, his brow furrowed. He had something to say, and he was just working out how to do it.

Eventually the path ended in a thirty-foot drop to the sea. We stopped at the edge and for a few minutes we both stood staring out over the waves as they rocked and raced. The wind brought tears to my eyes.

'Beautiful,' said Flynn.

I nodded.

He pointed, first to the Antrim coast and then across in the direction of Scotland, although there was nothing visible in that direction. 'Four times a day tidal pressure forces a billion tons of the Irish Sea through that gap between Torr Head over there and the Mull of Kintyre. On its way north-west it meets another current coming in the other direction and . . . whoa, then there's trouble. They meet over there, just off Rue Point – see the lighthouse?' I nodded. 'The waves are so violent you can hear them a mile away. Makes you appreciate the power of God.'

I presumed this was his way into *it*, but if it was deliberate he wasn't taking advantage of the opening. We were silent for a few more minutes. He opened his mouth a couple of times, about to speak, then just gulped in some more air.

I returned to a well-used tack. 'You know, Father,' I said, 'there aren't many things in life can't be summed up in a single sentence. It's a basic rule of sub-editing.'

Flynn nodded slowly then turned to me. His eyes suddenly looked a little haunted.

'I've been having visions,' he said, simply.

I nodded.

'I've been talking to God.'

I nodded again.

'He's told me the Messiah has been born. Here on Wrathlin.'

'Oh,' I said.

We began to walk along the edge of the coast. We were alone, barring rabbits. 'They're hares,' Father Flynn corrected, then added, 'You think I'm mad.'

'No,' I said, 'I'm sure they are hares.'

'I mean . . . the Messiah.'

'Not necessarily,' I said.

'It's why you're here, to write about me. To vilify me.'

'Absolutely not.'

He shook his head. 'If only you knew,' he said.

I stopped, snagged his arm. 'Tell me,' I said.

'You think I need this plastered all over the papers?'

'I'm sure you don't. And I don't intend to. If you don't want to tell me what you're on about, fair enough, let's get on with our walk. But I think you do.' I gave him my reassuring smile. It rarely works. 'All you have to do is say the magic words.'

'What, like, please leave me alone?'

'No, like, *off the record.*'

He smiled. Nodded. 'I always did like you.'

I shrugged. 'So what about the Messiah?'

It was cold. I put my hands in my pockets. I switched the tape on. He never did say the magic words.

'You should understand first,' he began, 'that I never have been particularly religious. That may seem a strange statement for a priest, but it's the truth. Becoming a priest can sometimes be like becoming a plumber or an electrician, something you go into because it's a secure job or because it's something for which you have a natural aptitude. It isn't necessarily something you have a particular love for. You learn it off by heart. That's how I was before my operation. I was doing a job. Just a job. Then I had my illness. Then my transplant.'

'And that made a new man of you, and alienated your flock.'

'Yes. A new man. A man with a greater appreciation of life. Of science. Of love. But not necessarily of God.'

'But that's changed.'

'Yes. Of course. It started with the sweats.'

'A lot of things do.'

'Really intense sweats. Seven nights in a row. Absolutely drenched, the entire bed, soaked through. I was scared. Very scared. I thought my body was rejecting the heart. I was too scared to go to the doctor. I didn't want to know. I thought I was dying all over again. Then on the eighth night I had this most incredible vision. The most perfect night of sleep and then this wonderful, wonderful vision.'

'A dry dream.'

'Dry. Comfortable. Warm.' The words were coming quicker now; he was slightly breathless, he moved his hands a lot as we walked. 'I was climbing stairs, old stone stairs, like in a castle. There were windows cut in the wall and every few yards I could look out over the most glorious countryside, all bathed in the most beautiful light. There was such an overwhelming feeling of peace and tranquillity.'

'You weren't in Crossmaheart, then.'

He laughed. 'No. Clearly. It was like heaven. Or what I imagine heaven to be like. And then I got to the top of the stairs and there was this great wooden door and it opened before me and I entered this circular room. There was a great window at the far end of it and shutters had been pulled back to give this wonderful panoramic view over hundreds of miles. Before the window there was a sofa, and on the sofa there was a man, and that man was God.'

'How could you tell?'

'I just knew.'

'What did he look like?'

'He was small. Heavy-set. He wore a black, wide-brimmed hat. Small eyes.'

'Sounds like Van Morrison.'

Flynn shook his head slightly. 'He turned to me and said: "Hello, Frank, it's good to see you," and I knew immediately that I was with the warmest, most loving man in the universe.'

'It wasn't Van Morrison then.'

'No. Not Van Morrison. God.'

'And then?'

'And then I woke up.'

'A bit of an anti-climax that.'

'No. Not at all. The next night the same thing happened. Almost before my head hit the pillow I was back in the castle, in that room, with Him. He sat me down and we talked and talked and talked.'

'What was he like? I mean, as a person?'

'What can I say? Omnipresent. Omnipotent.'

The only other word I knew starting like that was omnivore. I chewed that thought over for a moment, then said, 'Then he told you about the Messiah.'

Flynn nodded. 'He told me mankind had had two thousand years to improve itself since it crucified His son. That it was to be tested once again. That the Messiah was to be born, and that He was entrusting the Messiah into my hands.'

'And then you woke up.'

'And then He told me when and where.'

'When, then?'

'June 13.'

'This year?'

'Four years ago.'

'Four years ago – before you came back here.'

Flynn nodded. 'Aye. The address was Furley Cottage.'

'He gave you an *actual* address?'

Flynn gave me a half-smile. 'Incredible, isn't it?'

'Incredible,' I agreed.

We had come to a dip in the path that had formed itself into a small but murky-looking pond. Flynn interrupted his story long enough to wade through it in his boots then reach out from the other side and help me across. His grip was strong. I thanked him and stood for several moments catching my breath again. 'So,' I said, as we resumed his leisurely and my arduous walk, 'first thing in the morning you were straight round to Furley Cottage to hail the new Messiah.'

Flynn smiled. 'There is no Furley Cottage. I checked next day.'

'Bummer,' I said.

'So I went to bed that night to ask Him was He sure – yes, I know it sounds ridiculous – but I just had a normal night's sleep. Same the next night and ever since. I convinced myself I was just having crazy dreams. Until one day I was busying myself about the church and old Mary Mateer came in. She does most days. She's about ninety. Husband died ten years ago. Electrocuted himself trying to fit an electric shower. The shock knocked him out and he drowned in the bath. What do you say to someone widowed under those circumstances? Anyway, she's our oldest resident, so I said to her, "Did you ever hear of a Furley Cottage, Mary?" and she said she fancied one of the old cottages on Main Street was called that when she was a girl, but had been changed years and years ago, for whatever reason. I checked it out in the parish records and she was right. Furley Cottage, sure enough. Somewhere along the way it just lost its name.'

'What you're saying, Father, is that God is working from an old street directory.'

'I didn't say I could explain any of it, Dan, I'm just telling you what happened.'

I shrugged. 'Fair enough. So what happened? You went round . . .'

'I felt incredible. Euphoric. Scared. Nervous. Elated. Almost too scared to go . . . but I had to, of course. I walked down the hill, along the front. I stood outside the cottage for ten minutes. I didn't know what to do. On the one hand I was dying with excitement, on the other hand desperately embarrassed. I mean, how do you walk up to a house and enquire if the Messiah is at home? Has the Messiah finished his homework yet?'

'I can see where there might be a little awkwardness about it.'

'Indeed.'

'So what did you do?'

'I prayed, I took a deep breath, then I walked up to the front door, rang the bell, and waited to see what happened.'

'And?'

'Well, nothing happened. The bell wasn't working. A bit of an anti-climax really. I knocked on the door, but there was still no response. So I went round the back way, came up the garden path. There was a woman washing dishes in the sink. I half recognised her from church. She saw me. I stopped. We watched each other for a few moments. I wasn't sure what to do next. Then she peeled off these rubber gloves and opened the back door. She said: 'You've come about my daughter, haven't you?'

10

Patricia and I lay in each other's arms, listening to the rain. Storm clouds had gathered during the evening, dithering for hours as if waiting for us to go to bed so that they could cause the maximum annoyance by unleashing their venom just as we were dropping off. Great crashing rolls of thunder chased the sleep through our brains and out of our ears.

But we weren't intimidated. We snuggled up on fantasy island. It was nice.

After a while the thunder moved on, leaving behind a wind-scattered rain which wasn't steady enough to encourage drowsiness. Our tiredness had moved on as well. We lay with the covers thrown back. Little Stevie had gurgled happily in his sleep through the storm. He was giving every indication of being a trouble-free child. There was time yet, of course. I'd never recovered from teething. But then there wasn't any reason why he should have anything in common with me. The only thing we shared was Patricia.

It seemed like a good time to talk. In fact, it seemed like a good time for sex, but Patricia was still on the mend.

'I'll let you know,' she said.

'Thanks.'

'It could be weeks.'

'But not months.'

'I don't know. I'll keep you posted.'

'Thanks.'

'Could be years.'

'You won't be able to resist me that long. I'm banking on days.'

She snorted, which wasn't very encouraging, let alone pleasant. I changed the subject. I told her about the remote possibility that the daughter of God was living half a mile down the road.

It took me ten minutes to convince her that it wasn't a wind-up. That Flynn, deranged or not, was perfectly serious.

'He seems so normal,' she said eventually.

'I know,' I said, stroking her brow. 'Generally they're the ones you have to watch. The question is, has he really been entrusted by God to look after His daughter, or has his head been invaded by little pink marshmallows? Your immediate reaction is what?'

'You knew about it before you came here.'

'I did not. Next reaction?'

'You're lying.'

I tutted. 'Exactly what sort of a man do you think I am?'

'I don't think. I know. You're devious.' She gave me a friendly poke in the ribs. 'You knew about this.'

'I didn't.'

'Admit it. I can tell by the colour of your face.'

'We're in the dark, if you haven't noticed.'

'I know we are. But you're glowing.'

She knew me well. 'Okay. So I was vaguely aware of it. But that isn't why I came. I came to write. You know that. It's all I've talked about for ten years.'

'Yeah. Talked about.'

'Look, I don't prepare my lies that far in advance. Anyway, I'm hardly going to uproot you and a new-born baby, transport youse across the sea to a backward hole like this purely on the off-chance of making a few quid on the back of a ridiculous claim by a religious crackpot, now, am I?'

'Dan, nothing would surprise me. I note you've thrown yourself into writing your novel with your customary sloth-like enthusiasm.'

'Will you give me a chance? Jesus, we're only here forty-eight hours. Rome wasn't built in a day.'

'But the earth was created in seven.'

'And it hasn't moved for you in months.'

'You can always twist things back to sex, can't you?'

'I try.'

'Well, enjoy talking about it. It's all you'll be doing.'

'I might get lucky with someone else, if you're not more accommodating.'

'Aye, with a rabbit, if he'll have you.'

'The girls might fancy a bit of strange. I'm sure it gets a bit incestuous in places like this.'

'What is it they say, keep incest in the family?'

'You should know.'

She started giggling. Then we kissed. She broke off to say, 'God, wouldn't it be amazing if it really was true. The Messiah, here on Wrathlin. And a girl.'

'I'm not sure which bit worries me more – the Messiah coming back, being born in Ireland or being a girl. Actually, they all worry me about the same.'

'It would be . . . wonderful.'

'You think so?'

'Well, *different*. I mean, the world's so different now . . . I mean, I can't imagine Jesus on the Internet, or using a mobile phone.'

'I can't imagine *me* on the Internet or using a . . .'

'You know what I mean. A girl. A woman. I mean, the closest we've come to a woman of power before was Margaret Thatcher.'

'Not that far removed. A Messiah to some, Antichrist to others.'

Little Stevie woke up. While Patricia heated milk in the kitchen I cradled him in my arms. When she reappeared with the bottle she stood in the doorway for a moment watching us. A loving smile. Then she came across and took him from me.

'Did Father Flynn ask you not to write anything about the Messiah?' she asked, sitting on the edge of the bed. 'Is that why he came to see you?'

She said 'Messiah' so easily, as if there was a possibility. I lay back, my arms folded behind my head. 'On the contrary. He wants me to write it all down.'

Patricia nodded thoughtfully. 'Well, that's good. Even if he is nuts, you'll make some money from it.'

'It's not quite as simple as that. He wants me to write it all down, and keep writing it down, not for a newspaper, to make a complete record of anything and everything that happens to Christine . . .'

'Christine?'

'That's her name. A bit of a coincidence, I thought.'

'Or divine inspiration.'

'Yup, there's that. But he wants me to be, if you will, the official chronicler of everything pertaining to the life and times of Christine.'

'You mean he wants you to write the sequel to the Bible.'

'He didn't say so in so many words, but yes, I guess that's what he's getting at. One of the better commissions, I'd say.'

'And what did you say?'

'What do you think? I enquired about royalties.'

'No, seriously.'

'I did. I thought it was important to keep everything on a vaguely humorous level. At least until the straitjacket arrives.'

'And what did he say to you about you saying to him?'

'He just sort of smiled.'

'And what did that mean?'

'I don't know. He asked me to go to church in the morning. To meet Christine. He seemed to think that might convince me.'

'And you're going?'

'I am. You were going anyway, weren't you?'

'I thought I was.'

'You mean you're not?'

'I mean I've nothing to wear.'

I tutted. 'Why is that always a woman's first reaction?'

'Well, I haven't. It's a fact.'

'What the hell did you bring in all those cases then?'

'I've nothing churchy, Dan.'

'Does it really matter? You're not going to be refused entry to heaven because you haven't anything churchy. Jesus.'

'But what if I have to meet the Messiah?'

'She's not long out of nappies, for Christ's sake. She's not going to strike you dead for dressing down.'

Patricia shook her head wearily. 'Sometimes I get really tired of you, y'know?'

11

Sunday was another fine day. Skies blue. Sea calm. Patricia stormy. She screamed.

I was still in the land of Nod, that small kingdom between sleep and going to work. She'd gotten up early to do some more cleaning.

'Daniel!' she screamed again and I pulled myself up to a sitting position. She only uses the full Daniel when there's an emergency or I've done something wrong, which is generally one and the same thing.

'What?'

A herd of elephants in the hall. Then she was in the doorway. 'There's a rat in the bath,' she said.

'Is he enjoying it?' I asked blearily.

'Daniel, there's a rat in the bath.'

'Jesus,' I mumbled.

'There's a bloody great rat in the bath!'

I tried to shake the sleep from my head. I climbed out of the bed and tottered for a second while I got my land legs.

'There's a rat in the bath,' Patricia shouted, 'there's a rat in the bath! Get rid of the rat in the bath!'

She was white. She held Little Stevie to her. 'Rats eat babies' eyes,' she said. She stepped aside.

I walked down the hall and cautiously put my head round the bathroom door. There were some dark hairs in the bath. I turned back to Patricia. 'He's gone,' I said, shaking my head, 'although he seems to be going bald.'

Patricia put her head warily out of the bedroom doorway. 'Not that bath. The one in the front garden.'

I rolled my eyes at her. She rolled them back. 'You can't have rats around children,' she said.

'Might do us all a favour,' I replied under my breath, but not under enough.

'What was that?'

'I said, do us a favour and try and find something heavy for me to blatter it with, while I pull my trousers on. Okay?'

'Okay,' she said sullenly. 'But don't let it in the door. Make sure you close it properly. I hate rats.'

I got into my trousers. Pulled on a T-shirt. Patricia gave me a mean-looking hammer. I opened the front door and blinked for a few moments in the sun. Then I advanced on the bath with hammer raised, feeling vaguely ridiculous. I trod softly across the grass; the element of surprise would be important, and also I was afeared that any sudden activity might cause the satellite dish to fall off the wall and kill me.

The bath was tilted to one side and was maybe a quarter full of stagnant water. It stank. And there was an animal in it, but it wasn't a rat. Not even a drowned rat. A hedgehog.

Patricia, disregarding her own advice, had advanced to the door. 'Bash it,' she said. 'Bash its brains out.'

I turned. 'What school did you go to? It's a bloody hedgehog.'

'Aw,' she said, and hurried across, apparently not dizzy at all from her 360-degree turnabout.

She peered in over my shoulder. 'What's it doing in the bath?'

'Hold on, I'll ask it.'

'Ach – is it drowned?'

'I presume so . . .' I leant in further. It was breathing. Vaguely, like it was undecided about clinging to life. I pointed to the side of the bath. 'It's fallen in and not been able to get out. Look at all the scratches on the enamel. Poor wee thing.'

'Aw.'

It moved. Just a little. Weakly. 'Life in the wee bugger yet,' I said and leant down to pick him up. I got spiked for my trouble. 'Aaow,' I said.

I ran back into the house and returned with the old sheet I'd used to protect the satellite dish on its journey across to the island. I wrapped it round my hands. Then I gently lifted the hedgehog out of the poisonous water and set it on the ground.

'Aw,' said Patricia.

'We should just leave it be. Let it make its own way.'

'Nonsense,' said Patricia, 'it's too weak. I'll go and get it some bread and milk. That's what they eat.'

67

'Bollocks.'

'It is. Honestly, Dan. Bread and milk . . .'

'Aye. That's it, that's their natural food . . . they stay up all hours of the day and night baking wee loaves for themselves.'

'No need to be sarcastic, I'm only trying to help the wee thing.'

'I know. I'm sorry.' I looked at the critter again. 'They're meat-eaters, love. It needs . . . dog food or cat food or something. Will I bring some back from church?'

She looked at me, her face fallen. 'Does that mean I'm not going?'

'You said you'd nothing churchy.'

'I know, but . . .'

'Well, make up your mind. It's nearly time to go.'

Her face fell a little further. Much more and it'd be in amongst the daisies. 'I'll stay then,' she said sadly. It was an old ploy. The I'll-be-the-martyr ploy. Apt, really, for where I was going.

'Look, I'll wait. But you'll need to hurry.'

'No, you haven't time.'

'I'll wait.'

'No.'

'I'll wait!'

'It doesn't matter. I'll be okay.'

'Jesus!'

I went back into the house and had a wash and shave. The water was cold. When I emerged from the bathroom Patricia was standing in the hall, beautifully attired. A summer dress. Flowery, but not overly so. Her hair was pulled back into a ponytail.

'You look lovely,' I said.

'I changed my mind.'

'Good. You've broken the land speed record.'

'We can if we try. We just don't try very often.'

'Is that the third secret of Fatima?'

'Wouldn't you like to know?'

'Maybe I will. I'll ask Christine.'

'She won't tell,' Patricia said, shaking her head slowly. 'Don't forget, Dan, she's one of us.'

And it stopped me for a few seconds, that.

Patricia was right.

Christine was. One of *them*.

A little involuntary shudder ran through me.

68

12

I stopped the car at the foot of the hill. I had the window down and my sunglasses on. A nice breeze was blowing in off the sea. In my own mind I looked pretty cool.

'What the hell are you at now?' Patricia demanded, snapping me out of the moment. She pointed up towards the church.

'I know where it is. I'm just . . .'

'I'm not carrying Steven all the way up there, I'll tell you that for nothing. I'm still weak.'

'I just wanted to take a look at Furley Cottage.' I nodded over her shoulder. 'The stable, as it were.'

She gave me the steady look, perfected over a century of marriage. 'Aye, away in a manger, Sherlock,' she said, then shook her head malevolently. 'Let's get the church over with first, eh? Do your nosing in your own time, okay?' She tutted. 'Some people have no consideration.'

I tutted myself. She had already shouted at me for driving too quickly. And then for driving too slowly. Sarcastic driving, she called it. I knew to expect mood swings after the birth of a baby. I'd read a book. But Patricia had spent our whole married life practising for them.

The former Furley Cottage was at the end of a long whitewashed terrace. It seemed unremarkable. Small. A sturdy wooden door with the number 14 on it. A Mickey Mouse fluffy toy propped up against the main window. I hadn't known what to expect, but I was disappointed to see Mickey there. He was a fantasy figure bringing a touch of reality to what promised to be a bizarre story. Still. Maybe there had been an equivalent propped up in Mary and Joseph's front window way back when. Mickey of Arimathea. Or a Happy Herod.

I started the car again and moved it slowly up the hill. All the shops were closed. Of course, it was Sunday, but there was *always* one that stayed open. For milk. Bacon. Papers. Headache tablets. But nothing. We parked without problem in the churchyard. There were only three or four other cars and a couple of unsecured bicycles. Wrathlin village was small enough for most everyone to walk.

We were late. I opened the church door as quietly as I could, and we slipped in. The hymn singing mostly covered us. But there was nowhere to sit. Not a single space was free. People lined the back of the church and sat cross-legged the length of the aisle. A few heads turned as we entered. One of them was Duncan's. He nodded at me. He smiled at Patricia, then indicated that she and Little Stevie should have his seat. She shook her head. He waved her on. She looked at me. I nodded. She went down the three rows and took his place. He came and stood beside me. I nodded again.

'Full house,' I whispered.

He nodded.

'Sorry about the other day,' I whispered. 'Hangover.'

He nodded.

Father Flynn's voice was the dominant one. Booming, but tuneful with it. As the hymn drew to a close he smiled at the congregation. A movement to his left caught my eye. Another man, another priest, was climbing easily up into the pulpit. Small. Well-built. Elderly. Wispy-bald.

'Who he?' I whispered.

'Father White.'

'Visiting?'

'I wish.' He said it with just enough of a cynical glint in his eye to suggest that I might have judged him too quickly.

Patricia looked back at me. I nodded. She waved Little Stevie's left hand at me. I winked.

'So here we are again,' the priest said, scanning the congregation, his voice thick, as if his nose was clogged. 'How long is it now, since we broke the news?'

The congregation was silent. Not subdued, exactly; not wary, either; maybe a little lost. A boy near the front, hair cropped, said, 'Six weeks, Father,' and the congregation visibly relaxed. A few giggled.

'Six weeks indeed – and look at you. You're all still here. Father Flynn and I thought you'd have given up on us by now.'

There was a little light laughter. I tried not to bust a gut. That was Trisha's job. There wasn't even a grin from Duncan.

'We are touched by your faith.'

'Thank the Lord,' someone said.

'Amen,' said another.

'AMEN,' said everyone.

It seemed a little spontaneous for the Catholic Church. But then I thought, maybe it wasn't the Catholic Church any more. The transubstantiation wouldn't seem so important if you had the actual Messiah in your midst. You could just ask him about it. Or her.

'But it's not really your faith in us, is it?'

Silence.

'It's your faith in the one among us.'

Murmurings. Positive murmurings.

'It's your faith in the one among us!'

'Yes!' shouted someone.

'YES!' said the congregation. A couple near the front stood up and clapped.

'Let us remind ourselves,' said the priest, waving a calming hand. 'Sean, now,' he said, pointing at the boy who'd shouted out, 'what was the first miracle?'

Sean stood up. 'Father?'

'Yes, Seanie, what did Christine do first . . . what incredible thing did Christine do first?'

'The bull, Father.'

'Yes, the bull, Seanie. What did she do with the bull?'

'She was in the field by herself, Father, and the bull charged at her.'

'And what would the bull have done to little Christine, Seanie?'

'It would have trampled her, Father.'

'But what happened when it reached her, son?'

'She put her hand out to it, and it lay down.'

'And what do we call that, Sean?'

'A mirkle.'

Soft laughter and *aws*, a couple of amens.

I leant across to Duncan and whispered. 'True?'

He nodded.

'And what little boy or girl will tell me about the second mirkle?'

A little more laughter. Three or four hands went up. The priest pointed: another boy, same cropped hair: 'Her bloody feet, Father.'

Some more laughter and *aws*.

'Yes, Brian, what happened to her feet?'

'They were all covered in blood.'

'Yes. Good boy. Now what is the significance of that?'

Brian looked confused. He dropped his arm for the first time, then looked round at his mother, who gave him an encouraging smile.

'What did her bloody feet remind us of?' asked the priest.

He looked at his mum again. She raised her hand to scratch her nose, and said something under cover of it.

'Jesus on the cross, Father!' Brian yelled triumphantly.

'Good boy!'

The congregation burst into applause. Brian giggled and sat down. His mother gave him a hug.

'Now, boys and girls, you're all at school with Christine, aren't you?'

Scattered yeses.

'And haven't you all promised to remember that although she's a very special little girl, a very special little girl indeed, she's there for the same reason you all are – to learn.' Nodding heads. 'She isn't there to perform little mirkles for you. She isn't there to help you with your homework. She isn't there to fill your orange bottle up after you knock it over. And she certainly isn't there to put a spell on anyone who annoys you, is she, Martin Maguire?'

Four rows down a small boy ducked out of sight.

The priest leant down on the pulpit. The smile slipped from his face. His eyes, colder now, scanned the congregation again. 'And it isn't only Martin Maguire. He is a child and knows no better. There are some parents here today who might do well to remember the lesson too. Christine is a child, and while she is a child it is our duty to look after her, to protect her, to help educate her in the ways of man, not to exploit her or seek favour from her. Her day will come.' He waved a finger. 'You may look upon our little island as the new heaven on earth. As the new Garden of Eden. But remember, as beautiful as the garden was, there was always the serpent lurking nearby, ready to pounce, to sin, to destroy. It is our duty to God and to Christine to be good, and true, and kind, and watchful. Only one person is important, that is Christine. So have faith! Be proud! Show love! But be on your guard!'

He stepped down from the pulpit to warm applause.

Father Flynn took centre stage again. 'Thank you, Mark,' he said quietly. He turned to the congregation and nodded slowly. 'Remember,' he said, 'to thank God for this.'

'Thanks be to God,' said the congregation.

'And now for some general announcements. There will be no playgroup on Monday because Mrs McCleavor is down with a nasty flu bug. There will be a meeting of the parents' committee . . .'

I waited with Patricia in the churchyard while the congregation filed out of the church. Duncan stood with us. I shook a lot of hands. Little Stevie was cooed over. Shiny happy people.

'What do you make of all that stuff about miracles, Duncan?' Patricia asked. 'About the bull.'

He gave a little shrug. 'It's what happened. Or so I'm told. I didn't see it myself.'

'Who did?' I asked.

'Most everyone. A church picnic. The other side of the island. I wasn't there that day.'

'What about the bloody feet?' asked Patricia. 'What are they trying to say, that the blood is like . . . from a wound?' She looked at me. 'What am I trying to say?'

'I don't bloody know.'

She tutted. 'What's the word I'm looking for, Duncan?'

'Like she's a stigmatic,' Duncan said.

'That's the one. Like she's been nailed to the cross. Stigmatic. Is that what it was like, Duncan?'

'So I'm told. She just appeared in church like that one day. I wasn't there.'

'Who was?'

'Most of the church.'

'The same most?' I asked. 'Or a different most?' I nudged him. 'The most with the Host, in fact.' I smiled. He didn't. It seemed unlikely that we would ever spend a lot of time cracking jokes together.

I had no idea what Christine looked like, but I was pretty sure I would have noticed her leaving the church. Talk would stop. People

73

would stare at her halo. But everyone stood around chatting. So normal. So normal it was abnormal. When the church was empty I said to Duncan, 'So where's the Messiah?'

'Christine,' he said bluntly, 'is probably in the back room. She usually waits in there with her mum until everyone's gone home. She doesn't enjoy all the attention. She gets upset.'

'Imagine the Messiah having a tantrum,' said Patricia. 'You'd think the earth would spin off its axis.'

'Out of control into the universe,' I added.

'I'm only thinking out loud,' Patricia snapped.

Duncan looked embarrassed. 'I'd better get on,' he said.

The congregation was dispersing, making its way out of the churchyard and down the hill. Brightly coloured hats flapped in the wind. Snatches of the last hymn, hummed, blew back towards us.

'They're really sucked in by all this, aren't they?' I said.

'Dan . . .' started Patricia.

'Well, I . . .'

'Well, nothing, you should respect what . . .'

'I'd better get on,' Duncan repeated.

'I was hoping you might take us backstage and introduce us,' I said.

'To Christine?'

'Aye.'

'You make it sound like showbusiness,' said Patricia, 'backstage at a gig.'

I shrugged.

'Could you?' Patricia asked, hoisting Little Stevie up onto her shoulder. 'Father Flynn did invite us, didn't he, Dan?'

I nodded.

'I wouldn't like to,' said Duncan.

'Ach, go on,' said Patricia.

'No, no, thank you. I really can't. I'm late as it is. I'll really have to go. Listen, go back yourselves.' He turned suddenly, thrust his hands into his jacket pockets, and began walking towards the churchyard gates. 'I'll see youse around,' he called back.

'Can we give you a lift?' Patricia shouted after him.

'No. No, thanks,' he shouted back, and gave her a little wave.

When he was out of earshot Patricia said: 'He's a moody one, isn't he?'

I watched him lope off down the hill, round shoulders bunched up. I shrugged.

Patricia furrowed up her brows, shook her head slightly. 'Maybe he's got ME.'

'You mean that yuppie flu. Myalgic . . . whatever?'

'Nah,' she said, turning back to the church, 'Messiah Envy.'

13

The churchyard was finally empty, save for a big woman by the gate, sitting astride an old boneshaker, her face turned up to the sun. Patricia looked at her watch. 'Do you think they'll be long?' she asked and looked anxiously first at the back door of the church, and then at Little Stevie. 'He's due.'

'A couple of minutes won't make any difference,' I said.

'Try telling him that,' she replied, turning the baby towards me.

He didn't look too worried. Nevertheless, I put up a placatory hand. 'I'd rather not,' I said. 'Hold on, I'll check. See if it's worth waiting. You want to see her too, don't you?'

She nodded vaguely. I walked up to the back door. There came a murmur of voices from within. I knocked lightly. The murmuring stopped. A key was turned and a man stuck his curly head out.

'Oh. Sorry. I was looking for Father Flynn.'

'Aye. He's here.'

I moved forward. He didn't move back. I could just see past him that there were maybe a dozen people in the room, seated around a long table. 'Sorry,' he said, pleasantly enough, but forceful with it, 'we're having a meeting. We'll be finished in twenty minutes, if you want to wait.'

I shrugged. He nodded, then closed the door.

Patricia didn't want to wait. I did. I cited important research and journalistic curiosity. She cited warm milk and nappy. We agreed to differ. She would take the car and I would make my own way home with news of the Messiah. I kissed her goodbye. I shook Little Stevie's hand. He gurgled. He liked me. Then she drove out in a cloud of dust she would have chastised me for creating.

I kicked around in the yard for a while, enjoying the sun. I tried to eavesdrop on the meeting within, but there was nothing decipherable, only the dull throb of urgent voices. At the gate, the woman on the bike had produced a book from her saddlebag and was now earnestly studying it. I wandered across.

'Afternoon,' I said, a couple of yards off.

She looked up, startled, and for a second looked as if she might lose her foothold and tumble from the bike. She had a round, warm-looking face, a little flabby. Her eyes were large anyway, but were accentuated by sturdy black-framed glasses with thumb-thick lenses. 'I didn't see you,' she spluttered.

'I'm sorry,' I said, falling naturally into the Ulsterman's misplaced acceptance of the blame. 'I didn't mean to . . .'

She smiled. 'Lovely day, isn't it?'

I nodded. 'Did you enjoy the service?'

'Yes. Lovely.'

We looked away from each other for a few moments, our conversation already exhausted. Her eyes flitted briefly behind me, then back to her book. I squinted at it. The New Testament.

'He dies in the end,' I said. 'Then he comes back.'

She looked at me. Dead straight. 'I know.'

I kicked my feet in the dust. Behind me the back door opened and people began to emerge. 'Excuse me,' I said quickly and turned back.

I stood to one side of the church while a line of serious-faced men walked slowly past. Several nodded. A couple said hello. Then came Father White. He didn't speak, but his eyes ran over me like a car. It gave me the oddest feeling. Then Father Flynn was in the doorway. 'Dan!' he said enthusiastically, and reached out to me. I stepped forward and shook his hand. 'I thought it was you. Come on in.'

He ushered me through the door. At the far end of the room, at the head of the table, sat a woman; on her knee sat a child.

Flynn took my elbow and led me across. I don't know what it says about my attitude to life, but I looked at the woman first. Then the possible Messiah. She, the cat's mother, looked to be about thirty-five. She had dirty blonde hair, cut short. Eyes blue. Nose just a little turned up, but not unpleasantly so. She was smoking. A cigarette. I was shocked. Genuinely. It seemed incredible that the instrument through whom God had chosen to recreate his image on earth should also feel the need to shell out money on twenty Benson & Hedges. Bad enough that alcohol was banned in the name of religion – the very same alcohol which Jesus himself, a drinker if ever there was one, had gone to the trouble of creating through a mirkle to satisfy his thirst – without promoting cigarettes. B & H would have a field day if ever they got hold of a photo of the mother of God as I saw her then, a stream of smoke shooting out of her nostrils. Caught in the sun, the smoke had an almost mystical sheen, a lethal kind of mystical which, if inhaled passively, could still line your lungs with poison and allow you to die a horrible, pain-racked death completely free of charge several years down the line.

I reached out and shook the woman's proffered hand and reminded myself that she was not the mother of God. And that the girl on her knee wasn't the daughter of said supreme being.

The child was blonde as well. Blue-eyed. Perfectly Aryan. A smiler, too.

'Hiya,' she said.

'Hiya,' I replied.

'Dan Starkey,' said Flynn, 'Moira McCooey and, of course, Christine.'

'Hello,' said the mother, stroking Christine's hair.

'Dan's agreed to write the book about all this, Moira. He's a brilliant writer.'

I hadn't, but I was. Modest, too.

I nodded anyway. 'I'll give it my best shot.'

Moira held her gaze steady on me. 'I hope you won't be crucified by the critics,' she said lazily, her voice drawled out, tobacco-husky. She smiled up at me. 'Relax,' she said, 'we don't bite.'

I gave a nervous laugh. 'I'll be needing to have a few chats with you, if you don't mind.'

Moira shook her head and stubbed out her cigarette in a small glass ashtray. There were five or six others in it. 'Yeah, sure, any time. Sure, why don't you walk down the hill with us, and tell me what you'll need?'

'Yeah. Great. If you don't mind.'

'Not at all,' Moira said.

I winked down at Christine.

Christine turned her face up to her mother. 'He has a hedgehog,' she said.

Moira lit another cigarette as we left the churchyard and began descending the hill towards the harbour. Christine skipped happily in front of us. Flynn remained at the church.

'You look a little pale,' Moira said.

I felt a little pale. Unexpected references to small spiky animals tend to do that to me. I looked up at the sky. 'We writers don't get to see much of the sun. We spend a lot of time in darkened rooms.'

'You must work very hard.'

'No, generally we just spend a lot of time in darkened rooms.' Moira smiled politely. I nodded at Christine. 'She seems a very happy wee girl.'

'She is.'

'Of course, she should be, seeing as how she's the daughter of God.'

Moira stopped. 'I thought you might be taking that line.'

'What line?'

'The cynical line.'

'Who mentioned cynical?'

'You don't have to mention it. It's an attitude. It's written all over you.'

I shrugged as nonchalantly as the situation allowed. I would have to do something to combat the cynicism. It wouldn't do my cause any good. I wanted to get on with these people. I might one day want to shamelessly exploit them for large amounts of cash.

'I'm sorry,' I said, 'I'm afraid it tends to go with the territory. I'm trying to develop an open mind. Any help you can give me would be much appreciated. And remember, when this gets out, it won't just be one cynic like me you'll have to contend with – there's millions of them out there. And that's just in Belfast.'

Moira flicked her cigarette butt out into the road. 'We'll see,' she said simply. We started walking again. 'So what will you be wanting to know?'

'Everything, I suppose. Everything you're prepared to tell me. Are you prepared to tell me everything?'

'Frank seems to trust you. I don't see why not.'

'Good. Much appreciated. I'm not really that bad. What about your husband, will he . . . ?'

'What husband?'

'Oh.'

'Oh . . . what?'

79

'Oh, nothing. I . . .'

'You just presumed.'

'I just . . .'

'This is the twentieth century, y'know . . .'

'What, on Wrathlin? Are you sure?'

She smiled. 'Okay, fair point, but . . .'

I pointed skywards. 'You mean He's the only . . .'

'Mr Starkey . . .'

'Dan . . . please.'

'Dan . . . Christine was conceived during a time when I was having a relationship with a man on this island. A single man. That relationship is now over. Somewhere along the line God got involved, and I bore His child. I don't know the whys or the hows or the biology . . . I didn't feel the earth move . . . the heavens didn't split open and bathe me in angelic light . . . but I know as sure as I'm standing here that Christine is God's child and I will do everything within my power to protect her, to bring her up properly until the time comes for her to inherit the . . .' She cut herself off, laughed lightly, almost embarrassed.

'The earth,' I said, and gave her a little smile. I tried not to make it seem too cynical. 'And when do you think that might be?'

'I have no idea. At the moment she's just a perfectly ordinary little girl . . .'

'Although she's done a few mirkles.'

'. . . just a perfectly ordinary little girl who happens to have performed a few miracles . . . just a perfectly ordinary little girl who has no real idea of her own destiny, of her own potential . . .'

'But when . . .'

'Dan, there's no timetable for things like this. It's only happened once before, and we messed it up then. Frank thinks we might see her coming into her own around about the time of puberty. Girls grow up so much more quickly than boys.'

'It could be one hell of a first period then.'

'If you wish to reduce it to that level, well, yes, it could.'

Christine was out on the road now, kicking her sandalled feet through the gravel.

'Ma,' she called, 'come 'n' play.'

'Get off the road then. What have I told you about playing on the road?'

I stepped off the path and reached a hand out to her. She stepped back and kicked some gravel at me.

'That's not very nice, now, is it?' I said.

She gave a mischievous smile. 'Yes,' she said.

'I'll give you a good slappin', girl,' said Moira, wagging a finger.

'Are you allowed to do that?' I asked.

'Of course I am.' She gave a wink. 'The good thing is, Christine then has to turn the other cheek.'

'And does she?'

'Of course not.' Moira laughed. 'She doesn't know who she is yet.'

Christine reached out and took my hand. 'Will you play with me?' she asked.

'Of course,' I said, and kicked some gravel over her sandals. She squealed with pleasure and pulled away.

'You're asking for trouble,' Moira warned.

I took a step towards Christine. She took a step back, then raised her foot ready to aim some more gravel at me.

I took another step forward, stopped, raised my foot to attack.

We faced each other, smiling, mock-frowning, eyes locked. Moira walked ahead. The only sound was the gentle breeze, the far-off cry of a gull and . . . and something . . . whooshy . . . whooshy . . . which for a second confused me, something familiar yet strange, like blowing through a comb . . . getting closer . . . closer . . . and then I twigged . . . a sound I remembered best from childhood games and I looked quickly behind me, back up the hill, and in that moment it was already too late to do anything about it.

The woman from outside the church was racing down the incline on her bike, her legs firing like mighty pistons, her fat form raised off the saddle, her head and chest bent down over the handlebars, her hair flying behind her, mouth gaping, eyes fixed horribly wide behind her glasses. She was screaming.

She was not out of control.

She was *in* control, and coming straight for me.

Only at the very last moment did she veer away, but before I could even think *Thank Christ* I knew that her change of direction was no accident.

She was aiming for Christine. Dead centre.

The little girl stared at her, transfixed.

Moira turned, already screaming, but she was too late, she was too far away.

14

A whiff of alcohol, a sniff, a pale imitation of the real thing, a hint of booze consumed, attacked by the stomach's natural acids and belched back up as an unattractive, stale, harrowing gas. But alcohol, nevertheless. A suggestion of barley. Of Scottish Highland streams. Of smoky back bars. Of chat and crack. I opened my eyes. Fluttered them in the harsh fluorescent light. A pain in my head. A dryness in my mouth. A shadow to my left, moving closer. I tried to focus.

'Hello,' the face said. Jocular. A swollen, deep-jowelled, crusty-eyed face. And a white coat. 'I'm Dr Finlay.'

I croaked.

I was lying on a black leather couch. There were various certificates on the wall. A bookcase. Dr Finlay's bookcase.

'How are you feeling?' he asked.

'Sore,' I whispered.

'That's understandable.'

'How . . . ahm . . . where . . . uuuh . . . how long have . . . ?'

The doctor shook his head kindly. 'You've been unconscious for about six hours. I sent a message to your wife – told her you were okay and not to worry. Can I get you a wee whiskey?'

The room was too bright for my sore head. 'You must be able to read minds,' I said.

He shook his head. 'I read lips.'

I scrunched my brow. 'I didn't ask for . . .'

'No, but I saw you licking your lips, the classic sign of an alcoholic.'

'I'm no alcoholic.'

'Oh, no offence.' He had been perched on the side of the couch. Now he stood up and crossed to a mirrored wall cabinet. He opened the door and examined the rows of bottles within. Little brown medicine bottles. Unencouraging little brown medicine bottles. 'You won't want a drink then?'

'On the contrary. I'd love one.'

A memory stirred in me suddenly. The enormous woman. Her screaming face. The rush of the wind through the spokes of her bike. The squeal of pain that came from one of us. Or both of us. 'I think I was run over.'

He gave a throaty laugh. 'You were. By a whale on a bicycle.'

He turned. He had a small bottle in his hands. A pill bottle.

'About that drink . . .' I said.

'What drink?'

'The whiskey.'

'What whiskey?'

'You offered me . . .'

'I was only checking if you were concussed. But you seem quite capable of reasoned conversation. You're fine. You'll have a sore head. But I'll give you some of these. They'll do you rightly. Then you're free to leave.'

'So there's no drink?'

'No. Only medicine.'

'Not even for medicinal purposes?'

'Especially for medicinal purposes. We'd never get anything done if I started dashing out wee drams to every poor sod who came in here feeling under the weather. It is illegal, you know.'

'I know.'

He nodded. 'Sorry,' he said.

'But . . .' I began. He plainly wasn't aware that his own breath carried the stale whiff of the distillery. 'You can write me a prescription for it.'

'Can. Won't.'

'You're saying you have none?'

'I'm not saying anything. Or, if anything, I'm saying *you* have none. You know, alcohol isn't the answer to everything.'

'Are you sure?'

We regarded each other silently for a few moments. If anything stood testament to the evils of alcohol, it was his face. But it didn't seem the time to say so. If he had a precious supply of alcohol and was a drinker himself, he couldn't go dishing it out to all and sundry. I could understand that. But there was no need to preach about its evils. Less of the Hippocratic, more of the hypocritical.

I touched my head for the first time. A bump. Big one. Sore too. 'You examined this, then, when I was out.'

He nodded. 'You're okay.'

'I don't feel okay.'

'That's understandable.'

'My head feels . . . broken.'

'It will. For a while. But you'll be fine.'

'You don't need to scan it or anything.'

'I did scan it.' He held up his hands. 'With these. Still the best in the business.'

I tried to give him an appreciative smile, but my lips were too sore. His hands were nicotine-stained. The entire hands. Not just the fingers. I'd once, briefly, known a woman with nicotine-stained hair. But these hands were virtually golden. Physician heal thyself. I was glad that there'd been no cause for an internal examination. As far as I knew.

I had a sudden vision of a whale on a bicycle. 'What about the . . . Christine? The wee girl . . .'

'She's fine. She was waiting outside for ages. With her mum. But they had to go on. They wanted to stay. But Father White insisted. I told them you'd be okay. They were very grateful for what you did. Protected Christine like that. Saved her life, they said.'

I shrugged. If I had, it had been an accident. I must have tripped, or fainted. I wasn't a hero. There were dozens of people who could testify to that, some of them dead. 'What about the woman on the bike?'

'Oh, she's fine. She bounced. On you, actually. They brought her here too. Then Constable Murtagh took her away. Ran the gauntlet, rather. Someone hit her with a rock. She's fine. Under lock and key.'

I took a deep breath, yawned and stretched. I ached. 'What'll happen to her?' I asked, drearily.

Dr Finlay tipped a handful of small white pills into his hand, then dropped them into mine. 'I don't know. Depends what the charge is. What would you call it? Careless driving or attempted murder? Careless attempted murder, perhaps. I hear there's a crowd out at Murtagh's place wants to string her up. She's not a popular woman.'

'Why would she want to . . . I mean, what did she say? What was her excuse?'

'She babbled a bit. But then she's always been a bit of a babbler. Mary Reilly. You hadn't met her before?'

I shook my head, which was a bad idea. I told him that I'd spoken to her briefly at the church and that she'd seemed perfectly normal.

'Well, she would. That's what happens, one moment she's normal, next she's away. If we'd a home for the mentally deranged out here she'd be a permanent fixture, but we haven't. I recommended her removal to the mainland years ago, but people were reluctant. Up until now she's been pretty harmless.' He paused for a moment, as if deciding whether to go on. 'She's a medium, you know.'

'Strikes me as more of a large,' I said.

'You know what I mean. Spirits, and all that. People used to laugh at her on the one hand, then sneak off to see her on the other. That was before all *this* started, of course.' He gave me the kind of conspiratorial wink that suggested he wasn't altogether convinced by it either.

I pushed myself gently round on the sofa and placed my feet gingerly on the carpet. I felt a little dizzy. 'So was it the spirits that told her to try and kill Christine?'

The doctor shrugged. 'That's not for me to say.' He turned and placed the bottle of pills back in the cupboard.

'Do you believe Christine is the Messiah, doctor?'

'Of course.' He kept his back to me, busied his hands twisting a few medicine bottles round until their labels faced in the right direction.

I stood. The dizziness washed over me and then, abruptly, was gone. I smiled. 'Well,' I said, 'that feels okay.'

Dr Finlay turned from his cupboard. He looked me up and down. 'Fit as a fiddle, what did I tell you?'

I gave him a little nod and then thanked him.

'Can I order a taxi from here?' I asked.

'No,' he said.

'Oh.'

'Insofar as there are none. Island this size? Sure a strapping young lad like you could walk home in no time. It's only a couple of miles, isn't it?'

'I've just been in an accident.'

'The walk'll do you the world of good. I'm a doctor, believe me.'

'Aye. Right.'

He opened the surgery door for me. A mother and child sat in a sparsely furnished waiting room. They smiled at me. I smiled back. 'Thanks again, doctor,' I said.

'No problem. Sure I'm sure I'll be seeing you soon. You've a young child out at the cottage, haven't you?'

I nodded.

'I'll be needing to call out then, won't I, check everything's okay?'

'Of course.' *And I hope you'll be fucking walking*, I nearly added.

He followed me out of the surgery and stood before his patients. As I crossed to the door on the other side he barked, 'What the hell's the matter now?' at the mother, but as he lifted the child into his arms I saw that a look of bright concern had enveloped his ragged face.

15

It took me an hour. It had got a bit chilly. My bones were sore. I'd been in a serious accident and I was being made to walk home. My head hurt. The seagulls calling way up there sounded like they were laughing. Maybe they'd seen me being flattened by a big woman on a bike. Maybe they knew I was getting myself involved in something rather strange. Maybe they were just chatting about the price of fish.

I lingered for a few minutes by the shuttered pub. I leant against the wall. I tried to seep in some of its alcoholic energy, but all I could manage was some essence of cold brick and my legs felt heavier. I might have saved the life of the Messiah, but I couldn't buy myself a drink. I tried to cheer myself up by taking the long view: that maybe one day people would speak my name in the same awed manner in which they spoke of John the Baptist and Moses the Lawgiver – Dan the Accidental Hero – and preach earnestly of my suffering.

There were blessed few people around. I walked along the edge of the harbour, looked at the fishing boats gently bobbing in the greeny water. At Charlie McManus's ferry. No sign of him. There wasn't even an ice-cream man. Or a child running or a parent shouting at him not to go too close to the water. There was a dead calm. It was odd. Or normal. I didn't know.

I trudged the trudge of the lonely trudger out to Snow Cottage. It might as well have been ten miles as two. I was miserable.

I stopped at the end of the lane. There was a light in the window, welcoming – yes, but odd too, different. Instead of knocking on the door I peered through the window. Patricia. Rocking gently in a chair before a coal fire. A lamp on a table – oil or paraffin – throwing out a weak, gentle light. A table set. A baby asleep on a cushion on the floor. And suddenly I had a lump in my throat and a tear in my eye because it all just looked so bloody beautiful. Time-warped and soft. Shortbread tin and Oirishy both, but beautiful.

I tapped lightly on the door. Patricia answered it quickly. She was wearing a long skirt. A brown shirt, slightly frilly. No make-up to speak of, but a smile that made the need of it superfluous.

'The French Lieutenant's Woman,' I said. I held her by the arms. 'Or Lorna Doone?'

Her smile widened. She reached up and kissed me. Then touched my forehead. 'Are you okay?' she said.

I nodded. 'Fine.'

'They said you were fine.'

'Who did?'

'The priests came by to tell me about your . . . bravery.'

I shrugged.

'When I saw them, the two of them, coming to the door, I knew something had happened. And the way they started, all grave and gloomy, I thought they were going to tell me that you'd been killed in an accident. That I'd left you to make your own way home and you'd been knocked down by a car or a cow or struck by lightning or fallen down a hole and drowned. And I just thought instantly about how much I loved you and how much I would miss you and about how awful I've been to you. And then they told me you were okay and I just burst into tears. And now I'm going to do it again.'

And she did. She threw her arms round me and we hugged for a long time.

She pulled away. 'I made you some dinner,' she said proudly, 'it's in the oven.'

'No microwave?'

'No microwave.'

'I forgot the cat food. For the hedgehog.'

'It doesn't matter. He's in a box in the yard. I made a little house for him. I tried a little of your dinner out on him first. He gobbled it up. He seems to be thriving, so it can't be too poisonous. Have a seat.' She pulled the chair out for me. I sat. She opened the oven door. Lifted a steaming casserole across to the table.

'Looks delicious,' I said. 'Smells divine.'

'Wait till you try it.'

'I can't wait.'

She started to serve it up. Then abruptly she set the ladle down again and turned to a cupboard. She reached up. 'I forgot this,' she said, beaming.

I had to look twice.

'Jesus Christ,' I said.

A bottle of wine.

'Where on earth did you get that?'

'I brought it with me. From home.'

'But . . .'

'But I wasn't going to drink it until we had something to celebrate. And now there isn't anything better to celebrate than the two of us.' Little Stevie stirred on his cushion. 'The three of us,' she corrected. Patricia put her hand out to me and I took it and together we looked down at him stretching.

'Do you think you could love him?'

I nodded.

'Really?'

I nodded.

'I think you could too. If you give him a chance.'

I nodded.

She took my other hand.

'Dan?'

'Mmmmm?'

'I've been practising my pelvic floor exercises.'

'We don't have a pelvic floor. It's wooden, I think.'

'Dan . . .'

'I'm sorry . . . I . . . ?'

'Dan . . . you know what I mean. It's time.'

'Time for what?'

'Time to make love again.'

'I'll drink to that.'

'We'll do that too.'

I squeezed her hand. I felt elated. But mildly panicked. 'Are you sure it's okay?'

'Yes.'

'You're all healed?'

'Yes.'

'Are you sure?'

'Yes, Dan.'

'I don't want to hurt you.'

'I'm okay . . .'

'It just looked so . . . painful. Having Little Stevie.'

'Steven. It was. But I'm better now.'

'It's very soon.'

'Dan . . .'

'I know, I'm sorry. It's just . . . all the blood, the . . . mess . . .'

'Dan . . .'

'It was like a mortar bomb had scored a direct hit on an abattoir.'

She squeezed my hands firmly. Then pressed her lips to mine. 'I want you, sunshine,' she hissed. 'Now eat your dinner. Drink your drink. Then take me to bed.'

'Okay,' I said.

We made love in the still of the night, the quilt thrown back, the baby oblivious. Gentle. Slow. Gentle. Slow. As sweet and tender as the first time, but with the assured touch of familiarity.

We'd saved a glass of wine for the after-love. We clinked in the dark and whispered sweet everythings.

Patricia could be quite passionate with her words, and I basked in it.

'I love you more than all the grains of sand on all the beaches on all the planets in the universe,' she whispered breathily.

'Aw.'

'I love you more than all the waves in the sea, all the seas in the world.'

'Aw.'

'I love you more and more with each passing day, from here to eternity, to an eternity of eternities.'

She nestled under my arm. Stroked my stomach. 'How much do you love me?' she asked quietly, after a while.

'Lots,' I said.

16

The next morning, armed with a tape recorder and a swagger which comes with the love of a good woman, I set out for Moira's cottage. I didn't take the car. There was a cold breeze, but I was all man, plus a big fluffy coat with gloves. Along the way several people said hello to me, one person thanked me and a woman scrubbing her doorstep offered me a boiled egg. I was a made man. A hero, and I had bicycle spoke lacerations to prove it. I gave Moira's door a confident rap and stood back expectantly.

She answered with a snapped, 'Do you smell vomit?'

I shook my head. It was one of her less memorable lines. It probably wouldn't make it into Bible II. She was wearing a pink house coat and had a can of pine-fresh Haze in her hand.

'Somebody sick?' I enquired, stupidly.

'Christine,' Moira said, and turned on her heel. I followed her into the kitchen. 'Just a bug, but you never can get rid of the smell, can you?'

'I don't smell anything.'

'That's very kind of you, but I know there's a stink of boke.'

'No, honestly, I don't . . .'

'Don't contradict me, Dan, I'm the mother of God.'

'Sorry.'

She paused and rolled her eyes. 'I'm only raking.'

'You mean you're not the . . .'

'No . . . I mean you can contradict me.' She tutted. 'This is the problem. People don't know how to take me. I'm perfectly normal.' She thumbed upstairs. 'She's the odd one.'

I asked why she was pointing upstairs, seeing as how it was a cottage. She said the roof space had been converted, and did I want to see. I said why not and she took me up. It was all pretty mundane stuff. I don't know what I expected. Heavenly choirs and shafts of Godlight, not posters of Cliff Richard and a smell of vomit.

Christine was lying in bed, flicking through a book of nursery rhymes. There was a blue plastic basin beside her bed. It was empty. 'How're you doing?' I asked.

'Bokey,' Christine said.

She looked a little pale, but hardly at death's door. Moira said, 'There's a bug going around.' She felt Christine's brow. 'Normal,' she said. 'Christine. Do you remember Dan? This is the man who jumped in front of the bike? Remember the woman who nearly crashed into you?'

Christine nodded.

'What do you say?'

Christine shrugged.

'How about thank you?'

'Thank you.'

'No problem,' I said.

As we were going back down the stairs I said, 'I'm a little concerned.'

'She's fine.'

'No,' I said, 'about the Cliff Richard posters.'

Moira giggled. It was a nice giggle. 'You're not a fan?'

'Sue Barker's made better records. Though she hasn't.'

She paused, mid-step. 'I'm sorry, you've lost me.'

I cleared my throat. 'It's a joke lost in the mists of time.'

'Please explain it to me. Who's Sue Barker?'

'It doesn't matter.' I smiled. 'There's nothing worse than explaining a joke. Especially a weak one.'

We continued on through to the kitchen. It was a little after 10 AM. Ten seven, to be precise. I remember the time because it has historical significance. It was the time that Moira opened the fridge and said, 'Do you fancy a beer?'

I was staring through the door. There was a crate of Tennent's, with only three or four missing from the torn plastic wrap. I was mesmerised. It's not that I'm an alcoholic, you understand. It was just the surprise of it. 'I thought . . .'

Moira smiled. 'Do you think any of *them* have the balls to stop me?'

I shook my head.

'As far as I'm aware,' Moira said, removing two cans from the wrapper, 'these are the last on the island.'

'I feel very privileged.'

She was just handing one to me when she stopped and a mischievous grin crossed her face. 'So who's Sue Barker?' she asked, then tilted the can temptingly towards me, then away again.

'It's no secret,' I said.

'Tell.'

I gave her a nervous smile. '*Now* she's a television sports presenter. But way back she was a tennis player, reasonably good in a British way, hopeless on the world stage. She was close friends with Cliff Richard. All the tabloids claimed they were having an affair, but they both denied it. Still do – but as far as the greater public is concerned, it's the closest he's ever come to having sex.'

Moira nodded, handed me the can, then sat at the kitchen table and popped her Tennent's. I sat opposite her, and popped mine. 'Cheers,' I said.

'Cheers.' She gave me a quizzical little look. 'Do you know,' she said, 'that Cliff Richard is Christine's father?'

I spluttered some.

She laughed and took a drink. 'Thought that would get you going.'

'Cliff . . .'

'Not *physically* . . .'

'Oh . . .' I nodded, and looked for the emergency exit.

'I mean . . . the night she was born, I went to see his gig in Belfast. He shook my hand. There was something passed between us . . . a *warmth* . . . a *feeling* . . . *something* . . . and later that night I gave birth. I've always felt that he was in some way responsible, that a little bit of him was . . .' She trailed off into a shrug. 'You know what I mean.' I nodded, although I had no idea. 'He's so *spiritual* . . . I mean, he's been like the stopgap between Jesus and Christine . . .'

'And he's been crucified too,' I contributed, 'although only by the critics. But then he does keep coming back . . .' I smiled.

'You're taking the piss.'

I shook my head vehemently, then smiled again. 'Partly,' I admitted. I looked about the kitchen. It was modern, new; there was an Aga, a dishwasher, a washing machine, a microwave with grill facility. They were looking after her. She was watching me. I put down the can and produced the tape recorder from my pocket. 'Do you mind if I ask you a few questions?' She shook her head.

* * *

94

I don't know why it surprised me, but Moira had her head screwed on pretty tight. I mean, clearly she was deranged, thinking *that* about her daughter, but *that* aside, she was pretty well clued in. She knew what she wanted to do, where she was going, and how best to protect herself. 'The way I figure it,' she said, 'it's all a matter of keeping control. It's like the Spice Girls times a million. The reason they were so big, they had a good manager, they kept control, they had a piece of everything . . .'

'We're talking *girl power?*'

'After a fashion. Dan, life isn't a charity – or it isn't yet.'

I sat back and smiled. 'Now there's a frightening thought – the world being run by Combat Cancer and Dr Barnardo's and everyone having to wear little pink ribbons on fucking Aids Day. They don't even call it Dr Barnardo's any more because it doesn't fit in with some fucking marketing . . .'

'Dan . . . *you're* interviewing *me*.'

'Of course. Where were we . . . ?'

'I . . . don't know.' She laughed. She got me another can, and one for herself. She sat, thought for a moment. 'Back in Jesus Christ's day,' she began again, 'it took literally decades, maybe hundreds of years for his message to spread . . . but now, y'know, with television and satellite and the Internet, I mean, once we let this out *everyone*'s going to know about it in a matter of, like, *minutes*. There's going to be pandemonium.'

'I thought the idea was to keep it secret?'

'It is – until she's old enough. Doesn't mean things can't be set up in advance. Deals and things.'

'*Deals* . . . ?'

'I can't just stick her on a soap box and say, "Here's the Messiah." She'll be swamped. Or destroyed. She'll need to be protected. Represented. We'll need someone who knows television rights, someone who's promoted rock festivals – y'know, Woodstock or Glastonbury or something . . . we need to do it *big*, and we need to do it *right*.'

I opened can five. 'Excuse me . . . but you're not in this for, y'know . . . the money, by any chance?'

'Of *course* not. I don't mean it to sound that way. You think I'd choose to live *here* even if my daughter wasn't the Messiah, if I was interested in money? I'd have a decent job in Belfast or somewhere . . .' She sighed. She closed her eyes for a moment, as if the possibility of ever going to Belfast to get a proper job existed now only in her dreams. Then she opened them again, took another swig of her Tennent's and burped. 'Excuse me,' she said, then tutted. 'I hate to keep bringing this back to pop music, but youngsters can be destroyed by too much exposure; think how much worse it's going to be for Christine.'

'But she's the *Messiah* . . . surely she can . . .'

'We don't know that!' Moira cut in. 'How do any of us know what she can do? All *I* know is she's my wee girl, or nine tenths my wee girl and the other tenth is His . . . *I* don't know whether she's going to do party tricks or destroy the world, all I can do is provide the best possible environment for her: for now it's Wrathlin; by the time she's up a bit and wants to get her message across, she's going to need *deals* to enable her to do that. Do you understand?'

I nodded. In a strange way, I did. I was probably the only person on Wrathlin who would understand. Besides Patricia. 'I take it you haven't discussed all this with Father Flynn. Or his gloomy sidekick.'

'Father White?' She shook her head. 'They wouldn't get it. Flynn . . . could probably be persuaded. He's a nice guy . . .'

'His heart's in the right place.'

'Stop it. But I think the concept of a world stage is a bit beyond him. I don't think he can imagine much more than a revival meeting on the Ormeau Road. White . . . he's just creepy.'

'He reminds me of Telly Savalas.'

'Who?'

'Doesn't matter.'

'*Dan* . . . ?'

'He was Sue Barker's doubles partner. But no, I think you're right. I don't think either of them are equipped to take this onto a world stage. You need a mover and shaker. Like a Richard Branson or a Bill Gates.' We nodded together for a while, imagining. 'Come to that, you don't need me to write the book, you need a Shakespeare.'

'No, I need it to be understood by the man in the street.'

'Shakespeare was the people's . . .'

'Pish, I haven't a notion what he was rattling on about, and I'm not stupid.'

I would have argued, but she had a point. 'Fair enough. So you'd be going more for Tom Clancy than Salman Rushdie.'

'No, I'd be going for you.'

'Flattered as I am, why me?'

'Because Flynn recommends you. And you seem like a nice bloke. And you're sitting here having a can with me instead of slabbering round me or kissing my arse like the rest of them. I reckon you'd get the message across okay, whatever it turns out to be.'

I shrugged. It was quite a compliment, under the circumstances.

I opened another can and said, 'There's so much I have to ask you about all of this.'

She smiled. Warmly. 'Ask whatever you want, Dan. But, first, can I ask you something?'

'Sure.'

'Do you want to fuck?'

17

There are some questions a lady should not ask a gentleman. But then it was suddenly obvious that Moira was no lady and I'd never been accused of being a gentleman. I was red-faced, spluttering, and Moira was grinning widely.

'That was a bit out of the blue,' I managed.

'I haven't had sex in such a long time,' she said wistfully.

I nodded. She handed me another can. She wasn't much under five seven, standing; she'd a nice, trim figure and a sarcastic charm that was quite alluring. She'd long removed the pink housecoat. Beneath it were black ski pants, gutties, and a fading blue T-shirt with *Bahamas Yacht Club* written across her breasts, which were neither mountains nor molehills. Somewhere in between. Drumlins. Her skin was pale and she wore little make-up. Her nose was short but sharp. Her teeth were white and her smile keen. She said, 'Are you sizing me up?'

'Yes,' I said.

'Do I frighten you?'

'No.'

'Do you think I'm drunk?'

'No.'

'So give me one good reason why we shouldn't go to bed.'

'I'm married. I love my wife. Your daughter is sick upstairs. You're the mother of God.'

'That's four reasons.'

'Although I wouldn't want to jump to any hasty decisions. Opportunities like this don't come along every day.'

She smiled. 'You've been unfaithful to your wife before.'

'Did Christine tell you that?'

'No. Father Flynn.'

I nodded.

'And she to you.'

'It was a while back. We're better now.'

'That's not your son, is it?'

I shook my head.

'I don't see anything of him in you.'

I shrugged. I shifted in my seat. I glugged. It *is possible* to have sex with someone without being unfaithful to your partner. If it is just an opportunistic physical act which will have no consequences for those involved or connected to those involved. Just a moment or two of pleasure stolen from a difficult life. It can be a giving experience: helping somebody sad and lonely or in pain to get through their moment of crisis; you don't necessarily have to enjoy it yourself. And it beats the hell out of masturbation.

'If you sit there long enough,' Moira said, 'you'll analyse yourself out of it. Why not just come upstairs and fuck?'

'Because I don't delude myself that I'm that attractive. There . . .'

'. . . must be an ulterior motive? Dan, believe me, the ulterior motive is having sex with someone nice and there being no strings attached. You'll go back to your wife, and soon enough you'll pack up and go home, and if I'm lucky, if you're lucky, it'll be a nice wee memory for both of us. I don't see the problem.' We looked at each other across the table. After a little bit she said, 'Why is your knee drumming against the table?'

'Nerves.'

She pushed her chair back and stood. She reached across and took my hand. 'I can cure nerves,' she said. I stood. She led me out of the kitchen towards the stairs.

Halfway up I said, 'What are you going to tell Christine?'

'I'm not.'

Three quarters of the way up I said, 'What about birth control?'

'What about it?'

'To have one Messiah is understandable, but two would be plain careless.'

She squeezed my hand and said, 'Don't worry, I'm covered.'

'You make it sound like an insurance policy.'

'Well, isn't it?'

'Third party fire and conception.'

At the top of the stairs she stopped and looked into my eyes. 'Are you sure about this?'

I nodded.

There was a knock on the door.

Moira hissed a frustrated '*Fuck!*' and then put a finger to her lips. We stood at the top of the stairs while the door was knocked on again. 'They'll go away,' Moira whispered.

Then the bedroom door opened and Christine shouted: 'Mummy! There's someone at the door!'

'*Fuck!*' Moira hissed, followed by, 'Hussssssh darlin' . . .'

'Mummy! There's someone at the door!'

And then we both dissolved into giggles. Moira peered around the corner of the stairs in time to see the letter box flap inwards. She tugged Christine back from the top step, but it was too late. A slightly hoarse but still familiar voice called up towards us: 'Christine! Where's your mummy?!'

Moira kicked her heel against the wall, cursed again, then stepped out onto the landing. 'Down in a minute!' she called. She glanced back at me. 'It's Father White. Shadow me down the stairs so he doesn't see you, then get into the kitchen and tidy up those cans. Stick the empties out the back door or something. Spray some of that Haze. I'll stall him.'

We began to move down the stairs, Christine first, then Moira, then me hiding behind. 'I thought you said they couldn't stop you drinking . . .'

'They can't. I just don't want to flaunt it.'

'Chicken,' I said.

There was another knock on the door. 'Hold on!' Moira shouted, then added, 'Impatient son of a bitch,' under her breath. At the foot of the stairs I slipped past her into the kitchen and rapidly emptied the dregs into the sink and washed them away, then put the empty cans, and there were *lots* of them, into a plastic bag and placed them outside the back door. I sprayed some Haze, then sat at the table just in time for the kitchen door to open. Moira entered, followed by Father White, with Christine in his arms. 'I'm very sorry,' Moira was saying, 'I was having a shite.'

Father White cleared his throat, then stopped and his brow furrowed as he saw me smiling up at him, quite at home.

He stayed long enough to drink three cups of tea and scoff two fifths of a Battenburg cake. While Moira moved about the kitchen his eyes followed her, except when Christine was moving about at the same time. White was concerned about her ill health, and somewhat more concerned that he hadn't been told. The Messiah only stayed long enough to say hello and then Moira packed her back off to bed.

While Moira took Christine upstairs Father White shook my hand and thanked me effusively for saving her life, although such effusive thanks somehow seemed less than truly effusive. It was a new word for me and I was determined to wring the life out of it. I asked him what was going to happen to Mary Reilly and he stirred his tea for several long moments before looking up and saying that it was up to the Council. 'Not the police?' I queried and he mumbled a less than convincing 'Of course.'

Moira hurried back in, gave me a half-embarrassed smile, and sat at the table. She cut herself a slice of cake, took a bite, then asked, 'So, to what do we owe the pleasure?' spitting crumbs at the elderly priest in the process.

He seemed awkward in my presence, and I was unsettled by him. I was hardly listening to what he was saying because it seemed to me that there were secretive glances passing between them, that I was being excluded. It even crossed my mind, though only fleetingly, that if Moira was such a hornball, I mightn't be the only person she'd asked to bed in the recent past. What if Father White had called on the off-chance . . .

Shit. I'd known her five minutes and I was already thinking jealous thoughts.

I cut myself a slice of cake. There were only glances between them because they knew things about the McCooeys, about Christine, about the island, that I didn't, that they didn't want to share with me yet. That was understandable. I was only a journalist, I wasn't a mover and shaker. Nor, for long, would White be. Moira had told me that much. I smiled at her. She was an actress, then, and quite good at it.

After a while I got the impression that he was waiting for me to leave, but I stayed where I was, sure that Moira would make it clear one way or the other whether she wanted me to go. She said nothing, just flashed me a nice smile once in a while, so eventually it was the priest who stood and sighed after Moira said, 'We have to finish our interview.'

He looked at me, nodded and turned for the door. He paused with his thick white hand on the handle and looked at me. 'You know,' he said, 'it's Father Flynn who's in favour of this record being kept, not me.'

I shrugged. He left. Moira came back in. She opened the fridge and took out two cans of beer. There weren't very many left. She gave me one and popped open one for herself. 'So,' she said, 'where were we?'

It was dark when I left Moira's cottage. I hated myself deeply. I walked along the weakly lit Main Street and shuddered against the freezing wind blowing in off the sea. It was only when I reached the end of the street and was heading back out into the country that I realised I'd left my gloves behind. I tutted and walked on. Too awkward. We had hardly exchanged more than half a dozen words since we'd left her bedroom.

At the door she'd said, 'Was it that bad?'

And I'd hugged her and said, 'Moira, it was *fantastic*.'

'Then . . .'

'Don't ask.'

I kissed her and called goodbye to Christine, but there was no response. We'd kept things quiet, although I'd never been one for shouting. Whispering sweet nothings had always seemed a bit effusive to me.

Patricia, I . . .

Was drunk.

Was horny.

Will never know.

There was an anchor in my stomach and cement in my shoes. There was a persistent throb at the back of my head that was a sure-fire indication of a mean hangover to come. All-day drinking had once been my forte, but age and lack of practice had laid waste a once great talent. I had a can of Tennent's in each pocket, possibly the last two on the island. I had swiped them from the fridge when she wasn't looking. I felt mean about it, but not as mean as I felt about betraying Patricia.

I opened a can and kept walking. I'd forgotten how dark the countryside could be. I was a streetlights-and-shopwindows kind of a guy, not a pitted, muddy, splashy-lane bloke. As I walked, the can grew so cold that I was reduced to holding it between the two sleeves of my coat, supping at it like a leper, or so I supposed. I didn't have a lot of experience with lepers, although I soon would if Patricia ever found out I'd made love to Moira McCooey.

I'd been walking about twenty minutes when I heard a splash behind me. There had been other splashes, of course, rabbits or hares frolicking, raindrops on roses, whiskers on kittens, but this was different, *heavier*. I turned and stared into the darkness, but it was pointless. I could see nothing beyond the vague outline of the track leading back to town. I walked on. I dismissed it. A few minutes later there was another. I strained my eyes, but still nothing. A nothing I didn't like much. I was thinking of ghosts. Headless horsemen and wailing banshees. My heart was speeding up. I finished my can. I knelt down and placed it sideways in the road between two wide puddles. If there was someone following he would have a choice to make, either vault the low stone walls on either side of the road and continue after me over some very rough ground or wade through the puddles and really give himself away; much more sensible to walk the thin strip of dry track between the puddles. I hunched my shoulders and hurried on. I'd barely gone fifty yards when I heard the rattle of the can being accidentally kicked.

It could just as easily be someone else on the way home.

But I'd been in trouble before, many times in many places, and I knew better than to think bright, positive thoughts.

I started to run.

Whoever it was must have realised. There was a flash and a roar and for a split second the lane was illuminated, not that I had any intention of looking back. I knew what a shotgun sounded like. I had the sensation of something hot and dangerous shooting past my head, but I couldn't judge how close. On the same island was close enough. I let out a little shout of surprise then vaulted over the wall to my right.

There was only a short drop, three or four feet at most. My landing was soft. I put my head down and started to run. The grass was thick but the ground pitted from rabbit tunnelling. I stumbled and fell three or four times before I dared to look behind me. When I did, my blood froze. The night sky was lit by the beams of several high-powered torches. They were coming after me at speed.

18

Obviously they didn't know who they were up against. I had been a crack member of the Boys Brigade before being thrown out for drunkenness. And I had read *Bravo Two Zero*. If they wanted to get involved in a firefight, well, they'd better have matches.

I giggled and ran, then fell, giggled, ran, fell, giggled . . . it assumed a rhythmic but never monotonous pattern. There were advantages and disadvantages to the chase. I had the advantage of darkness, they had the advantage of torches to stop them falling down every hole they came across. I had the advantage of alcohol in my blood and the proof from past experience that a drunk can cover vast stretches of terrain without even being aware of it. He can leave the pub and one minute later wake up in bed, albeit with his trousers on fire. They had the advantage of knowing the land, knowing the island, knowing that it *was* an island and that eventually, if I didn't outwit them, they would drive me into the sea.

I crouched in the long grass for several moments, catching my breath and taking stock. There were six of *them*, spread fairly evenly apart. The ones on the outside were moving quicker or had easier terrain to cover and so had forged slightly ahead of those in the middle, creating a loose semi-circle. The speed of the chase, inevitably, meant that they couldn't cover every square yard with their torches; it wasn't inconceivable that I could lie down in the rough grass and hope that they passed over me. But in the end that would be down to good luck, two words which didn't figure large in my vocabulary, unlike effusively.

I started running again. There was a shout as one of them spotted me, and the torch beams began to converge. With a little zigzagging I managed to lose them again. I giggled. This was so *fucking stupid*. I wanted to stop and shout, *Are we playing hide and seek?* I wanted to shake my finger at them and tell them to catch themselves on, grown men chasing a wee fella like me. But I didn't even know if they were men at all. For all I knew it could be the women of Wrathlin on my tail. God knows, they're big enough and hairy enough. The thoughts piled in on top of each other as I charged breathlessly across the fields: had they been after me all along, or had they found out about Moira and me? Had Father White sent them? Or Christine?

The ground had been rising for several hundred yards. Even though I was running into the teeth of the wind the incline allowed me to put a little extra space between me and my pursuers. I'd been a runner at school and still played five-a-side, the hardest sport on earth, twice a week, so my legs were reasonably fit, even if the rest of me was a bag of bones. With the thin light from the stars I could see that I had reached the top of the island's central saddle, the highest point on Wrathlin. A mile ahead of me there was the chop of the waves, further still the lights of the mainland, civilisation. Snow Cottage was about a mile in the opposite direction. By accident rather than design I had led my pursuers away from it, which was good news for Patricia and little Stevie but somehow made my own safety seem even more remote.

There was a whirring sound ahead of me. I slowed up, suspicious. As I drew closer I could just make out the most bizarre outlines: like three helicopters had crash-landed and buried themselves in the soil, leaving only their rotorblades revolving. Still, they seemed less threatening than what came behind. When I was right up close it was suddenly obvious that they were wind turbines, and, once identified, that I knew something about them. Father Flynn had spoken glowingly about them. He'd helped engineer a European grant for them. They provided two thirds of the island's electricity. He'd even told me their names. Conn, Aedh and Fiachra. I had the info on tape, and had reviewed it the previous day while trying to make some sense out of Flynn's visions. If I'd had the inclination I could have waited for my pursuers and explained that the turbines had been named after the three sons of the mythical chieftain Lir, who'd been turned into swans by their wicked stepmother and spent hundreds of years floating on the Seas of Moyle around Wrathlin. Like most natives, the chances were that they didn't know much and cared less about their own history; they were too busy catching fish and killing rabbits and generally surviving to give a toss about myths and legends. If there was even a slight inclination to stop for a chat, my mind was made up by the sudden shotgun blast that whooshed past my ear and snapped an arm off one of the turbines. We live in an information age, but it's not much use to you if your head is splattered all over your computer. I ducked and ran.

As my fatigue grew, the icy wind began to catch me, cutting into my chest. I had run myself sober. In a different environment I could probably have stayed ahead of them indefinitely, as long as I didn't do anything stupid, like twist my ankle, because I was sure they weren't super-fit athletes either. But I had to face up to one indisputable fact. Sooner or later I was going to run out of land.

As I ran I tried desperately to remember the map of the island I had pored over before leaving Belfast or the route of the walk I had taken with Father Flynn. I tried conjuring up the points of the compass in my head: the old schoolboy method of remembering the order in which they came – *Never Eat Shredded Wheat*. North, east, south, then west. I'd walked west on leaving town, heading home, then been shot at and started running north; after a while this had taken me onto the higher ground where the turbines were, and now I was heading down towards . . . what was it, Artichoke or Altachuile Bay and the freezing . . . Straits of Moyle? It was coming back to me. I giggled again. It was like the moment of clarity which precedes death. I cursed. My teeth were starting to chatter. I needed to find another way, and fast. The sea was no use to me. To the east I could see the beam of the East Light, one of the three unmanned lighthouses on the island. Close by it, I knew, was Robert the Bruce's cave. It was probably the first place they'd look, figuring me as a mainlander and a tourist. Even if I went for it, it was also only accessible by boat, and the last thing I intended to do was venture anywhere near a boat.

I stopped for a moment and desperately tried to catch my breath. I looked back. The beams seemed further away now. Behind them, and therefore useless to me, was the town, then the southern leg of the island, with the second lighthouse in the far distance at Rue Point. I turned to my left. The third light, the West Light, winked into the darkness. It was the only way to go. The west of the island offered the greatest stretch of land for me to outrun them; eventually, of course, I would come to the sea again, but somewhere between there and now I would have to find help or a way of doubling back on them and seeking salvation in the town.

I took a deep breath and started to run again, keeping my head as low as I could.

I'd been moving for about five minutes when I chanced another look back.

The lights were gone.

My heart would have skipped a beat if it hadn't been too busy racing itself to death.

I stood gulping in the freezing air, trying to work out what was going on. I allowed myself a brief flurry of hope before settling into a more familiar mode of black pessimism. I made a quick calculation of the possibilities. 1) They'd given up. 2) They'd decided the torch lights were giving me too much of an advantage and had switched them off. 3) Their batteries had run out. On the whole, I thought number two was the most likely. But the only way to be absolutely sure was to wait and find out, and I didn't think that would be very healthy.

I pressed on.

Another fifteen minutes and there was still no indication of anything behind me. I had slowed down, and not just from extreme tiredness, but also because the absence of lights had somehow lessened the horror of being chased by men with guns. *What you can't see can't hurt you.* Was that the expression? If it was, it deserved pride of place in the *Big Book of Stupid Fucking Expressions*. I had just reduced my pace to a hurried stroll and was focusing my attention on reaching the West Light when there came a sudden fit of coughing off to my right, barely a dozen yards away. I turned, panicked, lost my footing and before I could right myself I was tumbling down a small hill. In a matter of moments I went from fleet-footed escapologist to sad drunk entangled in gorse.

And then there was a torch beam blinding me.

The voice, English, said, 'What on earth are you doing down there?'

Instinctively I said, 'Hunting for blackberries.'

There was a pause, and then, 'You won't find any blackberries down there, old son, not this time of year.'

'I know,' I said. 'Only joking. 'Fraid I got lost.'

A hand, thick and hairy, warm, reached down to me and dragged me screaming from the thorny gorse. My rescuer, or cunning executioner, shone the torch in my face, then in his own. He was wearing a big green parka with a fur-lined hood. His face was bearded and round and he had bottle-thick glasses and an eagle smile. There was a pair of binoculars around his neck. No sign of a gun.

'Look at you,' he said, 'you're freezing. Come on down to the caravan for a cuppa.'

He turned his back on me and started walking. 'Thanks,' I said, after him, and followed. I looked warily about me, waiting for the surprise attack, which would therefore, of course, not be a surprise. The ambush, then. But there was nothing, just the wind and the whispering grass and this rotund furball with the endearing smile and the kind invitation. I said, 'I know you, don't I?'

He shrugged, without turning. 'The caravan's just down here.'

'Where do I know you from?'

He shrugged again. 'I'm the warden. Maybe you visited the platform.'

'What platform?'

He stopped, looking at me oddly as I caught up. 'The birds.'

'What birds?'

He sighed. 'Oh dear,' he said. 'You're just a drunk, then.'

'What?'

'Just over here.' He pointed, and started off again. There was a small caravan, a two-berth at most, sitting rusty and neglected on a steep incline about twenty yards back from the edge of a large concrete platform. There was a y-framed metallic clothes line spinning at a hundred miles an hour in the wind beside the caravan. Three sets of bulky binoculars were set into the platform wall, with coin slots beneath them, giving a kind of Edwardian-looking pay-per-view over the cliffs and wild sea beyond. Only as we drew close could I hear the sound of thousands of seabirds over the roar of the wind.

'Bird observation platform,' I shouted.

He nodded. The wheels of the caravan were anchored into place by several breezeblocks. He yanked open the door and ushered me in. The inside smelt of burnt toast. There were piles of clothes lying everywhere. He had a flask of tea already made. He poured me a cup and even though I never drink the stuff, I was so cold I supped it eagerly just for the heat.

He had pulled his hood back now and I got a better look at his face. He was in his mid-fifties, probably, but his red cheeks and blond eyebrows gave him a boyish look.

'You're lucky I found you,' he said. 'I take a walk around the platform about this time every night. Just in case. Usually don't go over where you were, but I was having a pee-pee. Bucket gets full up in here, makes the place a bit whiffy. Anyway, welcome to my humble abode.'

'You're the warden?' I said.

He nodded. 'Bill.' He reached his hand out to me and we shook. 'During the summer I have a couple of assistants, but the winter I'm here alone. We're not officially open, but I never turn anyone away if they make the effort. You're not a twitcher, then?'

'Sorry?'

'Ornithologist. Bird watcher.'

There were answers to that, but they would take me into *Carry On* territory and I wasn't in the mood. I shook my head.

'You don't know what you're missing.'

I had a fair idea, actually. Lots of birds.

'Finest breeding colonies in Ireland,' he continued. 'Do you know anything about birds?'

I shrugged.

'What would your favourite be?'

'Sparrow. Blackbird. My wife has a lot of experience with thrush.'

If he got it, there was no reaction. 'Kittiwakes, guillemots, razor-bills, fulmars and puffins . . . oh, it's a sight, it's a sight indeed. Tens of thousands of them, beautiful . . . not so many places like this any more . . .' Bill looked dreamily out of the window. Then abruptly snapped out of it. 'Still, no concern of yours, eh . . . what was it, wandered off from the pub?'

'*What* pub?'

His brow furrowed. 'Jack's . . . Jack McGettigan's . . .'

I cleared my throat. 'The pub's been closed for months. Drink has been outlawed.'

'Out . . . ?' Bill looked at me for several moments as if I was mad. Then he shook his head and said, 'Oh dear, oh dear. They really went ahead and did it, did they? Oh my.'

Now that I was a little more settled, I could see that every available space in the little caravan was stacked with cans of food and bottles of mineral water. 'You mustn't get into town much,' I observed.

'No,' Bill said, 'nothing much there for me. Used to go for a beer, occasionally, bit of a sing-song, but they stopped that. And then no one seemed to drink any more. I only went for the company, didn't seem much point after that. No, I keep to myself up here, right through to summer. No family, see? Not any more, any rate. I suppose I do get a little out of touch.'

'But you'll know about Christine. The Messiah?'

He laughed. 'Oh yes. All that bloody nonsense. No time for that, have I? Anyway, I thought it would have all blown over by now, but if they've closed the pub I guess it hasn't.' He sighed. 'I don't see anyone now, really, not till summer. There's a radio down in the storeroom, chat with headquarters sometimes, keeps me in touch with the football results on a Saturday, but that's about it.'

I looked at my watch. It was a little after 9 PM. I'd been on the run for less than an hour, although it seemed like seven. I'd not given Patricia any particular time for my return, but with no pub on the island to distract me she would probably be concerned by my failure to return. I didn't mind that. What I did mind was her going to Moira's looking for me and Moira letting something slip. Or Christine. I shivered.

'What you need,' the warden was saying, 'is a hot whiskey.'

I looked up, smiling.

'It's a pity I don't . . .' At that moment the caravan moved. Just slightly. '. . . have any.'

We looked at each other. I could tell by the surprise on his face that it wasn't a regular occurrence.

'Wind must get pretty wild round here,' I said.

The caravan moved again.

'You must have it pretty securely anchored,' I said, 'with that strong wind.'

He was nodding, but it was not a confident nod. His hands were gripping the table. 'The thing is,' he said, 'the wind's blowing in the other direction.'

There were voices outside. Then the caravan gave a massive shift forward, throwing us both out of our seats.

Then we were moving downhill at speed. Somewhere in the background I heard excited yells. And somewhere ahead of us, and getting closer, there was a very tall cliff, an angry sea and some very sharp rocks.

19

As we trundled towards the edge of the cliff and the three-hundred-foot drop to death, I had one of those moments of frightening clarity with which I was becoming increasingly familiar. I looked at Bill beside me, helpless on the grimy birdshit-spattered floor of the caravan, and said, 'You used to be in *The Goodies*. You're Bill Oddie.'

'This isn't the time!'

'I know, I've seen the repeats.'

For the second time in a couple of minutes he looked at me like I was mad. I could have explained to him about defence mechanisms and the trouble they'd gotten me into, but he was right, this wasn't the time. He had been a television comedy star in a previous incarnation, but now he was just a bird warden scrabbling along the floor in a desperate attempt to get to the door of a caravan moving at speed towards disaster. Every time we hit a rock it threw the front of the caravan up in the air, and him back towards me. I tried myself, with no better results.

And then it was too late.

We struck something solid, we were tossed forward and then the whole caravan was over the edge and falling. We both smacked into the glass at the front with five hundred cans of food for company.

Remarkably, the glass held.

Big deal as we . . .

Then there was a sudden jolt and we stopped dead in the air . . .

No, not dead . . .

Swinging.

Back and forwards, like the pendulum on a grandfather clock.

Bill was clutching the back of his head where he'd cracked it on the glass. He groaned and moaned, 'What's . . . what're we . . .'

I stared at the water barking and biting far below. It was almost hypnotic. 'The answer, my friend,' I said slowly, 'is blowing in the wind.'

He eased himself up into a sitting position. Tin cans rolled off him and cracked into the glass. Still it held. I love glass now. Some people say it's a pain, but it saved our lives. For the moment.

Bill said, understanding dawning, 'The gas canisters . . .'

I rolled my eyes. 'You mean we're going to *explode* as well as . . .'

'No! The caravan . . . connected to half a dozen gas canisters . . . they're hidden in bushes so the tourists don't see them . . . but they're in a metal cage so no one'll steal them . . . they're keeping us up!'

But for how long?

What if whoever had pushed us over knew about them?

How long before they cut the line?

'We have to get out of here,' I said, a statement of such overwhelming obviousness that Bill didn't even acknowledge it.

We began to pull ourselves cautiously up the caravan. The hundreds of cans didn't help. Swinging from side to side didn't help. But the thought of never seeing my wife and child again did. I loved them both dearly and would never be unfaithful again. I would go to church more regularly, though not necessarily on Wrathlin. I would cut down on the drink. I would do good deeds. I said, 'Did you ever see *The Lost World*?' as we moved inch by inch. Bill shook his head. 'The sequel to *Jurassic Park*?'

'Will you just *shut up*?'

'Sorry. But there's a scene just like this. Caravan over the edge of a cliff, hanging on by a thread.'

Bill cursed as a tin of Heinz Spaghetti and Sausages shot off a shelf and whacked into the back of his head.

'Okay . . . *okay* . . . ! What happens?'

'I can't remember.'

'God!'

'Sorry . . . sorry . . .' I was moving up behind him. He had reached the door now and was carefully opening it . . . then the wind caught it and ripped it off. It slapped back against the side of the caravan and then disappeared. The whole vehicle shivered, shifted, then dropped several feet. We both let out involuntary shouts and held on for dear life.

It steadied again. 'Tell you what,' I gasped, 'if we get out of this, we'll rent it out, see what happened.'

Bill was shaking his head. He pulled himself back into the doorway, then peered out. For several moments he crouched there, contemplating, then looked back in at me. 'I don't have a bloody video player.'

'That's okay,' I said, 'you can borrow mine.'

He nodded. Then slowly raised himself to his feet. He reached out of the door and began to feel for something to grip on the outside of the caravan. He didn't need to tell me what he was doing. He had to get onto what *was* the side, but was now the top of the caravan. Once up there he could shimmy up the gas line to the top of the cliff. Easy-peasy. As he continued to feel for a grip a bird, a guillemot, a razorbill, *something*, squawked momentarily through the open doorway at me then flew off.

Bill found what he was looking for. He took a deep breath then started to pull himself up. As his legs disappeared I reached the door and peered out and up. The wind was terrifying, and wasn't made any friendlier by the excited calls of the seabirds flapping round us in the dark.

Shit!

I hated climbing. You have an aptitude for some things, and climbing wasn't one of mine. I'd hated trees as a kid. Chop 'em down rather than climb up 'em. And this wasn't even a tree. This was a caravan swinging in a gale two hundred feet above razor-sharp rocks.

Fuck!

If it had been an episode of the *X-Files* I could have whipped out my mobile phone and called for help. But it wasn't and I'd never owned one. Instead I cursed again and hauled myself out of the door, feeling desperately for the grips Bill had found.

It was freezing. My legs were jelly. My arms were jelly. *Oh God . . . wake up . . . wake up!* But there was nothing but the wind and the horror.

'There! *There* . . . !'

I looked up. Bill's head was just visible around the curve of the caravan. He had made it safely onto the 'new' roof and was now pointing . . .

I reached hesitantly out. My fingers curled round something, something curved and metallic.

'That's it! Now come on!'

Fuck!

Just take a seat in the caravan. It's relatively warm. There's lots of nice tinned food. Make yourself some supper.

Fuck!

I pulled myself up. There was a narrow ridge around the top of the doorframe on which I could just about support myself on the tips of my toes.

Just about . . .

No!

One foot slipped . . . then the other . . .

Fuck!

I was swinging on my hand grip, my legs whipped out from under me by the wind. I was a flag. A flag of surrender.

My fingers were like ice.

Just let go . . . just let go . . . float . . . float on . . . float on . . .

Fuck! Who sang that?

Float on, float on . . .

It would have to be the fucking Floaters . . .

I had a big book of hits at home . . .

'Take my hand! *Take my hand*!'

Bill was reaching down to me.

'I can't!'

'You can! You have to!'

'Fuck!'

I looked up again. Birds were swooping around his head. I'd no choice.

I let go with one hand and stretched, *stretched* . . . I caught his fingers, but he wasn't interested. He inched on down to my wrist, then started to pull.

'Let go! Let go with the other!'

'But I'll . . . !'

'Let go!'

I let go and he heaved and he hauled me up those few feet to the top of the caravan.

The wind hit me and nearly blew me over. Bill held onto me. We hugged each other for several moments, then the caravan shifted again and we grabbed desperately for the thin rubber pipe which was the only thing keeping us in the air.

We both looked up. It was about thirty feet to the top.

I looked doubtfully at him. 'We toss for who goes first, then?'

He shook his head. 'I have to go first. This is Royal Society property, I have to report it.'

'Fair enough,' I said.

A black and white bird swooped in at us. I felt its claws in my hair. I nearly lost my footing as I swiped at it.

'Razorbills!' Bill called. 'They're getting protective of their nests.'

'Excellent!' I shouted. 'That's all we need.'

'It'll be okay. There's no young ones to protect this time of year. No eggs. We'll be fine.'

That was okay. All we had to do was worry about the climb from hell.

I looked up again. The gas line was stretched tight. It went straight up for several yards, then curved around an outcrop. We couldn't see beyond that; we could only hope that the line straightened itself out again for the run in to the edge of the cliff.

Bill put both hands around the gas line. He looked at me and gave a little shrug. 'Why would anyone want to push my caravan over the edge?' he asked.

I shook my head.

'Vandals,' he said glumly.

'Good luck,' I said, and he pulled himself up. His foot crunched into the side of the cliff for support, dislodging a shower of twigs and moss which was immediately whipped away by the wind. He grinned back at me, then went for it.

It was okay for him.

He probably spent his whole life in the open air. This wasn't bad weather for him. It wasn't even cold for him. He probably felt *warm*. He was an outdoors man. A rough, tough birdman trained to scale cliffs to rescue injured birds, to fight off international birds'-egg smugglers. Whereas I could type *really* fast.

Fuck!

I ducked down again as another razorbill dived in at me, then looked back up to Bill.

He was at the base of the outcrop now, the most difficult point of the climb. But he was distracted. The razorbills were swooping in on him as well, but in greater numbers. He was closer to their nests, I supposed. He raised one hand to protect his face, then threw it out at them. The wind was howling, but I was sure I could hear him shouting at them to get away. Spend half your life helping birds, then in your moment of need . . .

And I would have to go up there in a moment.

I peered out over the edge of the caravan at the sea churning below. The rocks were set in a rough semi-circle, a toothy smile with flecks of mad spume.

The only way is up.

Now who sang that?

This time there was a scream from above, no doubt about it.

Bill was enveloped by razorbills. He had one hand over his eyes, but something about the way he was clawing at the birds suggested that he had tried to protect his eyes too late, that one of the birds had flown straight into his face and started pecking. He was holding on with one hand, swinging helplessly in the wind. I couldn't see his face, but I could almost feel his distress; he was beating, beating blindly at them. Then there was another flurry of wings and a wind-suckered shout and suddenly he let go of the rope.

He plummeted.

He was past me in an horrific instant. There wasn't a sound. Just a bulky coat in the dark. No scream. No last shout for help. Just a blur. I screamed after him. But there was nothing. Not even a splash or a thud; the wind was so loud that Bill's death was silent.

Jesus Christ.

Or Christine.

Alone on the roof of a caravan, swinging. Razorbills and an impossible climb above, certain death below.

I'm not afraid to cry. I'm not beyond rolling on the ground and begging for help. I would not stand up under torture because my legs would get tired.

Fuck!

I cursed everything there was to curse, and then looked up the gas line, at the outcrop and the birds, and tightened my hands on the rubber and started to pull myself up. There was no alternative. I had to try. The alternative was suicide.

One hand above the other. Pull.

Foot in the cliff. Push.

Not that far really.

Already my fingers were numb on the rope.

Already the birds were swooping in.

Fuck! Something thudded into me.

I kept my eyes closed and my head down.

Pull.

Push.

Pull.

Push.

Fuck! Something ripped into my cheek.

Then my neck. They were tearing my hair out. Ripping my fingers.

Keep those hands on the rope!

Eyes closed!

Push! Pull! Push! Pull!

I was at the outcrop.

There was wind, but it was drowned out by the cries of the razorbills. I heaved myself up, cracked my head on the outcrop, nearly dropped, swung for a few moments, wings lashed into my face, there was blood trickling down my brow. I started to move again. *Slowly, slowly, push, pull, push, pull* . . .

I was *on* the outcrop.

Whack, something hit me on the back of the head.

Fuck, they were throwing stones at me!

I heaved, I pulled. *C'mon Dan, c'mon! Drink! Sex!*

C'mon!

The attacks were easing off. I opened my eyes, half opened them; they were sticky with blood and I couldn't spare a hand to wipe them. *No nests here, no birds, must be* . . . I looked up. *Jesus Christ, only a few more yards!*

I'm going to make it!

What if they're waiting at the top?

The guys with the guns and the over-developed sense of fun.

What if they throw me straight back over?

No alternative . . . no alternative!

I pulled, I pushed, twice more, and then I was up and over and lying flat out on the sandy ground at the top of the cliff. I forced myself onto my knees and crawled forward several metres just to be sure the ground didn't suddenly give way on me or a gust of wind blow me back over.

I rolled over onto my back and stared at the stars. I gasped,

'Throw me back over if you want. Right now I don't give a flying fuck.'

And then I closed my eyes and waited, but there was no response. Just the wind, and fading cries of angry birds.

20

There's only so long you can spend lying on top of a cliff, feeling like death, before you start to feel stupid. Before you realise you're not going to suddenly wake up in bed. Nobody's going to rescue you. You're not mortally injured, you're just tired and a little bit battered. You know you've a long walk home. Once there you'll try a lame, 'Guess what happened to me,' and no matter how good you are at telling stories, you know that no one is ever going to quite understand. *You were on top of a caravan? Over the edge of a cliff? It was really windy? He fell off? Oh-ma-God, you poor thing, and pass the salt, would you?*

It had clouded over. It was starting to spit. Bill was dead. I had no idea if he really was Bill Oddie. Not that it mattered. He could have been Gunga Din or Adolf Eichmann. Nobody deserved to die like that, except of course Adolf Eichmann. I was covered in birdshit and blood. I was frozen and everything that could ache, did.

I thought about taking the circuitous route home, for safety's sake, but I was beyond caring, I was too miserable to continue playing commandos. There was a road leading from the bird observatory back towards town and I stuck to it. I tramped, head down, too tired to think, but thinking nevertheless. I had to go to the police, tell them what had happened. The mainland would be the best bet, but I'd get the ball rolling with the cop stationed here on the island first. But not yet. It was late and there was one thing I needed first: a hug. Someone to pat my head and tell me everything was all right. Patricia. She mightn't really believe my story, but she could provide a big pot of sympathy. Then a sleep. Then I'd be okay. We could be packed up in a couple of hours and off the island. Fuck it, forget the packing, just get on the first ferry then send for the stuff. The Cardinal had asked me to investigate a child who claimed to be the Messiah, not to get involved in murder.

Murder. A small, close-knit community.

Who was to say that *I* hadn't thrown Bill over the edge?

I had been down the road of being presumed guilty before.

My fingerprints all over the caravan. My footprints at the top of the cliff. My drunkenness on leaving Moira's. Even if she didn't finger me, Father White surely would.

Shit.

In took three quarters of an hour to walk home. It was a quarter to eleven as I struggled into the lane and saw Father Flynn's battered Land-Rover parked outside the cottage. I froze, even more.

Were *they* waiting for me? Were they in the bushes?

No. They would presume I was dead. *So they've come for Patricia. Even now they're* . . . no, what would be the point? What did she know? Come to that, what did *I* know?

The lounge curtains were closed, but there was a small bare side window. As I cautiously approached it there came a scuffling sound from behind me and I spun, ready to make a fight of it or at least beg for mercy, but it was only our friendly neighbourhood hedgehog out on patrol. I tutted and turned back to the window. I edged up to it and peered in: Patricia, cup of tea, baby asleep on sofa, Flynn, cup of tea, animated mouths, but smiles not scowls. Small talk and wee buns.

I knocked on the front door. Patricia opened it. Her first words were, 'Where the fuck were . . . ?' but then she trailed off as I stepped into the light and she saw the state of me. 'Jesus Christ, Dan . . . what happened?'

She ran to me and hugged me and I winced. Her fingers traced the dried blood on my face. She stood back and held me at arm's length. 'Dan . . . ?'

I shook my head and shuffled past her. Father Flynn was standing in the lounge, cup and saucer in hand, an odd mix of concern and awkwardness on his face. 'Dan . . .' he said, without any hope of completing the sentence.

Trish came in behind me and said, 'Dan . . .'

So we'd established my name. I looked at Patricia and said, 'Sorry.'

Her head moved a little to one side. '*Dan* . . . ?'

I looked at Father Flynn. 'Accidents will happen.'

'Oh dear . . .' he spluttered, 'you had a . . .'

'Self-inflicted.'

'Self . . . ?'

'I was coming home from Moira McCooey's. It started to rain. There's a dilap . . . dilapa . . . an empty farm house down the road a bit. I took shelter. I was nosing about waiting for it to go over. Found a couple of bottles of sherry hidden behind a broken old bookcase.' I took a deep breath. I sighed it out. 'I drank them. I think they were past their drink by date. Next thing I knew I was throwing up. I tried to get home, but I blacked out. Must have fallen over a wall or something. Woke up in a gorse bush about half an hour ago. Sorry.'

'Oh love . . . are you okay?' It was said sympathetically enough, but I knew the tone, and I knew the look of barely concealed loathing in her eyes. If Father Flynn hadn't been there she would have beaten me to a pulp.

'Felt better,' I said. I nodded at Father Flynn. 'I guess I was pretty stupid.'

'It's one of the reasons we outlawed the alcohol, Dan.'

I nodded. 'I'm never drinking again,' I said.

'I came to thank you personally for saving Christine. It was a brave and selfless act.'

I shrugged.

'So we'll say nothing more about the alcohol.'

'Thank you.'

'Now I better run along.' He smiled across at Patricia, then handed me the cup and saucer. 'We've had a great wee chat. She thought you were never coming home.'

'I always come home,' I said.

Patricia glared at me, then led Father Flynn to the door and bade him good night. She stood in the doorway until he'd started the engine, waved back at her, then driven off. The instant the door was closed . . .

'You stupid fucking . . . !'

'Shhhh!' I said, putting my finger to my lip, and hurrying to the curtains. I peered out after Flynn's disappearing vehicle.

'Don't you fucking shush me, you . . .'

'Trish!' I stuck a finger out at her, something she hates. 'Stop it! Stop it now . . . I'm serious.'

'I'm fucking serious! What the hell do you think you were . . . ?'

I checked the road outside again, then pulled the curtain tight. 'Pack up what you can. We're leaving.'

That stopped her. 'What . . . ?'

'We're leaving. First thing in the morning. Just the essentials. We'll never get all this shite in the car by morning, so just what's easy. We're catching the first ferry.'

'Dan . . . ?'

'There was no sherry, Trish. No *dilapidated* farm house. I got attacked on the way home from Moira's . . .'

'What . . . ?'

'*Attacked*. Me. Attacked. Trish, I can handle out-of-date sherry. Look at the state of me, for fuck's sake.'

'Mugged on Wrathlin?'

'Not *mugged*. Attacked. Shot at. In the dark. Guys with torches. They've been chasing me all over the fucking island for the last two hours. They were trying to kill me.'

'*Dan* . . . ?'

'I'm serious! *Jesus*! I knew this would happen!'

'It's not that I don't . . .'

'It's *just* that you don't, Trish, I'm *serious*.'

'Well, did you see who they were?'

'It was pitch dark.'

'You mean you were in Moira's all that time?'

'Yes.'

'Interviewing her from first thing this morning?'

'Yes.'

'You've never taken that long to interview anyone in your life.'

'She's the mother of the Messiah. I needed to go in depth.'

'So where did you get the alcohol?'

'What alcoh . . .'

'Dan, I'm not a fool. You smell like a brewery.'

'Moira had a couple of cans in the fridge.'

'Uh-huh.'

'It was just a couple.'

'Enough to keep you there all day.'

'Trish, for fuck's sake, we're getting away from the point here.'

'Are we? You got drunk at Moira's, made an arse of yourself, and some guys had to come and chase you away. Would that not be closer to the mark?'

'No!'

'Dan, tell me the truth.'

'I am telling you the truth!'

'Father Flynn said you were drunk at Moira's. So was Moira for that matter.'

'*What?*'

'Father White told him. It's true, isn't it?'

'No! Yes! For fuck's sake, Trish.'

'She's an attractive woman.'

'Trish!'

'And I know we're not back to normal in bed yet, but that'll come, I just need time to . . .'

'Trish, will you stop being stupid? For Jesus' sake. Look. I had a few cans of beer while I was interviewing her. She was fascinating. It's a *fascinating* story. But it's got nothing to do with bed . . . Trish, listen to me. I was walking home. I was fine. I heard something behind me. Then there was a gunshot. Then there were torches, half a dozen of them, then they were chasing me. It was like a rabbit hunt, except I was the rabbit.'

'Are you sure it *wasn't* a rabbit hunt? You just got in the way.'

'Do I look like a rabbit?'

'Sometimes. Besides, it was dark. Maybe . . .'

'Trish. They tried to kill me. There is no doubt about it. Now. You are here with me. Your baby is here . . .'

'*My* baby . . . ?'

'*Our* baby . . . I am not exposing you or him to that kind of danger. More importantly, I'm not exposing myself to that kind of danger. We have to get out of here.'

She sighed. 'Dan, it's not that I don't believe you . . .'

'It's just that you don't believe me. Fuck it, Trish, you wouldn't believe me if I came in with one arm blown off and an eye missing.'

'Yes, I would. If you'd witnesses.' She smiled. I scowled, but it slipped into a smile too. 'Dan, have a bath, let me look at those cuts, have a sleep. We can't go anywhere tonight. If you still feel the same way in the morning then we'll go.'

'I'm not drunk,' I said.

'Okay. I'll run the bath.'

'I'm not drunk,' I said again.

'I know.'

She ran the bath. I looked at Little Stevie, still asleep on the sofa. 'I'm not drunk,' I said.

Maybe I was a little. I fell asleep in the bath and drowned.

Or would have if Patricia hadn't prodded me back awake and then carefully cleansed my wounds. I didn't tell her about the birds, though she enquired about the birdshit. I should have told her everything, but I had never told her everything. Once you start down that road it's difficult to get off it. Besides, she would find out eventually. She always did.

I went to bed. She stayed up to settle Little Stevie. I was out like a light, and didn't wake until eleven the next morning. The first ferry of the day was long gone. The bedroom door opened and I was halfway through snapping a 'Why didn't you . . .' when I saw that Patricia was carrying a tray. There was an Ulster fry, a can of Diet Pepsi and a Twix on board, and you can't shout at someone who does that for you. 'What's the occasion?' I asked.

'I love you,' she said.

'I know. What's the occasion?'

'I love you.'

She put the tray on my lap, kissed the top of my head, and left me to think.

I loved her deeply and had betrayed her far too many times. It would have to stop. That and the drinking. I had been drunk. But I had been chased and Bill Oddie or somebody who looked like him was dead. We still had to get off the island.

And yet it was a pleasant autumnal morning. The sun was out. The grass was dry. The hedgehog was sleeping peacefully in his box. Last night's nightmare seemed just that.

I stood in the grass, contemplating. Patricia came up behind me and slipped her hands round my waist. 'Do you still want to leave the island?' she asked.

I nodded slowly.

'Not so sure,' she said.

I nodded some more.

'It could have been a mistake,' she said. 'Or deliberate. But there are bad guys everywhere, Dan. In Belfast. In New York. Everywhere you've gone there've been bad guys. You don't run away from bad guys, it's not you.'

'I didn't have a baby before.'

'That's nice. But it's no reason to run away.'

I loved her. I looked at her. I wanted to tell her about Bill.

'Look,' she said, 'let's just drive into town. There's a policeman, why don't we tell him you were attacked? Make it official. It's only a small place, he might have an idea who . . . he'll know who has guns, won't he? If they shot at you, there'll be, y'know, *cartridges* or something, won't there?'

I sighed. Then tutted. 'It all seems pretty lame now, in the cold light of day. Some-big-boys-hit-me kinda stuff.'

'It's up to you.'

It was. Bill was dead. I had to tell someone. But not the police. Not on Wrathlin, at any rate. I would tell the Cardinal. I needed reassurance. I needed to make my report, make sure he could cover me if I got into deeper trouble, that he could send in an emergency rescue squad if I needed it. Or at least say a prayer for me. He could thank me for doing a good job and tell me to leave, or tell me to stay and offer me more money. Or I could demand more money. Danger money.

We got ready and drove into town. We had the windows down. It was really nice. The sun was squinting in off the ocean. Patricia was all excited. We would get the one o'clock ferry, she'd do some shopping for baby clothes and non-microwaveable meals in Ballycastle while I called the Cardinal. If he agreed to my terms I'd get a big carry-out and hide it under some rugs in the back of the car for our return to the island. I was never drinking again; it would just be a comfort to know it was there if I really needed it.

We'd half an hour to wait for the ferry. We sat on a wall at the harbour, enjoying the sun. I felt refreshed. My bird pecks were not serious. I'd slept through the hangover, or the adrenaline of the night before had destroyed it. The ferry was just pulling in when we heard a commotion coming from the Main Street.

A tractor with trailer was rolling along the street, the farmer behind the wheel blasting his horn the whole way. People were peering out of shop doorways wondering what his problem was. Patricia smiled at me. 'Must have discovered the mother of all carrots or something.'

I smiled back, but there was already a sick feeling in my stomach. The tractor pulled to a halt outside the police station. It was just a terraced house with a small office at the front, not even a sign that said POLICE or anything. The farmer jumped down and hurried inside. A crowd started to form around the trailer. Patricia raised her eyebrows. I nodded. She took my hand and we stepped across in time to see the police officer, Constable Murtagh, come hurrying out of his house, halfway through buttoning his jacket.

We joined the small crowd at the back of the trailer. They parted for Murtagh and the farmer. There was a old tarpaulin lying on the floor of the trailer, covering something. Murtagh shook his head at it. Patricia squeezed my hand and the crowd held its breath as the farmer caught the edge of the tarp, looked once at Murtagh, who nodded, and then threw it back.

There was a gasp of horror from the crowd, and from Patricia, and from me, even though it wasn't a surprise.

Bill was lying there, blue, bloated and broken.

Patricia was looking at me. She could see that the colour had drained from my face. She felt me shiver.

'Dan . . .' she whispered, 'are you okay?' I nodded unconvincingly. 'Do you know him?' she asked. 'Do you think he was one of the bad guys?'

'No,' I said, 'he was one of the goodies.'

21

Constable Murtagh cancelled the next sailing of the ferry, just until
he could look further into the death of the bird warden. Patricia was
all for complaining, but I didn't want to make too much of a fuss in
case it seemed suspicious. So we just stood around with the rest of
the locals, shaking our heads and tutting. They said Bill had been on
the island for four or five years. They said he drank. They said most
likely he'd gotten drunk and knocked the brake off his caravan, then
trundled over the edge. They said his name was Bill Oddesky and
that he'd claimed to be of Russian descent. They said a lot of things,
some of which I knew to be false, some of which I was prepared to
believe. I watched the crowd in case they were watching me, in case
they suspected me, or gave some sign of having tried to kill me. I
detected neither or both, it was difficult to tell. Patricia whispered,
'What are we going to do?' and I said, 'Go home.' 'Swim?' she said.
'No, Snow Cottage, I mean.' She gave a little smile. She didn't seem
too disappointed. Somebody else, thank God, asked Murtagh how
long he was going to suspend the ferry for and he shrugged and
went back into his office. Dr Finlay arrived and asked the farmer
to bring the trailer up to his surgery and for a couple of fit men
to accompany it to lift the body in. I didn't want to seem like I
was ingratiating myself with the locals, so I held back. Big Duncan
Cairns stepped forward, and another two I didn't recognise. Patricia
looked at him, appreciatively.

On the way back in the car I said, 'For all we know, Duncan might
have been one of the ones who tried to kill me.'

'Don't, Dan.'

'*Don't Dan*, what?'

'Don't talk crap.'

'Might have been.'

She was shaking her head. Little Stevie was in the baby seat,
sleeping. 'How did you know him, the guy in the trailer?'

'The day I went walking with Father Flynn. Met him then. Stopped by his caravan. Nice guy. Thought all this Christine stuff was ridiculous. Right enough, his caravan was a bit close to the edge. Did he remind you of anyone?'

'Remind me?'

'Yeah. Like someone who used to be on TV?'

Patricia drummed her fingers on the dash for several moments. Then she shook her head. 'The only thing that comes to mind is *Blue Peter*, but I think that's just because he drowned. Why, do you think . . . ?'

'Nah, just reminded me of someone, can't think who, though.'

She was looking at me. She said, 'Dan, are you telling me everything?'

'Always.'

'Dan, please don't keep secrets from me, I'm a big girl.'

'You're not that big.'

'Dan . . .'

'Honest. I'm past that stage, love. There's nothing between you and me.'

'You mean there's nothing secret between you and me.'

'Something like that, yeah.'

She smiled, we pulled into Snow Cottage. Or the lane outside.

Somewhere around midnight, Little Stevie started to cry. At first we both ignored it, hoping his soft mew would settle into sleep. Then we whispered soothingly through the gloom and at first he responded but, as his discomfort began to increase, the cries grew louder, more insistent, demanding.

I said, 'I'll see to him.'

'What's come over you?'

'Nothing. Just doing my share.'

'It's not like you.'

'If you're going to make an issue of it I'll get back in bed.'

She made a zipping motion across her mouth. I pulled on my boxer shorts. We'd left the lamp on in his room. We had a contraption for warming bottles, which I flicked on as well. He wailed again as I picked him up. I joggled him a bit and did my baby talk. He wasn't impressed. I walked him into our room.

'He's hot,' I said.

'Very hot?'

'I don't know. Hot.'

Patricia tutted and got out of bed. She took him from me, cradling him with one arm, feeling his head with her free hand.

'You're right,' she said. 'Would you get me the thermometer?'

She gave me directions, but it still took me five minutes hoking through the Mafeking supplies to locate it. She snatched it from me, wiped it clean, shook it and slipped it into Little Stevie's rear end.

'That's the last time I put that in my mouth,' I said. I giggled. She didn't appreciate it. The look she gave me reminded me of the words thunder and funeral. 'Sorry,' I said. Then added needlessly: 'It's just a temperature.'

'A lot you would know about it.'

'I mean it's probably . . .'

'Who do you think you are,' she snapped, 'Mr Spock?'

'I think you mean Dr Sp . . .'

'Will you just shut the fuck up and go and get me some cold water and a flannel?'

My own temperature was starting to rise. I bit it back. She was right to be concerned, I was wrong to be flippant. It was my nature, but it was a bad time for it to blossom. I knew a baby's health was a finely poised thing for its first few months. Of course I knew it. 'Maybe he was too close to the fire. The heat built up in him and . . .'

'Dan. Get them. Now.'

I padded off to the kitchen. I'd read a couple of baby books. Patricia's baby books. When she wasn't in. I knew what to expect.

I got a can of Diet Pepsi. I took a couple of rapid gulps. Better to be safe than sorry, they all said. Always better. I found a basin, then the baby's flannel, soaked it in cold water and brought it back to the room.

'I'm worried,' said Patricia.

Baby wailed again. She hugged him close.

I held up the basin, and for a second she seemed reluctant to set him down.

'It's okay, love,' I said. I set the basin down on the bed and eased Little Stevie out of her arms.

'I'm really worried.' She knelt on the floor by the edge of the bed. She removed the thermometer. Stared at it. 'This isn't good,' she said, 'this really isn't good.' She squeezed out the flannel and bathed his face. He screamed some more. 'We should call the doctor. This isn't right. He shouldn't be like this.'

'Honey,' I said, 'give him a chance. You're only trying to cool him now. Give his body a chance to react. Let it cool itself. Christine – Moira's Christine, daughter of God, etc etc – wasn't well when I was there yesterday. Maybe there's a bug, maybe I brought it home.'

She turned her head back sharply. 'Did Christine have a rash?'

I shrugged. 'Not that I'm aware of.'

'Call the doctor, Dan. This isn't right.'

I peered over her shoulder. 'Maybe it's nappy rash.'

'On his chest? Jesus, Dan. Call the doctor.'

'We haven't got a phone.'

'Go and get him then.'

'It's the middle of the night.'

'I don't care if it's fucking Christmas Eve! Go and get the fucking doctor.'

I made the mistake of tutting.

She leapt up and slapped me in the face. Hard.

I stepped back, shaken. By the time I raised my hand to fend off another blow blood was already streaming down my nose. I looked into her eyes. I saw anger, of course, but beside it, vying for supremacy, fear. 'I'm sorry,' I said quickly, 'of course.'

I pulled on my jeans. Zipped up my tracksuit top. Grabbed the keys. 'I'll be as quick as I can,' I said.

One thing, I wasn't going to get caught in a Wrathlin traffic jam. The only thing that moved between me and the doctor's was a collie out sniffing and the odd spot of blood still escaping from my nose. I burnt rubber. Or as close to burning rubber as you can in a Ford Fiesta.

The doctor's house was in complete darkness. I banged on the door. For several minutes. Eventually there was a light, a single bolt was shot back and the big door opened a fraction. An elderly woman, blue dressing gown, hairnet, peered out.

'Is your husband there?'

She shook her head vaguely. Stifled a yawn. Said, 'I was asleep,' through bunched fingers.

'Where is he?' I demanded.

'He's . . . up on the hill . . . but . . . ?'

'What hill?'

She shook her head again. 'The hill. The cemetery.'

I let out a deep sigh. 'What's he doing there?'

'I don't understand . . .'

I tutted. I leant into the door. 'I'm looking for the doctor.'

She shook her head, rubbed at her eyes. 'Oh . . . yes . . . I'm sorry . . . you're looking . . . I was asleep. Of course. The doctor. I thought you meant my husband . . . silly . . . he's been up there these twenty . . . I'm sorry . . . the doctor . . .'

'Yes. The doctor. Where is he?'

'He went out. Earlier.' She turned and, twisting her head, examined a grandfather clock in the hallway. 'Much earlier. I'm sorry, I . . .'

'Can you bleep him?'

'I'm sorry . . .'

'Page him. Can you page him?'

'. . . page . . . ?'

'Jesus,' I spat.

'I'm sorry . . . I . . .'

'Do you not even know where he went?'

She shook her head.

'Is he seeing someone? Is he on call?'

'I'm sorry, I . . .'

'Is there anyone else?' I snapped. 'Is there another doctor? A nurse?' She looked confused. 'A fucking witch doctor?'

I turned on my heel. I got back in the car. I drove right up the hill and into the churchyard, then round the back. I banged on Father Flynn's door. He answered in half a minute. He was in his bed gear. I explained my situation to him.

'Oh dear, oh dear,' he said earnestly. He beckoned me into the hallway as he searched about for his shoes. He found them, began to push his feet into them without untying the laces. 'He does have a habit of disappearing off. And old Mrs McTeague's no better . . . she's really not *compos mentis* these days at all.'

'There must be someone else.'

With a grimace he finally lodged his second foot into its shoe, smiled, then put a reassuring hand on my shoulder. 'There's always someone, Dan. We'll go down to the McCooeys'.'

'Father, I don't wish to seem ungrate . . .'

'Dan, now calm down. We'll drive down to Moira's.'

I snapped my shoulder away from him. 'I've no time for this shit, Father. The baby's sick, I need a doctor. I don't need the fucking Messiah right now. I'm sorry, but I don't.'

'Dan . . .' He shook his head sympathetically. 'Calm down now. Moira McCooey's a trained nurse. She only gave it up when she had Christine.'

'Oh.'

'Oh indeed.' He squeezed my shoulder again. 'Trust me, Dan. Now let's go.'

22

Patricia opened the door. Her face was white.

'Oh Jesus,' I said.

She shook her head. 'He's unconscious . . . I think he's in a . . .'

Flynn came in after me. Then Moira. Behind her, still in her pyjamas, Christine.

Moira carried Dr Finlay's bag. I'd briefly explained the symptoms to her and she'd insisted we call round by the surgery to see if it was there. The old woman at the door had given some fleeting resistance but the combined attack of Father Flynn and Moira McCooey had soon swept her protestations aside and after a little poking about we found it. Evidently the good doctor wasn't out on call.

We followed Patricia into the bedroom. Little Stevie was on his back, naked, sprawled out, still.

Moira knelt to examine him. She touched his head. Pushed up an eyelid. 'Did you take his temperature?'

Patricia nodded. 'Hundred and four.'

Moira nodded. 'Has he vomited?'

'A little, a little while ago. Just a bit.'

Moira ran her fingers over his skin, tracing the rash. She opened the doctor's bag, took out his stethoscope, looked back quickly at Patricia, then at me, a look that said, *I'm only a nurse.*

She listened.

We waited.

A watch ticked.

Christine scuffed her feet on the carpet and peered round her mother's shoulder. 'Is he sick?' she asked.

'Shhhh,' said Moira.

She took the stethoscope off again.

'How serious is it?' Flynn asked.

Moira shook her head. 'I'm out of practice. It could be . . . this . . . it could be . . . that . . .'

Patricia tutted. 'Where's the doctor?' she snapped.

'Missing, presumed drunk,' I said.

Flynn gave me a look.

'It's just . . .' Moira began, 'most of the symptoms of measles are there . . . the fever, the rash . . . there's nothing in the mouth, though . . . I think it's measles . . . but . . . I mean . . . it's so long since I . . . he shouldn't be unconscious . . . there's the outside chance that it could be meningitis as well, which is altogether more serious . . .'

'Oh, my God,' Patricia cried.

'I'm not saying it is meningitis.'

'Well, what are you saying?' Patricia yelled.

'I'm saying I think it's serious!' Moira yelled back. 'I'm not a doctor!'

'Well, that's a fucking big help!' Patricia looked desperately from Moira to me to Flynn and back. 'Why don't you do something? Give him something.' Tears began to cascade down her face. 'My baby's dying.'

I put my arm round her. 'He's not going to . . .'

She pushed me away. 'You brought him here!' she screamed. 'You brought him to this bloody hole!'

'Trish, I . . .'

'Do something!'

I shrugged helplessly.

'Perhaps we should say a prayer,' Flynn suggested.

Patricia flew at him. 'Get out!' she screamed. She pushed him in the chest. Stunned, Flynn fell back.

'I'm sorry . . .' he began, but she shoved him again and he retreated ashen-faced into the hallway.

Patricia turned, her face a sorry mask of tears. 'What can I do?' she sobbed and lunged at the bed.

Moira intercepted her. Caught her by the wrists. Patricia stopped with a start. So to speak. Moira went eyeball to eyeball with her. 'We can start by remaining calm,' she said sternly. After a few moments of defiant straining, the fight seemed to go out of Patricia. She shook her head. Tears flew off.

'I'll do what I can,' said Moira. 'I'll give him some drugs. I'll do my best. He'll be okay if we all work together. I want Father Flynn and your husband and anyone else you can round up to track down the doctor wherever he is. He can't be that far away. In the meantime we're going to have to get a boat ready to take us over to the mainland just in case we need it. And raise Constable Murtagh, he might even be able to summon up a helicopter.' She shook Patricia's wrists. 'Do you hear me?'

Patricia nodded.

'Good. Now go and make a cup of tea or something. And while you're there, say a prayer.'

Patricia stared down at Little Stevie. Looked briefly at Christine, standing mesmerised by the commotion.

'Who to?' asked Patricia.

'Anyone that comes to mind,' said Moira.

It was a scintillating run. Gerry, not normally noted as an athlete, had suddenly found Billy's boots and beaten two players on the wing, cutting in towards the penalty box and then chipping over the on-rushing full back, leaving me clear just about dead on the penalty spot. I brought the ball down on my chest, let it fall onto my knee, bounced it up once. The left-footed volley gave the keeper no chance. Like a bullet into the back of the net. I turned, waved at Gerry, then saluted the crowd.

For a moment the surroundings failed to register.

I had been vaguely disturbed by this dream for some months. Normally, naturally, I dreamt of beautiful women, of sexual exploits, and woke with an erection. But in recent months I had begun to dream of scoring in an important football match and woken with sore legs. Maybe it was age. Perhaps it was the knowledge that while I had every expectation of continuing to experience and enjoy sexual activity for many years to come, the likelihood of me scoring a vital goal in an important game of football was receding with every day that passed.

The kitchen: me in a chair. Sore back. Sore legs. An arm dead from sleeping on it. Cold in the grey light of dawn. A can of Diet Pepsi half-drunk on the table. I got up, stretched. I checked my watch. Eight AM.

It had been a long night, a short sleep. Flynn and I had searched the island. The doctor couldn't be found. We called on Duncan Cairns, apparently the doctor's close friend, to see if he had any ideas. But the teacher wasn't home either. We knocked up a dozy fisherman and got him to ready his trawler for a quick dash across the water, but we hemmed and hawed so long about the wisdom of it that, by the time we did decide, a thick fog had rolled in and scuppered the plan. The fog would have ruled out the helicopter as well, but that wasn't even an option. Constable Murtagh said someone had broken into his office – the back room of his house, actually – and vandalised his radio. He was investigating. There was no other legitimate means of contacting the mainland, he said.

Patricia cursed me high and low. Cursed Moira high and low. Cursed Flynn low and high. She'd even started on Christine, but I managed to calm her before she went too far. Just in case.

Little Stevie didn't deteriorate. He slept. Hot. Fever. Rash. Laboured breath. But breath. Moira kept a close eye on him. Flynn finally got to say his prayer, though Patricia kept an eagle eye on him in case he attempted the last rites. At one point she broke down and seemed on the verge of having him christened, then she backed out, said what was the point, God didn't exist.

About four, I left the room. Patricia was stretched out on the bed, dozing. Moira laboured with fluttering eyes to keep watch over the baby. Christine had dropped off to sleep on the floor. Flynn carried her into the lounge and pulled a rug over her. He sat in an armchair and began to study his Bible.

I stood in the garden for a while, breathing deeply. I felt odd. Little Stevie was so small and helpless, and I was so big and gormless.

I felt an arm snake round my waist and squeeze. I turned hopeful of Patricia with good news, but it was Moira. She felt me tense up, and removed her arm.

'Sorry,' I said, 'I'm . . . it's just . . .'

'It's okay.' She put a hand on my arm. 'No comebacks, Dan. Have I said anything? It was good fun, wasn't it?' I nodded. 'And if you're not at my house for more sex by lunch tomorrow I'm going to tell your wife.'

'Moira, for Jesus' . . .'

'Only joking. Keep your hair on.'

I sighed. 'Sorry. I'm not . . .'

'It's okay.' She reached up and kissed my cheek. 'But if you do happen to be passing.' She winked and went back inside.

*　　*　　*

I dreamt of football and woke. I took a drink of the Diet Pepsi. It was flat, but it was Pepsi. Then I crossed my fingers and mouthed a silent prayer on Little Stevie's behalf. I walked up the hall and quietly opened the bedroom door. Patricia was still stretched out on the bed. Moira was in a crumpled heap on the floor. Someone had put a blanket over her.

Little Stevie was gone.

Biting back a surge of panic, I checked quickly on both sides of the bed in case he'd rolled off like an orange in his sleep. Nope. Then under the bed. Nothing. I stood and looked about the room. Although Patricia and Moira looked to be in pretty much the same positions as when I'd left them, it wasn't beyond the bounds of possibility that they'd moved the baby while I was asleep. I turned and walked quickly through the house, silently checking the rooms. I didn't want to take the chance of waking Patricia. If she didn't know where Stevie was, she'd freak out. If there was a simple explanation, then she wouldn't need to know that I'd nearly freaked out. Finally I approached the living room.

The door was ajar. I peered in. Flynn was slumped in the chair, the Bible open in his lap. Christine was gone too.

I shook Flynn awake.

'Whatsit . . . ?' he murmured groggily and made a protective grab for the Bible as it slipped to the floor.

'Where is she?' I hissed.

'Whaaaa?'

I tutted. I upped the hiss factor. 'Christine . . . where is she?'

He rubbed at his eyes. Shook himself awake. He jumped up, joints clicking, and crossed to the sofa. He pulled the blanket back, even though it was obvious she wasn't there. 'Why she was . . .' He looked sharply back. 'Is something wrong?'

'Youse didn't shift Stevie while I was asleep?'

He shook his head.

'Someone did,' I said.

'What do you . . . ?'

'He's gone. And you don't have to be Sherlock Holmes to work out who took him.'

Flynn shook his head again. 'She wouldn't do anything . . .'

'There's no accounting for kids, Father.' I turned for the hall. 'I once buried my gerbils alive and dug them up six weeks later to see how they were getting on. We'd better find her.'

'You've checked the rest of the house?'

'There's not much to check.'

We went outside.

If anything, the fog had intensified. Usually I would have been inclined to slap anyone who would call it a real pea-souper, but I let the priest away with it. I just cursed. They could be anywhere. Three metres or three hundred.

My baby.

My baby.

Yes, well. He had grown on me.

Flynn snagged my arm and pointed towards the upturned bath. He walked quickly and I followed. Slowly, through the fog, I began to see a figure, small and pale and damp-looking.

It was Christine. She was cradling something in her arms, something hidden in a bunch of blankets.

As we approached she looked up and smiled, at first, then quickly noted our demeanour and the smile faded into a worried grimace. She squashed the blankets into her chest.

'Oh . . . Christine!' Flynn cried.

As he stepped towards her she pulled the blankets protectively to one side. 'Mine,' she said.

'Oh, Christine,' Flynn said, softer now, moving closer.

'I was looking after the little baby,' Christine said.

Flynn stopped. 'But, Christine, he's not well, you have to be very careful.'

'I was.' He reached tentatively out, but Christine held the bundle close.

'The baby was sick . . .' she said, the smile edging back onto her face as she looked down into the blankets.

'But, Christine, if you could just let me . . .'

I put a hand on Flynn's arm. 'Excuse me, Father, but bollocks.' I stepped up to Christine and wrenched the bundle from her grasp.

She let out a wail.

I unwrapped.

Little Stevie, cool, calm, collected, smiled up. I smiled back. I let out a sigh of relief. His brow felt normal. His skin was pink, a little flushed, but the rash had faded. No, not faded. Gone. Gone completely, as if it had never been there.

Flynn turned from consoling Christine. He peered over my shoulder. 'Is he dead?' he asked matter-of-factly.

'Dead good,' I said.

The priest's jaw dropped as he saw the extent of the transformation. 'My goodness,' he said.

'Aye,' I said.

He looked a little closer. 'But he's . . .'

'Aye.'

He shook his head. 'It's a miracle,' he said.

'Mirkle,' I said.

He grabbed my arm suddenly. 'No. I mean it. It is. It's a miracle.'

'Father, I . . .'

'It is. It's a miracle! Christine's done another . . .'

'Father, the baby's better. It happens. It's not a m . . .'

'Dan, you don't understand,' he said excitedly. 'It *is* a miracle!' He grabbed my shoulders. 'Moira told me herself last night she didn't expect him to last the course. She was absolutely certain he had meningitis . . . thought he was a goner for sure. But now he's . . . it's wonderful!'

I shrugged him off. Little Stevie gurgled. 'Okay. If you insist. It's a miracle.'

A broad grin split the priest's face. He threw his hands up in the air. Caught them, too. 'A miracle!' he shouted. 'Thank God!' He turned to Christine. He tousled her hair. She slipped off the bath, pulled at her nightdress where it was stuck damp to her legs. He knelt beside her. 'What did you do to make the baby well, Christine?'

She ran the back of a hand across her face to remove the tears. Sniffed something back up her nose. 'I took him out of the room, Father.'

'And why did you do that?'

She bit at a finger. Twisted her head left and right. 'Because,' she said.

'You knew the baby was sick, didn't you? A very sick baby.'

She nodded.

'Then you brought him out here? What did you do?'

'Nothing. I sat on the bath.'

'What did you say to the baby?'

She shook her head.

140

'You said nothing at all?'

'I sang a song, Father.'

'What song did you sing, Christine? Was it a good song?'

She nodded. '"Jesus Loves You".'

Flynn gulped. It was a loud gulp. As loud a gulp as you're likely to hear this side of Gulpville, Indiana. When he turned back to me his eyes had filled with tears.

'It's a miracle!' he cried.

I nodded and turned for the house. It was time to bring the tidings of great joy to my wife.

23

Dr Finlay arrived at Snow Cottage a little after noon. For the purposes of the day it might as well have been called Fog Cottage. Or the Wrathlin Convention Centre. The previous three hours had been spent entertaining with steadily diminishing good will members of Flynn's congregation anxious to hear at first hand the miracle of the baby brought back from death's door by the infant Messiah.

Uhuh.

Patricia seemed to enjoy the attention.

'Out shooting,' was the doctor's explanation for his unavailability.

'We looked everywhere,' I said.

'Not everywhere,' he said.

'I mean . . .'

'Rabbits,' he said. 'We're coming down with the little bastards, Dan. Just doing my bit to help. I'm surprised nobody realised.'

I wasn't absolutely convinced by his story. His eyes were bloodshot from lack of sleep. There was a split shotgun in the back seat of his car and, sure, he had four bloody carcasses lying on some plastic sheeting in the boot, but I still had my doubts. I supposed great white rabbit hunters (that's the hunters, not the rabbits) *could* go shooting at night time, using their car lights to blind the rabbits or guide the shooting, but I had my doubts about how successful such an expedition would have been in the fog. Perhaps he'd managed to bag them before it descended.

I didn't even know if they *were* rabbits.

But I suppose I was too happy about Little Stevie to split hares.

'They're such a bloody hardy lot,' he said, bending back into the vehicle for his keys.

'The rabbits?'

'The people. They seldom have any use for me. I suppose I should have let Mrs McTeague know where I was going, but she's such a dozy old biddy it seemed pretty pointless. Anyway,' he said, abruptly changing the subject, 'what about you, lad? Howse the head?'

'Fine.'

'Told you. Okay then, we'll take a look at this kiddie, will we? Told me down home there'd been a bit of a miracle. What do you say?'

'I really couldn't say. I don't see them that often.'

He gave me a thin smile. 'Of course,' he said, and walked ahead of me into the cottage. 'Moira has my case, has she? Good on her.'

Father Flynn had fallen asleep in one of the armchairs. On the narrow settee Moira and Patricia were chatting animatedly, a pot of tea on a tray balanced precariously on a small stool before them. They both turned and looked at me and for a very brief moment I thought perhaps they'd been discussing me and my propensity for unfaithfulness, but then I realised that Moira's head was still attached to her shoulders and not nailed to the wall, so she mustn't have brought it up.

Christine was tickling Little Stevie on the floor.

'Well!' boomed the doctor, bending down and scooping the baby up. 'Let's see the wee man then.'

Flynn bounded suddenly from his chair. 'Whoooooah!' he shouted. We stood in shock for a moment. Then the priest reddened up. 'I'm sorry. I was asleep.'

We all nodded sympathetically at him. He sat down again. Dr Finlay took the baby into the bedroom to give him a thorough examination. Flynn tried to follow, but the doctor insisted on privacy. Patricia and Moira returned to their chat. I strolled out into the garden.

I walked round to the side of the cottage and found the box in which Patricia had placed the hedgehog. It was empty save for some leaves and a side plate.

Then Flynn was at my elbow. As I turned, he stifled a yawn. 'Sorry,' he said, 'I'm not as fit as I used to be.'

'You didn't used to be fit. You had a heart transplant.'

'You know what I mean.'

We looked at the garden for a while. The jungle. I shook my head at it. A jungle it would remain. I had once tried to weed a window box by spraying petrol on it from a soda siphon and setting fire to it. A neighbour had called the Fire Brigade. It wasn't even my house. I was just passing by and trying to be helpful.

'You know,' Flynn said, 'you've had quite an impact, and you're only here a few days.'

'Aye,' I said.

'First you save Christine's life. Then she saves your son's. I hope you're writing all this down.'

I nodded. I would have to. Once I bought a quill.

'We were hoping – the Parish Council, that is – we were hoping that you'd come along to our meeting tomorrow night.'

'Oh aye, what's up?'

'Just our regular weekly meeting. But there's been so much happening that we have to talk about. And there's a lot would like to meet you properly, and thank you for what you've done. Would you come along?'

'Love to,' I said.

Patricia stood in the hall, cradling Little Stevie. It was the first time we'd been alone since he'd taken ill.

'Happy?' I asked.

She smiled at the baby. 'Relieved.'

'Do you think it was a miracle?'

'I don't care, Dan, as long as he's alive.'

'Fevers break,' I said.

'I know.'

'Rashes disappear.'

'I know.'

'It happens.'

'I know.'

'But . . .'

'I know it.'

24

Of course I was late. Patricia and I bickered the whole way. My driving too fast in the fog, which stubbornly refused to lift. My clothes. My lack of assistance with the little one. My attempts at assistance with the little one. The little one cried healthily throughout.

I wore black jeans and a black shirt and my black zip bomber jacket. My wife wore culottes. For fifteen years I thought a culotte was a badly pronounced idiot, but then you learn something new every day. She looked lovely.

I dropped Patricia and the baby halfway up the hill at the end of the narrow lane which led to the schoolhouse. She'd accepted an invitation to a gathering of the church mothers. I was surprised that she'd accepted so readily. Before, she'd have laughed heartily at the suggestion that she might get involved with the sort of women who spent their time discussing the social history of linen or how to create flower arrangements depicting a five-point fall in the Dow Jones Index. Maybe giving birth changes you. Maybe having a six-pound ginger bap fighting his way sideways out of your birth canal for eight hours fucks up your mental faculties. I don't know. Maybe men and women are just different.

She gave me a sarcastic smile and slammed the door. I blew her a sarcastic kiss then sped off in a cloud of ironic dust. *Yeah.*

The church loomed up out of the fog like a big churchy thing in a fog. It was cold and a little creepy. There were two other cars parked at the rear, and three bicycles were propped up against the wall. I locked the car, stepped up to the hall door and knocked. A bolt was pulled back and the same curly-haired man who'd opened the door to me before stuck his head out.

'Yup?'

'Dan Starkey. I was invited . . .'

He smiled. 'Of course. Come on in.'

He stepped back, held the door open for me. Inside there were a dozen men grouped around a long table. All eyes were upon me. Flynn's. Father White's. Twenty others. Twenty-two, in fact, for beyond the table, in a single chair, set lower than the rest, sat Constable Murtagh. I hadn't been formally introduced, so I ignored him.

I smiled. 'I'm sorry I'm late, I . . .'

Father Flynn, at the head of the table, stood up. 'Gentlemen,' he said, 'this is Dan Starkey. The saviour of the saviour.'

The councillors stood immediately and turned eager faces towards me. I was enveloped by a spontaneous round of applause.

I put up my hand modestly. 'Please,' I said.

The clapping got louder.

'Well done, that man,' said someone.

I did what I do best in difficult situations. I shrugged.

After a century or two it died down. They sat. As they did, I noted that the police officer had not stood at all.

'Please, Dan,' said Father Flynn, 'take a chair.' He indicated one at his side. 'We're all indebted to you.'

Flynn quickly ran down their names and professions for my benefit: butcher, baker, candlestick maker. I wasn't really taking it in. I wasn't used to being the centre of attention. I nodded and smiled, nodded and smiled.

One, Carl Christie, bearded, solemn-faced, reached laboriously across the table and shook my hand. 'Is the baby all well again then?' he enquired sombrely. He ran the Credit Union.

'Seems fine,' I said.

'And the doctor's seen him?'

'He has. Says he's fine.'

'And would he be agreeing it's a miracle?'

'I really couldn't say.'

'What *did* he say?'

'Just that he couldn't find any trace of anything wrong.'

'But he didn't think it was a miracle?'

'He didn't say.'

He turned to the rest of the table and shook his head slowly. Several others shook too. The curly-haired man, Michael Savage, wrote something in a spiral-bound notebook.

Father Flynn raised his hands. 'Before we begin, we'll say a prayer.'

Heads bowed. He began. I watched. Father White watched me. He was the only one with his eyes open. I held his gaze. It wasn't malevolent, exactly, just kind of stern. As they came to the end of the prayer he finally closed his eyes and repeated *amen* with the rest of them.

Then they launched into half an hour of discussing items on a curiously mundane agenda. A parish fete. Secretary's report. Honorary treasurer's report. Minister's report. Births: none. Marriages: none. Deaths: one.

'Constable Murtagh,' Flynn said, 'would you care to address us on this subject? A tragedy, I'm sure we all agree.'

There were nods all around the table. If any of them were feeling guilty it didn't show. Murtagh rose slowly to his feet. 'My investigations,' he said lugubriously, 'are continuing.' He paused, and for a moment it looked like that was all we were getting. 'But at the moment everything points to an accidental death.'

'Was he drunk?' Father White asked.

'Not according to Dr Finlay. It does look as if his caravan broke loose from its, uhm, moorings and toppled over the side. However, I will make my report to my superiors and it will be up to them to decide if it warrants any further investigation. There will also have to be a full post mortem on the mainland. We will get the body across as soon as we can.'

There were murmurs from around the table, but nobody spoke. Murtagh took his seat again and Flynn stood. 'And now,' Flynn asked, 'is there any other business?'

Several hands went up. Flynn pointed first to Michael Fogerty, the butcher. Rotund, bull-like, he nodded in my direction. 'We obviously owe a lot to Mr Starkey, but I was wondering about the dish?'

I furrowed.

So did Flynn. 'The . . . ?'

'The satellite dish.'

'Ah. Of course. Your dish, Dan. Noticed it myself.'

'What of it?'

'I'm afraid it'll have to go.'

I looked quickly round their nodding heads. 'For why?'

'It's against the law,' said Carl Christie.

'What law?'

'Parish law,' said Flynn.

I cleared my throat. 'Oh,' I said, 'I didn't know.' I looked around the table, rather sheepishly. 'And, would that, like, stand up in, y'know . . . *court*?' I tried not to make it sound too obstreperous.

'Very well, actually.' Flynn laughed. 'In our court. And ours is the only one that matters here. With all due respect to Constable Murtagh.' He nodded across at the policeman, who sat impassively. 'The simple thing is, Dan, we're trying to create as near perfect an environment as we can for Christine to grow up in, and we believe that your satellite dish might threaten that environment.'

'Might I ask how?'

'Pollution, Dan. Pollution. It's all around us already, but we don't need to invite any more in. We know about satellite TV, Dan, we know what kind of channels it contains.'

I shook my head. 'I don't wish to cause a fuss, but it's not much different to ordinary television.'

'We've outlawed ordinary television as well.'

'Oh.'

'Dan . . .' Flynn began.

'But what else is there to do?' I asked. I was flailing about, hopelessly.

'Oh Dan,' Flynn said with a rueful shake of his head. 'You do live such an empty life. You don't need television to enjoy yourself. You don't need alcohol to have a good time.'

'Who mentioned alcohol?'

'You've been asking questions, Dan. We don't *need* any of those things. We have everything we need' – he clasped his hand to his chest – 'right here in our hearts. All you have to do is open your heart and all the answers you seek will be forthcoming.' He smiled warmly. 'Y'know, Dan, there are momentous events coming, we all need to be ready.'

The next momentous event on my calendar was the world heavyweight clash between Tyson and Lewis. They didn't know that my satellite dish was useless in its present state, but now they seemed intent on robbing me of the chance to see even the edited highlights on terrestrial television.

I tried to smile back, to show them I was taking it in jocular fashion, but it wouldn't quite come. All they saw was a hint of a snarl and all they heard was a mediocre whine. 'But surely television isn't so . . .'

'It's dangerous, Dan. Poisonous. We don't need it here.'

I tutted. 'Okay . . . you know, I respect your beliefs here, Father, everyone, I understand where you're coming from . . . I don't want to upset anyone, but can we just, ahm . . . *discuss* this for a moment? Just widen it out a little . . . I mean . . . if you think about it . . . y'know . . . even *shoes* are dangerous, Father, in the wrong hands. Or feet for that matter. I mean, a good kicking with a pair of Doc Martens can kill you, but you don't outlaw shoes. If you see my point.'

'I see your point, Dan. But let's just say that we're not in a *discussive* situation here. The law *has been* passed. It's *the law*.' He smiled at me again. 'We love you, Dan. You've already made a massive contribution to our lives here. But the law is the law and must be obeyed by everyone. It may seem dictatorial to you. But everybody voted for it, so it's democratic as well.'

Yes. Indeed. Everyone gets equally fucked.

I shrugged. Not one of my more convincing shrugs, but a shrug all the same. 'Well, okay,' I said, 'if that's the way youse feel, who am I to argue? You've God on your side.'

'We have,' said Flynn.

Father White knocked suddenly on the table. 'Might I suggest that Mr Starkey bring his satellite dish and television into town as soon as he can? Just to put temptation out of his way. Constable Murtagh can look after them until he leaves the island. Agreed?'

I opened my mouth to say something about good faith being a fundamental tenet of Christianity, although I had no idea if it was, but before I could say anything there was a sudden rush of *ayes* and Father White's proposal passed. I slumped down in my chair.

25

I knew from my long years of reporting council meetings that anything and everything could crop up under the Any Other Business heading. It sat misleadingly at the tag end of an agenda, like an afterthought, but invariably became the longest and most emotive part of any meeting, and those were meetings where the most important item for discussion was usually the collection of garbage, Sunday opening of shops or the amount of dogshit to be found on the local pavements. This one, on (one would be tempted to say *godforsaken* if it wasn't a trifle inappropriate) Wrathlin, was no exception, save that it dealt with less mundane subjects like the attempted murder of the Messiah, divine retribution and crucifixion.

I was still monumentally pissed off. I could survive a murder attempt, but how was I going to get by without drink *and* TV? And what would Patricia say? At least I could write my novel. What was she going to do all day with just Little Stevie to look after? Sew?

Sew my feet together, then lop off my head with an axe.

My head was still getting to grips with their simple lunacy, when they moved quickly on to a much grander form. Flynn asked if there was any further any other business, a mouthful in itself, and in response Father White stood and looked gravely about him.

Until that moment I hadn't thought to ask why there were *two* priests on such a small island. There had been bigger questions. White was much older than Flynn, but still well short of doddery. There was a feeling of power about him which Flynn lacked, although he made up for it with a certain kind of restrained charisma. Flynn was the more senior of the two as far as the running of the church and, indeed, the island was concerned. They had a common goal, but I suspected two different approaches to it. White was old school, Flynn was new. White was the rhythm method and Flynn was strumming guitars around the campfire.

I had thought at first that Father White might be the priest that the Primate had dispatched to the island to investigate the Messiah, who had been converted, but something about him made me doubt that.

Flynn looked a little pained as White waited for complete silence around the table, then tried to hurry him along with an abrupt, 'Yes?'

'The small matter of the attempt on Christine's life, Father Flynn.'

'I thought that had been resolved.' He nodded towards Constable Murtagh. 'She's still in your top room, isn't she?'

'Yes, Father, till this bloody fog lifts and we can get her across to the mainland. Her 'n' the bird warden.'

'And it's a watertight case, isn't it?'

Murtagh rubbed at his chin for a moment. 'That's not quite so straightforward, Father. Legally, she should have had access to a solicitor by now. We don't have any, of course, but since the radio went down we can't even speak to one on the mainland. It could cause problems later.'

I turned to the man beside me and whispered, 'Aren't there *any* phones on the island?'

He shook his head. 'We passed a law,' he whispered.

'Figures,' I said.

Father White knocked on the desk again. Flynn looked round sharply. 'Father?'

'I was thinking, do we really want this to go to court at all?'

'She is a danger to Christine, I think it's best that she . . .'

'But we don't want a trial on the mainland, do we? There's no telling what might come out. I mean, about Christine. We don't want that yet, do we?' He was very fond of the *do we*'s. He glanced at me. I held his gaze until he looked away.

Father Flynn sighed. 'What are you suggesting?'

'That we find an alternative solution.'

'Well . . . suggest one. *Anyone?*'

There was some uncomfortable shifting in seats. It seemed obvious, at least to me, that Father White had already thought of an alternative, but was holding off until he saw what the competition was.

There was movement to my left. Carl Christie swung back on his chair, two legs of it off the ground. 'You mentioned an airtight case a moment ago, Father,' he said.

'Watertight.'

'Well, I have one at home we could lock her in. Then take her out and toss her in the sea.'

It sat in the air for a moment while everyone looked at him. Then the low rumble of laughter began to make its way ponderously around the table, only stopping when it reached Father Flynn, who looked at Christie blankly and said, 'Thank you, Carl, for that contribution.'

Jack McGettigan, the elderly publican who had done most thus far to upset my stay on the island, stood up, leant on his knuckles on the table. 'I don't think we need to bother about a trial, Father. Just get her off the island. Ship her out. She didn't actually harm Christine . . . I don't know if Mr Starkey intends to press charges . . . ?'

I shook my head. I hadn't even thought about it.

Flynn nodded for a moment, then turned again to Constable Murtagh. 'Legally, Bob . . . ?'

'If she was in a parish house, sure, we could evict her, but then there's her mother could take her. But as far as I know she owns that shack of hers outright. Getting her to court, that's the best bet. I can't keep her in the back bedroom much longer, either.'

'I think we're overlooking the obvious solution,' said Father White.

'Crucifixion,' I muttered, not quite as under my breath as I had intended, for Flynn flashed me a look of annoyance, then sighed again and returned his attention to Father White. 'Which is, Father?' he asked, somewhat testily.

'We ask Christine.'

I snorted. I couldn't help it. I made a show of looking for a tissue in my pocket, and then blew my nose properly. Half masked by the tissue, I looked round the table to see if anyone else was trying to stifle their laughter, but I was the only one. They weren't jumping up and down like madmen, but the very fact that they proceeded to discuss it made it abundantly clear that these guys were two psalms short of a book of psalms.

'It makes sense,' said Father White.

'She's too young,' said Father Flynn.

'She's the Messiah.'

'She's a child.'

'She's still the Messiah.'

'When she's a child, she speaks as a child, Father.'

'She's still the Messiah.'

'I take your point,' Flynn snapped. He blew air out of his red cheeks and his eyes darted about the table, looking for but not finding any encouragement. 'So, for example,' he began, 'if she pulls some ridiculous punishment out of the air, say, say . . . this woman has to do the community centre dishes for the next year, then that's all she gets?'

'That's all she gets.'

Flynn darted a look at me, then back to White. 'And what if, by some stretch of the imagination, she pronounces the word crucifixion, what then . . . are we going to *crucify* the poor woman?'

'She isn't a *poor woman*. She tried to *murder* Christine. If Christine says crucify, then who are we to go against her?'

'This is ridiculous. Father, this is the Second Coming, it's about love and a new beginning, it's not about . . .'

'You can't say that! We don't *know* what it's about. *You* brought Christine to us, Father. *We* believe. We cannot pick and choose the good bits. This time we might get a vengeful God, Frank, it's happened before.'

'So . . . so . . .' He was starting to get a little flustered. He could see the argument running away from him. 'So . . . you would . . . go along with a child's tantrum, you would say this was God's word?'

'Has Christine *ever* thrown a tantrum?'

'No. She hasn't. I just fee . . .'

'She is the daughter of God. Would you deny her right to pronounce judgment?'

Flynn's eyes circled the table again. He saw a lot of serious faces looking at him. He avoided mine. 'No, of course not,' he said. There was a look of stifled desperation in his eyes. 'Father, all of you, I know Christine better than most of you. I know her ways. She is good and kind and pure, we should not ask her to do this. Please leave it to Constable Murtagh. Let him deal with it. I propose . . .'

Father White rapped on the table again. 'And I propose we ask Christine to decide! We put it to a vote, we do it now.'

Flynn leant forward to speak, then sat back again and sighed. 'Very well,' he said, 'we'll put it to a vote . . . I only trust that common sense will prevail. All those in favour of letting Christine decide, raise your hands.'

Father White's hand went straight up. The others were slower to follow, everyone watching each other, looking for a lead. A bald man opposite me, whose name I'd forgotten, was the first to raise his; then there was another, and another until most of those around the table had theirs in the air. Fifteen seconds later only Father Flynn, Carl Christie, Michael Savage the curly-haired note-taker and Jack McGettigan the ex-publican had failed to raise their hands.

'The ayes have it then,' Father White announced, beaming.

'They do,' Father Flynn said simply.

'Shall we fetch Christine?' White asked.

Flynn shook his head. 'Not now. I will speak to Moira. If she doesn't agree then it doesn't happen.'

'But we vote . . .' Father White protested.

'Christine isn't some sort of puppet to be wheeled out every time we need something done, we don't *own* her . . . I will communicate the vote to Moira, and we'll take it from there.'

'Perhaps I should be with you when you tell her, Father, just to ensure that . . .'

Flynn cracked his hand down on the table. It was so unexpected that half of them jumped in their seats. 'Are you suggesting . . . !'

Father White, surprised himself, blurted out, 'No, of course not,' too quickly, and knew immediately that he had lost ground he was not going to recover. Flynn took full advantage, snapping to his feet and sweeping out of the meeting. As he reached the door he glanced back and said, 'We will reconvene tomorrow, gentlemen.'

Then he pulled open the door and was gone.

I waited behind as the Parish Council filed solemnly out of the hall until there was just me and Constable Murtagh left.

'As a member of the Royal Ulster Constabulary,' I said, 'where do you stand on a defendant being sentenced by a four-year-old Messiah?'

'Have that satellite dish down here by first thing tomorrow, son,' he replied, 'or *I'll* have *you* crucified, okay?'

'Okay,' I said.

26

Rain drummed against the windows. I knelt on the arm of the chair and stared out into the drizzled darkness and reflected on how I had managed once again to get myself involved with loonies.

Before, in Belfast, in New York, it had been individual loonies, a magic mushroomed comedian or a detective who snipped fingers off with rose-clippers, but this was a different kind of loony altogether. It was a collective looniness. The council of loons.

Patricia could see that I was troubled. She hovered about me. Little Stevie slept. 'I'd make you a cup of tea,' she said sympathetically, 'but you'd only tell me to stick it up my hole.'

I smiled. I shrugged. I looked at the rain again.

'And I only brought the one bottle of wine, so there's no answer there.'

She put her arm about my shoulders. I rested my head against her for a moment. She felt warm. Smelt nice. I put my arm round her waist.

'I'm sorry I can't help,' she said.

'There's nothing wrong.'

I dropped my hand onto her rear and it sparked off a thought. I looked up at her hopefully. A way to forget my troubles.

She moved slightly away, then squeezed my shoulder and looked at the ground. 'I'm having trouble with thrush,' she said, her voice barely a whisper, shy even after all these years.

I dropped my hand. 'You shouldn't put so much bread out.'

She laughed and slapped the back of my head, then turned quickly on her heel. 'Well, I'm going to make a cup of tea.'

I stared into the blackness for a little longer. It would be easy just to pack up our belongings and get on that ferry in the morning. To forget about all the nonsense. I already had enough evidence for the Cardinal to send in the ecclesiastical stormtroopers. I'd earned the money, was maybe owed some more for the bicycle injuries.

I'd never even thought to ask about whether I was covered by any kind of insurance, whether Patricia would gain anything if a spoke entered my eyeball or a plague of locusts took a sudden interest in me. Third party fire and pestilence.

I followed her into the kitchen. I took a can of Diet Pepsi from the fridge and sat at the table. 'The way things are going,' I said, 'they'll probably outlaw this too, and then I'll really be stuck.'

'Dan, you'll never be stuck.'

'We should go home,' I said. 'These people are nuts.'

She shook her head. 'Dan, you won't go home till you see this through. You know that.'

'Jesus was thirty-odd when they got round to crucifying him. You want to be here that long?'

'And what's Jesus got to do with it?'

I grinned. She was right. 'Good point.'

'Besides, girls grow up so much quicker than boys.'

I tutted. 'Are you being sucked into all of this?'

'No more than you, sweetie.'

Her evening had been better fun. The ladies of Wrathlin seemed a nice bunch. What they lacked in sophistication they made up for with old-fashioned charm and a contagious homeliness. The social evening was nothing more than a chin-wagging session, with Patricia the centre of attraction. I'd given her her instructions, of course, but by the time she'd talked through her life and times the evening was drawing to a close and she very nearly failed to steer the chat round. She'd been worried about how to introduce the subject of the Messiah in the first place, and had hoped that it would come round naturally, but nobody mentioned it all night. Finally she just plunged in and hoped for the best. She tapped the knee of the woman sitting next to her and whispered, 'What about this Christine then? What's the gen on her?'

The woman smiled at her. 'It's great, isn't it? Our wee Christine – such a star!' And that had set the whole lot of them off.

Patricia poured her tea. I drummed my nails on the side of the can.

'It was like Christine had won a bonny baby competition or a talent show or something. They just seemed genuinely proud of her. Local girl does good.'

'Loonies,' I said.

'Maybe they're just right to treat it like that, love.'

'Aye. Drink your tea.'

'But . . .'

'Trish, if you'd seen my lot . . .'

'Well, maybe if there were any women on that Council, this might be a better place to live.'

'I can't imagine Wrathlin *ever* being a better place to live. Unless they reopened the pub.'

'You know what I mean.'

'Anyway, I'm not rising to the bait, Trish.'

'What bait?'

'You know what I mean.'

'I haven't a notion what you're talking about.'

'You know rightly. All that feminist crap.'

'What feminist crap?'

'About women ruling the world and . . .'

'I never mentioned women ruling the world!'

'You were getting there . . .'

'I . . .'

'Just finish your tea and do the dishes, love,' I said. Then I ran into the front room laughing.

'Bastard!' she shouted.

But it was okay. She was laughing too.

My idea was to write a big epic novel about the history of Ireland. It had been done before, but never properly. None of them had ever been funny, and the history of Ireland was nothing if not a laugh. Before, I'd had the thoughts, but never the time to write them down; now I had the time but the thoughts were driven from my mind by visions of the Messiah.

Patricia went to bed. I sat in the corner of the spare bedroom I was using as a makeshift study and passed ten minutes staring into nothingness and sniffing at a thick black felt pen. It smelt pretty good. After a while I started to feel a bit light-headed and set it down. Then I switched on the computer and started writing a report for Cardinal Tomas Daley. I tried to keep it objective and concise. The word loony only crept up twice. It took me about half an hour. Then I sat and pondered a while on how to get it to him. I had an Internet connection and a speedy modem, but no phone line. I could post it, but I had some doubt about how wise it was to let it out of my hands. No, I needed to get on the ferry, phone or fax him the report from Ballycastle. Hell, while I was there I might be forced into an off-licence. I spent a few minutes trying to work out how many cans of Harp I could squeeze into the car (a) without anybody on the ferry noticing, and (b) without sinking the ferry. I reckoned about two hundred in the boot. And a crate of Diet Pepsi in the passenger seat to throw the alcohol police off the trail.

After I printed out the report I folded and sealed it in an envelope and put it in my jacket pocket. I didn't address it. It contained no reference to the Cardinal.

I got another can of Diet Pepsi, then sat in the lounge for a while, back before the window. I watched the rain again. It was quite soothing. A mental massage. I started picking out raindrop patterns against the glass. It obviously hadn't been cleaned on the outside for a while, and the dirt encouraged the rain into various shapes: a map of America, a strutting peacock, an old woman's fleshy face.

The old woman's fleshy face smiled suddenly and then a fist banged on the window.

I shot backwards, toppling off the arm of the settee. 'Jesus Christ!' I shouted, but it was more like the Wicked Witch of the North West.

I lay on the floor, heart pounding. The face moved away. After a few moments there was a rapid knocking on the front door.

I took several deep breaths and cautiously raised myself. I was getting on in years now and my diet didn't allow me too many sudden shocks.

I steadied myself against the living room door. Patricia's head appeared at the end of the hall. 'Who is it?' she whispered.

'I don't bloody know yet,' I snapped.

'*Sorry*,' she snapped herself and ducked back into the room.

I opened the door.

The old fleshy face blinked at me in the light. Then the body it topped shook itself like a Labrador and while I was distracted by the spray she stepped into the hall.

'Come in,' I said.

'Sorry, love, did I give you a fright?' the woman said, her voice cigarette-craggy. 'I thought I'd take a wee look and see if anyone was up before I knocked. It's late on.'

'It is. And, no, you didn't.'

She nodded. 'I wanted a wee word.'

'Have several,' I said, 'it looks like murder out there.'

Behind me, down the hall, Patricia's face poked out again. 'What does she want?'

'I don't know!' I turned back to her. 'What do you . . .'

But she'd taken advantage of the distraction to walk past me into the lounge. She was sitting on the edge of the settee, a damp stain of rain already spreading out behind her.

'Have a seat,' I said.

She wore a purple anorak that fell as far as her knees. Her face bulged red out of its hood. Raindrops ran to and fro in the gullies between the wrinkles on her forehead like irrigation. Her Wellington boots were caked in mud. Her hands were pudgy. There was something familiar about her face.

The woman leant forward. 'You're the one saved the wee girl.'

'Christine?'

'Aye.'

'I suppose so. What of it?'

'I want you to do the same. I want you to save another wee girl.'

'I'm really not sure what . . .'

'You did it once,' she snapped suddenly, her top lip curling up unpleasantly, 'do it again.'

There was no need for the nastiness. If I'd been drinking I might have picked her up by the ears and thrown her into the garden. And kicked her while she was down for good measure. I have never believed that old age is an excuse for bad manners. Or for anything besides incontinence. But I hadn't been drinking, so I counted to ten and said as placidly as I could: 'You'd better tell me what you're on about, Missis, because I haven't a notion.'

This time her bottom lip curled down in distaste. She had a remarkably mobile mouth. 'Are you not listening to me?' she hissed.

'Yes. I'm listening.'

'You saved that wee girl.'

'Yes. We've established that.'

'Now I want you to save mine.'

'And what's her problem?'

'They want to kill her.'

'Who do?'

'They do. The Council.'

'And why would they want to do that?'

'Because of what she did. On her bike.'

Ah.

The penny dropped. Mary Reilly. Mary Reilly's mother.

'They're going to do something awful to her. I know it. She doesn't mean any harm, she's just not well . . . will you help her?'

'They're not going to do anything . . . *awful* . . . I think . . . *they* think she needs some help or something. I mean, she's hardly the full . . .' I glanced back down the hall for some sign of Patricia. She was good at talking to old people, I'd seen her in action. I just felt like hitting them with a mallet. I'd no patience. Never had. 'But don't worry,' I said, 'she'll be fine.'

'You don't understand! They're going to kill her! They always get their way!' She jumped up with a sprightliness that belied her advanced years. 'I just want your help!' she cried. 'Will you help me? They're going to kill my little girl!'

Notwithstanding the fact that her little girl could never in all the world have been described as little, there was no mistaking the raw emotion in her voice. Tears appeared at her eyes and began to dribble down her face, mixing easily with the raindrops.

'I'll make you a cup of tea,' Patricia said from the doorway.

She calmed down a little. I stood in the kitchen with my arms folded while Patricia soothed her. She was very good at it. Trish came in for a refill, said, 'Poor woman,' and went back in again. You can only stare at cupboards for so long, so I moved to the doorway and watched them talk. I was hardly listening.

Her face reminded me of someone, and it took me a while to work it out. Her daughter, *of course*, but also someone else. Then it came to me: Marilyn Monroe.

Years ago I'd seen a picture in a cheap biography, an illicit shot of her in the morgue, laid out on a marble slab, her hair dank, face sagged, not a sex symbol at all, and it had haunted me. And that was how this woman looked in her anorak, as if, once, one solitary, wonderful day, many years before, she had looked ravishing, had spent her whole life building to that day, but when it had come nothing much had happened. She'd stayed in, listened to the radio, done her hair, gazed at herself in the mirror, imagining a life off the island and had gone to bed promising herself a change, but next morning she was older, she'd passed her peak, her twenty-year struggle to beauty had yielded one uneventful night at the summit and now it was all downhill.

Sometimes I think utter bollocks.

Patricia was saying something to me. I said, 'What?'

'She wants you to go and speak to them. She says they respect you. Ask them not to harm her little girl.'

'They're not going to listen to me. And they're not going to harm her. Father Flynn's not going to let . . .'

'They've already decided! It's all over the village!' Mrs Reilly shouted.

'Are you serious?'

'Yes! So please. At least try. No one else is going to help her. She has no one.'

'Why can't you . . . ?'

'They're not going to listen to me. They hate me as much as they hate her!'

'Why?'

'Because we don't believe in all that shite!'

I cleared my throat. You rarely hear old people cursing. It's not right.

Patricia put a hand on my shoulder. 'Maybe you should, Dan.'

I twisted round. 'But what can I do? What can I say?'

'Dan, put a spanner in the works. You usually do.'

I tutted. 'Thanks.'

'You know what I mean.'

'Will you do it for me, son?' She was right in front of me then, clasping my hand. Her touch was surprisingly gentle for a gorgon.

I sighed.

Mary Reilly was a medium who was a large who was a potential murderer. Anywhere else I wouldn't have spoken up for her. But the rights and wrongs of the situation were obvious even to an old cynic like me. Everyone deserves a fair trial, and, Messiah or not, letting a four-year-old girl decide verdict and punishment doesn't amount to a fair trial.

Patricia squeezed my shoulder again.

Mother Reilly rocked back and forth on her heels, eyes pleading, anorak still dripping.

There was one important question that needed answering before I volunteered my services.

'Mrs Reilly,' I asked, 'you wouldn't happen to know where I could track down some alcohol on the island, would you?'

27

My suspicions about Mrs Reilly were confirmed by her speedy acquiescence. She had the baggy jowls of someone who enjoyed a pint or twelve of Guinness. She couldn't come up with the drink there and then, but she said she'd see what she could do about locating some. I promised to see what I could do about having a word on her daughter's behalf. As she sopped back out into the storm she gave me a benign grin which suggested that she wasn't too bothered about the trade-off. Patricia was, though. She thought I was pretty pathetic, bargaining over Mary Reilly's future. I gave this due consideration, and then told her to shut up. I meant it jocularly enough but it didn't come across that way, so she punched me in the eye.

Later, in bed, I tried to explain myself, but I didn't stand up to close examination and we spent a long night as far apart as we could without falling onto the floor.

By morning the rain had stopped. The fog was gone. The ferry was waiting. But I had to intercede on behalf of Orca, Killer Whale. I rose early, did a press-up, then readied myself for the journey into town. From the bathroom I shouted: 'Why didn't you tell me I had black ink on the end of my nose?'

'I thought you knew,' Patricia replied.

'Thanks,' I said.

Showered, shaved, I returned to the bedroom and put on a pair of black jeans, a black jumper, my fading light-blue denim jacket and a pair of black Oxfords. Patricia nodded approvingly from the bed as I dressed. I'd already wormed my way back into her affections by making her a cup of tea, which was no mean feat. Little Stevie gurgled. I'd made him a bottle. There's nothing like a bit of glass-blowing first thing in the morning to put some colour in your cheeks.

According to parish law, I should have loaded up the satellite dish and the television in the boot of the car and taken them down with me to Constable Murtagh. But Patricia simply said no, they weren't getting the TV, and that was good enough for me. Although Little Stevie seemed in perfect health, she was still nervous about being left in the cottage with no means of communicating with the outside world if he did take another turn, so she wanted to hold onto the car as well. The closest thing we had to passing traffic was a not very dependable hedgehog. Had we a dog, a Lassie, he might have been able to race into the town in minutes and bark out precise instructions to Dr Finlay, but a hedgehog would take days to cover the same territory and only pass on a serious case of fleas.

So I set to walking, fixing my face in suitably martyrish fashion before kissing Patricia and the baby goodbye.

'Good luck,' she said, and then added, 'Don't do anything silly.'

'As if,' I said.

It was a pleasant enough walk, damp but not cold, and by the time I reached the edge of town I felt invigorated, which was a novel experience. I looked at my watch. Jesus. 7.30 AM. The last time I'd been up and about at that hour I'd been meandering home from a bar.

As I passed the harbour I saw in the distance Charlie McManus leaning over the side of the *Fitzpatrick*. He seemed to be looking in my direction, but when I waved there was no response. When I reached the T-junction at the foot of the hill I paused for a moment and looked up towards the church, sitting dark and cold. Then I carried straight on along the front towards Constable Murtagh's house. It was a whitewashed mid-terrace, two up, two down, distinguished from its neighbours only by the iron bars on the upstairs windows. It was about a hundred yards along the row, and the only interesting things between me and it were the two men who loitered outside it with shotguns hung loosely over their shoulders.

As I approached they pushed themselves off the wall, blocking my passage in the process.

'Morning,' I said and nodded at the guns. 'What's up?'

One, a short, balding guy in a Barbour jacket, dropped the gun casually from his shoulder until it pointed at my stomach. 'You tell us,' he said.

The other, with much the same build but plenty of hair and an ancient duffel coat, said: 'Where do you think you're going?'

'I've to see the Constable.'

'What about?'

'My satellite dish. It's been confiscated.'

The balding guy stepped closer. The gun moved with him, into my stomach. He peered into my face. His breath was stale and he had sleepywogs in his eyes. 'You're that writer fella, aren't you?'

'Aye.'

He turned to his companion. 'You know, the one saved Christine?' Abruptly he pulled the gun away. 'Sorry,' he said, 'no offence. We're all very grateful to you.'

The other smiled broadly and stuck his hand out. I shook it. It was cold and damp. 'Well done,' he said.

I shrugged. 'Youse look like you've been here all night.'

They nodded. 'Aye,' said Duffel Coat, 'wettest night in years and here we are. Great fun.'

'What's the story, then? What's with the guns? You look like a couple of vigilantes.'

The baldy one smiled sheepishly. 'Ach, nothing really. Father White asked us to keep an eye on the cop shop, in case that witch tried to do a runner.'

'Don't you trust the Constable?'

'Aye. Of course we do. But you never can tell. She has the Devil in her, y'know.'

I nodded. 'Of course. You're quite right.' I stepped between them. 'I'd better get on through here and get this sorted out. I'm sure it's the last thing he wants to hear about with the trial coming up, but the law's the law, isn't it?'

'Sure enough.'

They parted. I passed.

'Well done again,' Duffel Coat called after me, 'and watch out for her, she's an evil bitch.'

I waved back.

Constable Murtagh answered on the third knock. The door was still on its chain and his ruddy face peered out through a six-inch gap. 'What the fuck do you want?' he snapped.

'I see you've been saved too,' I said.

His hair, short, grey, stuck up at mad angles. He had his green police shirt and trousers on, no shoes. A revolver in his hand. He looked like he'd been up most of the night as well.

'Listen, Smart Alec, I'm busy. What do you want?'

'I've come to have a word with Mary Reilly, if I can. Her mum has asked me to speak up on her behalf at the trial.'

Murtagh looked me up and down. 'I thought you were the witness for the prosecution.'

'I am.'

'So?'

'I also think it would be a bit fairer to try her on the mainland.'

Murtagh nodded slowly. 'Aye,' he said, then unhooked the chain. 'Come on in then.' He opened the door wider. As I passed he looked out behind me at the vigilantes and shook his head disdainfully.

I walked down a dark hallway into a back room which had been converted into an office. There was a desk, two chairs, a small filing cabinet. Posters warning about rabies, drugs and terrorism adorned the walls. There was also a large crucifix.

From behind he said: 'Hands up.'

I started to turn, but a hand on my shoulder stopped me.

'As you are,' he said. He knelt behind me and his hand shot up my leg. Then it crossed my lower back round to my stomach, up the chest, along my back, along both arms and finished on the other leg. Then he checked the contents of my pockets. Thirty-eight pence and a Barney Eastwood betting slip.

'All clear,' he said finally and brushed past me to sit behind the desk. 'Sorry about that,' he said, 'but you can't be too careful. Used to be all you had to worry about was someone coming at you with a fish knife or a big stick. Nowadays you turn your back for five seconds and some bastard whacks you with the Gospel According to Luke. Have a seat.'

He placed his gun in a drawer to his left, but kept it open. He was trying not to look nervous, but he was.

'It must be difficult,' I said, pulling back a chair, 'living with this lot.'

'Impossible,' he said, 'and getting worse. You saw them 'uns outside? Bleep and fucking Booster.'

'They don't seem to believe she's very secure here.'

'Oh, she's secure enough. Don't worry yourself on that score. It's getting her to the church without that lot stringing her up that worries me.'

'So you are going ahead with it. The trial.'

He watched me for a moment. 'Of course.'

I shrugged. 'Fair enough.'

He blew some air out of his nose. 'You're thinking, if he's so pissed off with the McCooeys, why go along with the trial?'

I shrugged.

'Well, put it this way,' he said. 'I am actually a believer.'

'You said "fuck" a while back.'

'I did.'

'You said they were getting worse.'

'They are.'

'So . . .'

'There are believers, and there are believers. I believe. Just maybe not in the same way as the others. I believe in Christine. Really. I'm just not very good at it yet. Sometimes I still say "fuck". Sometimes I still covet my neighbour's chickens. I believe in her, but I don't think she's up to sentencing someone just yet.'

'You're a McCooey, but you're not quite a McCooey.'

'If you like.'

'You're the Provisional wing of the McCooeys.'

'If you want to stretch a point.'

'So what're you going to do?'

'Take her to trial. There's nothing else for it. I've no way of getting her off the island.'

'The ferry might be one way.'

'Charlie McManus has taken the ferry out of service. There *is* no way off the island.'

'Can he do that?'

'It's his ferry.'

'Like it's my ball and no one else is playing with it.'

'Something like that. He says it needs a refit or something. But I detect another hand at work.'

'Father White,' I said.

Murtagh looked at me, a hint of a smile appeared, just for a moment, then was chased away. 'Well, that's not for me to say. Whatever his reasons, he has the right. It's his boat. And it's not like I can summon help. Someone smashed my radio. While I was out, they were in. Stupid, really. I didn't lock the door. And me a copper.'

'You could commandeer the ferry.'

'Yes. And drown.'

I grinned. 'Yeah, I know how you feel. Will the police on shore not be worried about not hearing from you?'

He shook his head. 'Not a bit of it. Sometimes they don't hear from me for months. It doesn't worry them. I run the whole show here, and they're quite happy to let me do it. I mean, who else would, but someone born and bred here?'

We looked at each other in silence for a few moments. He seemed a decent kind of a spud, but a decent spud under pressure. He was having to deal with things way outside the remit of a lowly island copper. He was being asked to be at once a moralist, philosopher and lawmaker, a fearsome trinity.

'So there's no way of getting in touch with the outside world?' I asked.

He shook his head slowly.

'Isn't there a radio up by the bird observatory?'

It was out before I thought about it. There was a momentary look of surprise in his eyes which quickly settled into a steady gaze. 'And how would you be knowing that?'

I shrugged. 'I heard.'

He reached into the open drawer. Instead of the gun he took out a small black dictaphone tape recorder and placed it before me. It looked remarkably like my tape recorder.

In fact, it *was* my tape recorder.

'I recovered this at the murder scene.'

'*Murder* scene?'

He was nodding slowly. 'Is there anything you want to tell me?' he said.

Sometimes you can hear your heart beat louder than The Clash at full volume. This was one of those times. I scrambled for words. 'I forgot the satellite dish . . .'

'*Fuck* the satellite dish.'

'Okay.' We looked at each other. I had a decision to make. He was a McCooey, albeit a wandering one. If he was any sort of a policeman he'd have listened to my interview with Moira, then checked with her when it was recorded. He would know that it had happened on the day Bill had died. So I'd been up there and not volunteered the information. Suspicious or what? Yet he had not sought me out for questioning. I had come to him. So possibly he knew something about Bill's death which absolved me. Or he could be lazy, or slow. Where was I going to run to anyway? Wrathlin was an open prison. So now he had me he could arrest me, then send me for trial up at the church, with Christine as judge and jury. Should I act dumb? Should I tell all?

He was there in front of me and he seemed more normal than most anyone else I'd met on the island. He *cursed*. He seemed mildly cynical. He was law and order, yet he was as trapped on this island as the rest of us.

I'm not good at making decisions. I mean sometimes I am. Murtagh drummed his fingers on the table and said, 'If it helps, I know you were being chased.'

'What?'

'Tell me what happened up at the bird observatory.'

'I . . .'

'The truth. I know most of it already.'

'But who . . . ?'

'Dan, tell me what happened or I'll throw you in a cell.' He thumbed upstairs. 'With *her*.'

I told him.

He nodded. We sat in silence for several moments. 'Do you want to tell me what's going on?' I asked eventually.

He shook his head. 'Too much,' he said.

'But . . .'

'But nothing. Take your tape recorder. It would be good if you could say a few words on Mary Reilly's behalf.'

'But aren't you going to . . . ?'

'No.'

'You believe what I . . .'

'I do. Now leave it. Don't ask me anything else. When the opportunity arises, get off the island. That's my advice, Mr Starkey. Take your wife and child and get off the island.'

'Do you know who . . . ?'

'Leave it.' He stood abruptly and unhooked a set of keys from a hook on the wall. 'Now, you run up and see her now if you want. She's handcuffed to the bed, so she won't harm you if you don't get too close.'

'Permanently handcuffed?'

Murtagh nodded. 'I know it's hardly straight from the International Convention on Human Rights, but I only have the one cell and the lock on it wouldn't fox a reasonably bright four-year-old. And before you ask, she doesn't get a chance to stretch her legs because there are people out there who want to stretch her neck.'

'How does she . . . ?'

'Piss? In the pot. It's not very pleasant for either of us. But that's the way it is.'

'What about her mental state?'

'She's like Greenland. Big and empty. She's been quite upset. She didn't want to make a statement. She was quite brassy when I first saw her at Dr Finlay's, but then someone threw a brick at her as we were leaving and I think that surprised her. God knows why. It didn't hit her. Nearly broke my fucking foot. Ooops. There I go again.'

He led me up the stairs and unlocked the cell door. As he pushed the door open he whispered, 'Word seems to have filtered out, so try not to mention crucifixion. It sets her off.'

28

I had already observed two sides of Mary Reilly. The first, perched rosy-cheeked on her bike, placid, happily reading the Bible; the second, minutes later, cheeks aflame, bearing down upon an innocent child, seemingly intent on murder. Now there was a third: doe-eyed, colour-drained, straggle-haired, scared.

She looked fearfully up from the bed as the door opened, then shrank back against the headboard as I entered. Murtagh locked the door behind me. I leant back against it. The heavily barred window gave a view of the harbour. The grey box room contained just the bed, a chamber pot, and a copy of the Bible, which lay open on the quilt. Mary's right hand was handcuffed to the metal bedframe. The skin was red-raw at the wrist.

'That must be sore,' I said.

She looked down at the handcuffs, then gave a little nod. She began to massage the skin.

'Do you remember me?'

She looked up, nodded quickly again. There were no obvious physical signs of damage from the collision.

'Your mother asked me to come and see you.'

When she spoke her voice was as timid and high as a little girl's. 'Mum?'

'She asked me to see how you were.' I pushed myself off the door and stepped slowly towards the bed. As I sat on the end of it she cowered back even further. 'It's okay, Mary. I'm here to help you. Is there anything your mum can get you?'

'Why isn't she here herself?'

'She's not allowed, Mary. The Council won't allow her.'

'But why?'

I shrugged. 'I don't really know. I think they think you're bad.'

'I am bad.'

'You know that?'

She nodded sadly. 'Of course. I tried to hurt a wee girl. Of course I'm bad. What else could I be?'

'Why did you do it, Mary?'

'I was told to.'

'Who told you?'

'The man.'

'What man?'

'The man.'

'What man, Mary? What's his name?'

'He has no name.'

'What does he look like?'

'I don't know. Just a man.'

'Where did you meet him?'

'Somewhere.'

'Somewhere on the island?'

She shrugged. 'I don't remember.'

There was a dreamy quality to her answers, but the vagueness didn't strike me as deliberate. There was genuine confusion in her eyes.

'Mary,' I said as gently as I could, 'in a couple of hours you're going to be asked a lot of questions up at the church, about what happened. It's important that you tell me anything you can, so that I can speak up for you. Do you understand?'

She nodded slowly. 'They don't like me, do they?'

'Mary, it's not that . . .'

'They're going to hurt me, aren't they?'

'If you tell me what . . .'

'He said they were going to hurt me.'

'Who did?'

'The Father.'

'Father Flynn?'

She shook her head. 'The other one. He said they were going to punish me for what I'd done.' Suddenly she began to take great whooping breaths and tears began to course down her face. I patted her shoulder. 'They're going to hurt me!' she cried.

'They won't . . .'

'I want my mum!'

'Mary, dear, I can't . . .'

She fell forward and buried her face in my chest. For a moment

I held my hands up and away from her as she heaved against me. I'm not a touchy-feely person at the best of times and the thought of embracing an eighteen-stone nuthouse would not normally have appealed to me, but there was something touchingly helpless about her outburst. I let my arms fall. I hugged her. 'It's okay,' I said.

'I'm scared,' she cried.

'I know.'

'He said I was the Devil's work and I'd have a Devil's punishment.'

'He's just trying to scare you.'

'He's said he'd . . .'

'Mary . . . Mary . . . will you tell them that you're sorry?'

She nodded.

'Will you tell them that you believe in Christine? That you realise that you were wrong and that all you want to do now is pray and ask for forgiveness?'

'I will.'

'Do you promise me?'

'I do.'

'Good. Then I'll have a word with them all, and we'll see if we can't get it all sorted out. Is that okay?'

She nodded again against my chest. 'I don't want to go there,' she whispered.

'I know you don't.'

'Can you not go there for me?'

'I'll be there with you.'

'Will my mum be there?'

'She will.'

'Will she hold my hand?'

'If you're good, and you tell the truth, she'll hold your hand when you're finished. Is that okay?'

I unclasped my arms then and she sat back. She pulled her free hand across her face. 'I'm sorry for crying,' she said. She let out a little chuckle. 'I'm so silly sometimes.'

'It's natural.'

'I will tell the truth. I'll be good.' She shook her head sadly. 'I don't know what came over me. I'm just scared.' She rubbed at one eye with a knuckle. 'I don't really remember any of it.' Her voice was lower now, more adult as the words began to spill out.

'How I got to the church, how I came to be riding down that hill so fast . . . I remember you jumping out in front of me . . . and then waking up in Dr Finlay's . . . and all those horrible people shouting at me and throwing things and screaming and throwing and screaming . . .' Tears began to drip down her face again. 'They were like . . . like wild animals . . . I could see their teeth . . . all bared and sharp . . . I don't know what would have happened if Constable Murtagh hadn't been there . . . all those people, people I've known for years . . . I've told their fortunes . . . and made them lunch . . . and gone to their homes and then suddenly they're all screaming at me as if I was the Devil himself . . .' She pulled suddenly at her lip; her eyes were wide, begging. 'I'm not the Devil, am I? I'm not some . . .'

'Mary, I've never seen anyone less like the Devil.'

'Not even when I was coming down that hill . . .'

'Not even.'

'You will help me, then?' I nodded. 'And you'll tell Mummy I'm all right, and that I don't need anything. But you'll get her to come all the same, to look after me when it's all over?'

'I will.'

'Thank you. I'm sorry I'm so much trouble.'

'It'll be okay, Mary.'

When we were going back down the stairs, Murtagh said: 'She's a Space Cadet, isn't she?'

'Bonkers,' I agreed.

29

The sun was just pushing its face through the fast-dissipating mist as I emerged from the station and walked back along the sea front. The vigilantes nodded wearily as I passed. 'All sorted,' I said.

At the junction I turned up the hill towards the church. Halfway up I stopped at Dr Finlay's surgery to ask him if he would speak on Mary's behalf, tell them she had a split personality or bad mood swings or was largely harmless apart from isolated murder attempts, but he wasn't in. Mrs McTeague squinted up at me. 'I've no idea where he is,' she said, true to form.

It was a little before 9 AM when I reached the churchyard. Although the trial was still an hour away people were already milling about the yard, hush-talking in little weedy clumps. Half a dozen of them had gathered about the doorway and were staring intently at something. Curious as ever, I wandered over. One of them looked up sharply as I approached. He murmured something and the rest turned towards me. Two I recognised as members of the Council: Carl Christie the Credit Union man and the ex-publican Jack McGettigan. I nodded.

'Morning, Dan,' said Christie. He angled his head back towards the door. 'Did ye see this?'

He stepped back. A mess of blue-paint graffiti adorned the hall door: FREE MARRY RILY.

I resisted the temptation to smile. 'Jesus,' I said, almost as thoughtlessly, then added quickly, 'would not be amused.'

They nodded in agreement, and then, almost as if it was choreographed, they shook their heads in disgust.

'Jackie Lavery came to open up this morning, found it,' one of the men I didn't know said. Slim fella, ginger eyebrows beneath a tweed cap. A face as well. Hungry-looking. 'It was still wet.'

Jack McGettigan pointed further down the door. 'Ye see that too?'

I gave it a closer look. There was more writing, smaller, smeared across the bottom of the door. I screwed up my eyes. 'What's it say?' I asked.

McGettigan knelt down beside it. 'Says nothing. Just letters. Jackie started cleaning it up this morning, then thought better of it. You can just about work it out.' He ran his finger up the remains of the letters, tracing them out through the smear. 'A, F, L, R. AFLR. Whatever that means. Any ideas?'

I shook my head. 'Somebody's initials, I presume.'

'I was thinking maybe it was an anagram,' Carl Christie said. 'Y'know, a clue.'

I studied the remains of the letters for a moment, but nothing coherent came to mind. 'Going from the spelling above, it's not beyond the bounds of possibility that we have a dyslexic vandal called Ralf at work. Know anyone called Ralph?'

There wasn't anyone called Ralph.

I left them scowling in the doorway. There was now a steady stream of people coming through the gates. Whole families. It might have been the biggest thing to happen on Wrathlin for years, but for the little matter of a Messiah being born. Amongst the new arrivals was Father Flynn, chatting happily with a young couple. As I approached, they thanked him and turned away, hand in hand. We both watched them for a few moments.

'Ah, isn't it wonderful to be young and in love?' I said.

'Is it?'

'Sorry. Of course.'

He smiled, but it wasn't a real smile, just as his joviality towards the young couple wasn't real. His eyes were dark, red-rimmed, his face wan. 'Did you see the artwork?' he asked, nodding at the church.

'Aye.'

He rolled his eyes. 'All we need. Another crackpot.'

I nodded. 'Any idea who?'

'None. As if I haven't enough on my plate.'

'Aye. I know. You're still not convinced, are you? About the need for a trial.'

'What can I say, Dan? It was a democratic decision. How can I argue with that?'

'I don't think twelve fascists voting together makes it democratic.'

'You're very cynical.'

'I see plenty to be cynical about.'

'You've no faith, Dan, that's your problem.'

'You've too much, that's yours.'

He broke off as several members of his congregation wished him a good morning. He smiled wearily at them, spoke quietly. They moved on.

'I was going to ask you if you would mind if I said a few words on Mary Reilly's behalf,' I said.

It took a moment for my enquiry to register, but when it did his eyes sparked suddenly back into life and he reached forward and clasped my arm. 'Would you, Dan?'

'I was thinking maybe I should. I don't think anyone else will.'

'Dan, Dan, I would be absolutely delighted if you would.' He bent in a little closer, dropped his voice. 'I've been so worried about all of this. You've no idea. I didn't sleep a wink last night. You know it's not right that Christine decides the sentence. I know that too. But what can I do? I can't go against what the Council has decided. We have to present a united front. It's such early days for the whole movement, Dan, that if we start arguing now there's no telling how it will all end up. Do you see what I mean?'

'Up to a point, Lord Copper.'

'Lord . . . ?'

'I'm sorry, it's an old joke. Yes, I know what you mean.'

'Good. Excellent. I'm very pleased.' He rubbed his hands together. 'She needs someone to speak up for her. I'm just sorry it can't be me.'

'Well, maybe it'll help her, maybe not.' I kicked at the dirt. 'I'm not exactly Perry Mason, y'know? More like Perry Como.'

'Dan, you are less like Perry Como than anyone I have ever met in my life. But you'll do grand, Dan. I know you will. It's just that Father White is so keen . . . so *enthusiastic*, I hate to discourage him . . . that's why it really is a godsend.' He squeezed my arm. 'It's the right thing to do, son,' he said earnestly, 'and it won't be forgotten.'

I shrugged.

I didn't mind it being forgotten. I'd butterflies in my stomach and moths in my head. I was the only thing standing between a mentally unstable woman and the possibility that a four-year-old Messiah might order her crucifixion, or at least make her do a lot of dishes.

A tug on my sleeve turned me round. Old Mother Reilly, dressed in black. A morbid quiver of her lips, with a ripple effect down her chins, passed for an appreciative smile. Her hand lingered on my sleeve. 'I just wanted to thank you for speaking up for her,' she said.

I shrugged. 'You haven't heard me yet. But seeing as you're here . . .' I dropped my voice and moved a little closer. 'Any news on the alcohol front?'

'Not yet. But I'm working on it. I won't let you down. These things take time.'

'Not too much time, I hope.'

She gave me the slightest nod, and turned for the hall. As she went towards the steps, her head down, people moved out of her way, then whispered things to each other when she had passed.

'How're you feeling, love?'

Patricia, Stevie in the pram, had sneaked up. She put her hand where Ma Reilly's had been.

'I've been better,' I said. 'I thought you weren't coming. I thought you were concerned about the baby.'

'I was. Then after a while I wasn't. He's fine. Didn't want to miss the trial of the century.'

I rolled my eyes. 'This is going to be a disaster.'

'You'll be fine.'

I kicked up a gravel cloud with my left foot. Patricia turned the pram away to shield the baby. 'Calm down, love,' she said.

'I am calm.'

'You're not. Your nostrils are flared.'

'As long as my trousers aren't I'm not worried.' We exchanged weak smiles. Then Patricia's brow furrowed. She was looking behind me. I turned to see two men come running red-faced through the churchyard gates. They carried shotguns loosely by their sides.

'If they're outriders,' Patricia said, 'they've forgotten Mary Reilly. And their motorbikes.'

The men jumped the steps and disappeared into the church hall. Sensing that something was up, the crowd that had been loitering in the yard began to hurry up the steps after them.

'What do you think?' Patricia asked.

'I saw them earlier, they were guarding Mary Reilly.'

'I thought that was the cop's job?'

'It was.'

'So?'

'We better find out.'

I started to move towards the steps.

'You *are* going to give me a hand with this pram?' Trish said.

I stopped. I looked back. 'No,' I said, 'you shouldn't have gotten pregnant in the first place.'

I pushed through the church-hall doors. I half fancied that the word 'bastard' followed me in, but I might have been mistaken.

Inside a crowd had formed at the bottom of the hall, surrounding the door which led into the church. I spotted Duncan Cairns hovering near the back and gave him a tap on the shoulders.

'What's up?' I asked. 'Somebody win the lottery?'

'Lottery's banned.'

'Figures.'

'Sensational evidence has been found which proves Mary Reilly's innocence.'

'*Has* it?'

'No.'

He smiled.

A sense of humour.

Maybe he wasn't the complete arse I'd taken him for.

Then the crowd began to move back as the doors were slowly opened from within. Father Flynn appeared, followed by Father White and the members of the Council. They were all grim-faced. A dozen questions were shouted as they entered, but ignored. Flynn raised his hands, then moved them up and down like he was patting an invisible horse, waiting for quiet. The men with shotguns hovered by the church doors.

Slowly the excited jabber faded and Flynn lowered his hands. 'Thank you. Ahm, ladies and gentlemen,' he said gravely, 'I'm afraid there's going to be a bit of a delay in today's proceedings.' He glanced at one of the gunmen. 'In the eloquent words of Marcus Farrell, Mary Reilly has done a runner.'

Gasps.

'Yes, she seems to have escaped.'

Father White wasn't able to hold himself back. 'But she will not escape divine retribution!'

A roar of approval. A stamping of feet.

'No, thank you, Father, she will not,' Flynn replied with quiet authority. 'As I was saying, she has disappeared from Constable Murtagh's house. And so, it would appear, has Constable Murtagh.'

Gasps upon gasps.

Again he waved calming hands. 'Settle down. There's no point in getting into a state about it, let's all just try and remain calm. At the moment we just don't know exactly what is going on. The house is empty, the police car is still there, so they must be on foot. She may have overpowered the Constable and forced him to go with her. She might have injured him and left him somewhere. There's even the possibility that he has decided to go with her of his own accord. We just don't know.'

A man in the audience shouted: 'I thought we were keeping an eye on her?'

'Yes, Jimmy, we were. As far as we can establish they slipped out the back way. I should warn you all that Constable Murtagh has a gun, so we can only presume that Mary Reilly has access to it and is loose somewhere on the island. So we're all going to have to be very careful until she's back under lock and key.'

'What about Christine?' Duncan Cairns asked. 'What if Mary goes after her again?'

'Christine is already under armed guard. We also have men down at the harbour, so they won't be making their escape that way.'

'They won't be making their escape at all!' Father White bellowed, and got a rousing cheer for his effort. He stepped in front of Flynn. 'We need everyone who has a gun to go home immediately and collect it. Ask anyone who couldn't make it today as well. Meet back here in thirty minutes, then we'll search every inch of this island. She won't get away!'

There was another cheer for him.

'The rest of you, go on home, lock your doors and pray that we find her before she hurts anyone. Go now!'

It was last in, first out. I was carried along on a wave of aspiring vigilantes and deposited in the churchyard beside Patricia and the pram. She handed me a plastic bag. It was warm.

'What's this?' I asked.

'A bag of shite.'

'Right.'

30

By noon a rag-bag of some sixty agitated islanders had congregated in the churchyard. They were all men, and they all had guns. Most were shotguns, but there were a few weapons of an altogether more sophisticated hue, which was, frankly, surprising. I'd expected slings and arrows, cudgels, rolling pins, Moses crooks and fish hooks. Not AK-47 assault rifles.

Father White addressed them from the steps of the church. Father Flynn stood by the church gates. He intended to bless them as they went a-hunting. Not the gates, the hunters. He had delegated the actual mechanics of the search to Father White, although I wasn't altogether convinced that he had much choice about it. 'He's neither younger nor fitter,' he explained, 'but he could have planned the invasion of Normandy in half the time.'

It was said with grudging respect. He looked worried. His voice was dry, his eyes were pinched up pensive. The mob was excited, baying to be off, and though they didn't need it, Father White was whipping the frenzy up further. It was a simpleton's version of a fox hunt, chasing a big girl around half a dozen square miles of bramble, scrub and wind-bent tree.

'That's an awful lot of hardware for an island this size, Father. What's this, the forgotten wing of the IRA?'

He laughed. 'No . . . of course not . . . we get a lot of ships call by, and they're usually keen to trade. Particularly the Russians. God love their impoverished wee souls. There's a fair bit of bartering goes on.'

'You mean like half a dozen cabbages for a Kalashnikov.'

'Actually, you're not that far off. They've no shortage of weapons but their rations leave a lot to be desired. Poor scrawny half-starved wee men. You could probably equip a small army in exchange for sixty-four of Mrs McKeown's meat pies.'

'It looks like you have.' I shook my head. 'That's still an awful lot of weaponry to track down an eighteen-stone schizophrenic. She's not Rambo, Father, she's Dumbo.'

'Dan, she's with Constable Murtagh, and as far as we're concerned he *is* Rambo. He has a gun and he knows how to use it.'

'He's also the law, Father.'

'Not on this island.'

'Father, you know that's not right.'

Before he could respond Father White appeared at his elbow. He had a shotgun under his arm.

'You're still here, Starkey?' he snapped.

'No, I'm a hologram.'

If he heard it, or understood it, he decided to ignore it. Good thing too. He probably didn't know I was a master of kung fu. If I got really angry there were few ageing priests in the world who would last more than a few minutes with me in a tussle. No, he had more important things to do. 'If you're not joining the hunt,' he said urgently, 'I'd advise you to get on home and lock your door. You too, Frank, just in case.'

He turned then and waved his hunting party forward, then led them out of the churchyard.

I tutted. Flynn looked at me. 'What's wrong now?' he asked.

I shrugged.

'Dan, she needs to be captured. She's dangerous.'

'Maybe she is. I still think you're taking a sledgehammer to crack a nut.'

'Dan – you're going to write about all this, and I can't put any restrictions on what you write, all I can ask is that you try to look at this whole thing from our point of view. I know you're not yet converted to Christine, but we *are*, we've given our whole *hearts* to her, we're *devoted;* so when someone tries to harm her it's natural that we should seek to protect her, and make sure it doesn't happen again. Do you understand?'

I nodded.

'We have something precious here, and we don't want to lose it.'

We watched as the last of Father White's band of vigilantes turned down the slope from the end of the church lane onto Main Street.

Father Flynn delved into his jacket pocket, looking for something.

I heard rustling. He produced a crumpled paper bag and reached it out to me. 'Can I offer you a boiled sweet?' he asked.

'Are they brandy balls?' I enquired.

There are some foods Patricia can't prepare at all. For example, once when she attempted an Ulster fry she made so much that there was plenty for the firemen as well. But she does make a mean ham sandwich. Ham. Bread. Low-fat margarine. Colman's English Mustard. Just the basics, but perfectly assembled. With a whole loaf I could have bargained a nuclear sub off the Ruskies.

I had always believed that the way to a man's heart was a neat incision in the chest with an extremely sharp instrument, but Patricia's creations made me fall back on old clichés. I chomped a plateful at the kitchen table and it made me feel better about the long walk home and how I'd passed through the line of hunters stretched out across the island, coast to coast. It wasn't what they said that worried me. It was what they didn't say. Hard looks. If my coat had been any baggier they might have searched me to see if Mary Reilly was hidden in any of the pockets. Some of these men, I knew, had tried to kill me. As I walked ahead of them my shoulders were hunched up, as if that might be some sort of protection against a sudden shotgun blast.

I munched, Patricia looked out the window, and worried.

'So where'd you leave him?'

'Up the church tower, telescope in hand. You can see just about everything from up there.'

'And what did he see?'

I shrugged. 'I left him to it. He was hogging it.'

'Do you think the pressure's getting to him?'

'I don't know. It's getting to me.'

And it was. At home, no matter how much of a bind you were in, there was always the off-chance of being rescued by the police or army; there was always the reticence of the terrorist when it came to public appearances. Here there was no recognisable law. Here there were too many guns. Here there was no way off the island unless they wanted you to leave.

'They will be caught, won't they? Before the day's in.'

'I suppose. I mean, Mary and Murtagh are both island people, so it's conceivable that they know every last inch of the place and how to use it to best advantage. But they're hardly unique in that respect. Flynn seems to think they'll be captured in a very short while. He says there's a sort of historical precedent for it.'

'Meaning?'

'Meaning that about a hundred and fifty years ago there was another blow-up here. A Protestant minister and his family tried to set up a church, raised everyone's hackles in the process, and there was a trial.'

'For what?'

'I don't know. God. The meaning of life. The usual thing an island community likes to busy itself with. It seems – surprise, surprise – that the trial wasn't going in the Prods' favour, and they did a bit of a runner as well. So just about the whole of the island turned out to hunt them down.'

'And?'

'And they found them. And they hacked them to death.'

'Oh. Dear.'

'Of course that was then, and this is now. We live in altogether more enlightened times now.'

'Right.'

They came to Snow Cottage around six. Three of them. Two came up and knocked on the door, the other I saw pass the side window to take up a position in the back jungle. They were perfectly polite, even a little embarrassed, said they were checking every house, asked if we minded them checking ours.

'Sure, fire ahead. Any sign of them yet?'

'Nah. Jamie McBrinn found a shoe that might have been Mary Reilly's out by the lighthouse, but it could just as well have belonged to any big-footed woman.'

We stood respectfully back, let them get on with it. Patricia whispered to me about making them a cup of tea. I told her to catch herself on and reminded her about the cups of tea people had made for the British Army when they were first sent to Belfast; they'd enjoyed them so much they'd stayed for thirty years.

The searchers said hello to Little Stevie, the miracle baby. Little Stevie bubbled something thick and transparent out of his nose in response. They took a little longer in the garden because there was a little more of it. They found a wheelbarrow in the dark undergrowth,

185

but no killer whale. Then they thanked us for our patience and moved on. We watched them go through the kitchen window, noting the thin line of hunters spread out beyond the garden wall as far as the eye could see.

Patricia looked at her watch. 'It'll be getting dark soon.'

'Yeah.'

'They'll call the search off then, won't they, for the night?'

'I expect so. If Mary and Murtagh are out there together, I expect that's what they're waiting for. Do whatever they're going to do under the cover of darkness.'

'What do you think they'll do?'

'I have no idea.'

'What would you do, Dan?'

I shrugged. 'Cry. Call for momma. Incite insurrection amongst the rabbits. I hate to think.'

It was still pretty bright, but Patricia reached up then and pulled the curtains. She shivered.

'That doesn't make it go away, love,' I said.

'I know.'

I gave her a hug. And a kiss.

'What'll we do if they come here in the middle of the night, looking for help?'

'We tell them to fuck off.'

'We'd have to help, wouldn't we?'

'We'll jump off that bridge when we come to it.'

'So what now?'

I hemmed and hawed. Eventually I said, 'How about that pelvic floor?'

31

There were gunshots during the night. Isolated shouts. Cars roaring along the lane outside.

I was dreaming, of course, and soaked with it. The third time I shouted out Christine's name was enough for Patricia and she kicked me out of the bed with orders to take a shower and rid the demons, except there was no shower so a rub down with a cold flannel had to suffice. After that it was difficult to get back over so we lay in the semi-dark around dawn and bickered over who was taking up too much territory in the bed, all of it carried out in hissing whispers for fear of waking Little Stevie. At some point I asked her if she ever said her prayers, and she told me it was none of my business, which I took for an embarrassed yes.

By seven I was up and tracksuited. It was an old Liverpool Carlsberg tracksuit, and it had never seen a track. But it had seen action on several football pitches, most of them lovingly laid out by groundsmen who must have worked on the Somme. There were several cigarette burns on the sleeves, testament to close encounters with footballers with the same regimented approach to training as my own, and also to the dangers of passive smoking.

Before thinking about food I took a turn round the garden, at least those sections accessible to earthbound creatures. It was a bright autumnal morning, with a slight but not unpleasant chill in the air. Around the back, the hedgehog had returned to its box, the floor of which was now packed with leaves. I lifted the grimed saucer out and returned with it to the kitchen and placed some of the remnants of the ham from the previous evening on it. Then I left it back in the box. There was no reaction on the part of the hedgehog. He didn't wave a paw, or wink an eye; he didn't even bristle. Perhaps he found it difficult to express his emotions; possibly he was of English extraction. For a moment I pondered on how I'd come to acquire a pet hedgehog on an island of ten million rabbits, or hares. But not for a very long moment.

I made breakfast – toast, raspberry jam, coffee for Patricia; Diet Pepsi, a Twix for myself, and carried it through on a tray. Little Stevie would be catered for later, wife-willing. Patricia pushed her knuckles into her eyes and gave me a big open-mouthed yawn.

'Och, thanks,' she said. 'What's come over you?'

'Making up for the sweats and screams,' I said. 'Husbandly duties.'

'Love, honour and raspberry jam.'

'Something like that.'

We ate in silence, thinking our own thoughts.

It had come to me during the night where Murtagh and Mary might be, but I thought it better not to share the information, on the basis that what you don't know can't hurt you, unless you're at a Christian Brothers school.

The bird observatory.

Murtagh had not been able to hide his surprise when I told him about the radio shack up there. He was a prisoner on the island with no means of communicating with the mainland, but if he made it to the birdman's radio then he could summon help. They could be whisked off the island by helicopter. If I was right, then our troubles could soon be over. Once they realised what was going on, they'd have all sorts of police and social workers over. They'd probably take Christine into care.

They wouldn't have attempted a night landing on stormy Wrathlin, so it was all a matter of whether Murtagh and Mary had managed to evade capture until daylight. But it was past breakfast time, and there had been no sound of helicopters. Of course they could just as easily come on a boat. Or the radio could have been broken. Or that might not have been their intention at all.

'Will you stop fidgeting?' Patricia said.

'Sorry.'

'If you can't sit still, why don't you go and find out what's going on?'

I stood up.

'But first you have to help me with the baby.'

I tutted. She looked at me sternly. I withdrew the tut.

An hour and a half later we climbed into the car and drove into town. I was going for fresh bread and gossip. Patricia was going to a women's meeting. I primed her to prise all the information she possibly could out of them, so that later we could combine our findings into a rich rumour stew which, when boiled together, would leave a residue of truth.

Of course, she was used to me talking nonsense.

'It's not that sort of a meeting,' she said.

'You'll chat. Youse 'uns always do. It's in your genes.'

'We won't. We'll be too puffed. It's keep fit. Exercise.'

I shook my head. Snorted. 'Jesus. Youse are desperate. Keeping fit while the world goes to pot. It's like Stepford aerobics.'

'Maybe we're just keeping things in perspective, Dan. Besides, there's nothing wrong with keeping fit.'

'Fit to fight the good fight.'

'Whatever you say, Dan.' She tutted. She pulled her T-shirt half up. 'You know I've this stomach to lose.'

'What stomach?'

'Dan, please.'

'I'm serious.'

'Yeah, sure.'

'You're fine. Honest. I love you just the way you are.'

'Aye. Bollocks.'

'Besides, what does Little Stevie do during all this? I'll have you up for neglect.'

'Steven is in the creche.'

'A *creche* is it? Sor-rey.'

Where I came from a creche was a polite collision between two cars, but I let it lie. She said quite a few kids went to the creche, Christine amongst them.

I dropped her and the baby off in the churchyard. There were a few other women standing about. They waved over as she got out of the car. She didn't kiss me goodbye. She presumed I'd pick her up in an hour. She presumed a lot. Usually she presumed right. Then I drove back down the hill and parked on the seafront.

The gossip was fresher than the bread. The trial and subsequent hunt had disrupted the baking schedules, so the women stood about the grocery store rattling away about the night's events, or their version of them, waiting for the bread to be delivered.

I loitered amongst the frozen fish and listened in. Five or six of them – the women, not the fish – stood about the cash register talking ninety to the dozen. They were all fat and fiftyish and could have done with accompanying Patricia to the church hall to exercise their bodies instead of their mouths. The woman behind the counter, who'd been so welcoming on my first visit to the shop, scowled over from time to time. One had heard something in her garden and had gone out to investigate and nearly got shot for her trouble by one of the hunters. Another was convinced she heard a woman crying in her garden, but she hadn't dared look out. One said three or four cars had raced past her cottage in the middle of the night out towards the Magennis farm. Another slept like a brick and hadn't given the search for Mary Reilly a second thought.

There's a limited amount of time you can stand admiring fish before people start to become suspicious. I decided to give up on waiting for the bread and was just moving towards the door when the bell jangled and Duncan came in. He wore a big black donkey jacket and stained black jeans. The women stopped their jabbering when they saw who it was.

'What's the news then, Duncan?' the shopkeeper asked.

Duncan nodded hello to me then turned a serious face towards the women. 'Bad,' he said solemnly. 'It looks like they might have got away.'

'Aw, y'don't say?'

'Aye. I was just talking to Father Flynn. He says Carl Christie's wee motorboat is missing. He saw it tied up secure before he went to bed, then it was gone by seven this morning.'

'And he thinks . . . ?'

'Aye.'

'Oh dear,' said one of the women.

'We don't need that,' said another.

'There's nothing but trouble will come from it.'

'Nothing but trouble, no.'

'They'll be there by now.'

'Telling the world.'

'Aye. Telling all about us. She's a bad egg, that Mary Reilly. I always knew that.'

'So what does the Father say about it, Duncan?'

'He says life goes on as normal. We've nothing to be ashamed of. We've done nothing wrong. Besides, and I think he has a point, who's going to believe someone like Mary Reilly?'

'But what about Mickey Murtagh? They'll believe him, won't they now?'

Duncan shrugged. 'What can he say? That he deserted his post and ran away with a madwoman?'

'Aye. Right enough, Duncan,' said the shopkeeper.

I attempted to slip out the door, but the bell jangled again and they all stopped and looked at me.

'I'll come back for the bread, then,' I said. 'D'ye think it'll be long?'

'It all depends,' said the shopkeeper.

I smiled at their fat faces and went on out.

'He's an odd one too,' one of the women said just as I closed the door.

'Odd as begot,' said another.

I sat on the car bonnet for a couple of minutes until Duncan emerged with a bag of potatoes under his arm. He came straight over.

'You think they've really made it?' I asked.

He set the bag down on the car and ran a hand through his shaggy hair. 'Probably.' He looked out across the harbour. It was a smoked-out hive of activity. 'Father White and a hatful of his boys lit out in one of the trawlers first thing this morning to see if they could catch them. Pretty much depends what time Mary and Murtagh set out. There's not that much power in those wee boats. If there was a bit of a swell they might have found it slow going. But I'm thinking they probably had too much of a head start. Are you pleased, Dan?'

I shrugged. 'I'm pleased she's not been crucified. She needs locking up, not nailing up. What about you?'

'I'm in two minds.'

'Like Mary.'

'I mean, she didn't deserve a trial like that, or to be hunted down like an animal. At the same time, I dread to think what might happen once Murtagh starts blabbering.'

'You think he will?'

'What else can he do? He's not just going to turn up at the local police station with Mary, turn her in, then get the boat back over here, is he?'

'I suppose not.'

'He'll have to tell them everything about us. They probably won't be the slightest bit bothered about Christine, but taking the law into our own hands, well, that's a different thing entirely. There'll be helicopters coming over that horizon by tea-time, I'll tell you. Then your lot will follow, the TV, the radio . . . then everyone else. Half the world'll be laughing at us and the other half will be breaking their necks trying to pay homage to Christine.' He shook his head sadly. 'The place'll never be the same again.'

'But think what you'll make on the T-shirts.'

He lifted his potatoes and walked off.

Patricia emerged from the hall bang on time, then spoilt the achievement by gossiping on the steps for ten minutes while I drummed on the wheel of the car. Her T-shirt looked damp, her hair dank.

'Don't worry about me,' I said when she slipped into the front seat, 'I've nothing better to do.'

'True.'

'I was being sarcastic.'

'I wasn't.'

I started the engine. Little Stevie started crying. Patricia jiggled him about a bit. By the time we were out of the gate, he had settled again. He was his mother's son all right.

'Feeling good then?'

'Knackered.'

'And what's out of the Sisters of No Mercy?'

'Not a lot.'

I tutted. 'You had an hour.'

'I was exercising.'

'Nevertheless, you had an hour.'

She ran a hand through her hair, which couldn't have been pleasant. 'I hear they escaped. In a boat.'

'That I know. Nothing else?'

She shook her head. 'I'm not the journalist, Dan. We've had this out before. I work in a tax office. You work in a newspaper. Tax *your* brain on this, not mine.'

'Well, thanks for your help.'

As we reached the junction at the bottom of the hill Patricia pointed across at the harbour. 'Bit of a crowd gathering there,' she said, 'if that's of any interest to you, lover.'

'I'm not blind.'

I hadn't noticed it, in fact. There was a crowd, on the far side of the harbour, and getting larger. I turned the car right and drove along the front as far as I could, then parked. I opened the door and jumped out. Then I leant back in.

'Coming?'

'Wait until I get Stevie . . .'

I closed the door and hurried on along the harbour. Patricia yelled something after me, but I was too curious to pay attention. There were about thirty locals gathered at the end of the looping harbour. They stood at the edge, looking down towards the water. About half of them carried guns. I squeezed my way through to the front. Father White was just making his way up a set of slippery-looking steps from a trawler, his pudgy hand clamped around the belt of a man in front of him for balance. Behind him, seven or eight others waited to step off. A small motorboat was tied to the back of the trawler.

Puffed by his exertions, Father White stood sucking air for several moments. The crowd shuffled back to give him space. The other crewmen took the steps at a much faster pace and were soon gathered about the priest.

'What's the news, Father?' one of the crowd shouted.

'Did ye catch them?'

'Of course they didn't catch them; wouldn't they be in the boat, Dermot?'

Father White raised his hands. 'As you can see, we've found Carl Christie's boat. It was floating – empty – about three miles off Ballycastle.'

He reached into his pocket and produced a pistol, which he held aloft.

Murmur. Murmur. Murmur.

'On the boat we found Constable Murtagh's gun, his shoes and his warrant card.'

Murmur. Murmur. Murmur.

'We can only guess at what might have happened. Perhaps Mary Reilly, in her distressed state of mind, or in an act of remorse and contrition, threw herself overboard. Constable Murtagh, perhaps, dived in to save her, and both were lost. I don't know. It could have been like that.' He drew his hands together. 'Let us pray now for their lost souls.'

Heads were bowed. His wasn't. His eyes were wide and their glint was not one of sorrow for a tragic loss, but of triumphant elation.

32

For the following three days the island was quiet – too quiet, as they say.

A watch was kept along the coast for any sign of the bodies, but the perceived wisdom was that if they were washed up anywhere it would be on the mainland, and that might not be for weeks, months, or even years, such was the malevolence of the currents. A service of remembrance was hastily arranged in the church, and was well attended. The spirit of the service was one of relief rather than sorrow. Mother Reilly wasn't there. A woman who visited her said she had accepted the news with dignity. Constable Murtagh had no living relatives on the island.

I busied myself in the cottage, at my desk, making notes for my epic. This was relatively easy. Notes for a novel are a joy, because they require neither style nor cohesion, two qualities I've rarely been accused of. Patricia kept herself busy with the baby and coming to terms with using more than one ring on the cooker at a time. Moira and Christine came around one day for lunch, and the chat was good, perhaps because it did not dwell excessively on the obvious. The attitude was very much: *she's the Messiah, so what? Have a biscuit.* At one point Moira asked when I was coming round to do more interviews with her and my face went as red as a beetroot. Patricia was busy feeding Stevie and didn't notice. Christine busied herself in the garden, making sure that the hedgehog had enough undergrowth in its box to see it through the winter. She was remarkably patient, given the creature's lack of animation. As a child I would have clodded it with half bricks.

On the Thursday evening Duncan Cairns came for dinner. It was a star-filled autumn night. Patricia set a big coal fire which threw an ancient light upon our little dining room. I pulled the cot into this cosy setting, and after dinner we all relaxed and enjoyed the warming glow. Duncan seemed different: quieter, almost melancholic, his big frame squashed into a little armchair, his long legs stretched out in front of him. His face was dourly set; every so often his eyes would flash or darken in the half-light with some mysterious thought. We fell into periods of silence, punctured only by Little Stevie's contented gurgles and the spit and crackle of the fire. It was extremely pleasant. I didn't say a word out of place. I'd been given my orders.

Duncan broke one such silence with an 'excuse me' and pulled himself to his feet.

'It's just down the hall,' Patricia said, but he shook his head and smiled, then crossed to the door where his coat hung on a hook. He slipped his hand into a pocket. When he returned to his seat he held a bottle in his hand. He turned it towards me in the glow. The label said Bushmills. The capacity ten glasses. But the liquid inside was crystal clear.

'It's a cold night,' he said, watching me carefully, 'I thought we might have a wee nip of this.'

He reached the bottle across to me. Our fingers touched momentarily around it. Bonding for real men. I unscrewed the top. Positioned my nose above the neck with the precision of a docking Apollo. Smelt. *Whoosh!*

I passed it along to Patricia. She smelt it as well, and nearly toppled over. She passed it back. I took a sip, held it in my mouth, then thought I better swallow because my fillings were starting to melt. Down it slipped, like lava; if Patricia's impenetrable stew had not already laid down a diamond base in my stomach it would have burnt its way through to my feet.

'Jesus Christ,' I growled with an involuntary impression of Tom Waits. 'That's a bit rough.'

Duncan threw his head back and roared. I passed the bottle to him. He took a lengthier gulp, then sat back and let the joy course through him.

I looked at Patricia. 'Jesus Christ,' I said again.

He passed the bottle to Patricia. She sniffed it again. Her face contorted. Then she gave a little shrug, pinched the end of her nose between two fingers, then tipped the bottle back. She paused just before the alcohol reached her lips. 'If we're all blind in half an hour,' she asked with Minnie Mouse intonation, 'who's going to feed the baby?'

She wasn't looking for an answer. She took a slug, fought with it for a while, but eventually conquered it. A true Starkey. Then she gave a big smile.

'Gee,' she managed after a bit.

She passed the bottle back to me. I showed it to Duncan. 'You first,' he said.

I sat it on my knee. 'What's come over you, Duncan?' I asked.

He pursed his lips. 'Just thought you might like a drink. You don't object, do you?' I shook my head. 'Dr Finlay intimated that you might enjoy one.'

'Well, I do. I'm just surprised. At you. At it. I do believe you're starting to trust us.' I held the bottle up, swished the alcohol about. 'I take it this is very definitely against the law. There hasn't been a repeal of prohibition, has there?'

'No. Of course not. We make it ourselves.'

I took another mouthful.

While I was incapacitated, Patricia leant forward. 'We?'

'Uh, yeah.'

'We who?'

'Does it matter? Enjoy. There's not a lot of it about. And it's killed no one yet.'

'I like the "yet".'

'It's rocket fuel, Duncan,' I whispered.

He nodded.

In half an hour we were all drunk, and, as they do, tongues began to loosen. Duncan began to tell us a little more about his island. It wasn't a question of us – me – wheedling it out of him; he wanted to talk, and I fancied the alcohol had been his way into it, that he could say to us under the influence what he didn't have the confidence to talk about in real life. He was a big handsome fella, but he had the inert shyness of an islander, brought up to keep his own counsel. Now his mind was being asked to cope with things bigger than island minds were meant to, and he needed to talk it through in order to sort it out for himself. He started hesitantly – slow, slow, quick quick, slow, dancing around the facts, ignoring chronology, speaking as the ideas entered his head.

'There are six of us. Were seven.' He rubbed his hands quickly over his face, as if he were washing. 'Mickey. Mickey Murtagh. God rest his soul.'

'Seven what?'

'Seven of us as liked to drink a bit. We used to hang out together in Jack McGettigan's back in the old days.' He laughed suddenly. 'The old days. Last year or two ago. Then Jack saw the light, and the Council saw the dark, and suddenly there was nothing to drink any more. So we set about making our own. Took a while to perfect. We had some supplies of the old stuff set aside, thinking something like a ban was on the cards, so we've mixed and matched a bit. Not much of the old stuff left now.' He took another swipe at the bottle, then passed it back to me. 'That day Mickey Murtagh made a run for it – took us by surprise. The search 'n' all. I had to get out of there pretty quick, up into the woods to dismantle our stuff before they found it and thought about doing the same to us.' He shook his head sadly. 'Poor Mickey. Never was much of a swimmer, but still tried to save Mary. A good man, Mickey.'

I nodded sagely. 'Seemed like it.'

'I never met him,' said Trish.

'A good man,' Duncan repeated. He let his eyes linger on Patricia again; before, it had annoyed me, but now I took it for what it was, friendly eyes on a pretty woman.

'So there's a gang of youse meet up somewhere and drink,' said Patricia.

'Aye. Talk and yitter about all this, and what we can do about it.'

'And what can you do about it?'

He gave a sad laugh and rubbed his sleeve across his mouth. He said a quick sorry. 'Old habits die hard.' Patricia smiled. 'What can we do? Not much. Sad, really. Our leading light sails off and drowns. The most constructive thing we've done so far is a bit of vandalism on a church.'

The graffiti, of course. 'You did that?'

'Not me, no. I can spell. Willie . . . well, he was never one for the education. It was stupid anyway.'

'I got the Mary Reilly bit, but the letters, what was that all about? The AF . . . whatever.'

'AFLR,' said Duncan, spelling them out with a finger in the air. 'Obvious, if you think about it, Dan. Alcoholic Front for the Liberation of Wrathlin.'

He let it sit for a moment. And then we all dissolved. It was a wonderful thought.

Patricia, having drunk marginally less, recovered first. 'Are you serious, really? This Alcoholic F . . . thing?' she asked.

Duncan gave a little shrug. 'More serious than we should be. Less serious than we could be. I mean, what are we? A teacher. A doctor . . .'

'Dr Finlay,' I said.

He nodded. 'Anyway, half a dozen of us who aren't very happy about the way things are turning out.'

'Do youse believe in Christine?' Patricia asked.

'Believe?'

'You know what I mean. That she's the Messiah.'

'No. I don't think we do.'

'You don't think, or you don't?'

'We don't think. Maybe we should be the Agnostic Alcoholic Front. The point is, it's not Christine that we object to. It's what has grown up around her. The laws, the prohibition, the intimidation. The dictatorial nature of the Council, of Father White in particular.'

'But not Father Flynn?' I asked.

'Flynn's heart's in the right place, if you'll excuse the expression, but he's not a born leader. He's too nice. White's adept at playing people off against each other, at making promises, at pushing through repressive laws.'

'I thought you islanders were a really tight-knit bunch,' I said, 'but White's only been here a few months and he already seems to be running the show.'

'What gave you the impression he's only been here a few months?'

'I . . . well, I don't know. I thought . . . someone told me that he'd only recently arrived. I had the impression that he'd only recently converted to the McCooeys.'

Duncan shook his head. 'You couldn't be more wrong. Father White's been in on it from the start. Sure wasn't he priest here for thirty years before Flynn ever came back?'

'Seriously?'

'Yes! He retired about five years ago. Flynn came to replace him. Flynn had the original visions about the Messiah, but he didn't know what to do with them, who to tell . . . eventually he told White, and that's when all this really took off. It was White who worked at it, moulded the visions, moulded Christine, into the concept we live by today. Well, some of us live by.'

'But wasn't there a priest that came out here from the mainland, and got converted, then didn't go back? I mean, just a few months ago? I'm sure someone told me that. I thought it was you.'

'No. Definitely not. I mean, there may have been one across for a weekend or something, but Flynn and White have been pretty nervous about anyone in their trade getting in on the secret. They haven't given much away.'

Ignored for too long, Little Stevie suddenly let out a wail. It seemed to shake Duncan's confident flow. He set the bottle down at his feet as Patricia leant over to see to the child. 'I'm sorry,' he said, 'I've been running off at the mouth a bit.'

'Nonsense,' said Patricia, lifting the child from the cot, 'you've just been getting a bit off your mind, and opening our eyes a wee bit. It's what we needed.'

'Thank you. But I don't want to give you the . . . y'know, the wrong impression about our wee group. I mean, we're not really a . . . *rebels* or anything. It's mostly hot air. The sum total of what we've done is daub a slogan on a church wall. We wouldn't harm a hair on Christine's head, y'know? We just enjoy a drink.'

'Of course you wouldn't,' Patricia said.

'But things are getting more serious,' I pointed out.

'Aye. I know.'

'And sooner or later someone might have to do something in the way of standing up for what's right.'

Duncan nodded. He looked at his watch. 'Well,' he said, 'school in the morning.' He stood up, crossed to the door and slipped his coat off the hook. 'Thank you,' he said, suddenly awkward again. 'It was a lovely meal.'

'Our pleasure,' said Trish.

'Come again,' I said.

We followed him up the hall. He lingered by the door. 'Ahm,' he said, his gaze falling between us, 'I'd appreciate if you kept what I've said under your hat. I mean, not for my own sake, but for the others. We're, uh, just a bit of a joke really. Except no one has much of a sense of humour any more.'

I patted him on the arm. 'Don't worry, mate, we won't breathe a word. Besides, who would believe a name like the Alcoholic Front?'

He smiled grimly. 'Aye, I know. Stupid, eh?'

Patricia gave him a little hug. I stood by, without hitting him. Then I walked him to the Land-Rover. Patricia turned back in with Little Stevie.

'You okay to drive?'

'Who knows? It's a fairly straight road, but for the bends.'

I nodded. We shook hands. When I went back in Patricia was sitting in front of the fire with Little Stevie on her knee. 'Gone?' she asked. I nodded. 'Odd big lump, isn't he?' she said.

'I suppose. Yeah.'

'You know what the gossip is down in the church?'

'I don't particularly care.'

'That he's Christine's dad.'

'Jesus Christ,' I said.

'And Joseph,' added Patricia as I checked to see if there was anything left in Duncan's bottle.

33

During the night an intruder broke into the cottage. He made his way to our bedroom, curled back the quilt, then sliced off the top of my head and filled my skull with quick-setting cement. Then he stuck barbed wire up my nose and nailed my head, naturally enough, to the headboard. Patricia slept through it all.

The morning was one of the brightest and loudest since the creation of the universe. Even with the curtains closed.

Patricia stood at the foot of the bed, hair sleep-tousled, eyes dark, skin grey. Her dressing gown hung open. Little Stevie guzzled at a bottle. She kicked the bed's wooden frame. Earthquake. 'You never learn, do you?' she screamed quietly.

'Uuuuugh.'

'You only have yourself to blame.'

My head was revolving at 72 rpm, an unfashionable speed. 'Thanks,' I croaked, 'I need to hear that.'

'You *knew* how strong it was.'

'I can cope.'

'Aye, you look like it.'

I hid back under the quilt. 'Am I complaining?' I whined, from the safety of the cocoon. Staying up to finish the bottle had been a mistake. Like the Bay of Pigs.

I peeked out. She had that mock sympathetic look. 'Do you want a hair of the dog?' *Evil* smile. 'Do you want me to see if there's any left in the bottle?'

'There's none left.'

'Do you want something to eat, then?'

'No.'

'A fried egg sandwich?'

'Patricia. This isn't funny. Please go away.'

And she did. She rumbled about the house for a twenty-minute eternity and then shouted something about going down to the church for another social. She asked me to do the dishes from the night before. I gave an inconclusive grunt. The door slammed. The cottage seemed to vibrate and I tensed, ready for the ceiling to come down on my head. It didn't.

When I was sick for the fourth time that morning I made the promise. I was never drinking again.

It had worked well in the past.

Some time around four in the afternoon I began to get some feeling back in my legs.

I raised myself cautiously from the bed, then tested my feet out on the floor. I managed a few Bambi steps, then sat again. Then a few more. A seat. Then some more. In ten minutes I was back to the svelte fighting machine of the night before. After that, and holding my nose, I bent and lifted the basin from the side of the bed. I took it into the bathroom and washed it out. Yum. Then to the kitchen and a can of Diet Pepsi. And a chocolate digestive.

After letting that lot settle I pulled on my tracksuit again and took a dander round the accessible parts of the garden, breathing deeply of the fresh sea air all the time. Refreshing. Dizzy-making, but refreshing. I looked in on the hedgehog, but with all the dead leaves in the box it was difficult to determine if he was at home.

I was just turning back into the cottage when a Land-Rover eased its way down the lane and pulled up. The driver's door opened, banged shut, but for a moment, with the undergrowth/overgrowth, I couldn't see who it was; I heard a smoker's ragged cough, the flick-flick-flick of a cigarette lighter in a strong breeze, and then Dr Finlay's head appeared at the front gate. The rest of him too.

'Ah,' I said, which wasn't one of my better opening lines but the best I could do with a numb tongue.

'Starkey,' he said, 'I hoped you might be here.' He pushed the gate open and walked slowly up the path, shaking and flicking the lighter the whole way. When he drew level with me he gave a big tut and thrust it back into his pocket. 'Bloody waste of money,' he said. 'Do you have a light?'

'You didn't come all this way for a light, Doctor?'

'Don't be daft,' he said gruffly, stopping before me and holding his cigarette up expectantly. It was a self-rolled job, untidily done. I nodded back to the house. 'If you can work out how to turn the cooker on without burning the place down, you're welcome to a light.'

He followed me into the kitchen and fiddled with a ring. I hadn't touched a cooker in fifteen years and I wasn't about to start now. I worshipped at the altar of Pot Noodle and Microwave. And with Patricia I'd no choice.

It only took a few moments for him to get his cigarette lit; he straightened slowly, took a deep suck, held it, then puffed out contentedly.

'So, what's up, Doc?' I asked. He looked as if he hadn't heard the line before. Which was strange, considering the number of rabbits about. I tapped my skull. 'The head's all healed, if that's what you're here for. And the baby's away to town with the wife. And doin' fine.'

'No, no,' he said, 'it's not your health that concerns me. Or the family's.'

'And if you're here to recruit me for the Alcoholic Front for the Liberation of Wrathlin, I'm afraid you're too late. I'm going to sign on with the Pioneers just as soon as I get rid of the shakes enough to write my name.'

He blew a cloud in my direction. I waved it away with my hand.

'Aye,' he said, 'Duncan told me he'd told you about that foolishness. Pay no heed to him, Starkey, it's just a joke that got out of hand.'

'I know. You're just drinking buddies.'

'That's the sum of it.'

'Prone to a bit of vandalism.'

'That wasn't my idea.'

'I didn't think it was. So to what do I owe the pleasure?'

'I have a letter for you.' He reached inside his anorak and withdrew an envelope. 'It's from Mary Reilly's mother.'

I took it from him. I shook my head. I knew instinctively what it was. She was backing out of our deal now that Mary was dead. I couldn't be of any more use to her, so the bargain was off. I tried hard not to feel too despondent. It wasn't as if I was ever going to drink again anyway. 'The old cow didn't have the guts to come and tell me herself.'

'The old cow hung herself last night.'

'Oh.'

'Oh. Indeed.'

I looked at the envelope. It suddenly felt cold in my hand. It was a suffocation-blue airmail envelope. Most of my name was written on the front in pencil: DAN STARKY.

'Hung herself?'

'Aye. A woman who looks in on her from time to time found her this morning. She'd been dead for quite a while. A day, anyway. Hanging from a wooden beam in the kitchen. She used a pair of tights. Brown ones. From a different era. There wasn't even a run in them.'

'God.'

'Aye. Well. What can you say? Her only daughter dead. Ostracised by most of the people here. Nothing to live for. And all she left was a letter for you.'

I turned it over in my hand. 'Shouldn't you give it to someone else? The police or something?'

'There are no police.'

'The law, then. Father Flynn.'

Dr Finlay shook his head mournfully. 'There's no law, either, son.'

I waved the envelope in front of him. 'Won't people be wondering what . . . ?'

'If they knew about it, I dare say. We'd most of the Council round to see the corpse. But I thought it better to keep the letter to myself.'

'The woman who found it didn't . . . ?'

'Never noticed it. Too shaken up by the body.'

'So,' I said, and looked at the envelope again.

'Up to you now, son,' said Dr Finlay. He tapped his cigarette and a spray of ash flittered to the floor. We both watched it. He didn't apologise.

I tore the envelope and withdrew a folded single sheet of wispy-thin airmail notepaper. I unfolded it. The handwriting was spidery, starting flush with the top left-hand corner but descending in a rough diagonal across the page.

'You'll want to read it to me,' the doctor said.

'Of course.'

There wasn't much to it. But there was enough, after a suitable period of respectful mourning, to brighten my day and change my priorities.

Dear Mr Starky, – so this is the end, and at the end of it all, all I have to do is finish my half of our agreement. Go to Mulrooney's field. Fresh dug bit in the corner on the coast side. Buried there. Thank you for agreeing to speak up for Mary, I know it would have helped. It was very good of you.

I looked up at Dr Finlay. 'To the point,' I said.

He nodded. 'What's this agreement?'

'She promised to track down some drink for me if I spoke up on behalf of her daughter.'

'That was a bit mercenary.'

'I was a bit thirsty. It isn't the whole story, Doctor. Ask my wife. Sometimes I've to hide my own good nature under the guise of a commercial transaction.' The doctor nodded doubtfully. 'Besides, I thought you'd sympathise – particularly if you're drinking that muck Duncan was hiking around last night. It's lethal.'

'Yes. Well. It's an acquired taste.'

'Arsenic is an acquired taste too.' I held up the sheet. 'But this, this is a treasure map. Buried in a field, Jack McGettigan's horde of booze. Jesus, there must be tonnes of it.'

Finlay wasn't so sure. He took the letter from me and quickly ran his eyes over it. 'Why go to the trouble of burying drink?' he asked. 'You'd be better pouring it down the drain.'

'Unless you weren't quite certain about the future and needed something to fall back on. I'm sure Jesus did the odd bit of joinery when the alms collection didn't come up to scratch.'

He sucked in. His eyes closed slightly, letting out only a cool, appraising light. He blew smoke down his nose. 'You're very flippant about things, Starkey, aren't you?'

I shrugged. 'What can I say? I had the impression first time we met that you were less than devoted to the McCooeys. I didn't think you'd mind.'

'I'm not devoted to the McCooeys. That doesn't mean I'm not devoted to Christine.'

'Of course.' It was becoming a familiar excuse, or defence.

We were both silent for a while. He puffed again. He was

thinking. He looked at the letter again, then handed it back to me.

'She was a daft old bird,' he said.

'A blue bird now.'

'Aye.'

'And she enjoyed a drink. You could tell that from looking at her.'

'I suppose she did.'

'But she wasn't a member of your wee group?'

The doctor shook his head. 'It was a men's group.'

'But she knew where the booze was hidden, and youse didn't.'

'Well, that remains to be seen.'

'True. And there's only one way to find out.' I waited for him to say something, but he just kept a steady, thoughtful gaze upon me. I said it for him. 'We should go take a look. Are you game?'

He shifted uncomfortably from one foot to the other. 'The way things are now it would be madness,' he said. 'Father White and his crowd are all riled up. We get caught with a load of booze there's no telling what they'll do to us. Look what they tried on Mary Reilly.'

'I asked you if you were game.'

He sniffed up. Took another drag on his cigarette, the last, then threw the butt into the sink where it hissed in a soaking cereal bowl. We locked eyes for a long moment, then a tongue darted unconsciously out and licked his lips. His own tongue, of course. It was The Sign. He was hooked.

34

'I think youse are mad,' Patricia said from the doorway.

The four of us had shovels. Me, Dr Finlay, Duncan Cairns, Willie Nutt. I hadn't met Willie Nutt before. He was small and squat, his hair was close-cropped and he had the jangly eyes of a man who enjoyed living up to his own name. Both names, in fact. He had been responsible for the graffiti at the church. He kept a bottle of the AFLR's poison in his pocket and from time to time took a long slug. It didn't seem to affect him at all. We all refused when he offered it round.

As we climbed into Dr Finlay's Land-Rover, Patricia shook her head again. 'What's the *point*?'

Willie Nutt put his head out of the window. 'I haven't had a pint of Harp in eight months,' he said. '*That*'s the point.'

She moved around to the driver's door. 'You're only asking for trouble. Doctor – surely you see the stupidity of this.'

Dr Finlay smiled sympathetically. 'Of course I do, dear,' he said, and pulled the door shut.

She hurried round the front, catching me as I put one foot into the vehicle. 'Dan?'

'What?'

'Promise me one thing.' She grabbed my arm, then brushed her lips across my cheek.

'What?'

'If you find it, the drink, don't bring it all back here. We're in enough trouble.'

'I'm not stupid, Patricia.'

'Well, what do you intend to do with it?'

'Drink it, of course.'

'Every last drop,' said Willie Nutt, laughing.

'This isn't funny,' said Patricia.

Finlay started the engine. I gave my wife a loving shrug, then looked at my companions. With the doors closed and the windows up, I became suddenly aware of a strange, unappetising smell.

Finlay kept the lights off. The moon winked out from between storm clouds as we bumped carefully along the lane. The bumps could have been pot-holes or rabbit skulls. Willie Nutt sat in the back beside Duncan, softly laughing to himself and sipping.

'Is he wise?' I whispered to the doctor.

'Wise enough.' He looked up at Willie in the mirror.

Willie caught his eye, leant forward. 'I've betrayed Christine,' he said.

I looked at him. I didn't know what to say.

'I'm Judas,' he said.

I looked at him still.

He held up his bottle. 'And this is Judas's carry-out.'

He cackled once and sat back. I glanced at Duncan, but he wasn't listening. He was staring out into the darkness, his face shadowed save for a hint of white where he bit down on his lip.

'He's not wise,' I said to the doctor.

'Wise enough,' said the doctor.

I looked back again. 'You okay, Duncan?'

Duncan nodded absently. 'Sure.'

'Thirsty?'

He cracked a little. 'Aye.'

'Good.'

I nodded at Willie. 'So what do you do for a living?'

He gave a gap-toothed smile. 'What'dya think?'

I'd pretty much guessed already. 'Does it involve fish?'

'Aye.'

'Catching them?'

'Smoking them.'

'You smoke fish?'

'Aye. And cigarettes.'

'Which do you prefer?'

'Well, I don't lie back with a smoked herring in me gob after sex. He-he-heh.'

Finlay glanced back. 'Since when did you start having sex, Willie?'

'He-he-heh,' said Willie and snuggled down in his seat.

We drove in silence for about five minutes. There was no other traffic. Then Finlay nodded forward. 'It's only up the road here,' he said.

'This Mulrooney that owns the field. He'd know the drink was there, wouldn't he?' I asked.

'I don't know,' said Finlay.

'We can hardly ask him,' said Duncan.

'But it's not likely someone can bury the entire contents of a bar in one of your fields and you not know anything about it,' I said. 'He may be keeping guard.'

Finlay shook his head. 'Gerry Mulrooney is eighty-nine if he's a day and is mostly away with the fairies. You could build forty-eight bungalows in his front garden and he mightn't notice.'

'Oh.'

'So we're not likely to be disturbed,' he continued, 'at least not by him.'

'He-he-heh,' heheed Willie Nutt from behind.

'*He*'s already disturbed,' I said.

Finlay shook his head. 'Leave him be. He's as sound as a pound. He just enjoys his own company.'

The doctor pulled the car into an open gateway and then we trundled slowly along the edge of a field. When he stopped the vehicle and switched the engine off we were enveloped by the sound of angrily crashing waves. Spits of sea and rain stung us as we clambered out. At least the noise of it all would disguise our digging. About three hundred yards back up on the brow of the hill sat Mulrooney's farm. There was a light in one window.

Finlay produced a torch from beneath his seat and shone it around the corner of the field where it dipped towards the sea. The grass, knee length everywhere else, was noticeably shorter here, but that was to be expected with the sea salt and wind.

'I'm sorry, I only have the one torch,' Finlay said, 'but we should spread out along here, look for . . .'

'Look for this?' Willie Nutt shouted.

'Shhhh,' Duncan hissed nervously.

Willie had tramped some twenty yards back, unnoticed. His diminutive frame was almost lost in the dark, but as we hurried towards him we could see that he was standing by an untidy scar cut into the grass with a low mound of earth at its centre, like a scab.

*   *   *

Finlay clapped Willie on the back. 'You have a nose for alcohol, young William,' he said.

Duncan shook his head. 'Jackie didn't disguise it very well.'

'He's been careless because he's been nervous,' said the doctor.

We unslung the spades and stood on either side of the mound, each of us waiting for another to plunge the blade into the soft earth. The wind whipped through us. It was unpleasant business.

Willie Nutt offered his bottle round again.

We weren't that cold.

'Party time just around the corner, boys,' Finlay said finally and plunged his spade into the mound.

'Digging up our own pub,' said Willie, following suit. 'Kegs and kegs and kegs of beer.'

'I'm going to set a keg up in my back room,' said Duncan.

'I'm looking for a fine Irish whiskey,' said Dr Finlay, heaving his first shovelful carelessly behind. 'Black Bush. And a nice Guinness.'

'Strongbow cider,' I said. I set shovel to soil. It slid easily into the wet ground. 'I haven't had it for years. I've a real taste for it now. The apples. Worst hangover in the world, cider, but it's worth it.'

'A child's drink,' said Finlay.

'Kegs and kegs and kegs and kegs,' said Willie Nutt. And added, 'He-he-heh.' As a catchphrase it hardly dazzled, but it was not unendearing, and certainly preferable to the smell of smoked fish.

'Old Jack'll get a right shock if he sees the dark again,' said Duncan, 'and comes looking for it.'

'Serve him right,' said Willie, thrusting his spade into the black earth again. Soon the soil was flying backwards.

After a short while we needed a rest. It had been an undisciplined rush and we were already puffing. I rubbed my hand across my brow. Sweating hard despite the cold. I wasn't used to physical exertion. My muscles were already aching, despite my weekly press-up.

'Deeper than I thought,' said Duncan.

'Ach, not that much further,' said Finlay, 'and then a wee whiskey.'

Duncan sounded a note of caution. 'People are bound to notice the smell of alcohol. On your breath tomorrow.'

Willie stopped digging, spat. 'So?'

'We need a supply of breath fresheners,' I said with the confident authority of a professional, 'so people won't be suspicious.'

'People will get suspicious if we suddenly start buying breath fresheners,' said Duncan, resting his own blade for a moment.

'Ach pish,' said Willie Nutt and thrust his spade into the soil again. 'Breath fresheners!'

He wasn't the sort of man who had time for anything fresh. Besides, a quick gargle with the rotgut he was drinking would kill any unwanted odours. A bath in it wouldn't do him any harm either.

Clink.

Metal blade on something solid.

'Hallelujah!' exclaimed Willie.

Clink.

Duncan, about eight feet further along, hit something as well. He let out a whoop. 'We found it! The sly old sod did bury it!'

'You didn't believe me,' I said.

'I believed you, Dan,' said Finlay. 'I didn't believe Old Mother Reilly. But now I'm prepared to kiss her sweet blue lips.'

Yuck, I thought.

As we began to scrab away the remaining soil we began to see little glints of silver – but it didn't feel like keg metal. Willie, the most industrious of us all, dropped his spade behind him and stepped down into the shallow trench we had created. He knelt and pushed away handfuls of soil with his chubby fingers. Then he felt along the surface. The space he'd cleared was maybe three feet across. He searched for the edges.

He looked up at us where we stood leaning on our spades, steadying ourselves against the wind. We were keen to discover, but not keen enough to discover first. There is something eerie about dark holes on stormy nights. The rain had grown heavier and was cascading steadily into the trench, causing it to sludge up. 'What is it, Willie?' Duncan said urgently.

Willie shook his head. 'Like tarpaulin, silver tarpaulin. Thick as hell. Heh, bastard's wrapped the booze up tight in it. We'll have to dig right down the sides till we find the join. Less you've got something'll cut through it, Doc?'

Finlay shook his head. 'Not here. Maybe at home. I never thought.'

'Who could think of it?' said Duncan. He peered at the tarpaulin.

The rain and the digging had made the sides slippery and he was careful not to lean too far forward. 'How long do you think it will take, to dig down?'

Willie gave a little shrug. 'Not long. If we keep at it. No way of telling how deep it goes. But it can't be that far down. '

Duncan cast a nervous glance back towards the farm on the hill. 'Maybe we should leave it,' he said. 'Come back another night. Earlier.' He peered at his watch. 'It's four already. Soon we'll be stuck with all the booze and it'll be too bright to hide it. We should come back.'

'Aye,' said Willie, 'bollocks.'

He had a point. 'Duncan,' I said, 'we're nearly there. If we leave it now the trench'll only fill up with water and the job'll be twice as hard.'

'Maybe we should just leave it altogether.'

'You're getting cold feet, Duncan,' said Finlay.

'Cold and wet feet.'

'Then let's get the job finished, and then we'll bathe those poor feet of yours in whiskey.' He brandished his shovel again. 'Okay? It won't take long.'

Duncan lifted his shovel reluctantly. 'Aye. Okay. I suppose. Let's get on with it then. But let's hurry.'

The dig was on again.

This time, after half an hour, we each took a hefty swig of Willie Nutt's bottle. We were miserable, cold, tired, sopping. But the home fires were soon burning.

The soil was coming away very easily, but the more we tore at it the more Somme-like the conditions underfoot became. If we'd been kids, we'd have loved it. But we were grown men with a drink problem and it was no laughing matter.

And then we reached the bottom. Willie, of course, struck first. Blade on solid stone or rock. Again he dropped his spade and scrabbed away final handfuls of oozy mud. He picked up something and smoothed as much dirt as he could off it.

'What is it?' asked Duncan.

'Just a brick,' said Willie. He examined it briefly then tossed it in Duncan's direction.

Duncan ducked. 'Watch it,' he said.

Willie bent down again and, with his hands, began to trace, then dig, along his side of the trench, revealing as he went brick after brick securing the end of the silver tarpaulin.

'Jesus,' said Duncan, 'it's about bloody time. My hands are going to fall off.'

'Ach,' said Finlay, 'we're there now, aren't we?'

He carefully stepped out from his side of the tarpaulin and half slid in beside Willie and Duncan on theirs. I joined them too.

We paused for a moment, we four rebels, and smiled at each other. Then we bent and lifted the remaining bricks and threw them behind us. Willie finished first and started to lift the tarpaulin.

'Hey!' said the doctor.

Willie snapped round.

'Let's do this with a bit of style, our Willie. It's not every day you discover buried treasure.' He rubbed his hands together. 'Now, we each take hold of the tarp, and on the count of three, we throw it back. And then we crack open one of the finest alcohols known to man, the old Black Bush, and thank the Lord for watching over us.'

'Amen to that,' said Duncan.

'Yes, indeedy,' said Willie.

We took hold.

'One,' said Finlay.

'Two,' said Finlay.

Deep breath.

'Three,' said Finlay.

Up and away flew the tarpaulin, shimmering in a darting shaft of moonlight.

And our feet gave way in the tramped trenched mud as we scrambled back in panic. Down came the jumble of bodies, engulfing us in the rotting dead.

We screamed, louder than any wind, and tore at each other in desperation.

35

The day didn't break. There was no fracture of the night. The morning light oozed through the mist like sour cream from a depressed sponge.

Damp. Cold. Shivery. We sat in the Land-Rover, lost in thought, waiting for the light. We three. Dr Finlay drummed anxiously on the wheel. Duncan, beside him, nails bitten to the quick, stared ahead; I lay in the back, chipping the mud from my jeans. No words were exchanged. Lost in our own nightmares. Willie Nutt had run away. Out into the dark. Screaming.

In the scramble out of the trench Finlay had dropped the torch, and nobody was prepared to go and rummage amongst the dead for it. I had the memory only of hollow eyes and rigid bone and the crazy death smile of a decaying head thrown up at me by the avalanche of remains. Of scrambling up the side of the trench and feeling a hand grab my leg and pull me back and screaming myself and kicking out and then hearing the shout of pain and fear and realising that it was Duncan grabbing at me in his panic and not the living dead pulling me down to hell. The realisation did not halt me; there was no helping hand for him, nor for Dr Finlay, older, less agile, clawing at the slippery sides, eyes bulging, his professional familiarity with death of no service to him. I ran and threw myself through the hedge into the next field, ignoring, welcoming even, as a confirmation of life, the tear of thorn and bramble, the sting of nettle.

I lay for ten minutes, curled, trying to hear above the wind and the rain and my laboured breath. It was the doctor who gathered himself first, calling out, 'Duncan? Are you there?' in a shaky voice. 'Dan, are you there? Willie, are you okay? Can any of youse hear me?' And Duncan emerged from the grass not fifteen yards from me and I rose too and we worked our way silently back through the hedge to Finlay, leaning ashen-faced on the bonnet of the Land-Rover.

'Jesus,' was all we managed between us for a while, then we sought the poor comfort of the interior of the car. Daylight would provide answers to questions we scarcely dared think about. It wasn't much more than an hour to wait, but it stretched interminably; time had slowed . . . slowed . . . slowed until with the greying light we creakily climbed from the vehicle and stretched, an unpleasant stretch that emphasised our dampness.

'Bloody hell,' Dr Finlay said, his first words in some time. He looked older already, haggard, haunted.

'Bloody Mother Reilly,' I said.

'Aye,' said Finlay.

'That's what I like to see in an older woman,' I said, 'her sense of humour still intact. I'm glad her neck isn't.'

Finlay turned as Duncan joined us. 'You all right, son?' he asked.

Duncan nodded morosely and looked at his watch. 'I'll have to go soon,' he said. 'What're we going to do?'

'Take a look,' said Finlay, nodding across at the trench.

'Naturally,' I added.

'Must we?' said Duncan.

'We must,' said Finlay grimly, and stepped forward.

'Can't we just leave them?' Duncan said.

Finlay ignored him. 'It's too late for that, mate,' I said, and moved after the doctor. Reluctantly, Duncan followed.

The doctor stood at the edge of the trench, looking down, shaking his head. We joined him on either side, and were soon shaking our heads too. It was a mess. Human spaghetti, a mixture of the caved-in long-dead and the rotting newly dead, oozing together in the autumnal mud. Six bodies. Twelve feet, at any rate. Two of them, the bodies, not the feet, it was immediately apparent, were those of Mickey Murtagh and Mary Reilly.

Finlay stepped down into the trench. 'I'll need some help,' he said, looking back up.

I nodded and stepped down. Duncan stayed where he was. 'What're you doing?' he said, averting his eyes from the corpses.

'We're going to have to lift them out,' said the doctor, rolling up his sleeves, 'get them separated as best we can.'

'But why . . . shouldn't we leave them be . . . I mean . . . for forensics or whoever deals with . . . ?'

Finlay's head whipped round. 'Will you snap out of it, man!' he roared. 'No one is coming to sort this out! We need to know who these people are, and how they got here. We need to know the truth.' He shook his head, tutted, turned back to the corpses. 'For God's sake, Starkey, tell him, tell him to get back to the real world.'

The surreal world, actually, but he had a point. Duncan wanted to practise what I had preached, but not practised, which was hiding in bed until everything went away. 'He's right, Duncan,' I said, 'we have to find out for ourselves what happened. Nobody else is going to do it for us. Come on down and give us a hand – I mean, they're only dead bodies. They can't do you any harm.'

'Aye, you didn't feel that way last night.'

'It scared the shit out of all of us, Duncan, but it's different now. Come on down. Eh?'

'I don't like this at all,' Duncan said, but he carefully dropped down into the trench, steadying himself for a moment against me while his feet found their proper level in the mud. His nose curled up in disgust. 'They stink.'

And they did. They were gag-makingly rotten. Willie Nutt's aroma would have served them as an underarm deodorant, had their underarms not largely oozed away.

Murtagh and Mary were no trouble. We lay them in the grass. Each time, I grabbed a leg. A cold, hard leg, slimy with mud. Murtagh was heavy with death. Mary was just heavy.

The others, beneath, were not as fresh. Duncan was sick three times. Me twice. The doctor not at all, though he choked up a couple of times. It took us half an hour to carry, coax, cajole and yes, well, pour, the remaining bodies above ground. When finally they all lay side by side, Dr Finlay set about examining them properly. Duncan and I sat back against the car and tried to make small talk. It was very small. Every once in a while our eyes drifted back to the doctor, poking into ribs, carefully pulling apart rotting clothes, nodding, tutting, spitting behind him.

Duncan looked at his watch again. 'I'll have to go soon,' he said. 'I've school to teach. If the kids arrive and I'm not there they'll be suspicious. No, not suspicious, concerned. They'll tell their parents. *They'll* be suspicious.'

'Let them be, we've a mass murder here.'

'We don't know it's murder, Dan.'

I laughed. 'What the hell do you think it is? You think that every once in a while someone walks through this field and falls into a hole and is never heard of again?'

'It's not impossible.'

'You know it is.'

'You're jumping to conclusions. It could be old Mulrooney getting protective about people going on his property.'

'Like trespassers will be executed.'

'I'm not saying it is, I'm saying it could be.'

I shook my head. Dr Finlay spat behind him again.

Duncan looked at his watch again. 'It's gone eight,' he said.

Dr Finlay trudged slowly back to us. Ignored us, in fact, for a few moments while he leant heavily on the bonnet of the Land-Rover. There were tears in his eyes. He had come looking for fine Irish whiskey and ended up to his elbows in decaying people. He had a right to cry.

I put a hand on his left shoulder. 'You okay?'

He nodded wearily. His hair was plastered to his scalp; his jaw, thickly stubbled, hung down, heavy; his lips were dry and cracked.

'So what did you find?' Duncan asked bluntly.

Finlay pushed himself off the car. He held his hands up, level with his chest, looked about him, confused for a moment. Looking for somewhere to wash them. Then he shook his head. *Silly*, he mouthed. He rubbed them down his trousers. 'Well,' he said. And stopped. And looked back at death row. He gave a slight shake of his head. 'I don't ever want to have to do that again.'

'Who would?' said Duncan.

'What about Murtagh and Mary?' I asked. 'I take it death wasn't by drowning.'

'No. Of course not. They were both shot. In the chest. Looks like a shotgun did it. They're practically hollow.'

'Oh God,' said Duncan, turning away. He took a deep breath of the sea wind. 'Oh God,' he said again.

'And the others?' I asked.

'I'd say much the same. Difficult to tell. They're pretty far gone.'

'Have you any idea at all who they were?'

'Yes and no. Two of them I can make a stab at. One's a priest of some description; at any rate, he's wearing a dog collar, although I'm not aware that we've gone short of priests in the recent past.'

'How long do you reckon he's been dead?'

'I couldn't say, not accurately. It's not really my field. Six months, maybe. The other one, he's been under a good deal longer, but at least we can put a name to him. Mark Blundell. From Belfast.'

'You recognise him?'

'If I knew someone looked like that, I'd be worried.'

'So how . . . ?'

'Detective work. And this.' He reached into the side pocket of his jacket and produced a damp-looking leather wallet. 'Inside his coat.' He handed it to me and I flipped it open. The contents were remarkably well preserved, considering where they'd been; there were a few damp spots on the three twenty-pound notes I withdrew and the half-dozen fast cash receipts were badly faded. The Visa card looked as good as new. A plastic-coated Department of the Environment identity card. A driving licence. A curling photo of a woman with two toddlers.

Duncan took the driving licence from me. He examined the photo. Shook his head. 'He's changed,' he said.

I took it back. 'Thank you, Sherlock,' I said.

Duncan turned away again. 'I hate this. All of it.'

'What do they tell you, Starkey?' the doctor asked. I could tell he already knew.

I quickly re-examined the evidence. 'That he's been underground about six years. That's how long the autobank receipts date back. That he was based at the Department of the Environment in Belfast. That he was married with a couple of kids.'

'Anything else?'

'That he was probably here on a work-related matter. The receipts are dated for early February. You don't get tourists that time of the year, do you?'

Finlay shook his head. 'Rarely. Bird watchers, mostly. Some government people during the winter, but they're always Department of Agriculture, checking we're not exceeding our fishing quotas or trying to sell us on the benefits of myxomatosis. I can't think why someone from Environment would bother with us – and get shot for his trouble, if that's not going a bit far.'

Duncan nodded across at the line of corpses. 'The other two – one of them couldn't be his wife, could it? Maybe they're all bird watchers . . . an accident . . .' He trailed off. 'We sometimes get bird watchers during the winter, maybe the two of them . . . ?'

Finlay shook his head. 'They're both male. Young adults. Eighteen. Seventeen. God love them.'

'His wife's probably still sitting at home waiting for him then,' said Duncan.

'Four people don't just disappear without anyone noticing,' I pointed out.

'Not here anyway. I'd know about it. For sure.'

'So apart from Mary and Murtagh then, we can surmise that the four others are all from the mainland.'

'Aye. I suppose.'

'And we can also surmise that Father White and his fellow travellers, having made such a public show of the search for Mary and Murtagh and finding the boat and his gun and his warrant card, are not only involved in their murder, but in the murder of four others as well.'

'Aye, it would be looking that way.'

'But what would be the bloody point?' shouted Duncan, throwing his hands up angrily. 'It's all meant to be about love and salvation. Not this.'

'Well, that's the million-dollar question, Duncan,' I said.

Finlay shook his head ruefully. 'It doesn't make sense.' He slapped his hand down on the bonnet, then bunched it up into a fist and ground it into the palm of his other hand. 'That trial, that bloody trial, was all about protecting Christine. But it wasn't about *this* . . .'

'What about the priest?' Duncan asked.

I had a pretty good idea. The Primate had been wrong. I had been right. Murdered, not converted. I said, 'If he's only been dead six months, then the chances are he was visiting and found out too much . . .'

Finlay nodded. 'That's possible. But this chap from the Environment. My God, Starkey, if he's been down there for six years – that pre-dates any thought of Christine by two years. What's the bloody point in that?'

I shrugged. There didn't have to be a point, or if there was, it was a point of no return, a point we had just passed.

The whole notion of Christine as the daughter of God had been both disturbing and mildly comical. The flight of Mary and Murtagh had elevated it to the darkly bizarre. Their presumed drowning had transformed it into tragedy. Now, with the rotting corpses, it had metamorphosed yet again: now it was a horror story, and one that clearly had not yet reached its conclusion.

A slight drop in the wind made us turn suddenly back up the field at the sound of an engine. Another Land-Rover was just turning towards us through the gate.

'Oh Jesus Christ,' wailed Duncan, 'they're going to kill us too!'

His huge frame swivelled deftly, his eyes darted about, panicked. Then he dashed the few yards from the doctor's car to the hedge. He threw himself into it, head first, then thrashed about for a few moments before finally disappearing.

Dr Finlay turned to me. He nodded down at the line of corpses. 'So what's our story?'

'I'm working on it,' I said.

36

Duncan was too far gone for us to shout after him not to worry, his big loping strides taking him over the hill and far away when all he had to face was my wife, Little Stevie, Father Flynn, Moira McCooey and the manifestation of God Almighty on earth, or indeed Christine, trundling along the track we'd made the previous night.

I recognised the dent in the side of the car first, then as it drew closer Patricia stuck her head out of the passenger window and shouted something, but it was carried away on the wind. As the priest stopped the vehicle Dr Finlay strode forward with his hands raised.

'I'd stay where you are for the moment!' he bellowed.

Flynn, his door already open, hesitated. Patricia climbed out. Christine ducked out behind her. Moira held Little Stevie in the back seat.

Finlay tried to block her path as my wife ran towards me, but she dodged him easily. I was ready for the hug. A warm embrace. I'd missed her, albeit subconsciously.

But she was coming at me too fast, was too close by the time I recognised the venom in her eyes and the black pouches beneath them. I opened my mouth. She raised her palms and gave me a huge shove. I toppled back into the sodden ground. Christine let out a *Yippee* and ran behind, laughing.

'Where the fuck have you been?' Patricia yelled.

'Trish, for God's . . .'

'I've been up all fucking night, worried to death!'

Dr Finlay put a placatory hand on her shoulder. 'Mrs Starkey . . .'

'Fuck off!' she spat, slapping it away. She kicked out at me. I scrambled away. 'You've no consideration for anyone, have you? Not for me! Not for the baby! Anything could have . . .'

Christine screamed. Shrill. A scream of innocence tarnished. We all turned. She stood by the line of corpses, her blonde hair running away behind her in the wind, her tiny face blanched.

Moira struggled out of the car and hurried across, thrusting Little Stevie into Patricia's arms as she passed. Then came Father Flynn. I jumped to my feet and with a shrug for Patricia moved down to where Dr Finlay had already lifted Christine into his arms.

'It's okay,' he whispered, holding her close, turning her head. Her eyes tracked back to the corpses.

Father Flynn stopped, stared, stood with his mouth open. He crossed himself. Twice. Then his hand went to his chin, held his jaw, as if he feared it might drop off his face. He turned helpless eyes on Dr Finlay, then on me. 'What's going on?' he whispered.

'Don't you know?' I asked.

Moira looked quickly at the rotting line-up, then lifted Christine from the doctor and carried her back to the Land-Rover. Patricia stood beside me.

Father Flynn shook his head. 'How could I . . . ? What . . . ?' Tears started to run down his cheeks. He rubbed a hand across his face. 'My God, Doctor, what has happened here?'

'Hazard a guess, Father.'

Flynn turned away, then buried his head in his hands.

Patricia, calmer now, put her hand on my arm. 'You came to dig up booze and you dug up corpses instead. That'll teach you. Is it an old cemetery or something?'

I shook my head. She hadn't really looked at the corpses properly. It hadn't entered her head that she might recognise any of them. Then it entered mine that she'd never met the fat girl before. So I introduced them. 'And you've seen Constable Murtagh before,' I said.

'Oh God,' Trish said.

Moira returned, prodded one of Mary Reilly's feet with the toe of her shoe. 'I thought she drowned,' she said simply.

I shrugged. Moira grimaced.

The doctor stepped up beside the priest. 'Frank, if you don't know anything about this, you know what this means.'

Flynn turned wary eyes on him. His shoulders seemed to have collapsed. 'I daren't think it.'

'You've thought it already, Frank. I know you have.'

'He wouldn't resort to this. He's not that bad.'

'He has. He is. Count them, Frank, six bodies.'

Father Flynn took a deep breath, threw his head back, then blew it out. His eyes seemed to implore the heavens for inspiration. 'Who're the others?'

'One's a priest.'

Flynn looked quickly back at the line-up. He bit at a lip. 'There was a young buck came across a while back. The Cardinal sent him to check up on us. He seemed a nice lad.'

'And what happened?'

Flynn gave a little shrug. 'I told him the truth. He seemed quite excited by it all. We begged him not to tell the Cardinal, but he said he had to, that his first duty was to him. I accepted that. He phoned, then I spoke to the Cardinal; he wasn't impressed. But he went home, the priest went home, I walked him down to the ferry.'

'Well, if it's him, he came back, or never left.'

'And . . . how was he . . . ?'

'Shot.'

'My God,' said the priest, and crossed himself again.

'What about Mark Blundell, Father?' I asked.

'Mark . . . ?'

'Blundell. Right at the end there – laughing boy. Worked for the Department of the Environment in Belfast. Remember him?'

Flynn shook his head. Looked from the corpse to me to Finlay and back. 'Should I?'

I handed him the government ID card. Flynn studied it intently, then glanced back at the less healthy version. He shook his head again.

'He was killed and buried here about six years ago, if that's any help.'

'I wasn't here six years ago, Dan. You know that. I was still in Crossmaheart.'

I nodded. 'So you were. That's you off the hook then.'

'I . . .'

'Joking,' I said.

The priest turned watery eyes on me. 'What about the others?' he asked quietly.

'No idea,' said Finlay, nodding at the two still unidentified corpses, a little too slim now for their rotting jeans. 'Who knows what the poor sods did? Wrong place, wrong time. Didn't believe. Or believed too much. Or in something else.'

'This is crazy,' Patricia said, hooking her arm through mine.

'Madness,' said Moira. She shook her head. 'It wasn't meant to be like this.'

'What was it meant to be like?' I asked.

She shrugged. 'It's all . . .' she began, the freezing wind causing her to hug herself tightly, 'it's all been like a dream so far. Real, but not real, do you know what I mean? Just us, *here*, nobody could touch us. I didn't really have to think about what might happen next.'

'Others were doing that,' I said.

'Not like this,' said Flynn, 'not in a million years. I don't understand *why* . . .' He shook his head miserably. 'Why would anyone want to tarnish such a *wonderful* . . . ?'

'Power,' said Dr Finlay, 'and control.'

I nodded at his side. 'This is the biggest thing since sliced bread.'

'But this is about Christine, innocence and love and . . .'

'Father,' I said, 'it may have escaped your notice, but half the deaths in the whole bloody history of the world have been about religion. It's nothing new.'

'But it . . . *felt* like something new.'

'Aye, well,' said Dr Finlay.

Flynn suddenly stamped his foot in the mud. It wasn't the greatest idea, as mud flew everywhere, but nobody complained; the priest's jaw was now set firm and there was a new and determined look in his eyes. 'Moira, we can't let Christine's name be tarnished by all this. We'll go back to town. We'll call a meeting. We'll confront Father White. Expose him. Throw him and anyone else involved in this off the island. We have to bring all of this to an end.'

He wasn't looking for a debate. He turned and strode quickly towards the Land-Rover.

'Talk about mood swings,' said Patricia. I nodded. She was an acknowledged expert on the subject.

The doctor followed him. 'Frank, let's not be too hasty. There's nothing to be gained by rushing in.'

Flynn's eyes blazed with his new-found missionary zeal. 'Either come with me, or stay here, Doctor.'

The doctor turned back to us and raised his palms in exasperation as the priest climbed behind the wheel. Then Patricia and I, plus the baby, hurried to the vehicle. Moira hesitated, shaking her head vaguely at the corpses.

'Father,' she called, 'we can't just leave them like this.'

Flynn ignored her. He started the engine.

'Come on, Moira,' Patricia shouted as she shifted Little Stevie up onto her shoulder in order to climb into the back. 'They aren't going anywhere.'

But they were. Seagulls were circling.

We decided to leave Dr Finlay's vehicle for the time being. The inside was caked with mud and little bits of rotting flesh, so we all squeezed into Father Flynn's. It was a little uncomfortable, but not as uncomfortable as having your chest shot out and the maggots holding their annual convention in your lower intestine.

Patricia told me wordlessly to hold Little Stevie. I took him. I had a little ground to make up with her. About the size of Australia. Stevie's eyes were bright and darting. I cooed at him. His ginger hair looked a little darker than I remembered, and I thought maybe there was hope for him, anyway.

'How come,' I said as Father Flynn roared towards the town, 'you lot all arrived together?'

Patricia barely opened her mouth. 'Like I say, I was worried. God knows why, for all the consideration . . .'

'Just tell me, would you?' I snapped.

'I *am* telling you,' she snapped back. 'I was worried.'

'So you ran to Father Flynn.'

'No, actually.'

'You ran to Moira, then . . .'

'No, again. They came to me.'

'They just happened to come out on a social call – like at what, eight in the morning?' I glanced at Moira, and then away, just in case Patricia's mood was more to do with a sordid revelation than . . .

'Christine told us to come,' Moira said.

I sighed.

'She did,' Moira said. 'She was up half the night. Couldn't sleep. Having nightmares. I didn't know whether it was an upset stomach or the end of the world. She kept saying she had to go to the hedgehog house. I didn't know what to do. I mean, you can't do every silly thing your child tells you, but then . . .'

'The Messiah, yeah, I know.'

'So I took her to Frank's.'

'Lucky it wasn't Father White's.'

'Frank drove us out. And a good thing too. Patricia was in a real state.'

'I was not.'

Christine stood in the front, nose pressed against the window, head shooting from side to side with the rhythm of the windscreen wipers. Dr Finlay sat behind her, holding her waist so that she wouldn't take a tumble as Flynn urged the vehicle along the narrow lanes.

Patricia touched my arm. 'I didn't know whether to say where you were, but when you didn't come back, I thought something terrible had happened, that you might be . . .'

I lifted her chin up. 'Hey. You did the right thing.'

She gave me a wee smile. A kissy-on-the-nose smile. Which I did. 'Would you have done the same, Dan, for me?' she asked.

'Well, I might have given it a couple more hours,' I said.

At the edge of town, the doctor insisted that Flynn stop the car. And the priest did, but without good grace. 'What?' he snapped impatiently.

Finlay spoke calmly. 'Frank, I know you're angry, but are you sure it's the wisest thing to just charge in and accuse Father White like this?'

'I'm not accusing him of anything. There's nothing to prove. All the evidence is there.'

'Okay, granted. But think of it. You know as well as I do that Father White isn't responsible for those deaths alone. He had help. He didn't shoot six people dead, drag their bodies out there, and then bury them. Friends, followers, disciples, call them what you will, but he had their help, and most likely they're with him now. If they can kill six . . .'

'When I inform the Council, it will take the correct . . .'

'Damn the Council, Frank! Don't you think some of them must be in on it as well?'

It was an obvious thought, but one that had not occurred to him, and for a moment Flynn's new-found determination seemed to waver. His face looked as innocent as Christine's had been before discovering the corpses. 'I would have known about it,' he said.

Finlay raised his eyebrows. 'You think so?'

Flynn started the engine again.

I put a hand on his shoulder. 'White has the capacity to kill six people. Maybe we should think about dropping the women off. And Christine.'

'He's not going to shoot Christine!'

'We stay together, Dan,' Patricia said. 'Safety in numbers.'

'I don't think you should take our baby in there.'

'*Our* baby?'

'Yes,' I said.

'Well, if he's our baby, his place is with us.'

I turned to Moira. She shook her head. 'Christine's the boss, he wouldn't dare do anything.'

I looked at Finlay. 'Looks like the troops aren't falling into line,' I said.

He opened his mouth to speak, but Christine thumped the window and gave an excited little yell. She pointed.

The town was still out of sight around the next bend, but there was a very definite funnel of thick black smoke billowing up into the air above it.

37

Father White, grinning, sweating, signalled for the school gates to be opened, then watched as Father Flynn rolled our vehicle down the slight incline.

For a few moments after he pulled on the hand-brake, all we could do was stare.

A bonfire had been lit in the yard; children, working in relays, fed the flames with armfuls of books from the schoolroom. Round about them, shouting encouragement, stood half a dozen armed men. Worst of all: Duncan, hands tied, on his knees before the fire, grubby, muddy, a nasty-looking gash on his head, the side of his face caked with blood.

'Jesus Christ,' I said.

Curling black pages swirled upward in the wind. Sparks dashed everywhere.

Flynn recovered first. He jumped angrily from behind the wheel and hurried round to confront his colleague. 'What on earth is going on?' he shouted.

Father White smiled broadly. 'We're burning filth, that's what we're doing!' He turned to the kids and clapped his hands together. 'That's it! Pile them on! Burn them up!'

Flynn looked anxiously back at us as we climbed out. Dr Finlay came round to the front of the vehicle, shaking his head in disbelief. 'You can't burn books,' he said, flatly.

'Of course we can,' snapped White, 'when they're filth!'

The doctor kicked his foot into the dirt. 'This isn't Nazi Germany.'

'Actually,' I pointed out, 'it might be.'

There was a wild look about the priest. The adrenaline had taken over, or the madness. 'We're not burning *school books*!' he exclaimed. 'We're burning this pervert's private collection! A private library of filth! Would you believe he keeps it in the classroom where any child can be exposed to it?'

Duncan, his head hanging down, spat out a mouthful of blood. 'It's not filth,' he said groggily. I'd grown to like Duncan a little bit; he didn't strike me as the type to have kiddy porn; he was a single man on a remote island, you couldn't blame him for having *some* porn even if it wasn't much more than top-shelf stuff. But somehow I doubted that White's definition of filth coincided with mine.

Flynn was becoming increasingly incredulous. 'I can't believe you've done this,' he said, trying to get past White, towards the fire, or Duncan, or both. But White stayed where he was.

'He tried to stop us, Frank!' White hissed. 'We came to tell him first thing, to do it quietly, without fuss, simply take them away, but he wasn't here. And then he arrived covered in mud like a pig in a poke and attacked us. He's a dirty stop-out and he got hurt. I'm sorry, Frank, but it's the law.'

Startled, Flynn's head snapped away from the fire. 'What law? There's no law against books, man!'

'But there is, Frank. It's Council law.'

'What?'

Father White shook his head, mock sadly. 'Things have changed, Frank. How can I say it? You're not the power you once were.'

'You're mad! There's no law about *books* . . .'

Actually, it made sense. He'd already agreed to censor television, even phones; burning books was inevitable. But it wasn't the time to point it out. Maybe Flynn was seeing the light at last. Or *a* light. He rushed suddenly forward. White, taken by surprise, froze, but Flynn ignored him, crossing instead to help Duncan to his feet. 'You're okay, son,' he said urgently.

White glowered after him, then turned, his triumphant grin soured. 'He's corrupting our children, Frank! Dirt and filth, Frank, dirt and filth!'

'He's not. He's . . . *Duncan* . . .'

I could see it in his eyes: reality bites.

Flynn had been building his own little dream world, banishing the things he didn't like, but now someone else was muscling in on his utopia and he didn't like it. He had seen corpses and a bleeding schoolteacher and burning books and he couldn't cope with it.

Duncan swayed about on weak legs. 'I didn't . . . I couldn't . . .' he mumbled.

White nodded up the steps to the school where two of the men who'd been amongst the most enthusiastic members of the hunting party stood watching the altercation, their guns hanging lazily by their sides. They moved down the steps and took up positions on either side of Father Flynn.

The look of surprise on the priest's face was, well, surprising. In a second it was usurped by indignation as they each took hold of one of his arms. Duncan sank back to his knees. 'What *on earth* do you think you're doing?' Father Flynn demanded, pulling away from them quite easily. The gunmen hesitated, looking back at Father White for guidance. Flynn bent once again to Duncan.

White snapped his fingers. 'Take Duncan up to the church. Now. Frank as well.'

One of the men swung his gun down off his shoulder and poked it into Flynn's back. The other pulled Duncan roughly to his feet. Patricia slipped her free hand into mine and squeezed. Little Stevie seemed mesmerised by the fire. Christine had already run off into the schoolroom. Moira, with a concerned glance at Duncan, gave pursuit.

Flynn straightened, turned, shook his head disdainfully, then pushed the gun out of the way. He glared at the gunman. 'You wouldn't dare.'

'Please, Frank,' said White, his voice a little softer, 'go up to the church. Once we're done here I'll come up and explain everything to you.'

Flynn stuck out an accusing finger. 'You mean you'll explain about the bodies in Mulrooney's field?'

If he expected it to have dramatic impact, his expectations were sadly misplaced. It barely registered on the priest, and not at all upon the gunmen.

'If you wish,' White said matter-of-factly, as if he had been explaining a fine point of scripture to an intending communicant.

The gunmen began nudging the priest and the teacher towards the school gates. Flynn resisted for another few moments, then threw up his hands with an exaggerated sigh of resignation. 'Very well,' he cried. 'Have it your way. You just call the Council together, and we'll see about this. It's madness!'

As they passed, Dr Finlay stepped forward to take a closer look at Duncan's injury, but the gunman between them blocked his way;

the prisoners continued their march to the church. The doctor shook his head helplessly.

Then it was White's turn to point. 'Go on home, Doctor,' he growled, 'you're not needed here.'

'He needs treatment.'

'No, Doctor, he doesn't,' White said firmly. 'Perhaps it's you that needs the treatment. Why don't you go back to that little surgery of yours and fix yourself a little drink? Or organise another devastating attack by the Alcoholic Front for the Liberation of Wrathlin?' Finlay glanced after Duncan, but the teacher was already out of earshot. 'Pathetic!' jeered the priest. 'Go on home, Doctor. You might care to get rid of your supplies of alcohol before we come visiting, eh?'

Finlay held the priest's gaze for several moments. Then he nodded to himself, and started walking towards the gate. He didn't look at me as he passed.

Patricia, at my side, leant forward and caught Christine as she marched towards the fire with an armful of books. Two of the books fell to the ground.

Father White turned at the same time. 'Ah! That's my girl.'

Moira appeared behind her daughter. 'She's not your girl.'

'She knows what's right, Moira. Just look at her.'

'She's a kid,' Moira spat, 'she likes burning things.'

Patricia retrieved the books from the grass. Christine threw five others onto the fire. Then she clapped her hands and ran back into the schoolhouse. It was a big fire, and the kids were still trooping in and out. Duncan had a lot of books.

My wife rolled her eyes as she showed me the covers.

'So what exactly is your complaint about these, Father?' I asked.

'Filth,' he said.

'*The Lord of the Rings*?'

'Filth,' he repeated.

'It's one of the great classics, Father. A story of good versus evil, in which good triumphs. How can you object to that?'

He grabbed the book from my hand and threw it onto the fire. 'Pagan filth,' he said.

I tutted. 'Someone famous once said that when you start burning books, there's no hope for civilisation.'

'Someone got it wrong. We're about saving civilisation, and saving souls. We've invested all our hopes in Christine – and it is our duty to protect her from things just like *The Lord of the Rings*. Devil's stuff, and you know it.' His hand shot out and he grabbed the other book from Patricia. 'Or how about this? *Kane and Abel*?' He brandished the thick volume above his head. 'What should we make of this? A misspelt study of the Biblical story, is it, with valuable lessons for mankind?'

I shook my head.

'No, it's more filth! Do you object to me burning this as well?'

'No, actually, you can chuck that on. But that's just the literary critic in me coming out.'

White ignored me. Patricia giggled nervously. 'I'm sorry,' she whispered. She squeezed my hand. I squeezed back. The book burned.

For a few minutes we stood and watched the bonfire. Then, as the children began finally to run out of books, they gathered round as well.

Father White, all smiles again, clapped his hands together. 'A marvellous job, children!' he proclaimed. 'Well done!' They let out a cheer. 'Now, as a special treat for all your hard work, I'm going to give you the rest of the day off school. What do you think of that?'

Another cheer went up.

'Away on home with you now. Tell your mums what good boys and girls you've been – but don't forget to come back tomorrow.'

Yelling and screaming and laughing, the kids charged out of the gate. Christine returned to her mother's side. 'Can I go and play?' she asked.

Moira, though I could tell by the look on her that she was seething, patted her daughter's head gently and spoke softly. 'Of course you can, love. Will you walk me down home first?'

Christine screwed up her face. Mock. Then nodded and smiled. She took her mother's hand.

Father White put a hand on Moira's shoulder. She shrugged it off.

'Don't be like that,' he said.

'I'll be as I like.'

'I'll come down and see you later. Explain everything. It's all quite straightforward.'

'Don't bother. I know what I saw out there.'

She spun on her heel and set off across the yard, pulling Christine with her.

With a slight shake of his head, Father White said, 'She'll come around,' to nobody in particular.

Patricia disengaged. 'I'll go after her,' she said. 'See if she's okay.'

'She's okay,' I said.

She tutted. 'Dan. You're a man.'

'What's that supposed to mean?'

'Work it out for yourself.'

She started after Moira. Little Stevie, up on her shoulder, looked back at me. I gave him a little wave.

'Do you want me to come with you?' I called.

'No,' she shouted back.

I had some difficulty with this. It was a nice gesture, of course, going to the aid of a friend who'd just stormed off. Genuine concern. But it was an odd type of concern, because it didn't seem to extend as far as me, her loving husband, whom she'd just left alone in the company of a mass murderer and his henchmen without even the courtesy of a goodbye kiss.

Father White, at my side, shook his head. 'Strange breed, women,' he said.

It was the most human thing I'd heard from him since I'd arrived on the island, but coming from a man who'd most probably only ever had sex with his left hand it was also based on a complete lack of direct experience. 'Tell me all about it,' I said, nevertheless, and turned back to the fire. The four remaining gunmen warmed themselves by it, awaiting instructions.

White turned as well. He rubbed his hands together. The six of us stood in a circle. I should have been scared. These were evil men. My protector, Father Flynn, had been marched away. But I didn't feel scared. Not much, anyway. The barely disguised hysteria of the book burning seemed to have evaporated with the last of the books.

After a little, I said: 'You didn't seem unduly fazed by our discovery of those bodies.'

'I wasn't. I was surprised it took so long.'

'Youse shot Constable Murtagh and Mary Reilly.'

'We did. We'd no alternative.'

'Of course. And a priest.'

234

'We'd no alternative.'

'And a government inspector.'

'Him too. Same reason.'

'He was here long before Christine was even born.'

'True.'

'So why . . . ?'

'I'm not going to go through this twice. Come up to the church with me. I owe Frank Flynn an explanation before I owe you one. But I've no objection to you sitting in on it. You are the official historian, after all.'

'You want this written down?' I asked incredulously.

'Of course I do. It's important.'

He had me confused. Wrathlin had me confused, but Father White had me particularly confused.

'You're not concerned that history might portray you as a mad-man intent on murder?'

He stretched his lips into a half smile. 'An historian not in possession of all the facts might portray me that way. On the other hand, an historian able to take the long view, once he has listened to all the facts with an open mind, who is able to put them into perspective, might record something completely different.'

'But what if he doesn't or can't or won't?'

'Well, then he might end up in a shallow grave as well. It's quite straightforward. Do you have an open mind, Mr Starkey?'

He had a way of saying *Mister* which rolled off his tongue like a wave of nausea.

'Gaping,' I said.

38

Before we entered we could hear Flynn's hollow pacing along the floorboards. He wheeled round as the door opened. The short wait for our arrival had done nothing to cool his temper. His face was flushed. A dry white tongue flicked at his upper lip, his arms were clenched stiffly to his sides.

'Just who the hell do you think you are?' he spat immediately.

I shrugged, an involuntary reaction based on long experience. White ignored him. He turned and closed the door firmly, then stood with his hands clasped behind his back. Thin lines of sweat had dried on his head like vague river traces in an African landscape.

'Well?' Flynn demanded.

'Frank,' White answered softly, 'if we're going to get anywhere, you're going to have to calm down.'

Flynn's hands snapped away from his side. 'How can I calm down? You've turned this from heaven to hell! You've ruined it all!'

White shook his head. 'No, Frank, I haven't. You don't understand.' Flynn opened his mouth to speak, but White raised his hand quickly, then stepped forward. 'Have a seat, Frank. Let's talk about this rationally.'

'Rationally!'

It was not a word much used on Wrathlin, and there it was twice in as many seconds.

'Where's Duncan?' I asked.

'They took him away,' said Flynn. 'Why don't you listen out for the gunshot?'

White shook his head. He stepped behind the Council table and pulled a chair out. Intentionally or not, he ignored the Council leader's seat. Then he looked expectantly up at Flynn.

Flynn wavered. I touched his arm. He looked round quickly, as if he hadn't been aware of my presence. 'It can't do any harm, Father,' I said.

'Are you in this with him?'

'No. Of course not. Don't be daft. I'm the original impartial reporter.'

He looked doubtful. 'So you're not on my side either.'

'Father, hear what the man has to say. What harm can it do? He's calling the shots anyway. Literally.'

'Thank you,' White snapped, 'we can do without your contributions.'

I pulled out a chair for myself at the end of the table. Flynn looked from me to White and back. Then he rounded the table and for a moment I thought he was going to thump his usurper, but he stopped behind the leader's chair. His eyes betrayed a flicker of hesitation, then he drew back the seat next to it, so that they sat on either side of it. 'Very well,' Flynn said, sitting rigidly, 'I'll listen. I'll be fascinated to hear whatever explanation you can come up with. Fascinated to know how a man of God can justify the murder of six people.'

A face appeared at the window at the end of the hall. Bearded. A gun barrel over one shoulder. He peered in, nodded, turned away.

White hunched forward. He rubbed his hands together slowly. Looked at the ground. Flynn's eyes bored into the top of his head. White was searching for the right words. Finally he looked up. 'Frank,' he said quietly, his diplomatic hat finally in place, 'I must apologise, I . . .'

'An apology isn't going to bring . . .'

Firmer voice: 'I must apologise for keeping you in the dark. We thought . . . the Council thought it best, with your fragile heart . . .'

'There's nothing fragile about it!' Flynn boomed.

White raised calming hands. 'Frank! Please! Just listen to me. We knew you wouldn't go along with what we planned to do. But we thought we were right. We know we *are* right. Now listen to me.'

'I'm listening.'

'Right. Right.' White rubbed his hands together again. 'Just give me a chance. I've already explained about Murtagh and Mary.'

'You've admitted killing them. You've *explained* nothing.'

'I did explain. To protect the island. To protect Christine.'

'That's neither explanation or justification.'

White tutted. 'Bear with me, Frank, will you? Let me tell you about the one that really matters. The government man.'

'Mark Blundell,' I said.

'Whoever.'

'Killed before Christine was even born,' I said.

'Yes. Thank you,' said White, turning shut-up eyes upon me, then away. 'Frank. It's like this. This man. Blundell. He wanted us off the island. All of us.'

Flynn's eyes narrowed. He leant forward, suddenly intrigued. 'What do you mean?'

'What I say. He wanted to move every last man-jack of us across to the mainland. For good.'

'But why, for heaven's sake?'

'He said it was too dangerous to live here.' He let it hang in the air for a moment, then half whispered, 'Have you ever heard of radon?'

Flynn repeated the word silently. He shook his head. 'What is it?'

White glanced up the table. 'What about you?'

'It's a type of washing powder, isn't it?'

White tutted. 'Of course it isn't.' Back to Flynn. 'Frank, this fella, *Blundell*. Long before you came back, he came across to the island one day, unannounced, with all this equipment. Sneaked. Didn't ask permission. Just, just . . . did it. I watched him for a few hours, then I went down to see him. He wasn't going to tell anything, but I kept asking and he said he was doing a survey. What sort of survey, I asked, and why here? He said, not just here, throughout the whole United Kingdom, had been going on for years – just that Wrathlin had never been the top of anyone's list. It was a snide wee comment. I didn't like him. A superior type and nothing to be superior about. I was polite. He said it would only take a couple of days. He was looking for traces of radon. What's that? I asked. A radioactive gas, he said. Goodness, I said, that sounds scary. He laughed. Nothing to worry about. He said it was a natural gas they like to keep an eye on. Just a wee survey. I'll be gone before you know I'm here, he said.' White took a deep intake of breath. He shook his head. Looked at the floor. Dramatic pause.

'What happened?' Flynn asked.

'What happened, Frank, was that he scuttled away and continued his survey, and we put him up and gave him food and just made him welcome as we always do to strangers . . .'

'Did,' I said.

'Do, did – shut up, Starkey, and listen.'

'Okay.'

'The survey went on for several days. He was a curious wee man, always kept himself to himself, but the truth of the matter is, there was an evil streak in him, and in a way it's as well for us that there was. He should have taken his survey, gone home and reported the findings to his superiors, but instead he couldn't resist telling me – you could see the pleasure on his face – letting slip, almost by accident, but definitely by design, that he was getting readings that suggested an abnormally high radon presence.'

'But . . . but . . . but . . . what does that mean?' Flynn asked.

'Abnormal is abnormal, Frank,' White said drily. 'Said he'd never come across anything like it. Claimed it was extremely dangerous. That he was seriously concerned for the population and that he would be recommending an immediate evacuation of the island.'

'To which you replied?'

'I thought it was a little rash. I asked why he needed to recommend such a thing. What danger was there? He said he didn't know. He said there'd never, ever been such high readings, it was just such an incredible phenomenon that the safest thing would be to get everyone off the island until a team of scientists could investigate the situation properly. He wouldn't listen to me, Frank. I told him we'd an extremely healthy population. I told him that if he moved people off the island, the chances were that they wouldn't come back, that it would be the death of our whole community, but he wouldn't listen, said he had the power to have us moved off. There was no reasoning with him.'

'So you killed him,' I said.

'It wasn't as simple as that, Starkey. We insisted he stayed for a Council meeting.'

'Insisted?'

'We prevented him from leaving. But just so that the whole Council could hear it from his own lips. He wasn't happy about it, of course, being kept here, but at the same time he seemed to relish it, relished causing such an uproar. And there certainly was. But he wouldn't listen. He'd made his mind up and that was that.

Some of the boys had drink taken and it got a bit nasty. All sorts of name-calling. Childish, yes, I know, but you know how we are here, Frank. We're proud of this wee place. It got out of hand. Someone shot him. I'm sorry it happened, but it happened. And I can't say it wasn't the right thing.'

'You wouldn't care to recall who actually pulled the trigger?' I asked.

'No, I wouldn't. Blundell was beyond reasoning with. He would have killed the island without a second's thought.'

'He might have been saving you,' I said.

'You don't understand, Starkey. This gas. This radon. I'm not saying it's not there. I know it is. But it's there for a reason. We just didn't know what reason back then. We all knew something was happening. We could feel it in the air. A sense of elation. A sense of potential like you can't imagine. All of us felt it. Such well-being. You felt it, Frank, didn't you? You remember what it was like when you came back, there was a real buzz . . . I remember when you arrived . . . you weren't a well man, were you? But within weeks . . .' Flynn nodded thoughtfully, his anger now well subsided. 'We were so content . . . but at the same time waiting, waiting for something important to happen . . . and it was there all the time, little Christine . . . and it took you to lead us to her, and for that we will be eternally grateful. God through the might of nature had seen fit to create this, the perfect environment for his daughter to be born. This Garden of Eden. And we must do everything to protect it. Do you see now, Frank? Do you understand? *Think* about it, Frank.'

Flynn sat back in his chair and closed his eyes. He clasped his hands under his chin. 'You're right,' he said softly, 'I do need to think about it.'

White pushed his chair back and stood. 'Take as long as you want. You'll see the truth of what I'm saying. You'll understand why we've done what we've done. We've agreed all along that there's a new dawn coming, Frank, that it's starting right here. It's so vital that we do everything in our power to protect the girl, because when she comes of age the whole world's going to answer to her.'

Father White left us in the hall. When the door closed I said, 'Barking or what?'

But Flynn fixed me with such a look of disgust that I walked away from the table and stared out of the window. I had presumed, because of the bodies, that Flynn was now on 'our side', but I was wrong. He was still Father Flynn, champion of Christine and bloke who'd talked to God.

'They killed Blundell,' I said.

'Shhhh.'

'They killed the priest. The others.'

'Will you give my head peace?' Flynn snapped.

I shut up.

A little after noon the door into the church opened and Duncan limped in. Someone pulled the door closed behind him and locked it. Duncan had a plaster on his face but he was just as mud-grubby. 'Howdy,' he said disconsolately and sat on the edge of the table. 'What's been happening?'

I shrugged. 'Congratulations on your single-handed stand against censorship.'

He gave a weak smile. 'It didn't do much good.'

'Not the point. It's the effort that counts. We need books. So that we can look up words like radon.'

He gave me the *what?* look.

I told him what White had told us. The priest hadn't said those magic words, *off the record*. I kept it succinct and just short of *we're all going to die*. His initial response was a single raised eyebrow, which is difficult, and a 'Seriously?'

I nodded. Then he joined Flynn in some solitary thinking and I was left to my own devices for another five minutes. I could almost hear their brains whirring. I don't know why they needed so much time. It was perfectly clear to me what was going on: over the course of many years the radon had boiled all of their brains. And the longer Patricia, Little Stevie and I stayed on the island the greater was the likelihood of our own brains getting boiled.

Eventually Duncan gave a slight shake of his head and said: 'It does make sense, you know, if he's telling the truth about the radon.'

I was way ahead of him. 'He's a priest, of course he's telling the truth,' I said.

From the window, Flynn tutted.

'But it does make sense,' Duncan continued, unfazed. 'It explains quite a bit. Not about the murders, but about what's been happening here.' He patted his injured face lightly, winced, gave himself a *That was stupid* look. 'I know bugger all about radon, but if it's been at such a high level all along it's bound to have affected us.'

Flynn turned from the window. 'We've never been healthier, Duncan. You know that. Sure it's no wonder Dr Finlay's such a sad old drunk – he has nothing to do all day.'

'I don't necessarily mean physically, Father. Up top.'

'But we're not . . . well, backward,' said Flynn.

'Of course not!' said Duncan. 'We're *forward,* if anything. I mean, think about it . . . your visions, Christine's powers . . . even Mary Reilly – didn't everyone think she could talk to the spirits . . . what if she could . . . I mean, *see* things, just like you did, Father, just like Christine can . . . what if it's the radon, Father?'

'What if it's in-breeding,' I said, helpfully.

Duncan snorted. 'I know it sounds crazy . . . but is it any crazier than the Second Coming?'

I looked at Flynn. 'Could explain a lot, Father.'

He was nodding slowly. 'It would mean none of it was true. The . . .' He trailed off. There was despair as deep as the ocean in his voice. His eyes studied the pock-marked wooden floor. How many heels had left their indentations there over the years? *Lots.* I smiled, then tried to cover it. Nobody noticed. Flynn looked up at Duncan. 'What you're saying is that if Christine isn't the daughter of God, then she's some sort of a defective, a mutation caused by this gas.'

'No, I . . .'

'That everything we've done in her name has been because our minds have been altered by this *radon*. That I put it all in motion by having my visions, visions caused by this gas.'

Duncan was shaking his head. 'No . . . Father. Not at all. I'm not saying it's necessarily a bad thing, Father. If this radon really does enhance the power of the human mind, then the possibilities are endless . . .'

But Father Flynn was no longer listening. He stood abruptly and started for the hall door.

Duncan went after him. 'Father?'

The priest stopped, turned. 'Stay here, Duncan, there's a good fella.' Duncan stopped. 'I've made a big mistake,' Flynn said, and hammered on the door. 'I have to sort it out.'

39

Shards of light cut through the clouds, choosily illuminating the crucial aspects of an essentially tragic scene.

Tragedy and I are old chums. We've bumped into each other at parties, shared a glass or twelve of beer, reminisced about the dear departed. God is a bit more of a stranger, but it was nice of Him nevertheless to cast a little light on the situation. He had an interest, of course. So did Mother Nature, oozing up from below. I hadn't quite worked out if the two were the same, and if they were, if that made He a She, or them an It. It's funny what goes through your head as you kneel in the dust with a gun at your head.

I turned that head slightly. Duncan was on my left. He nodded helplessly. There was still shouting going on within the church. Father Flynn's voice, of course, and, higher pitched, Father White's. They had been at it for a couple of hours.

The Council was in there too, jabbering. The gunmen were outside. Threatening.

Duncan seemed resigned to his fate. 'I thought they were taking me off to shoot me last time. I look on it as having a last couple of hours to make my peace with God.'

I spat. 'God burnt your books this morning.'

'Not God, Starkey. You know that as well as I do.' His hands were behind his neck. So were mine. My neck, that is. It's not a very comfortable way to sit, but it's more comfortable than having a bullet make its way through your head at a hundred-odd miles per hour. Duncan pulled his elbows in until they met in front of his nose. 'But now I wish they'd get on with it,' he added.

'I don't,' I said.

Amongst other things never to have reached such a wayward out-post as Wrathlin – myxomatosis, satellite television, Lean Cuisine Tagliatelle – was a collection of old maxims, including two of particular relevance about shooting neither the messenger nor the piano player. But thus it had been ordained.

Father Flynn's attempts to explain to his colleague the error of his ways, that Christine was quite possibly the most highly developed human being on the planet but not the daughter of God, had obviously fallen on deaf or mutated ears. Definitely red ears, in any case, because White had come storming out of their meeting and ordered that Duncan and the world's most fearless reporter be readied for execution. It was a bargaining tool, but Flynn wasn't in the form to bargain, which wasn't good news for us.

Gunmen dragged us out, thrust us down, pulled us up to our knees, pressed cold metal barrels against the back of our heads. And then we had a temporary reprieve. It went to arbitration as the rest of the Council trooped in, barely looking at us as they marched past, stern-faced. Jack McGettigan, proving that there's nothing worse than a reformed drinker, slapped Duncan on his injured face as he passed and muttered something largely incoherent but involving the word 'pornographer'. Duncan let out a yelp.

'What a way to end up,' I said into the face of a cold, stinging wind. A tear or two rolled down my cheeks. I bit at a lip. I didn't want anyone to think I was crying. I was tough, a street-hardened cynic. I'd stared death in the face before. And cried.

Duncan spat into the embers of the fire. 'Aye. What a way to go,' he said.

'Shut up, will youse?' the gunman behind me ordered, nudging me with the barrel.

'Give me a good reason why,' I said, sniffing up.

'Because I'll shoot you if you don't,' he barked.

Duncan gave a sour laugh. 'Tommy, for God's sake wise up, you're going to shoot us anyway.'

'Well, just keep it down, eh?'

I looked at Duncan again. 'Thanks,' I said, 'for cheering me up.'

He gave a little shrug.

Tommy was the only gunman directly threatening us. The rest had retreated out of the wind to the shelter of the hall steps; they could also hear better the wind coming from within as Flynn fought his last stand. I hadn't met Tommy before; he'd stared in at us in the church hall earlier in the day; beardy, bulky, a sheep's lifeless eyes.

'You were in my class at school, Tommy,' said Duncan.

'So?'

'Nothing. Just that now you're probably going to have to shoot me.'

'So? You're a heretic and pornographer.'

'You believe that?'

'Of course I do.'

'Because Father White says?'

'Yes.'

'You believe everything he says?' I asked.

'Sure.'

'Why believe him and not Father Flynn?'

'Because Father Flynn's not well.'

'Who told you that?' asked Duncan.

'We know he's not well. He's mental. He's saying all sorts of crazy stuff.'

'Like what?'

'About stupid gas driving us nuts.'

'You don't think he could have a point?' I asked.

'Of course not,' he said and gave us a pity-the-poor-misguided-fools sigh. 'He's just lost the faith.'

'You don't think the likelihood of the Messiah being born on Wrathlin is just as crazy as some gas driving us nuts?'

'That's exactly the argument I'd expect a heathen to come up with.'

'Tommy,' asked Duncan, 'could you really shoot us?'

'I could.'

'You must really hate us.'

'I don't hate you at all. I just love Christine. And if Father White says killing you two will protect her, then that's fine by me.'

'It won't be on your conscience then.'

'No. Not at all.'

'Good,' I said, 'that's nice to know.'

A jumping to attention on the steps, then the door opened and Father Flynn, followed by Father White and the rest of the Council, emerged. They appeared, if anything, even more sombre than before, although sombreness is a difficult thing to judge where religion is involved; in a religious type, sombreness can often be taken as the equivalent of a broad smile in a non-religious type. It goes with the territory. A priest who comes on like Laughing Boy isn't to be trusted.

As the councillors formed themselves up, the gunmen hurried down the steps, then stood in a loose semi-circle behind Duncan and me. They gazed reverentially up at our jury. The councillors spread out along the top step, almost equally split around Father White. Flynn stepped down into the yard and walked the few yards to us. It was difficult to judge from the set of his eyes the outcome of those heated discussions. His face was pale, but so was everyone's; it was a pale afternoon, chilled by the grey clouds above and the rush of the freezing Atlantic winds up the hill to the church.

Flynn stood before us, nodding his head slightly, then clasped his hands behind his back.

'I never wanted this to happen,' he said simply, then sucked in his cheeks and looked beyond us, down the hill towards the harbour. Not finding any solace there, he turned slightly, then peered back at Father White, who nodded. 'I have asked that you two, and I, be allowed to leave the island immediately, and that we give our word to tell no one of what has gone on here.'

'Fair enough,' I said.

'Unfortunately this request has been refused.'

I tutted. Duncan's head dropped. My head rarely drops without the influence of alcohol. I tossed a defiant look in the direction of the Council. I would get to the screaming and begging soon enough.

'The thing is,' Flynn said, 'I fully understand the position Father White and the rest of the Council find themselves in. If you believe in something, especially if it is something as important as this, then you have to stick to your guns, literally, in this case. Give it everything. Don't let anyone put you off. That is what they are doing. I sympathise, because I felt the same way. Now, because of recent revelations we are all aware of, I am no longer able to believe in the idea of Christine being the daughter of God. She's a remarkable girl, but I can't say that she is anything more than that. I have argued my case, but I could just as well be wrong. I hope for the sake of the people behind me here that I am. But I see now that I cannot stand in their way.'

'That's a little short of an endorsement,' I said.

'I have pleaded with them not to carry out their threat to execute you and Duncan,' said Flynn.

'Thank you,' said Duncan.

'Unfortunately that has also fallen on deaf ears.'

'Oh.'

'So the story of Christine will never be written. At least by your hand, Dan.'

'That's what publishing's like, Father,' I said.

He gave me a sad little grin. 'Always ready with a good line, Dan, always ready.'

'Comedy is easy. Dying is hard. What's your punishment, three Hail Marys?'

'Oh, I don't think they could afford to let me away that easily, Dan. No. I'm afraid when it comes to punishment, I'm down there in the dust beside you. It's only right.'

And he sank to his knees. Then shuffled round.

The three of us looked up at Father White.

'I can't believe he's going to kill you as well,' said Duncan.

Flynn gave a little shrug. 'What else can he do?'

'What else indeed?' Father White stepped down into the yard. His face seemed to glow. Triumphant. All-powerful. He stopped before Duncan. He placed his hand on the teacher's head. Petted his hair for a moment, then suddenly clenched his fist and pulled his scalp sharply up, lifting Duncan's not insignificant body a couple of inches off the ground. 'What would you have us do?' he spat, his face snarling up. He forced Duncan's head round until it faced Flynn. 'This priest, this colleague, this friend of mine, this primary supporter of Christine, turns out to be the serpent in the Garden of Eden. What would you have me do, keep him alive so that he can spread more of his poison? So that he can infect everyone, turn everyone against Christine? No! Indeed, no!' He let go of the hair, raised his hand and punched a fist into the sky. 'God is watching us, and it's with God's blessing we're doing this!' he proclaimed.

'Amen,' said at least three of the councillors. The rest nodded. Sombrely.

It seemed about the right time to put my spoke in. 'Have you actually put it to Christine, then?' I ventured.

White snapped round. 'Put what?'

'Our execution.'

He blew air disdainfully out of his nose. 'I don't need to.'

'You made a big case for it before. Before Mary Reilly escaped.'

He grabbed my hair. Twisted. Quite possibly he wanted some of it for himself. He pressed his face into mine. Disappointingly, he had nice breath. 'Yes, we were prepared to try her, we needed to show everyone the evil that was abroad. That was important. But the sort of evil you three have been responsible for is of a much more insidious nature.' He let go of me. 'Mary Reilly was clearly mad,' he said, 'and thus more easily discredited by public debate, but you three are altogether more lucid, more capable of spreading your misguided rubbish than she ever was.'

I looked up at the councillors. 'And all of you agree with this?'

They nodded, one by one, no shyness about it, no avoiding the eyes of a doomed man. I shrugged. Perhaps my last shrug on this mortal coil. 'Oh well, fair enough then. Who am I to interfere with the democratic process?' I coughed up. I spat. 'Sorry, did I say democratic process? I meant mind-warped fascist fantasy bastards intent on murder.'

An evil smirk slipped onto Father White's face. 'Is that it?'

I shook my head. 'Led by a bald cunt who wouldn't know a Last Supper from a pastie supper.'

He shook his head mock-sadly. 'As a last will and testament, Starkey, it does you justice. Embarrassing and forgettable.'

'Maybe, but at least it makes me feel better, you arrogant self-satisfied radiation-saturated fucker.'

A couple of the gunmen let loose with a titter. A stern look silenced them.

'Not for long,' said the priest, then stepped along. 'Is there anything you want to say, Frank, before the end?'

Flynn nodded. 'I want you to know that I forgive you. All of you.'

'Thank you, Frank. And we forgive you.'

Another step along. 'What about you, pornographer? Anything to say to us?'

Duncan mumbled something. His eyes remained fixed on the ground.

'What's that?' White asked, kneeling down.

Duncan turned his head up suddenly, and spat in the priest's face.

The shock of it sent him sprawling onto his back in the dust. He righted himself quickly, heaved to his feet, just as Tommy the gunman crunched the butt of his gun into the back of Duncan's head. Duncan fell silently forward, instantly unconscious.

White ran a sleeve across his face, looked at the damp stain. 'Do it,' he said.

Tommy stood back a little, then raised the pistol and centred his sights on the back of Duncan's head. He looked up at Father White. The priest nodded. He looked up at the line of councillors. They nodded too. He looked at Father Flynn. He shook his head.

'Don't do it, son,' said Flynn.

'Shoot him and be done with it!' White shouted.

'He's Christine's father,' I said. 'Tommy, you know that, don't you?'

Tommy hesitated. Looked back at White. 'He's not, is he?'

'Of course he's not. God is Christine's father. You know that.'

'You'll go straight to hell,' I said.

Tommy looked back at Flynn, then realigned his shot.

'He's Joseph,' said Flynn. 'You're going to murder Joseph.'

Tommy looked up to the Council for help. They weren't much help. He looked round to his fellow gunmen.

'Pull the trigger,' one of them said.

Still he hesitated. A rolling sweat broke across his brow. Father White, impatient, moved swiftly across to the reluctant executioner and grabbed the gun from him. Tommy reversed out of the semi-circle. 'I'm sorry,' he said.

The priest cradled the pistol in his hand for a moment then stepped forward and stood above the unconscious young teacher. He straddled the body, raised the gun, mouthed an almost silent prayer, then shot him. Twice.

40

Blood, pumping like that, has its effect.

The gunmen, the councillors, the priest they were loyal to, had all been involved in murder before, but murder of a different kind. I could tell that from their hang-jawed faces: the government man, Mary and Murtagh, the young priest, the pair we would never identify, had all been killed in the murky dark of a Wrathlin night, in the panic of a drunken argument, in the leaping shadows of a wild-grown field. This was different: the shuddering body of a man they all knew, his life force spraying out of a butchered head, lying in a churchyard on a crisp autumnal day. They stood stock-still. Stared. No one objected when I reached into my pocket and produced a knot of kitchen roll and dragged it across my bloody face.

Father White, gun still in hand, administered the last rites. If anything represented the madness that had overtaken Wrathlin, it was this. And no one else seemed to think it strange.

Then he stood and looked at me. It could only have been for a few seconds, but it was enough time for me to cram through my mind what I needed to: my farewells. The bodies we had discovered in Mulrooney's field had been real enough, but long dead, and thus also a little unreal. Duncan's blood on my lips was the ultimate reality, the flavour of death.

If I was ever considered important enough to warrant an obituary in my local paper I hoped that this was what they would say: that he was a good man. That he was born with a bone deficiency: very few serious ones. That he laughed and drank and enjoyed himself because that was what life was for. That he regretted any hardship or pain or death that he had caused and hoped that It would forgive him. That he'd had a wonderful life and he wanted to thank James Stewart and Humphrey Bogart, *Zulu*, The Clash and Sugar Ray Leonard for all the good times, for the beat of Charles Bukowski and Dr Feelgood, for the taste of Harp, Tennent's, Rolling Rock and other absent friends. That he loved his wife. And that he loved his child.

I took a deep gulp of the wind, salt-ridden, biting, beautiful wind, and stared resolutely back at Father White.

'Good shot,' I said.

Beside me, Father Flynn was flying through a hundred whispered prayers, eyes shut tightly.

Death stepped behind me. Cool metal pressed hard against my skull. In those last moments I sought perfect composure.

Goodbye Patricia.

Goodbye my love.

Jesus, that's a Glitter Band song. I can't have that as my last . . .

Bang.

But not bang – honk.

Horn.

Honk.

Horn.

Hesitation. A relaxation of the metal.

Honk. Honk. Honk. Roar of heavy engine.

I opened my eyes. Turned, as everyone else looked behind me.

And over the brow of the hill came a tractor.

The tractor pulled a two-wheeled trailer.

And behind the trailer came people. Lots of them.

Father White stepped away from me, the gun hanging loose at his side. He looked back at the councillors, caught them swapping confused glances. With radon-inspired choreography they stepped down into the yard as one.

The tractor and trailer heaved through the gates. I could see now that it was driven by Dr Finlay. He was thumping his hand up and down on the horn. Beside him in the cab stood Moira and Christine and Patricia. Behind the trailer came the ladies of the parish, half of them in aerobic tracksuits. And behind them, stretched out way back down the hill, others, dozens upon dozens of ordinary people, the fishermen, the shopkeepers, the housewives, the kids. There was something about them, a look, a provocative tenseness that suggested that they were drawn to the churchyard by something more than their allegiance to Christine. It became clear what it was when Finlay wheeled the tractor round until it faced back out of the yard; he flipped a switch which disconnected the trailer. It rolled back a couple of yards and then flipped up onto its wheels, disgorging the rotting remains of six familiar corpses.

Finlay cut the engine and clambered unsteadily from the vehicle. He leant back against it. His lips were poteen moist, but his eyes were bright, thrilled, proud. Moira, jumping down from the cab on the other side, pointed at the bodies, then at Father White.

'This is what he has done!' she shouted as the crowd began to swell about her.

'Moira, please . . .' the priest began, half disdainfully. But half not.

'He's murdered all of these people!'

They'd been lured by the tractor's procession through the town, a mechanised Pied Piper, a Palm Sunday for the Millennium. Now they huddled forward to examine the stinking mass properly.

White spread his arms, wide and welcoming. Unaware still of the incongruity of the gun clamped in his left hand. 'You don't understand, Moira . . .'

Father Flynn struggled to his feet. 'Duncan, Moira, poor Duncan,' he cried, the emotion breaking in his voice. 'Look what they've done to the poor boy.'

Moira noticed the body for the first time. She put her hand to her mouth to stifle . . . something . . . Her eyes blazed. She ran forward. Knelt by the body. 'You've killed him as well?'

'Moira, now . . .'

'God help you!' She stepped forward and punched White hard on the nose. He stumbled back into the protection of his own men, dropping his gun in the process. They gathered about him, now facing on all sides the growing crowd. Maybe two hundred strong. Or weak. Or easily swayed. Or out for justice.

I got up too. My knees clicked. 'Nice punch,' I said and picked up his gun.

White's lip curled up towards a threat, but Moira stopped it. She pointed at Duncan. 'How could you do that?' she demanded.

'He was a pornographer and a . . .'

'He was Christine's father!'

'He was a . . .'

'He was her daddy!'

'Only physically, Moira. The spirit of the . . .'

She hit him again.

His protectors weren't very protective. They held him up. Kept him in the firing line.

White, rattled, nose bleeding, turned on them. 'Get them back!' he bellowed, waving his arms at the encroaching crowd. 'Get them out! This is God's house! It's no place for a rabble like this!'

Holding their guns out in front of them, they began to push out, slowly widening the circle. One shot into the air.

Screams came from those who couldn't see; there were some backward steps. But no panic.

A woman, a blue scarf tied about her throat, pushed through the throng and up to the man who'd fired. 'Jimmy, put that gun down and come on home with me, now.'

Jimmy looked at her. It wasn't a request.

'Stay where you are!' barked Father White.

Jimmy shook his head. He gave the priest an apologetic shrug and dropped his gun. 'Okay, love,' he said, and slipped into the crowd.

Patricia pushed through to me. Slipped her hand into mine. Squeezed. 'Are you okay?' she whispered.

'Fine,' I said.

I did love her. I would tell her later.

Moira still faced Father White. Blood dripped off his lip, off the end of his chin. She stuck a finger out at him. 'You've been making decisions on Christine's behalf for too long, Father!' she bellowed.

'I've been protecting her.'

'You've been murdering in her name. You think she wants people killed in her name?'

'They were dangerous.'

'To who? You?'

'To Christine.'

'There's no need for murder!' somebody shouted.

'No need to kill them!' a woman hissed.

'Duncan was a good boy.'

'Duncan was my cousin.'

'My nephew.'

'My cousin.'

'My uncle, and you killed him!'

'Look at him! He has no head!'

'What gives you the right?' Moira demanded.

'The Council decided.'

The Council suddenly didn't look so decided. Heads went together. Some of them cracked.

'Father,' said Jack McGettigan, 'perhaps we should reconvene.'

'We've made our decisions,' White boomed.

'But, Father . . .'

The crowd began to press forward again. The gunmen withdrew slowly. They cast anxious glances at White. The priest looked desperately about him. 'Bring Christine to me,' he shouted. 'Let her speak.'

'Do you want to kill her too?' someone yelled.

'Please, bring her here, let her speak . . .'

'She's only a child!' Moira yelled. 'She's scared.'

'She's . . .'

'Just a kid.'

'God bless her,' a woman called.

'God bless her soul,' echoed another.

'Keep him away from her.'

A roar of approval. The crowd pressed further in.

'Stop there!' White shouted. 'Stop this instant! I'll order them to shoot! I'm warning you. Go on home. We'll sort this out. In the name of Christine, go home.'

It had gone too far. They weren't for stopping.

'I'm warning you.' White turned and poked one of his men in the shoulder. 'You! Shoot one of them. Any one of them.'

The man raised his rifle. Lowered his rifle. Looked at his comrades. Shook his head. 'I'm sorry, Father, I can't.'

'I am the law. Shoot someone.'

'I'm sorry. Half my family's here. I didn't join to . . .'

'I don't care!'

White pushed the next man. 'Shoot. Anyone. Now. I'm telling you. Do it now!'

The second gunman shook his head. 'I can't,' he said. 'They're family.'

'Murtagh was family. Mary Reilly was family.'

'That was different, Father.'

'In God's name how?'

He looked at the ground. Mumbled. 'It was dark.'

'Good God, man. There's devils abroad in the daylight as well. Shoot!'

'These aren't devils.'

White grabbed at the gun. 'Let me show you how . . .'

The man held it tight. 'No, Father,' he said. 'I can't let you.'

White looked desperately from one to the other, right around his protective circle. He saw that none of them would back him up.

The priest swivelled back towards the crowd. His anguished eyes flitted from one to the other desperately looking for support, but there was none. 'Don't you see what's happening?' he cried. 'In God's name come to your senses before it's too late.'

There wasn't even sympathy. Just a hard island glare. He wilted under it. He dropped his head into his hands, then slowly slipped to his knees. He began to sob.

Flynn stepped forward and placed a hand on his old colleague's shoulder. 'We have come to our senses,' he said softly.

The crowd quieted, stood about him, transfixed by the sight of the priest's shoulders moving up and down as he cried uncontrollably. It lasted for several minutes.

When the tears had run their course he snorted up and down, then spread his fingers and peered through the gap. Like a child checking to see if the monster had gone.

One of Duncan's relatives bent forward and spat with perfect accuracy between index and forefinger into the priest's left eye.

'They're not as dumb as I thought,' I whispered to Patricia.

'They've had their eyes opened, that's all.'

'Just wait till they hear about the radon.'

'The *what*?'

41

Patricia peered into the box. 'What do you think?' she asked, pushing a loose strand of hair out of her eyes. She was happy. Her eyes sparkled. She was going home. So was I.

As usual, I shrugged. 'Up to you,' I said.

Apparently there's something thrilling about being up and about in a misty dawn. Something to do with the exhilaration of being in at the start of the new day; the cool damp is supposed to be invigorating. Lost on me. My trainers and the bottoms of my jeans were already sopping from standing in the dewed garden for too long. I was tired. We'd spent most of the night packing up our stuff, cramming it back into the car.

'What's that old saying?' Patricia asked. 'Home is where the hedgehog is?'

I tutted. She wanted to take the hedgehog home to Belfast. 'You agree to take responsibility for the fleas, and I'll go along with it.'

'But we've looked after him for so long.'

'Trish, it's only been a few days and he's slept for most of that. Catch a grip. Anyway, if he wakes up in Belfast he'll probably die of culture shock. All of those sophisticated hedgehog coffee mornings on the Malone Road, they'll give him the spiky shoulder.'

'I suppose I do get attached to things.'

'You could say that.'

'I got attached to you. And I already have a child to look after.'

'There's that.'

'And Stevie.'

'Oh hah-hah.'

Eventually, we reached a compromise. We agreed to transport the hedgehog across to the mainland and place the box in some remote undergrowth where he could sleep away the winter safe from the dangers of radon. He would not be the only evacuee, that was for sure.

The previous evening's town meeting had stretched through to the small hours. The packed hall had not needed much convincing of the existence of the radon, but the question of whether to press ahead with a full evacuation had left the small community divided. At first it was agreed that the children should go, then the mothers wanted to go with them, but wouldn't leave their husbands, who didn't want to leave at all, although they didn't mind the children going. Christine, playing at the back, had become almost irrelevant to the proceedings, demoted in a few hours from daughter of God to bright kid, and who likes a bright kid? She didn't appear to be particularly disturbed by it, though there was some doubt as to how long her good humour would last. The other children seemed to enjoy being able to pull her hair without fear of divine retribution.

Father Flynn, restored by popular acclaim to his seat at the head of the Council, although there was no Council to speak of, spoke eloquently and with authority about what had happened in the preceding months and years, and about the dangers of remaining on the island. 'Most of us have been horrified by what has gone on here in the past few days,' he said, his eyes falling on Father White, sitting head bowed in the front row, staring at the floor, 'but we shouldn't blame anyone. People have died. But we can hold no one responsible. That, I fear, is the nature of this radon, this gas which has corrupted all of our lives. Just as it seemed to bring us the goodness of Christine, it also brought us the madness of murder. Just as it brought us the bounty of good health, it brought us the unpredictability of insanity.' He clasped his hands before him, giving his words the emphasis of prayer. 'I honestly believe that it can only become more dangerous the longer we stay here. We should thank God for this brief interlude of sanity he has given us, and get off the island before its darkness descends upon us once again.'

One of Duncan's many relatives jumped up. I recognised him as the man who'd so expertly gobbed on Father White. He looked about ready to spit again. He jabbed a finger out in White's direction. 'You don't mean to let him go? After killing Duncan?'

White didn't seem to be listening. He didn't twitch.

'I hesitate to say, let he who is without sin cast the first stone, Shane, but it does apply here.'

'I didn't shoot anyone.'

'No, you didn't, but you did follow Christine just as much as anyone. I seem to remember you making a point of setting fire to your television set in your front garden, long before we decided to outlaw them. We've all been affected in our own way, Shane.'

'But I didn't kill anyone!'

'Neither did Father White. Not the Father White we all know and love. This radon has corrupted him as much as the rest of us, just in a different way. Our Council's the same. How can they be blamed for what the radon has done? I started all of this off with my visions of Christine. Blame me if you want to blame anyone.'

'You mean to just let him go?'

Flynn nodded. 'We're all guilty. We're all innocent.'

A skinny old man at the back of the hall rose unsteadily to his feet. 'The name's Gerry Mulrooney,' he rasped.

'Yes, we all know you well, Gerry.'

'The name's Gerry Mulrooney, and I've farmed here for the best part of sixty-five years, and there's not no one's going to throw me off of my land.' He sat down.

'Of course not, Gerry,' placated Flynn.

Mulrooney struggled to his feet again. 'And I don't know what the hell this radon stuff is, but I've not noticed it doing any harm.'

'Aye,' someone shouted from across the hall, 'you've not noticed half a dozen bodies in your garden either.'

Laughter. Mulrooney glared across the rows in front of him. 'What's that?' he growled.

'He has a point though,' said a man close to the door. 'I can't leave the farm the way it is. Not now. I've been there all my life, Frank. Can we not just forget about all this madness? We got caught up in it, that's all. Now we know what to watch for, won't we be okay?'

Flynn shook his head. 'My point is, Francis, that we just don't know how it's going to affect us next.'

Moira, about six seats up from White in the front row, stood up. 'Father, everything you say is right. But it could also be wrong.' She nodded round the audience. 'What I think he's saying is that we just don't know what's going on because everything we say and do is affected by this gas. We could all be talking nonsense now. Christine could still be the Messiah. We'll only really be in a position to know if we get off the island, away from its influence.'

Flynn nodded enthusiastically. 'Exactly, Moira. We need to get our people off, and those who do know something about radon on. Then maybe one day we can come back. When it's safe.'

Jack McGettigan, to Flynn's left at the Council table, shook his head. 'You know as well as I do that once people leave they'll never come back. It has always been like that.'

'Didn't I come back, Jack?'

'Aye. And look what happened. Maybe it was that Protestant heart.'

'Now, Jack,' said Flynn, and waved a finger in jovial admonishment, 'don't be saying that.'

As I stood in the garden, I flashed back to Duncan's head exploding. To the taste of him on my lips. The stench of piled bodies remained trapped in my nose. Flynn was right. There was madness in the air.

It was still before seven when we locked Snow Cottage up. There were no goodbyes. It had never felt like home. I'd written three words of a novel, and two of them I wasn't sure about. I'd come within a moment of having my head blown off and once again been saved by a woman. Women, in fact. It almost hurt to think it. Patricia, Moira, the women of the parish, had all along been more on the ball than their menfolk, had all along expressed their misgivings to each other but agreed to stand by their men until things got really out of hand. Oh, they'd believed in Christine okay, but they'd preserved a certain detachment. They'd allowed their menfolk free range on the decisions, and in the process proved that they were the real decision-makers. Moira and Patricia had spread word of the bodies, and the revulsion had inspired insurrection and suddenly the McCooeys were no more. It was a triumph for womankind.

Mind you, they'd needed Dr Finlay to start the tractor.

Patricia hummed gently as we drove. She didn't look back. Little Stevie was happy in her lap. The hedgehog box was wedged into the boot.

When we reached town I asked Patricia if she would miss the old place.

'Of course. Like a hole in the head.'

'We thought it might be a little paradise.'

259

'*You* thought it might be a little paradise.'

'I thought it might bring us closer together.'

'And do you think it did?'

I shrugged. 'I suppose so. What do you think?'

She shrugged too. Little Stevie opened his eyes briefly. 'I don't know if we were ever that far apart,' Patricia said.

I drove up the Main Street and stopped outside Dr Finlay's house.

'What now?' Patricia said.

'We should say goodbye.'

'We'll miss the ferry.'

'There's no shortage of ferries today, love,' I said.

'You don't understand. I want on the *first* one.'

'We'll *get* on the first one.'

I rattled the door. Dr Finlay's housekeeper was already up. She kept me waiting at the door. Several minutes later Finlay arrived, yawning, still tying his dressing gown.

'We're off,' I said.

He didn't look especially heartbroken. 'Oh. Right. Good luck, then.'

'You're staying?'

'Of course. I'm a doctor.'

'And doctors don't get sick.'

'Something like that.'

'Most people will leave, though, won't they?'

He nodded solemnly. 'They've been looking for an excuse for years. Christine stopped the rot. But now she's gone . . . not gone – what would you say – diminished?' I shrugged. 'Well, there'll be no stopping them.'

'Will I send you some whiskey across?'

He cracked a smile. 'That would be nice. I can't see Jackie opening the pub again.'

'I wonder if he ever did bury that drink.'

He yawned again. 'It would have aged better than what did get buried.'

'What about Duncan? There'll need to be a funeral.'

'Aye. I suppose. Same for the others. Don't worry about it. Go on home. You're well out of it.'

'And Willie Nutt? Did he ever show up?'

Finlay shook his head. 'Probably still running. Nah, he'll turn up. Bad pennies always do.'

For several moments we looked silently back down the hill to the harbour, and then on across the sea. The mainland was hidden by cloud and mist. 'All these deaths,' I said, 'do you think . . . ?'

'We'll get away with it?'

I nodded. The six in the field. Bill. Duncan.

'We're an island, we're used to keeping secrets.'

'That big?'

'One day I'll tell you about the others.'

I looked at him. He didn't smile. Patricia pumped the horn.

He put out his hand. I shook it. 'Good luck,' he said.

'Thanks.'

Patricia waved over. He smiled and turned back into the warmth.

Charlie McManus was busy on the *Fitzpatrick* as we drove onto the quay. A Land-Rover was waiting to board. I pulled up behind it. As we stopped, the driver's door opened and Father Flynn climbed out. A head turned from his passenger seat. Moira. She waved back and got out as well. Christine's face appeared suddenly in the back window, smiling and waving. Then she followed her mother.

I rolled the window down and Flynn bent in. Moira went round the other side to speak to Patricia. Christine beat her to it, reaching in immediately to pet Little Stevie.

'I didn't think you'd be first in the queue,' I said.

The priest shook his head. 'I'm just seeing Moira and Christine across. I've people in Ballycastle they can stay with. Then I'll be back over. They don't get rid of me that easily.'

'They nearly did,' I said.

'Nearly's a big word,' he said.

It wasn't. But I nodded. I knew what he meant.

Charlie McManus stuck his head above the quay. 'Yees can bring them on now, if you want,' he shouted. He pulled a rope back, secured it, then waved us on.

Father Flynn, Moira and Christine hurried back to their vehicle. He started the engine and carefully negotiated the ramp. I followed on. There was just about enough room for the two vehicles. Charlie secured the gate behind us. As he passed us on the way to the wheel I said: 'You'll be busy today.'

'Aye,' he said.

'How many runs do you reckon?'

'I don't know,' he said sourly.

He walked on. 'Expansive as ever,' I said. Patricia smiled. 'What was out of Moira?'

She shrugged again. It was fast becoming a family trait. If Little Stevie came off with one before his first birthday I'd be prepared to acknowledge some minor contribution to his genes. 'I think she's just relieved it's all over.'

'Yeah,' I said, 'I imagine she is. It must be difficult thinking you're the centre of the universe one day and just a single unemployed mother the next.'

'I don't think I could cope with it. I have enough trouble coping with you.'

'Seeing Duncan like that can't have helped. Did she ever say anything to you about him?'

'Not a peep.'

'Strange.'

'We're not all gossips, you know. Some women *never* talk about who they've slept with.'

'Really?'

A throbbing of the engines.

In a couple of minutes we were underway. In a couple more we were out of the shelter of the harbour. Grey sky merged with the grey sea ahead of us. The mainland was only thirty miles away, but it might as well have been three hundred for all that we could see of it. We gathered instead to the rear of the vessel, the six of us, watching the island slowly fade. Some people had arrived on the quay and were waving to us. We waved back. All their shattered hopes and dreams were on board. In fact she was sucking one thumb and had plunged the other into her left ear.

'There's coffee and stuff back there,' Charlie McManus hollered from the wheel, signalling behind him with his thumb, 'less those 'uns have scoffed it!'

Just about hidden from view was a small galley, four steps down. Half a dozen of the non-car-owning classes had already made it their home.

I was feeling unusually good. Perhaps it was the prospect of being

262

able to open a cool beer without being buried under a cascade of dead bodies. 'Do you want me to get them?' I asked.

Patricia turned surprised eyes upon me. 'That would be nice.' She turned to Moira. 'He doesn't even drink coffee, you know.'

'I know,' Moira said, and smiled warmly at me.

I hurried away. Coffee for three.

As I approached the galley a short, rotund figure in a priest's garb emerged.

'Oh look,' I said, 'it's Napoleon going into exile. I didn't realise you were on board.'

'Yes,' said Father White, perfectly pleasantly, and raised a gun, 'it's my final journey.'

42

A rogue wave crashed against the *Fitzpatrick*, throwing us, instantly drenched, to one side. If I'd bothered enrolling for the Alcoholic Front training I might have taken advantage of the sudden shift to overpower Father White, but as it was we just looked at each other helplessly for a few moments until the vessel settled. Then we shook ourselves like a pair of enthusiastic Labradors.

'Isn't it strange,' White said, holding the dripping gun steady on me, 'that all of the protagonists in this little drama should find themselves together right at the end?' With his free hand he wrung sea water out of his trousers.

'I'm not a protagonist,' I corrected. 'I'm an observer.'

The sneer didn't help his looks. Mad-jittery eyes did nothing for him either.

He indicated the direction I should move in with his pistol. A new pistol, of course. I'd picked up his old one the previous afternoon just after his transformation from front runner to beaten docket. It was now resting, between murders, in the boot of my car. I'd intended to chuck it overboard once we got underway.

I glanced behind him. Three figures were hunched around a Calor Gas single-ring cooker in the galley, taking a little heat from it while they waited for water to boil and paying us no attention at all. White followed my glance.

'The faithful?' I asked.

He shook his head. 'No. There's only me.'

'Aw,' I said.

'Me and Charlie. Charlie believes.'

I looked back along to the wheel. Charlie was watching. I gave a little laugh. 'What are you planning, Father, making a run for Cuba?'

'Somewhere much closer,' he said, then added, quite normally, 'Heaven, if you must know.'

'That'll be nice,' I said, then nodded up at Charlie. 'Who pays the ferryman?'

White glanced behind, then, brow furrowed, back at me. 'Meaning what?'

I said nothing for maybe ten seconds. Then I said: 'Nothing.'

He prodded me with the gun and I started walking. Behind me he said, 'You're referring to the ferryman who transports the souls of the damned, aren't you?'

I ignored him.

'That's what you're suggesting, isn't it? That the ferryman has his price.'

'No,' I said over my shoulder, 'it's just a line from a Chris de Burgh song, much as I hate to admit knowing it. It seemed a shame to waste it.'

'Charlie's as loyal as they come,' he snapped on my heels. 'With me to the end. This end.'

'Aye. Whatever you say.'

Perhaps I wasn't treating him with the respect he deserved. He had a gun and a belief in the Messiah that couldn't be broken down by mere logic. Perhaps I'd been too close to death to give it any respect at all.

We reached the rear of the vessel. Everyone looked surprised to see him. This was understandable.

'Just when you thought it was safe to go back in the water,' I said by way of introduction.

Flynn snapped from incredulity to anger in a couple of seconds. 'What on earth do you think you're doing?' he demanded, not for the first time.

White's smile was almost gentle, and all the more worrying for it. 'I don't intend to do very much on earth, Frank, not very much at all. Just what God has told me to do.'

Moira tutted. 'You're not still on that, are you?'

'I still believe,' White said softly, but now with a little tremble of his upper lip.

Moira's eyes blazed. 'Don't you listen at all?' she boomed. 'It's the radon! It's the bloody radon! God isn't speaking to any of us.'

White waved the gun in her face. Christine cowered back against her mother. 'You're a sad deluded woman, Moira.'

'Can't you see the madness of it?' Moira erupted again. 'Look at you – you're a priest, you carry a gun, you kill anyone who doesn't agree with you! Can't you see it?'

'I see what God wants me to see. I see that we had the whole world in our hands. Now you've thrown it all away.'

'We had nothing. We deluded ourselves.'

'We had everything. We had Christine. God entrusted us with the responsibility of looking after her.'

'I'm *still* looking after her!'

White reached his free hand out to Christine. Moira stepped back, pulling her away from him. 'No, Moira, you're not,' White hissed. 'You're taking her to the mainland. She'll lose her innocence. She'll be corrupted.'

'No, she . . .'

'She will! I've seen it happen.'

Flynn leant forward. 'Father, please . . .'

'Get back!' White shouted and thrust upward with the gun, glancing it off Flynn's chin. The priest's head rocketed back and he stumbled against the side of the ferry.

Abruptly Christine burst into tears.

White pulled suddenly away from Flynn, lurched with the sway of the boat towards Christine. Christine twisted away from her mother and ran crying down the ferry.

'You see what you've done!' Moira screeched and began to move after her.

'Stay where you are!' White shouted.

Moira twirled. 'What are you going to do, Father, shoot me?'

'If I have to.'

Patricia caught Moira's arm. 'Please, Moira, just . . .'

Moira slapped her away. Little Stevie started crying. Moira started after her daughter.

White raised the gun and shot once. Moira fell.

'Jesus Christ,' I said.

Anxious faces peered out of the galley. One man stood as if to go to Moira's assistance, but then pulled the door over.

Moira rolled over on the deck and clutched her leg. She raised a bloody hand to her face, then turned murderous eyes back at White.

'Let it bleed, Moira,' White called. 'It doesn't matter, you're guaranteed a place in heaven. Come with me, Moira.'

'There are a lot of places you're going,' Moira wrenched out, 'and heaven isn't one of them.'

White trained the gun on her again.

'That's just what I was going to say,' I said.

He turned to me, raising the gun. 'You always have too much to say.'

I nodded.

Flynn, pushing himself erect, a hand clamped to his jaw, stumbled towards Moira.

'Stay where you are!' White roared, moving the gun again.

Flynn stopped. 'Would you shoot me as well?'

'You know I would.'

Flynn hesitated. 'Are you all right, Moira?' he called.

Angry, in pain, Moira barked back: 'Of course I'm not!'

'Let me help her!' Flynn cried. 'She's Christine's mother!'

'Not any more,' White said simply. He moved forward, his gun tracing Moira's shape as he stepped around her. 'Christine!' he called.

'Please . . .' Moira moaned, stretching out a hand to grab him, but he avoided her easily and moved on up the ferry.

Christine's head ducked down behind the bonnet of Flynn's Land-Rover, but her blonde hair, whipped up in the wind, was clearly visible. As she peeked out one side, White grabbed her from the other. She let out a shrill little scream.

'It's okay, it's okay,' White intoned, but his whisper was rough, anxious, not soothing at all. She wailed. He clutched her arm tightly and dragged her forward. She let loose with a kick, but her legs weren't long enough. She turned a tear-streaked face towards her mother.

Our party moved cautiously up the boat. Father Flynn helped Moira to her feet. Patricia bowed her head and kissed Little Stevie on the brow as she walked.

Father White couldn't go any further. The waves spat angrily like pogoing punks. The elderly priest turned towards us. Christine tried to dash away. He clawed her back. Then he raised her and held her tight against his chest.

'This is the end of it all!' he bellowed.

'Please . . . !' Moira cried.

'In God's name . . .' muttered Flynn, edging forward.

I leant against the boot of the Fiesta. Patricia snuggled into me. 'Please, Dan, do . . .'

'I'm not bulletproof,' I hissed.

White rubbed spray from his eyes with his gun hand. 'You've taken everything from me, Frank!' he yelled. 'We were building heaven on earth, and you ruined it!' He squeezed Christine, bent and kissed the top of her head while she tried again to squirm away. 'For God so loved the world that he gave his only begotten son. That's what we lived by. For two thousand years. And then he gave us his daughter. And you want to do the same again. Destroy, corrupt, sacrifice! It can't happen, Frank! There's only one thing to do. Take her back to her father. He needs her back.'

He looked quickly over at the sea. Opened his mouth. He seemed to bite at the waves. 'We're going overboard, Frank. We're going into the sea. That's where God first breathed life into us, and that's where he'll welcome us back into his bosom.'

I glanced at Patricia. She turned disappointed eyes away from me. 'I want you to go up beside Moira,' I whispered.

'But . . .'

'I want you to offer him Little Stevie. Ask him to take Little Stevie to heaven with them.'

'Fuck off!'

'Please,' I hissed, 'I need the diversion.'

'Bugger the div . . .'

'Do it. Trust me. I can stop this.'

She bit something back.

'Please, love, it's the only way.'

'This is my baby.'

'It's *our* baby. I wouldn't harm a hair on his head. Please.'

I gave her a little nudge. She gave me a glance that carried a promise of bloody revenge, then moved reluctantly forward.

White had locked ranting eyes on Father Flynn.

I slipped a key into the lock, turned. I pulled the boot up a couple of feet and slipped my hand in. The gun was in there. Somewhere.

Patricia distracted White perfectly. She held Little Stevie out in front of her. 'Please,' she said, 'take him with you.'

'What?'

'Patricia?' said Moira.

Flynn reached out a beseeching hand. Patricia ignored it. She shook her head. 'He's right,' she said. 'This is no place for Christine. It's no place for any child. Their place is with God. Please take him with you.'

Jesus, where did I put the bugger?

White had a child in one hand, a gun in the other. He looked confused for a moment. Unsure.

'Let her go in Christine's arms. It will be an honour.' Patricia reached forward. Christine, calmed slightly by the presence of the child, reached out for Little Stevie. Patricia hesitated.

Jesus, where the . . . ?

Christine took hold of Little Stevie. Patricia wouldn't let go. Acting and fear would only take her so far. She wasn't going to let go of our baby. Christine pulled. White growled, 'Leave him then!'

Patricia glanced desperately back. 'I have to say goodbye,' she said.

Something sharp at my neck.

A low growl. 'Lost something?'

I turned slightly. Charlie McManus. A blade. A fishknife. Something.

I gave the tiniest shrug.

He nodded into the boot. 'Give me it. Now.'

The boat reared up. Father White stumbled forward; Patricia, better placed, put a hand out to stop him; she almost hugged him, and he took full advantage of it; he got hold of the baby, my baby, *our* baby, and shoved Patricia backwards. She fell, tumbling over ropes and loose crates. When she looked up White had Little Stevie and Christine tucked against his chest, his free hand still holding the gun tightly. A wave reached out to drench the three of them. Christine screamed. Little Stevie roared. Patricia raised her fingers to her lips, then thrust them into her mouth.

'Carefully,' said Charlie McManus.

I reached, carefully, into the cardboard box. I removed the hedge-hog from the scrummage of leaves.

Charlie's brow furrowed. The knife-prick relaxed. 'I thought . . .' he began.

With all my strength I thrust the animal upward. Charlie screamed and fell back, pawing as the sleeping creature instantly embedded itself a thousand times into his face. I plunged my hands into the boot again, frantically . . . I found the shoe. Inside it, the gun. I ran forward.

White was swaying back and forth, unsupported, mouthing a prayer, waiting for the next big wave to provide the imbalance required to topple him over the side into the grey waters with Christine and my son. He wasn't brave enough to throw himself.

I raised the gun. 'Let them down, Father,' I shouted.

His eyes slowly focused on me. A tiny smile. A little shake. 'You wouldn't dare,' he said.

As the bow rose, I shot him between the eyes.

He fell forward, the children toppling out of his arms. His head thumped off the deck.

Screams.

Patricia caught Little Stevie.

Christine rolled and surfaced, roaring.

I closed my eyes.

I took a deep breath.

I took another.

A hand on my arm. Father Flynn. 'They're okay,' he said softly, 'they're okay.' And then he let out a very deep breath himself and said, 'That was a very brave thing.'

I opened my eyes. The deck was awash with blood and sea water.

'How did you know he would fall forward?' Flynn asked.

'I didn't.'

'How did you ever manage a shot like that?'

'Luck.'

He clasped his hands. 'Truly God has watched over us,' he said.

'You bastard!' Patricia screamed, coming up the deck at speed. Before I could respond she kicked me hard where it hurts. 'You could have killed both of them!'

I collapsed.

But I wasn't angry.

There was nothing to be angry about. I knew that it had been done with affection.

43

Cardinal Tomas Daley, Primate of All Ireland and still the hot favourite to be the first English-speaking Pope since Robbie Coltrane, looked up from his desk. His face was the colour of crematorium ash. 'Well,' he said sombrely, 'it certainly makes quite an impact, reading it in black and white.'

'You should have been there, living it in colour.'

'I'm sure it was dreadful for you. What can I say? I had no idea.'

I shrugged. It wasn't a good idea. My head was playing host to a cement mixer. It had a little to do with the close, thundery weather and a lot to do with the two-day bender I'd just completed. It was in honour of Little Stevie and his christening. We'd gone to the Presbyterian Church round the corner from our house. It seemed so strange to be sitting in a pew and not be worried about having my head blown off.

'How's your wife . . . the baby?'

'Fine. Although I won't try to sell them another island holiday for a while.'

'Well, that's natural. And yourself?'

'Fine. I'm thinking about entering the ministry. It's a pretty exciting life.'

He held my gaze for a few moments. He lifted my report and tapped it gently against his desk. Then he stood up and crossed to the ornate fireplace that dominated the room. He looked gravely back at me, then threw the report onto the blazing fire.

We both watched it for several moments.

When, after several further moments it had still failed to catch light, I said, 'I could have told you that was an imitation fire. It's very life-like, isn't it?'

The Cardinal was shaking his head. 'I had no idea. I must confess I wondered when they never seemed to bring coal in.' He bent into the hearth and lifted the report again. 'I'll have it shredded,' he said, and walked back to his desk.

'You can shred, but I can't see how you can hope to cover up seven murders.'

'We don't wish to cover anything up, Dan. The . . . *radon* . . . is a very real threat and I'm sure there will be considerable media interest . . . but the murders . . . well, of course, they were a very terrible thing, but I don't see that there's anything to be gained by bringing them before the public. Nor this business about Christine being the Messiah. Exceptionally gifted, yes indeed, but no need to mention . . .'

'Cardinal, it's not that easy.'

'Isn't it? You know, Dan, I'm not without influence. The . . . *bodies* . . . have already been removed and disposed of.'

'Just like that.'

'Just like that. We've had lots of practice.'

'You've . . .'

'Don't ask, please.'

'But . . . anyway, I don't see you're going to shut eight hundred-odd people up. Odd being the word.'

'Again, Dan . . . you'd be surprised. Oh, I'm sure something might leak out eventually . . . but do you think those people are one bit proud of what went on out there? They're not only embarrassed, but they're afraid of being implicated . . . and don't underestimate the Catholic faith either . . . if it does one thing well, it makes you a little scared for your soul, do you understand?'

'I'm starting to.'

'Add in resettlement grants, employment grants, all the benefits the Mother Church can bestow on her flock . . . you *would be* surprised.'

'Expensive, though.'

'What isn't, these days?'

'Of course,' I said, without any trace of subtlety, 'I don't need a resettlement grant.'

'No.'

'Or, indeed, a job.'

'No, I presume not.'

'And I'm about as Catholic as Cromwell.'

'Are you trying to make a point, Dan?'

'A small one. What with all the life-threatening situations I got into in my brave attempt to save the Catholic Church from universal embarrassment, I didn't actually get started any of that novel I was supposed to be writing.'

'You did rather get overtaken by events.'

'I was thinking another writing grant mightn't go amiss. Just to see me through the next few months. A year, tops.'

The Cardinal nodded slowly.

'Of course I haven't quite decided on the subject matter. My characters don't have to be Catholic. Or live on an island. They wouldn't have to go within a hundred miles of an island, any island. They could be practically housebound. I'll put them in wheelchairs if you insist.'

'Blackmail is such an ugly word, I think,' said the Cardinal.

'So is starvation, it's much longer and worth a hell of a lot more in Scrabble.' I had no idea if it was, but it had the desired effect. He was reaching for his chequebook.

A few weeks later I bumped into Father Flynn. At first I didn't recognise him. He'd lost a lot of weight, his walk was stooped, his eyes hollow. He was looking in a Waterstone's window on Royal Avenue. I walked past him once, then checked back when I realised who it was.

He was pleased to see me. His handshake was weak, but keen. 'You haven't seen Christine or Moira, have you?' was his first post-formalities question.

'I thought you were sorting them out?'

'I was. I did. Then the Cardinal stepped in. He's moved them on somewhere. He thinks it's better that they have no contact with me. I suppose he's right. But I'm dying to see them. You get attached, y'know?'

We talked on for a little while, but there wasn't a great deal more to say. We exchanged telephone numbers. I took his on the back of a betting docket and lost it when I cashed it in the next day. A rare winner. I realised I was losing the number as I gave it in, but I let it go.

I hadn't lied to him, exactly. I hadn't seen Moira or Christine, and had no plans to. I'd been bad and would not stray again. Patricia had seen them, though. She'd been out for lunch with them a few times.

They had a flat about half a mile from our house. Moira was back working as a nurse. Christine was in primary school, a year early and top of her class. Settling well, apparently.

One day, when Moira went to pick her up from school, she didn't appear at the gate with the rest of the kids. Moira hung about, getting more and more anxious, then hurried into the classroom.

Christine was there okay, with a teacher, but she was barefoot. Her feet were bleeding.

Moira stood frozen.

It took a while for the teacher to convince her that it was just that Christine's shoes were too small.

We laughed about that. And it's nice, laughing together; it's what we do best, that and fight. Sometime we even get to make love on the Magic Settee.

People tell you that once you have a child your life is never the same again. They're right. You get marooned on a remote island and nearly murdered by a bunch of radiation-crazed religious maniacs.

We'd probably started out the wrong way with Little Stevie. We had enough problems to overcome with him not being mine, without subjecting the three of us to life on Wrathlin. The idea had seemed romantic, and it had stayed an idea. Often, romance is.

One night, when Little Stevie was just about six months, Patricia and I stood in his nursery, hand in hand in the half light, just watching him. He was beautiful. Even his hair. It looked like it might darken sufficiently for him to pass as an out-of-season strawberry blond.

'You do love him, don't you, Dan?'

'Of course I do.'

'As much as me?'

'As much as you love him?'

'No, as much as you love me.'

'Yes. I do. I really do. Honest.'

'Thank you.' She gave me a little kiss.

'Thank *you*,' I said.

She gave me another kiss, then slipped her hand from mine. 'Come to bed, lover,' she said.

She went ahead of me. I lingered by the cot. Little Stevie's eyes were open, there was the merest hint of a smile on his face. He was a great wee fella, and so what if he wasn't mine by blood. I'd look after him. I'd do him proud. Daddy Starkey.

Wrathlin might as well have been four years away as four months. He wouldn't remember it. He wouldn't remember Duncan, Duncan's death, the bodies, the mania; he wouldn't know how close he'd come to death himself, through illness, through my gambling his life on a hedgehog. Blissfully ignorant, smiling there in his cot at nothing, not a care in the big bad world.

I stood for another moment by the door, then slowly turned down the dimmer switch. 'Good night, son,' I said, and closed the door softly after me.

'Good night, dad.'

I was back through the door in a flash . . .

AUTHOR'S NOTE

Wrathlin Island is a real place, and well worth a visit, lots of birdlife, although it goes without saying that the people and most of the places mentioned in this story are completely fictitious, with the exception of the Messiah, who *is* coming, so get your act together. Radon, likewise, *does* exist and can be found at varying levels in many parts of the United Kingdom. I would like to thank Dr H. C. H. Glochamner of the Department of the Environment's Natural Gases division for his valued assistance in researching this novel. I would like to, but he doesn't exist, nor does his department. Dan Starkey will return shortly.

Divorcing Jack

Colin Bateman

'Richly paranoid and very funny' *Sunday Times*

Dan Starkey is a young journalist in Belfast, who shares with his wife Patricia a prodigious appetite for drinking and partying. Then Dan meets Margaret, a beautiful student, and things begin to get out of hand.

Terrifyingly, Margaret is murdered and Patricia kidnapped. Dan has no idea why, but before long he too is a target, running as fast as he can in a race against time to solve the mystery and to save his marriage.

'A joy from start to finish . . . Witty, fast-paced and throbbing with menace, *Divorcing Jack* reads like *The Thirty-Nine Steps* rewritten for the '90s by Roddy Doyle'　　　　*Time Out*

'Grabs you by the throat . . . a magnificent debut. Unlike any thriller you have ever read before . . . like *The Day of the Jackal* out of the Marx Brothers'　　　　*Sunday Press*

'Fresh, funny . . . an Ulster Carl Hiaasen'　　　　*Mail on Sunday*

ISBN 0 00 647903 0

Of Wee Sweetie Mice and Men

Colin Bateman

'A supremely entertaining piece of work' *GQ*

Smooth operator Geordie McClean has succeeded in setting up a gigantic payday (for all concerned) by arranging a St Patrick's Day fight in New York between his hopeless Irish heavyweight champ Fat Boy McMaster and Mike Tyson. Belfast journalist Dan Starkey is hired to write the book of the whole affair.

Dan is trying to persuade his wife Patricia to give their marriage another go, but he has not succeeded before boarding the plane with McMaster and his deeply suspect entourage. If he thought he was leaving the sectarian conflict of his homeland behind him, Starkey is quite mistaken and McClean's outfit soon falls prey to all the old enmities, while developing an uncanny power to outrage plenty of other interest groups at the same time.

Kidnap, romance and mayhem ensue . . . and all before a punch is thrown in the ring!

'Fast, furious, riotously funny and at the end, never a dry eye in the house' *Mail on Sunday*

'I have absolutely no interest [in boxing], but such are Bateman's skills with narrative and characterization that one is gripped to the last page, whatever one's sporting predilections' *Literary Review*

'If Roddy Doyle was as good as people say, he would probably write novels like this' *Arena*

ISBN 0 00 649612 1